FICTION    Gadol, Peter.
GADOL
           The mystery roast.

| DATE | | | |
|------|---|---|---|
|  |  |  |  |
|  |  |  |  |
|  |  |  |  |
|  |  |  |  |
|  |  |  |  |
|  |  |  |  |
|  |  |  |  |
|  |  |  |  |
|  |  |  |  |
|  |  |  |  |
|  |  |  |  |
|  |  |  |  |

# The Mystery Roast

Also by Peter Gadol

*Coyote*

The
Mystery
Roast

by

Peter Gadol

Crown Publishers, Inc.
New York

The author wishes to thank Jared Stamm and David Groff for their insight and their enthusiasm, and Mary Evans for her wisdom and her friendship.

Copyright © 1993 by Peter Gadol

Published by Crown Publishers, Inc., 201 East 50th Street, New York, New York 10022. Member of the Crown Publishing Group.
Random House, Inc. New York, Toronto, London, Sydney, Auckland

CROWN is a trademark of Crown Publishers, Inc.

Manufactured in the United States of America

Design by Lauren Dong

Library of Congress Cataloging-in-Publication Data

Gadol, Peter.
The mystery roast / by Peter Gadol — 1st ed.
I. Title.
PS3557.A285M9   1992
813'.54—dc20                                          92-7943
                                                        CIP

ISBN 0-517-576562

1   3   5   7   9   10   8   6   4   2

First Edition

For Stephen
and for my mother

# The Mystery Roast

One day midway through a winter of mystifying warmth, a polar bear escaped from the zoo. She was spotted charging north across the vast lawn of the park, an amorphous, vanilla beast making one mad, hopeless break for freedom. The zookeepers never figured out how she scaled the steep, cement walls of her cage, and a team of sharpshooters had to fire five tranquilizer darts into her rump to capture her. Around three o'clock, a helicopter weighted with an arctic pendant flew low across the western sky as it carried the doped truant back to her exile.

And yet no one in New York City that afternoon noticed the airborne bear. The city at that moment was united and preoccupied by an impending storm that promised to break the lull of unseasonable weather. In one hour, a blizzard would finally arrive. So children galloped home from school, and planes hastily spiraled down to the airports. The famous skyscrapers of glass rocked in the manic wind, and the blinking sass of Midtown marquees lost its lure in the fading light. Down in the garment district, two fleets of dress racks collided and sent the latest twills flying. Farther downtown two men used the antennae of their portable phones as sabers in a struggle over the last free cab in Manhattan. Doormen paced back and forth under their canopies, shoppers returned holiday sweaters as if tomorrow all exchanges might be outlawed, and terriers accustomed to being walked at dusk barked and winced to no avail when rushed through early rounds. Broad sidewalks became virtual rivers of pedestrians flowing in frantic errands, in a run on delis and video stores for noodle soup and film noir. Packed shoulder to shoulder, subway riders couldn't turn their paperback pages, and amid one traffic jam on a cross street, three women in saris passed among stalled cars and earned irregular profits by selling individually wrapped roses, each a surprise beacon of red in the gothic mist. New York was practiced in panic, usually prepared for or at the very least hardened by steam pipe explosions and blackouts and stock market dives and sanitation strikes, yet this storm, a predicted and overdue turn of weather, had inspired a more chaotic retreat than normal.

Eric Auden, however, was not running for cover. He had woken up before noon for a change and emerged today from his mother's apartment for the first time in a week. While the rest of the city braced itself for a midwinter apocalypse, he paced through the New York Museum of Art and at long last got on with his life.

Eric had come to the museum on a unique mission. It was located in the neighborhood where he had grown up, and it had provided the stage for art appreciation classes when he was seven, countless school field trips, and a few adolescent dates. When his father came to town, they would meet for lunch in the frescoed cafeteria. His high-school graduation had been held in the medieval courtyard. So to gain perspective on his past, to move beyond its hold, its reach, he walked briskly from room to room and made sure everything was in its place: the suit of armor against which he used to measure his evolving height, a favorite Flemish portrait of a man and woman on their wedding day, a Byzantine mosaic he once copied in crayon, and a bronze cat from Ancient Egypt, green with time, only one gold earring left. He used to nag his mother until she lifted him up so he could look at the cat head-on, so he could stare into its vacant, metallic gaze.

The museum was empty today, entire cultures abandoned. He hurried past the tall lion-gates, the winged beast-gods that guarded the collection of blue glazed Fertile Crescent bricks that had been collected, imported, and reassembled to re-create part of an Assyrian palace. In front of a bas-relief of one particularly gruesome battle (Ashurbanipal had really had a good day), a man and a woman made out. From the way they tied their sweaters around their necks and from the high hem of their jeans, Eric assumed that they were visiting from abroad. He nodded to indicate that he was sorry that he'd interrupted them, and they smiled back, glassy-eyed, and kept on necking.

Eric walked through every collection, addition, period room, and wing as if he were skimming a novel he had read many times before. So he was naturally disappointed when he arrived at the rooms of Greek Antiquities only to discover the arched main entrance barricaded with a whitewashed, plywood wall. A door had been cut into the barrier, and it was padlocked shut, patrolled by a man in a gray uniform who directed patrons toward other exhibits with more officiousness than a traffic cop.

"It's closed?" Eric asked the obvious.

"Closed, sir," the guard said. "Yes."

"Do you know when it will be open again?"

The guard shrugged. "They just closed it off a few days ago."

"Really? Why?"

"They're renovating the whole wing."

"So it's going to be months."

"Months. You just missed it, sir. They just closed it off."

Eric lingered for a moment, thinking he might cajole the guard into letting him have a quick look inside, which was all he wanted. He knew that he was being sentimental and only putting off what came next on his agenda, so he reluctantly gave up and headed toward the Pre-Columbian Wing. One wall of the gallery was a two-story slope of windows. He stepped past a boat made of bark, beyond a line of totem poles, and leaned against a lower pane. Outside, a sidewalk flame thrower in search of an audience was reduced to performing for a pretzel vendor. In the park beyond the museum, the tree branches bobbed and swayed in an erratic dance. Enough was enough: He had to move on. First, he would use the men's room, then he would buy a newspaper, skip downtown to a diner, and check the apartment listings. Want ads, too. That was the plan. He had to stick to the plan.

Eric sped through American Art, then up a flight of stairs and ended up in European Prints, where he knew there was a men's room somewhere. He passed a new special exhibit that hadn't opened yet, something about Dutch landscapes, and ultimately, he found a men's room. Then he would leave the museum and for the first time in a long while truly take charge, ride off into the snowstorm, his newfound momentum leaving him dizzy but sure. He lost his pace, however, when he swung open the door to the men's room and saw a nude woman.

Not a nude woman exactly, but a drawing of a nude woman taped to the tiled wall facing the door so that it was the first thing that any man would see when he entered. Other drawings covered the mirrors over the sinks, larger drawings hung above the towel dispensers, on the panels of the stalls, everywhere but the urinals. Then a blond man turned toward him and said in a voice that was at once familiar and distant, "This is an exhibit. Admission is fifty cents."

Eric looked at the man and his heart raced.

"If you don't want to— Eric? I don't believe it."

"Timothy. Hello. Wow, hello." The two of them shook hands and then fell into an awkward hug. In the years since they'd last seen each other, Timothy had become almost unrecognizable. His haphazard blond mop was redder now, cut short and urban, his patterned shirt was buttoned to the collar and adorned with a silver bolo, and he wore cowboy boots. Timothy's eyes had always been a solid blue, but now they looked polished to a luster that seemed sinister. "It's good to see you," Eric said—and he meant it—but he immediately began to feel overwhelmed with nostalgia. Once they had lived like brothers during summer vacations. At the beach they were an inseparable pair: Timothy was the one who decided that they would ferry across the bay and explore a deserted fish factory, and then once inside the ghost of a plant, Eric navigated the abandoned gutting and canning assembly line.

"It's good to see you, too," Timothy said. "It's been a long, long time."

They had been about to start the last year of high school when they abruptly split apart. Eric did the math: "Ten years."

"Damn." Timothy shook his head in disbelief.

The more Eric stared, the less the new Timothy connected with the old, and the stranger leaning against a men's room sink could very well have been an impostor. Eric wanted to run out the door.

He scanned the drawings on the walls. A posterboard sign propped up in a corner read: TIMOTHY RAMPLING—TEN DRAWINGS OF MY FRIENDS ANDRE AND INCA. In childhood, Timothy used to draw elaborate illustrations, doodles really, penciled networks of bridges and trawlers and local lighthouses. Clearly he had graduated to a more complex artistry (less line, more shadow), yet the drawings seemed far too sophisticated to belong to the boy who used to sit in Mae's Diner and scribble on paper napkins.

"So . . . you drew these?" Eric asked.

"Ten years is like almost a third of our lifetime."

"And you're showing them here?" Eric began to tour the room, an automatic move after all, since he was in a museum. "Oh." He fished for coins in his pocket.

"Forget about it," Timothy said. "What brings you to New York? Are you just visiting or living here again?"

"I was in Washington for a while, but I've been staying here for the last six months."

"No kidding. You and your wife? You got married. I think that's what someone told me."

· They had reigned over the moss-covered bluffs and rotting piers of Long Island Sound. At the end of each summer, Eric had returned to school in the city and left Timothy at the beach, where he lived with his real family for the rest of the year.

"That's what someone told—"

"I got married," Eric said. "Right. So you're still drawing. I like your work."

"Yeah, I became an artist. Thanks." Then Timothy laughed. "This is really weird. Don't I know you from somewhere?" His familiar chuckle reduced the tension in the air. "No, seriously: How have you been?"

"I'm fine." Eric tried to sound blasé.

"Just . . . fine?"

"I'm great," Eric stated with more solid footing. He noticed that Timothy was playing with a rubber band. He always used to be doing something with his fingers—long, thin fingers, which Eric's mother had decided were perfect for the piano. What a stretch, she liked to say though Timothy never played. She repeated this often around the time that Eric was giving up lessons. "So why are you hanging your drawings in a men's room?"

Before Timothy could explain, a man burst into the room like a gunslinger barreling into a saloon. Presumably he expected to use the facilities (Eric himself didn't have to anymore). Timothy greeted the man with a grin and an upturned palm. "This is an exhibit. Admission is fifty cents."

The man eyed the towel dispensers and appeared ready to complain, but Eric, who nonchalantly examined the drawing of the woman opposite the door, must have suggested something legitimate about the exhibit, so the man pulled out a dollar bill, then pocketed the change. "This is a show? Didn't they just build a new wing?"

"They did," Timothy said, "but my work is in here. Drawings, which you're welcome to purchase."

"I don't think so," the man said before actually touring the makeshift gallery. "And this is all of it?"

"I hang different drawings each day," Timothy said.

The man slipped on his reading glasses and poked his head into the wheelchair-accessible stall.

Timothy turned toward Eric. "I don't have enough in my portfolio really to go around to real galleries just yet, not the good ones anyway. So I thought I'd try to make a splash this way. People who come to museums are interested in art, right? I'm hoping that they'll come in, take a look, buy something. Spread the word."

The man stared at Timothy over his glasses. "They're, um, quite nice." When he passed a sink, he looked into the few inches of an exposed mirror and combed a single tuft of hair across his head.

Eric examined the drawings. They were all portraits, each in charcoal with some blue and white chalk for accent, all nudes. Timothy had drawn the contours of a man's or a woman's body with bold, sweeping lines and then turned inward and concentrated on a few details. Andre was teddy-bearish with curly, receding hair, small ears, a little extra flesh at the hip. Timothy had drawn him standing, and the man looked like he was awaiting a Simon-says instruction—except in one drawing he pointed an accusatory finger at the artist and viewer and seemed to be saying, Don't take that picture, don't you dare. What kind of a name was Inca? The woman was tall and angular, and four times out of five Timothy had depicted her lying down. Only in one drawing was she sitting in an armchair, one knee pulled up to her chest. She had a chic, short bob and long dancer's legs. It was difficult to tell much from Timothy's sketching, but Eric was attracted to her in the way he could be teased by a fashion ad. She looked like she was laughing easily at whatever jokes the artist was telling her while she posed. When she was prone, one breast melted into her chest and the other fell freely downward.

"Do you know these people?" Eric asked.

"They live in my building," Timothy said.

The man was eyeing the urinals now.

"There's another men's room downstairs," Timothy informed him.

"Well, very provocative," the man said. He pushed open the door and left.

"Have you sold anything?" Eric asked.

"No, but I am definitely getting high grades."

"How long have you been doing this?"

"Three weeks."

"Don't you have problems with the security?"

"They know. I'd been coming here a lot lately—visiting the museum, that is—to copy paintings. I'd get permission to bring an easel in, sell the stuff to tourists on the street—you know the routine, it's a living. I got to know some of the guards."

"Friends in high places."

"That's why I have to charge admission. It's for them. Plus they take a commission on sales. If there are sales someday."

"Haven't the curators caught on?"

"Not yet." Timothy padded across the room to a drawing of the man which he had been staring at. He pressed his thumb against the man's left big toe and tried to erase a smudge with his finger. "I forgot to fix this one. It's a mess. I mean fix with fixer." He only made it worse. "So, Margot Brandon—she's your wife."

"Margot," Eric said. "Right."

"A celebrity. I see her on television all the time."

"Me, too."

"She seems smart. Well, on TV anyway. . . ."

"She left me. We're divorced." Eric felt as if he were detailing somebody else's life, his mother's for example, not his own.

"That's too bad." Timothy looked away from the man with the smudged big toe. "I'm sorry I brought it up."

"No, I'm okay." Eric made another pathetic attempt to sound cheerful. "Really."

"I'm sort of in the process of breaking up with someone myself."

Eric had heard rumors that Timothy had been living with a man out at the beach. "A lawyer?" That was what he had been told.

"Heavens. That was ages ago. No, this is a guy in the city. It's sort of been a light-switch deal."

"A light-switch deal?"

"Off and on," Timothy explained. "The bulb is about to blow for good."

"I'm sorry."

"Don't be. If someone makes you unhappy, you have to move on, you know? That's my rule." He looked like he expected a response.

"It's a good rule," Eric said.

Timothy washed his dirty thumb in the sink. "And how is your mother?"

"Same as she ever was. She married again."

"I heard."

"She's single now."

"She sold the house out there, right?"

"Not too long after I went away to school. The boat, too."

"Not the *Lydia*."

" 'Fraid so."

"Have you been staying with her here in the city?"

When Eric fled Washington, he had moved back into his mother's apartment fully expecting to bicker the way they did when he was in high school. To his amazement, they had ended up renting movies and supping together in front of the evening news. Until last night, they had lived together in easy commune, and even last night, they'd managed to stop arguing before getting nasty. "I've overstayed my welcome," Eric said. "I'm looking for a place."

"It's funny you should say that. I'm living down in the West Village—"

"You live here now?" Of course he did, but the idea was foreign: Timothy belonged in the country, on the beach.

"All the way west." Timothy grinned. "Not for everyone. It's kind of remote, kind of bleak."

To Eric, *bleak* sounded cathartic and therefore appealing. "Oh, yeah?"

"There's a great café in the building. And on the floor below me, there's a loft owned by a cinematographer. He owned the whole building, but he's sold most of it off. Richard mostly lives in London, all the time in fact, and he called me to ask me to find someone to rent his place to."

"I should check it out."

"Definitely. Richard wants whoever I find to paint the place. He wants it all gray."

"I could use something to do. I'm looking for work, too."

"There might be something in the café downstairs. I'm not sure."

"Perfect. I can't believe I ran into you." Eric was full of questions about how his spaced-out teenage comrade had evolved into this savvy, groomed man who had the temerity to set up shop in the world's greatest museum. But to find out about Timothy would mean reciprocating with the facts of his own life; Eric had an equal decade to account for. And he might discover that all they had in common now was a childhood which they no doubt remembered with different degrees of fondness and regret.

A woman shot into the men's room. "Thank God, I finally found you," she said to Eric. Her cheeks were flush, her fingers cold when she grasped his hand. "I knew you were in a rest room, but I wasn't sure which one. I've been to them all." She took out a dollar bill to hand to Eric, who pointed to Timothy. "My friend Lila came here last week. Remember her? Tall, blond-gray hair. Forties? Well, fifties. You don't remember her? My name's Lila, too. I feel sort of funny in a men's room, don't you? No, you're men!" Lila wore flared slacks and a vest and a thin tie. She readjusted a nylon pouch belted around her waist. "Neat stuff. Which one of you is Timothy Rampling? You? You. Well, well, well. I see a lot of Modigliani here, I must say. Quite a bit." She made a fast assessment, nodding her head and clenching her hands. "So much mystery, so many questions. And flourishes one finds in Titian's cartoons." The woman obviously had only come by to drop names. "Dare I invoke Millet's pastoral realism, or even the heavy forms that populate the sculpture of Maillot?"

"Be my guest," Timothy said.

"That one." Lila wagged a finger at the man with the smudged big toe. "That piece there."

"Yes?"

"It's so—how should I put it?—so École des Beaux Arts. Reminds me of what I used to see in a gallery on the rue Jacob."

"No kidding."

"How much?" Lila asked.

"How much?" Eric echoed her unintentionally, offended that this name-dropper was bothering to inquire.

Timothy also appeared to be thrown off guard. "Well . . ."

"I have to get out of here before I get caught."

"Three hundred?" Timothy suggested.

"I came prepared," Lila said. And she pulled six fifty-dollar bills out of her marsupial hip-purse. It all had happened so fast, the woman's inspection of the room, her purchase. After Timothy had removed the drawing from the wall and rolled it up, Lila opened the men's room door, peered into the hallway to make sure no one was looking, and then rushed away with her new investment tucked discreetly under her arm.

Timothy flipped through the crisp bills. "I actually sold something, how about that. Not that I'm in this for the money."

"Congratulations."

"I should have said four hundred." Timothy checked his watch. "They're going to close this place soon." He pulled out a portfolio case from one of the stalls and began to remove the pages of nudes from the walls.

"I'm glad I stumbled in here," Eric said. He helped take down a drawing of the woman from a mirror. Silently, he and Timothy dismantled the exhibit, working as efficiently as they had a dozen years earlier painting Eric's mother's porch.

They went downstairs, and on the first floor, Timothy proudly announced, "A sale," when a museum guard approached him. The guard, who probably wanted his cut, pointed Timothy toward a side gallery, where the payoff was made.

Outside, Eric skipped down the fan of steps. A man wearing a poncho of plastic garbage bags was washing his hands in the rusty trickle from a verdigris-stained drainpipe. He dried them in the heat of the floodlights aimed at the museum's columned facade.

"Well," Timothy said, "I'm glad you stumbled in, too. I have to say, I've thought about you now and then."

Eric shivered. He pulled his scarf up over his mouth like a bandit.

"Come downtown sometime and check out that loft."

"I will." Eric didn't want to let him go, not after finding him after all this time, but he didn't know what to say, he never did. He was practiced at losing friends and lovers, at falling out of touch, at drifting away, not at finding anyone, not at renewing old alliances. They shook gloved hands.

"I'm in the book," Timothy said. Then he turned, half-saluted, and began to walk south with the traffic.

Eric watched him float off. "Wait!" He wasn't sure if Timothy was still in earshot.

Timothy pivoted.

"I might as well come look at the place now, if it's okay with you."

Eric felt a crisp flake of snow hit him on the cheek and stick to his skin for a brief moment before flipping over and landing on his scarf. He blinked as he jogged toward Timothy, and in the instant of a blink, he forgot what it was that had prevented him for so long from getting out of bed in the morning, from sleeping at night. Not too far away, two hansom cabs, for lack of fares, were drag-racing in front of a grand hotel. In the cathedral, priests abbreviated the Mass. Herds of commuters poured into the train stations like crazed pilgrims converging on shrines, and scalpers couldn't give away tickets to the evening's musicals. Across the park, children released from the chores of math and table-setting played cops-and-robbers on an idle carousel.

He lived in a metropolis where people did not travel from place to place in leisure, not without a plan, not without a sense of immediate destiny: Wandering aimlessly went against the ethos of bustle and survival. With a simple subway ride downtown, Eric fell into the rhythm of the city.

I t used to be a factory," Timothy said. He pointed at the tallest building halfway down Forelle Street, but Eric was surveying the rest of the block, what he could see through a thickening squall of snow. A truck garage as large as a plane hangar stood at the far corner. It faced a windowless warehouse, which Timothy claimed was one of the last refrigeration companies operating in the meat-packing district. Forelle spilled into West Street, and beyond West was the highway—beyond the highway, in sight, the dark and depthless Hudson. Forelle Street was an appendage to the grid, an added block as the island widened moving north. It was not aligned perfectly with the rest of the lattice of streets, and so according to Timothy, the turn onto the quiet east-west street from the busier north-south one was sharp and dangerous, hazardous when it rained. Just last week a bakery truck had crashed into a lamppost. A few stale brioches still lay scattered on the sidewalk.

"I live at the top," Timothy said. "Richard's place is right below mine."

The building rose two floors above its neighbors and was fortified by the abutting structures, but to Eric's eye, all three edifices listed in a Pisan tilt. He glanced up at the roof and then slowly followed the seven stories down, seven stories of peeling eggshell paint, until on the street level he saw a green awning, retracted, and the sparkling windows of a restaurant. Propped up by the door was a chalkboard with the day's specials spelled out in an illegible cursive. Gold lettering on a black sign stretched the length of the storefront: THE MYSTERY ROAST.

"It's known for its coffee," Timothy said, following Eric's eye. Ten years ago, Timothy would come into the city and visit Eric during the school year. Eric played the Sherpa, Timothy the explorer, and now the roles were reversed. "Wanna see the apartment?"

The entrance to the residential part of the building was to the right of the café. Timothy pushed open the gate to a freight elevator. "The passenger elevator doesn't work," he explained. "If this one breaks, use the back staircase. And don't go up to the roof. There's something wrong with the door and it's a cinch to get locked up there."

The already gray walls of the cinematographer's loft looked pristine. The place was cavernous, an entire floor. "It's huge," Eric said, his voice echoing. With all that gray and so little furniture, the loft was as serene as a dance studio. And along one wall, there was a continuous, gallery-like line of framed photographs, silvery stills of box-office deities from Hollywood's Golden Age.

"If we become neighbors," Timothy said, "I promise not to make a lot of noise."

"You won't play bocci?"

"No bocci. I paint. Painting is quiet. Sculpture would be another thing."

"So what does this Richard guy want for it?"

"Not much."

"Good."

"Seventeen fifty."

"One thousand seven hundred and fifty dollars?" Eric's jaw dropped. "Every month?" No way could he afford that, no way. He stepped over to the windows and looked down at the street. Both the front and back walls of the loft were almost completely glass, tall expanses broken down into a graph of smaller panes.

"You should see it when it's sunny out," Timothy said. "It gets a lot of light." The storm was in full gear now, a white haze making it virtually impossible even to look across the street. "It's blindingly bright."

"One *thousand* seven hundred and fifty dollars?"

"That's nothing for a big loft. You've been away. Believe me, it's a bargain."

"Not if you don't have a job. Hasn't there been a rise in crime around here?"

"It's the deal of the century," Timothy said. "In the front windows, you've got the Empire State Building, and in the back, the World Trade Center. When it isn't snowing. The painting shouldn't take long."

"It's not that I don't think the place is perfect—"

"You have to see it when it's light."

"It's more than—"

"I'll give you the keys." Timothy dangled a key ring. "You can come back tomorrow and see it when it's sunny. Or whenever. I promise not to show it to anyone else."

"Well . . ." Eric knew better than to entertain the remotest possibility of such an extravagant commitment. His mind was made up, but he was flattered that Timothy was trying so hard to sway him. "Okay, I'll come back."

"Not to be a broken record, but you'd like it here. The coffee in the café is the best in the world. Here, take the keys."

Eric slipped the key ring over his forefinger and clutched the tangle of metal with his palm. "Richard won't want the place back any time soon?"

"Maybe never."

"Would I have to paint the place gray?"

"Gray, yeah."

"Okay, gray." Eric glanced around the loft once again, trying to record its dimensions in his mind. "Gray is perfect." Gray was healing. No, no, no. He would come back for a second look, but ultimately he would have to return the keys.

Eric worried that if he went home underground on the subway, his good fortune might change, and when he emerged on the street, he would discover that he had been dreaming all afternoon. So he headed through the blinding snow over and up to Fourteenth Street and then, soaking, hopped on a bus across town. Another one carried him north.

He was in a mood to cook (an urge he felt often but only acted on once in a great while). When his mother, Lydia, arrived home later, she stepped into the kitchen and sniffed the garlic aroma. "What's the occasion?"

"I just felt like cooking." Eric opened the oven and checked the roast. He sliced a cucumber.

"Smells like my favorite dinner." Lydia set her briefcase down and took off her flake-covered overcoat.

"Plus I'm making some salad with my famous Russian dressing." Roast chicken, stuffing, and salad was Eric's favorite menu, too, mostly because it was the only one he knew how to prepare.

"You're sweet. What a dreary day. D.O.D. cutbacks, a big bore."

The news was on before dinner was ready, so mother and son sat down with cocktails. Sharing a fondue fork, they passed a jar of marinated, smoked mussels back and forth as improvised hors d'oeuvres. At the end of their marriages they had forged a peculiar kinship. Actually, Lydia had been legally separated from Anders Bruckner for a while, more than four years. For tax reasons, they had never formally divorced, but this winter Anders wanted to remarry. Even if all had been said and done in this union long ago, her new legal status had seemed like something to celebrate, so when Lydia became lawfully unwedded for the third time one day last month, she had brought out a bottle of very dry, very expensive champagne. Eric had clinked his glass with hers and dutifully drank his half-bottle, not in celebration but with a profound and crippling sadness. Eric had never known Anders all that well, but Lydia on the other hand was quite friendly with Margot. She liked her, Eric knew, but she accepted her departure from the family with curious aplomb, which Eric took to mean that she had always expected and was not surprised by this outcome. Lydia always claimed that she had married Eric's father when she was young, too young, and so Eric had followed in his mother's footsteps, which bothered him deeply.

Once respective divorce documents were signed, Eric was left to mourn the past alone while his mother, he was sure, was eager to move on to the next romance in her long career. There had been men after she and Anders had parted, but none in the previous year. She had barely gone out, and neither had Eric. Instead they had giggled their way through videocassettes of screwball comedies, the skirmishes of the past forgotten until last night. Now Lydia was ready for new things in her life, but there lay Eric, sprawled out on a couch, unable to face his own future. This was what he imagined his mother believed, that she couldn't move on when there was this kid at home to take care of.

The anchorman delivered his reports with practiced cheer: cold weather in the Northeast, a new civil war in Africa, another failed bank, a corrupt Senator. Eric popped into the kitchen to check on the chicken, and while he was away from the TV, his mother blurted, "Margot," as if she were issuing a warning, Heads up.

"Margot?" Eric's first response was to glance toward the foyer to see if she had walked in. He came back to the television and sighed: She had entered through another sort of door. He folded his arms tightly across his chest. "Hi, Margot. How's your Q-rating?"

"Perez is running for Mayor after all." Lydia was clearly trying to pretend that the news was significant and the fact that Margot Brandon delivered the report was no big deal. "I knew he would."

A wider shot of Margot and the candidate made it clear that they were in downtown Brooklyn. "I can't believe she's in the city," Eric said.

"You certainly don't expect her to call you, do you?"

Thankfully, no. But he had New York and she had the rest of the country. Margot was combing her part farther down the left side of her head now, or maybe she was simply wearing her hair longer. Eric heard her voice, a deeper alto than he recalled. Finally, he focused on the report: A local hero had announced a campaign for the mayoralty.

"It would be wonderful if Rob won," Lydia said. "It will never happen, but I'll still vote for him."

Eric's mother's endorsement seemed more like a vote for Margot than for the candidate, as if her coverage indicated good taste on her part, as if in following the man thus far, she had proven once again to be the young woman Lydia had always admired and perhaps envied. Eric had grown rather accustomed to seeing his ex-soulmate on the network news, but tonight, he was more annoyed than usual. Last week, she had been in Boise reporting on heroin in the heartland, so why had she come to New York? Just to torture him with her proximity?

"It's a great gig for her," Lydia said. "Even you have to admit it, Eric, it's a prize-winning assignment."

"I don't see why she's covering a local story on network TV."

"You missed the lead-in. This is part of a new series, 'Electing the Future,' and Margot is following several races all over the nation—federal, state, and local. Bright and brilliant leaders making bold bids for key offices. Sounds like fun."

"Fun. Sure."

When Margot signed off, Lydia said, "The chicken smells tasty." This was more of a reminder than a compliment.

Eric dashed into the kitchen. Only the right wing of the bird was charred.

"Delicious," Lydia said. They dined during the rest of the broadcast.

"So you'll never guess who I ran into in a NYMA men's room today."

His mother was munching on a large piece of romaine and couldn't respond.

"Timothy."

"Our Timothy?"

"He was exhibiting his drawings. He's an artist. I only saw his drawings, but—"

"Wait." She wiped a gob of dressing off her chin. "He was showing you his drawings in the men's room?"

"Not just me. Everyone. He's mounted a show there." Eric described Timothy's nudes. "It's how he hopes to make a splash in the art world."

"Are you sure that art was all he was selling?"

"You're the one who taught me to be open-minded."

"It just sounds a little lurid to me, a tad juvenile."

"Don't be stuffy. It's working. While I was there, two people came in, delivered raves, and one lady even bought a drawing for an exorbitant price."

"Timothy always was original."

"He seems to have his shit together. And I looked at an apartment this afternoon."

"Already?"

Already? She had practically tossed him out last night.

"Where?"

"The West Village, Forelle Street. A loft in Tim's building. It's cheap for a loft. Seventeen hundred and fifty." As Eric repeated the rent, the notion of paying out this much money on a monthly basis seemed ludicrous and impossible. Maybe he could find something cheaper farther west. Like New Jersey. Money was going to be a problem if he was going to move out. Unfortunately, although conveniently, his great-aunt Lucia had died a couple of years ago. Lucia Madsen had made some experimental films in the Bohemian Twenties and then gone on to make a fortune in the fashion business. Eric only remembered her as a terribly old woman who would disrobe at the dinner table. Her estate had gone to her only niece, Lydia, and Eric had been lucky enough to receive about twenty thousand dollars after taxes. He had lived on this legacy after losing his job, after Margot had moved out. In fact, he lived on the money for a year, but now he had only five thousand four hundred dollars in the bank.

"You'll have to get a job," Lydia said.

Why, Eric wondered, when all of New York City had to know this fact by now, did she find it necessary to proclaim anyway? "I'm probably not taking it."

"I'm glad. I'm glad you're making a move," Lydia said, eyes on the set. She did not sound like she was saying what she was thinking. "I'll miss you, of course."

Eric was annoyed by the false note that he heard in her voice, a hint of disapproval. He was never sure what she wanted from him.

Lydia climbed into bed earlier than usual, dragging an overweight novel with her. She had made a second career out of rereading nineteenth-century classics, and Eric often wondered when in life she had decided to ignore everything written after 1900. Late in the evening, he noticed that she had fallen asleep with her night-table lamp on. He stepped into her room and delicately placed a marker in the book butterflied over her hip. When she slept, the lines of her face, crow's feet and brow, and the ridges in the veins of her hand clutching a pillow seemed smoother than when she was awake. Eric remembered how when he was little and his mother napped, he would play with his Matchbox cars, racing scaled-down Jaguars and Porsches over the contours of her back, hip, and shoulders. He turned off the lamp, and in response, his sleeping mother mumbled something to someone in her dream.

Eric spooned out a bowl of coffee ice cream and hunkered down to watch his favorite late-night news program. A different issue of the day was explored at length each evening, and although he didn't know what to expect, he certainly thought that the story of the new mayoral candidate had been fully explored, at least for today. But there was Margot, delivering the ten-minute "dummy piece" that opened the show. There was not enough room for his heart in his chest.

"Robinson Perez grew up on mean streets . . ."

"Margot, Margot, Margot," Eric chanted. He repeated her name until it sounded nonsensical. "Margot, Margot, Margot, Margot." Impossible: Margot still meant Margot. Margot from Fargo, that was how she had introduced herself during Freshmen Week. They were just friends the first year, and then the following fall they became lovers. They were married a week after graduation and stayed together three and a half years.

"He went to school here, in a building that ultimately would become a notorious crack den."

"How have you been?" Eric asked the set.

"His first political post was the vice-presidency of the student council."

After college they set up their apartment in Washington, where Margot had spent her summers as an intern and was able to grab the job she had always wanted, as an assistant to an associate news producer. She got Eric a job at the station, too, a tedious research position for the evening news, but he didn't care because he was content simply to be married. Domestic life was new and exciting. Often Margot worked late and came home long after he did, and each night her return seemed like the ending to a fairy tale. Her body was always plentiful with new places to kiss, like between her right shoulder blade and her leaflike spine, like just above her left breast in the flat plane beneath her collarbone. Margot came home, they made a mess of a never-made bed, and afterward she whipped up something to eat in the time it took to boil pasta water. She took whatever was in the refrigerator and cupboards—broccoli, capers, walnuts—and tossed it all into a skillet to create the most fabulous sauce. Eric was always in awe of anyone who could cook well, but even more dazzled when a true chef could throw a meal together in a flash. He loved to lie on the bed in their cluttered studio and watch her work her magic: She would be naked except for a long apron. She cooked, and this was the source of mystery, astonishment, and envy. They ate pasta à la Margot in bed, spent and purring, watching talk shows, and after a syndicated cop serial they followed together, they fell asleep.

"A much-publicized event in Rob Perez's life occurred when he was Borough President. He was mugged by a homeless woman with a switchblade. Perez credits this incident for what admirers have called an unusual sensitivity for the impoverished."

"Margot, Margot, Margot." Eric knelt in front of the television. "Margot?"

After the first year, she began her ascent, the sort of rocket-rise yapped about in gossip columns. She became a full-fledged producer. And why not? She was smart, worked hard. Her ascension became industry myth, and to Eric she confessed that she was toying with going in front of the camera. She became busier and busier, and one lucky day—just as in the movies when the understudy starlet gets her break when she goes on for the ailing diva—Margot had to deliver a story when a snowbound reporter could not make it to the scene. As a reporter she traveled more, and Eric saw less of her. At some point he became paranoid: Did she have a fling with that White House reporter with the broken nose, Jeff Shaft? Eric never found out. He missed her terribly, he ached for her, yet when she came home at night, exhausted, she seemed to resent him and his dependence on her. In retrospect, she might have been afraid of her ambition, of the meteoric arc her career was tracing. At the time, Eric had no idea why they were fighting. He was never sure what their disputes were specifically about. And then he lost his job.

He had long before stopped appreciating the squalid grind of the media business, and then one day at 6:24 before the 6:30 feed, he was instructed to put together background for an obituary hot off the wire—and so what if there was a little miscommunication? So what if Eric supplied the dates and biography for an All-Pro defensive end instead of a former Secretary of Defense? His boss caught the mistake before it went into the newsreader's script anyway. Should he have been dismissed? He was married to Margot Brandon after all, which did not save him, not this time. It wasn't his first blunder. A staff cutback was the network's excuse, and Margot never tried to rescue him. He was banished, and he hardly saw her at all, not even at the water cooler.

"On the House floor, Perez used his acerbic wit to distinguish himself and spark fear among his opponents."

"We started out together," Eric whispered to the television. "Isn't that worth something?" He slapped the top of the set. He did not have to watch Margot when she came on the air, yet he did. He always tricked himself into being surprised when she appeared, but in truth, he would flip to her channel looking for her.

It was three-thirty in the morning when Eric awoke. He thought he heard a noise in the kitchen. He had fallen asleep on the couch with the television on. In a dim alley, a woman with long hair and a trench coat was holding a gun against her stomach, aiming it at a man who looked like he could use a shave and a meal. The man was saying something like, Wait a minute, sweetheart, you don't know what you're doing. Eric flicked off the TV as his mother walked into the room carrying a glass of milk.

"Don't stop watching on my account," she said. The milk glowed in the dark.

"What are you doing up?"

"I couldn't sleep. What are *you* doing up?"

"Bad dreams?"

"I just couldn't sleep."

"I don't think milk is the sort of thing you're supposed to drink if you want to fall asleep again. It's an old wives' tale, you know, about warm milk and honey."

"I've been an old wife longer than you."

Eric wondered if there was liqueur in the milk, a thimble of Amaretto. He knew better than to stay here, than to talk to his mother now.

"Two thousand dollars a month is a lot to come up with," she said.

"Seventeen fifty. I probably won't move down there. Anyway, I'll find work."

"You know I could call your father. Much as I don't like talking to him, I'd call him for you and ask him to ask one of his friends if there's anything for you downtown."

"Don't call Dad." The last thing Eric wanted was to owe his father a favor. He spoke with him once or twice a year. He hadn't seen him in two.

Lydia sipped her milk. Milk and liqueur, Eric was sure: Some sort of aperitif was making the glass luminous. "I remember," she said, "when you were eight or so, and you used to tell me—"

"Don't."

"You used to tell me that on Monday—"

"Please."

"On Monday you were going to be a doctor, and on Tuesday you were going to be a lawyer. On Wednesday an artist, on Thursday an architect. On Friday . . ."

Over the years this snapshot of precocity had evolved into a self-incriminating confession that Lydia either deliberately or inadvertently used against him. "Don't get into the job discussion."

"I didn't say anything about jobs. That was life-talk, not job-talk. Ambition, *weltanschauung*. Don't you have any desire to *be* anything?"

Eric was tired of his mother's redundant prods. "So what will you do?"

"What will I do when?"

"What will you do now that I'm moving out, now that you're free of me?"

"*Free* of you? Let's not get carried away. Look"—now, as always, his mother pretended to be the one who was in the benevolent mood, not the person who had thrown down the glove—"you should be happy. You're getting started—"

"You keep telling me that I have to jump-start my life."

"You do. Margot left. You were down. Enough's enough."

"Mother, you're just projecting." This had been on Eric's mind for some time. He had nearly said it the night before.

"It's late." Pause. "Is this something you found in one of those magazines you sit home all day and read?"

Eric went into his bedroom.

"How am I projecting?" Lydia was framed in the doorway, casually sipping her milk as if she had stopped by to help Eric with a bit of trigonometry.

"I mean that all this talk about me getting on with *my* life," Eric said, "is fucked up. What you are really worried about is getting on with *your* life. And I get the feeling that you think that you need to get me out of the way first."

"This is silly. I'm going to bed." She stayed put.

"The truth of the matter is," Eric continued, "that you can get on with your life no matter what I do, and that's what will happen. And that's the way it always has been, even when I was younger. You do what you do. That's it. I'm not in your way, if you want to get on with things. I have never been in your way. You'll marry whoever you're going to marry next. You'll get divorced. You'll move on. You do what you do."

Lydia set down the milk on top of a dresser. "Why are you telling me all of this? You know why, right? If you hadn't become so goddamned self-absorbed lately"—over the years she had called him selfish, she had labeled him arrogant, but never self-absorbed, which for some reason stung more—"you'd see that you just think you're in my way, as you put it, and you obviously feel guilty about it. You feel guilty but you want *me* to do something, not you. If you were less self-absorbed and you thought you were in my way—whatever that means, and I'm not sure I really know—then you would just take matters into your own hands and get out of the way yourself, if that's what I need. Or what you think I need. I don't even know what we're talking about, it's so convoluted." She threw her arms up and disappeared into the hallway, only to return moments later. "But I do know, unfortunately, that you never seem to do anything to help anyone else. And that's the way it always has been, and quite honestly, it never surprised me that Margot . . . that she . . ." Lydia stopped, mumbled something to herself, and left the room. Eric heard her bedroom door close. She had left her glass of milk on the dresser.

The last six months were embers now, smoldering. Weren't they supposed to be friends at this point in life? Eric was ready to storm her room and flail his arms and demand an apology. Her myopia was maddening. At the same time, he wanted to wrap himself in the quilt folded over the foot of her bed and calmly explain his numbness, his inertia, but then allay her maternal worrying: He was moving on, after all, moving out. As usual, he didn't know how to say any of this—words eluded him, with his mother, with Margot, and conflicting sentiments of indignation and empathy, as always, paralyzed him. So he bottled his emotions. He sank into his bed.

At a younger age, he might have cried. But tonight—today—he knew that his family life, if you could call his partnership with his mother that, no longer mattered. He had hardened. And so as he mindlessly studied the objects on his adolescent desk—a rubber dolphin from the Aquarium, a pile of arrowheads, a pocket compass that permanently pointed southwest—his thoughts were not mournful or even angry. Instead he calculated expenses in his head: how much it would cost if he went to the airport tomorrow and flew to a city that made him happy, Paris, for example, and how long he could afford to live there.

Ihe next morning after his mother left for work, Eric got up and packed everything he wanted to take with him in a duffel bag. Shirts, socks, jeans, loafers, only the essentials. He wrote a terse note to say he would call her soon, and he left her spare set of keys on the kitchen counter.

The city moved in slow motion. The temperature remained low enough that the previous evening's snow did not begin to melt away under a bright sun. Drifts amassed against brownstones. Doormen shoveled paths, ploughs cleared the avenues. Despite the wind, Eric let his long camel-hair overcoat fly open as he walked toward the museum, his scarf waving Isadora Duncan–style behind him. First, he would find Timothy to tell him that he would not be taking the loft. Eric regretted having to say good-bye so soon after finding his old friend, but he knew that he had to get out of the city while he still had the means. He would say good-bye, take a cab to the airport, and escape to Paris. That was the plan.

The museum was even emptier today. Eric headed directly for Timothy's men's-room gallery but on the way was stopped by a guard who informed him that first of all he had to get rid of his bag, and secondly he needed to pay the admission fee. Eric obeyed, checking his luggage, but kept his coat on. He clipped the day's green NYMA button to his scarf.

From the checkroom, he opted for a shortcut through the galleries of ancient art. He glided past a display of portrait-busts of Roman Senators, past a Demotic scroll stretched the length of a wall. He was all set to dash up the stairs, when he noticed the blocked-off entrance to Greek Antiquities. The white plywood wall looked flimsy next to the solid, century-old plaster arch that embraced it. But where was the guard? Eric spotted the man several rooms away, where a group of grade-school children edged dangerously close to an equestrian bronze. The guard's back was turned. And then Eric noticed a temptation too wonderful to ignore.

The door cut into the temporary wall was open a crack. Eric assumed that someone was standing on the other side, clutching the knob. And then again . . . A peek was all he wanted. He pulled the door back cautiously, met no resistance, and tiptoed into Ancient Greece. He left the door ajar exactly the way he'd found it. No one stopped him. He felt like a cat who needed to inspect Toll-House cookies just out of the oven, cooling on a plate. He would sniff and lick and paw what he could and see how far he could go before someone came along and returned him to the floor.

The galleries looked exactly as he remembered them. The renovation had apparently only just begun, and removal of the art was the first chore. Crates were pushed up against the walls, yet most of the artifacts were still on display. He coasted past an impressive breakfront of red-figured vases, and then a heroic bronze helmet which floated in a cabinet all its own. He moved swiftly from room to room and didn't encounter anyone, no curators, no renovators. Anyone could have wandered in here. He proceeded further into the depths of the lost empire, backward along the time line. Several of the glass panes on the display cases had either been removed or were tilted open like transom windows.

He came upon the prized Brazewell Krater, a massive urn which in the early Seventies had won a spot on all the front pages because it was the most expensive museum acquisition to date. His hands tingled when he realized that he could commit a forbidden act. He ran his fingertips gently over the painted scene of orgiastic revelers gulping wine and dancing in the moonlight. On the other side of the urn, a regiment marched off to defend the city-state. The clay was cool to the touch. He traced the fretted decoration around the brim. He stood on his toes and peered inside the oversized vase. Nothing but ancient darkness. He tried to look deeper inside, but his long scarf brushed against the urn. Then he heard a high-pitched, metallic ping.

And footsteps. Someone was coming. He took a step back and held his breath, but no one appeared. In another room, a case of bracelets and rings was open, too. Eric removed one gold ring with a carnelian setting. He checked again to make sure that no one was watching him and slipped the ring over his pinky. A loose fit. The metal adjusted to the temperature of his flesh. He returned the ring to the case, turned around, and then an object across the room caught his eye.

A marble face, blank and smooth. A face belonging to an idol as white as the sun in a pale winter sky. He must have seen this object dozens of times before, but he didn't remember it. He drew closer and became hypnotized, transfixed. The features of the idol's face had worn away with time, like words lost on a tombstone. She had no eyes, no ears, no mouth, nothing but a prominent, triangular nose. The small statue of a woman was only a foot tall. Her head would fit in his palm, a head with a broad brow and a strong chin tucked into an elongated neck, which was supported by a wafer-thin body. At her widest, across her square shoulders, the idol spanned the length of his longest finger. At her thickest, at her neck and rump, she was no more than an inch. Her bony arms were folded one over the other and reached across her waist as if she wore a straitjacket. The arms, like her tapered legs, were demarcated with carved lines. A triangle of lines, too, for genitalia. Subtle swellings formed her breasts. Her thighs and feet were pressed together, and she stood on her toes, awkwardly balanced and requiring a Lucite base at her heels to hold the pose. She bent her knees slightly. She rocked her head back in laughter.

The panel of glass in front of the object was held open by a metal arm that unfolded from the pedestal, supporting the case. Something about the idol—her featureless face, her simple geometry, her whiteness— something that he could not quite pinpoint intrigued him. He glanced at other objects in the glass case, amulets and gold chalices, a scrap of dolphin fresco, but he kept returning to the idol. He read the card positioned next to the artifact:

CYCLADIC FIGURINE, C. 2500 B.C. KNOWN AS THE "AUSGRABEN IDOL." WHITE MARBLE. FROM THE AEGEAN ISLAND OF NAXOS. ATTRIBUTED TO THE NAXOS MASTER. GIFT FROM THE NORBERT STEWART COLLECTION.

The arms of the idol were crossed as if she were waiting for Eric to answer a question. Or her arms were crossed because she shivered. Her knees were bent as if she davened in fear. Or maybe her head was tossed back with confident satisfaction, with delight. The identification card offered more information:

MICROSCOPIC TRACES OF PIGMENTS WERE DETECTED ON THE FIG-URINE, INDICATING THAT IT WAS ORIGINALLY PAINTED. MOST LIKELY, THE FACE OF THE IDOL WOULD HAVE BEEN DETAILED WITH THE LARGE, ROUND EYES AND STRAIGHT SMILE CHARAC-TERISTIC OF THE PERIOD. FIGURINES SUCH AS THIS ONE WERE INTENDED TO BE POSITIONED HORIZONTALLY ON THEIR BACKS, AND NOT PROPPED UP AS SHOWN HERE. SCHOLARS BELIEVE THAT

THE SLOPED-BACK HEAD DENOTES A MOMENT OF ECSTASY. THE
BENT KNEES MIGHT REFER TO A RITUAL DANCE. THE ARMS FOLDED
ACROSS THE WOMB INDICATE FERTILITY.

He squinted and tried to imagine a pair of *large, round eyes,* but he only
focused on her sundial-shaped nose. The urge, the need, to follow the
slope of the small woman's neck down to her shoulders, to trace the arch
of her back with his finger, the curve of her bent knees all the way down
to her lobed feet, overpowered him. He swooned, resisted a magnetic
pull at first. Then he reached for the idol. The marble looked smooth,
yet it had a granular, porous quality when he touched it. The Cycladic
idol was so airy that he thought for a moment that the piece was a hoax,
painted balsa perhaps, or pumice. Yet the woman was solid like stone,
cold like marble when he cradled her back in his palm. The *Cycladic
figurine, c. 2500 B.C.* came from a world he could never know, from time
lost. It had survived history that no one alive could truly understand
with certainty.

Eric suddenly noticed people at the other end of the wing, a man in
a suit, two women in overalls, a ponytail dangling from one. They were
standing around a table, drinking from Styrofoam cups, munching on
doughnuts, chatting. A coffee break during the renovation of Greek
Antiquities, it seemed, and although their backs were turned away from
him, Eric knew that he had to escape right away. So he stepped back,
out of the alignment of passageways and presumably out of their sight-
lines.

He stepped back, but he held on to the idol. He unwound his crimson
college scarf from his neck, wrapped it around the artifact, and gently
placed the idol into an inner pocket of his coat. Because it was unbuttoned, the bulge was relatively inconspicuous.

He walked fast but didn't run. Behind him, he heard the museum
workers laugh. He glided through the doorway in the temporary wall.
The guard was still busy with the children, kneeling in front of them
now, ballooning his cheeks into fish-faces. Eric moved quickly but not
with any more noticeable determination than anyone else passing from
point A to point B in the museum, or like him, toward the checkroom.
He retrieved his bag.

He didn't realize how much he had been sweating until he plunged
into the cold wind outside. The sky had shifted from blue to gray: A
second storm waited just beyond the city limits. Eric immediately
headed downtown. Cabs and buses followed one another's tracks down
the ploughed avenue. People on the sidewalks negotiated a layer of ice.

No one noticed him, as far as he could tell, yet there were people out and about, too many people, so he slipped through the entrance of the stone fence of the park.

Eric took off. He galloped. He ran due west, he ran as fast as he could over the snow. His chest, his lungs, opened up to let in more thin air, to take in more oxygen. Instead of following a path, he cut directly across the lawn, leaving the first boot prints in the pure field. He looked at these prints as he made them, but after a while he began to go snow-blind. At first when he glanced up toward the trees ahead, all he saw was empty air. Eric held his coat closed around him as he ran. He wondered what he looked like, his duffel bag slung over his shoulder, the tail of his coat pulled up to his gut. He was sure that no one else was in the park with him, not on this cold morning, not in the immediate vicinity at any rate, and he began to feel safer as he retreated farther from the museum.

The faster Eric ran, the weirder the landscape through which he raced became. It wasn't snow-blindness. He felt as if he were swimming through a frozen pond, and while he knew that the people above the surface were panicking about his welfare, he was actually quite warm and alert, even if he couldn't find a place to pop up for air. Strange: Along the rolling terrain of frozen lawn and amid the pockets of dense woods, pieces of his past life in this city came rushing at him. High-school boys jogged by in a pack, a cross-country team making its way through the park. They weren't really there, Eric knew, but they looked completely three-dimensional, far off but real. He passed a crowd gathering for a summer concert, spreading blankets. There he was, age five, launching a toy sailboat in the lagoon. There he was again, sitting under an ageless oak, on a date, too frightened to kiss, too scared to say anything lest his voice crack. And then paces later he saw himself one more time, tossing a Frisbee, playing with a friend's collie.

Eric calmed himself. He was drunk on adrenaline, that was all. He focused on running. He sprinted faster. By the time he passed the rear of the open-air theater, he was fairly certain that he was not being followed. He stopped and nearly gagged on the congealing gas of his own breath. He opened his duffel bag and pushed aside half of the shirts and socks and formed a comfortable and well-padded bed for the figurine still wrapped in the scarf. He pulled back the wool enough to see her head. "Wow," he said to the idol. "Wow," to the elm trees and the snow while he was at it. He was delirious, starting to feel very foolish, but high nonetheless. At the same time he had to ask, "Now what?" Rather than answer the question, and not wanting to stop long enough to tire, he closed the bag and continued running. He crossed a road and then swept through the rest of the park, skipping off a path and up a hill directly to the stone fence, which he climbed over to reach the street. The subway was a block or so south.

He only had twenty-dollar bills in his wallet, so that was what he handed the woman in the glass booth. The C train came down the tracks. Eric received a handful of tokens and some change, and as the train sidled up, he dropped one token in the turnstile but spilled half of his supply on the platform. He hopped into the car as its doors closed. As the subway hurtled downtown, Eric regained his breath. The car became crowded. A man stretched out and slept, yesterday's tabloid as his pillow. A woman entertained a child whose snowsuit made a swishing noise when she tried and failed to stand up on a seat. Old men read newspapers printed in dying languages. People got on and off, and for the first time, Eric felt lucky to live in an overpopulated city where it was easy to travel in a swarm.

He rushed down Forelle Street, which was beginning to cloud with a freezing mist, a thickness that was neither snow nor rain. He rode the freight elevator up to the sixth floor, managed to turn the lock next to the elevator buttons, and once inside, once the door was shut, gasped a sigh of relief and collapsed to the floor.

The sun faded away—the new storm was darker, windier than the last—but Eric left the lights off. He opened his bag of clothes and removed the idol from the scarf with great care and reverence. He set it down on his lap. The gravity of his act hit him like a blow to the back of his skull.

Okay, okay, he thought—his heart finally slowing to a normal pace, the beat of reason and clear thinking—he would just hold on to the idol overnight. He'd had his fun. Tomorrow he would go to the police. He would concoct a perfectly plausible story. He'd play the bystander who had rescued the stolen treasure. He would say that someone else had been making off with the forty-five-hundred-year-old Greek figurine, and he, Eric Auden, citizen-turned-hero, had wrestled the priceless statue from the thief. He'd get his picture in the paper. Yes, he would go to the police, and tomorrow afternoon the ancient idol would be back home in the museum.

**H**eads, she went out; tails, she went home. Lydia tossed a quarter into the air but fumbled the catch, and it landed on her computer keyboard lodged between the T and the Y. She regularly received invitations to benefits from an array of institutions that were less interested in flattering Lydia Carver, the person, than they were in luring Lydia Carver, the senior member of an international-relations think tank. People liked to be associated with a high-profile, well-funded organization like the Thornton Institute, and in the case of the New York Museum of Art, the fact that both groups shared the same neighborhood contributed to the cordiality. There were two other invitations for the evening that she could have accepted instead, but she stuck with her first choice. Go, she pushed herself, just go.

She stuffed project reports and grant proposals into her briefcase. She had no intention of doing any work tonight, yet she couldn't very well descend the main staircase of the mansion-turned–think tank empty-handed. She was supposed to be a very important person. Talking-head news programs still came to her for sound bites, although lately she didn't return the producers' calls. Before she'd gotten into the business, she always imagined that a think tank would be a place where pipe-smoking men in tweed and brainy women like herself would sit around in cracked leather armchairs in paneled rooms and say nothing. They would merely exist in a thick funk of heady thought, thought too complex to articulate aloud, thought reserved for telekinetic transmission within the confines of the oak sanctum. What Lydia actually did these days was answer the Thornton Institute's financial needs by heading up the aeronautical division of the think tank's Defense Department contracting concern, which meant that she oversaw the development of software-training programs for fighter pilots. Aviation companies built the guts of planes and the think tanks worked through the bugs in the brains. She had been at

Thornton for four years, having taken the position when it became too difficult to work with her boss at the Matting Foundation, a man who happened to be the same Swiss-born, increasingly politically conservative, chain-smoking Anders Bruckner whom she had recently divorced. She had left Matting, too, because the place had drifted so far to the right during her tenure, although that didn't explain why she ended up doing mostly defense work at Thornton, whose letterhead boasted at least five former Republican cabinet officials and three hawkish generals emeriti. But Thornton was closer to home and paid well. She was bored but comfortable, and at this point in her life, another change seemed like a lot of bother.

As she climbed the museum steps, she sipped the cold, clean air. The city was smog-free after a prolonged snowfall. Yard-long daggers of ice hung from the museum pediment. This was quite the place to be tonight, the first museum event since the theft two days ago. Admittedly, this was why she had broken her habit of throwing away NYMA invitations without opening them. She could see strands of red tape around the trees where the police had closed off a piece of the park. The stolen idol was still at large.

As a rule Lydia did not read the tabloids, but since she cared about the New York Museum of Art and since a crime had been committed in her neighborhood, she indulged herself. Besides the weather, only a trial or scandal could bring New York to any sort of temporary unity or focus, and it had been a winter of sleepy headlines so far. Plus, this was not the everyday crime of violence or financial impropriety that the city had grown accustomed to. The museum theft offered a new brand of mystery: It was a crime that had never before been committed here, and so the papers and media ran wild with the story. The day after the theft, the *News* devoted its front page to a photo of the Cycladic figurine, and the headline was a single word: STOLEN! Today, another picture of the statue had run in the *Post* under the banner: COPS CLUELESS IN MUSEUM HEIST: ANCIENT LADY LOST FOR GOOD?

Lydia read that museum officials were in a state of shock. If the place was going to be vandalized, they had always assumed that someone would break in at night. The fact that the burglary had occurred in broad daylight was not only embarrassing but also revealed a previously unknown vulnerability. The *Times* labeled it a trend: Not too long ago, three museums in Paris had been victimized on the same morning when thieves cut canvases from frames—the thefts were carried out while the museums were open to the public. Now NYMA, once considered impregnable, was no longer safe. The museum, observing a policy of never publicly discussing its security—a convenient out, Lydia thought —refused to offer any explanations as to how such a theft might have been accomplished.

Many questions remained unanswered. A relatively obscure item had been stolen. Why, given all the magnificent relics of civilizations past and present, exotic and mundane, did an art thief (or thieves) target such a minor, albeit exemplary idol? The Brazewell Krater was in the next room. Why were no other objects also taken? Sure, the Cycladic statue was valuable (estimates went as high as eight hundred thousand dollars, and one auctioneer thought that the idol, given current prices and its well-preserved state, might fetch three million), but some experts argued that there had to be a motive that ran deeper than mere money. The museum director had dramatically declared, "The very randomness with which the Ausgraben Idol seems to have been singled out and victimized is indicative of the profoundly random violence raging in our city and of the terrorism in the world we now live in. Our last sanctuaries are being spoiled."

Lydia flashed her invitation at a guard, and then a second one checked her purse and briefcase. She stepped through a metal detector. When a third guard looked her up and down, she thought that he was going to complain that her work clothes weren't dressy enough for the occasion. He directed her toward an elevator up to the exhibition.

A sign neatly painted on a wall read: DUTCH LANDSCAPES—MAPPING A WORLD. The place was packed. Lydia thought that at the very least she would get to see some of the paintings with more leisure than when the museum was open to the public. Wrong. While a few party-goers studied the blue skies and flatlands and cows, most of the guests stood with their backs to the oils, watching the crowd, blocking the art.

Whenever some of the well-dressed patrons shifted to one side, she sneaked a peek at a gabled church or a tulip field or a windmill. She concentrated on the buffet of Cajun shrimp, overcooked and too spicy, and fois gras, served on limp toast points. The stuffed grape leaves were greasy, and the smoked salmon leathery. She knew that she should have been attempting to meet new people, but she didn't spot anyone she wanted to get to know. With some gentle nudging she won a full view of a painting, a splendid scene of an amber field and a distant cathedral town.

A man with an overgrown mustache and Victorian sideburns tapped her on the shoulder. "Excuse me, but aren't you Lilliane Dutoit, the great Belgian actress?"

"Sorry, no." Lydia tried to step back from the landscape to study the angular light, the meek sun giving way to looming rain clouds.

The man called across the room. "Justine, Justine. Come meet Lilliane Dutoit." To Lydia: "I don't know why you don't allow anyone to take your picture. You're as lovely as ever. Please meet my wife, Justine."

Justine bowed hello. She hooked her husband's arm. He looked as though he might appropriate some salt shakers and sugar bowls to depict a military campaign from the Boer War. Justine wore a dress too red for her pale complexion and looked consumptive. "I own all your movies," she said. "On video, that is. It's wonderful the way we can own movies now."

"I'm afraid you have me confused."

"I've heard how publicity-shy you are," the man said. "You've been found out. But you're among friends and admirers!"

Lydia glanced at the landscape once again, longingly. She wished she were there.

"You do look marvelous," Justine said. "What's your secret?"

Lilliane Dutoit had to be eighty. Strangely enough, this was not the first time that Lydia had been confused for her. A long time ago, but still many years after Lilliane Dutoit had appeared in her last black-and-white, hooker-with-a-heart-of-gold spy flick, a man had snapped a photo of Lydia thinking she was the reclusive actress. That was at a time when maybe, just maybe, Lilliane Dutoit might have looked glamorously younger, and Lydia something like her. "You have me confused," she said more forcefully. "I create training programs for fighter pilots."

"Fighter pilots!" the man roared. People looked at him. "That's killing." His laugh evolved into a choking cough and he withdrew an enormous monogrammed handkerchief and patted his lips.

"I'd rather be working on the Sino-Cambodian project we've got going," Lydia said, "but I'm stuck training fighter pilots." She knew that whatever she said was lost on the man. Poor Lilliane Dutoit, she thought. The paparazzi were always hanging out at the corner deli near her building hoping to catch her buying a peach.

The man laughed hard again. "Please stop, you're ruining me. Come, Lilliane. Let us show you our contribution to this little show." The man tugged gently on Lydia's elbow until she followed him and Justine halfway across the exhibit.

The painting that they had loaned the museum was small by comparison to most in the show. It was a miniature version of the others, perhaps included only because it was by a well-known artist. The plaque next to the frame indicated that *A Field Near Delft* hailed from the Phillip and Justine Brick Collection. "It's lovely." Lydia was polite.

"Fighter pilots!" Phillip Brick tapped his paunch and chortled.

"I've always wondered," Justine said timidly, "why you didn't show up for your marriage to John Henderson. You looked like the perfect couple in the movies."

Lydia remembered hearing about this famous Hollywood episode when she was a child. "Yes, well, what you probably don't know," she said, "is that John slept in a hair shirt and liked to flog himself. Or have me . . . well, you know. At San Simeon, he was fine company. But most of the time . . ."

"How odd." Justine cocked her head. "In the movies, he always seemed so . . ."

"All-American?" Lydia suggested.

"Precisely."

"Do you like my painting?" Phillip Brick was attempting the impossible task of sucking in his belly and straightening his back. "Justine, maybe Lilliane would like some of what you're drinking." His wife dutifully retreated to the bar. When he was alone with Lydia, he said, lowering his voice, "You know, I have quite a collection."

"Do you?"

"I've been amassing it for some time."

"Have you?" Rescue me, Lydia prayed, someone rescue me.

"Excuse me, Miss Dutoit?"

"What?" Lydia accidentally answered and turned around.

"I apologize, Phillip," a man said. He had the faintest trace of an accent. "I didn't mean to interrupt. I just want to take her over to meet Cy Rothman. He's in another room." And striking blue eyes, as clear as aquamarine. "He hasn't seen you in so long, Miss Dutoit, and he doesn't know you're here."

"I'm not," Lydia muttered. But looking again at the jowly man who held her captive, who was pouting at the second man's ill-timed intrusion, she opted for the prettier face. She allowed the man to escort her away from the Phillip Brick Collection. Over her shoulder, Lydia saw Justine return with two foamy glasses. "I'm not—"

"I know," the man said. "I was eavesdropping."

"You're saving me."

"Maybe I'm dragging you off to save *me*. I'm tired of talking to the same old people." As the man led Lydia past groups of guests, she noticed that everyone either raised his glass or nodded a silent hello. When they arrived safely at a remote corner in the next room, having acquired fluted glasses of flat champagne on the way, Lydia started to giggle.

"You looked like you were in agony," the man said.

A young woman popped her head in. "Marek, Scott Mathers is leaving."

"Say good-bye for me, and tell him I'll call him tomorrow."

Marek? Lydia pulled the invitation out of her purse and read the name at the bottom, the name of the organizing curator: *Marek Vanetti* was printed in elegant, fine type. "This is a lovely show," she said.

"It was great fun to throw together," Marek Vanetti replied. He squinted at the invitation in Lydia's hand. "I know you're not Lilliane Dutoit. But . . . I'm sorry, I don't know who you are."

"Lydia Carver. I'm always getting invitations to come to these openings, but I never do, but what with the theft and all—"

"Shush."

"Sorry."

"It's just that I'm too young to have an ulcer, and I'm starting to get one. Look, I know this is a pick-up line, but I'm sure we've met before."

It was a tired come-on, but how long had it been since any line had been used on her? "I live nearby and come to the museum often enough. Or I used to when I was trying to acculturate my son."

"Jason. Jason Maldemer."

"Do you know Jason?" Funny: Just the other day Lydia had been thinking about her second husband.

"Not anymore. I did something to upset him, and like so many others, he dropped me. But Scott Mathers—he just left—he—"

"I thought that name rang a bell." Lydia was facing a painting of a harbor city. A pool of cool water bounced against the pier, and a canal-street of thatched roofs rose beyond moored boats. "I was married to Jason for a while, as you probably know."

"You're Lydia *Carver* now?"

"My maiden name."

Marek nodded. "Are you in touch with Jason?"

"Me? No." Not in years. "Who is?" The pop-philosopher of the Sixties and Seventies had closed himself off and was living as a recluse, possibly still in the city: That was the rumor. Now and then at a party, she used to hear that a Jason Maldemer manuscript had arrived at his publisher's, but then a book never materialized. Rumors were Lydia's only connection to the man, and even they had petered out.

"I don't want to alarm you," Marek said, "but I just heard something about Jason from Scott Mathers."

"Is Scott in touch with him?"

"No, but his wife is a literary agent who has a client who told her that she had heard from someone else that Jason was ill."

"Oh, no." Lydia felt ill herself, hot in the room filling up with more bodies.

Marek slapped his palm to his forehead. "I'm a buffoon. Of course, this news would upset you. I shouldn't have so casually—"

"No, really, it's fine. Obviously I'm concerned, but that's okay. I'd rather know than not know." What Lydia had been thinking about the other day was that one morning she would wake up and simply read Jason's obituary.

"Nevertheless, I'm sorry I dropped it on you."

Lydia did not remember meeting this man before, though his accent was familiar, and so were his slender hands, which kept passing a champagne glass back and forth, a glass from which he refrained from sipping. "You know," she said, "I haven't really had a chance to look at the art. Maybe you can show me around."

"Have you seen *The Hunting Party Near Haarlem*?"

"I think there's a conspiracy to block the walls."

"Come. I want to talk to you some more, but really, I should mingle."

Marek walked in front of Lydia, holding a drink in one hand and Lydia's hand in the other, and wove his way through the crowd of collectors, museum patrons, socialites, and Dutch art scholars, all courtiers who paid homage to the curator-prince when he passed. They seemed drawn to him, attracted. Lydia was. His skin was dark, his hair long in back. He had to be ten years younger than she was. His suit was wrinkled in places, and instead of a handkerchief, a pencil peeked out of his breast pocket: He didn't appear entirely comfortable in this costume.

They arrived at the painting he wanted her to see. "They had a deep need to map out their landscape," the curator noted. "You see the men and squires here in the foreground carrying their rifles, and the man with the dogs has gone ahead. They're walking away from one forest, moving along the river toward another. But look, that's really only about a quarter of the picture."

"Most of it's a landscape," Lydia said. She remembered an art history class she took in college thirty-plus years ago. She'd had a crush on her professor.

"Exactly. I'm not boring—"

"Not at all." Say anything, she thought, ramble about the cows.

"You can see the church there"—Marek pointed at the painting with his pinky as if he were afraid of offending the artist—"and you see the town over there. Really, this is a geography more than anything else. The hunting party approaching the viewer even tells you what's off the map, namely more forest."

A man whispered something in Marek's ear, and soon Marek was shaking another man's hand, accepting congratulations. While he engaged in necessary small talk, he grinned at Lydia. It was either the champagne or it was Marek Vanetti, the curator with the clear blue eyes and a rumpled suit—one of the two was making Lydia light on her feet, high, lofty in one of those pale skies on the wall.

Marek returned. "You don't know how I hate these parties."

"I can imagine."

"You met Phillip Brick. You know what it's like. Everyone so eager to impress everyone else. The collectors and people from other museums wielding their power, and the pandering scholars—brilliant though they are—kissing up to the collectors, especially the private ones, because if they don't, they won't get to see the prints. Alas," Marek said as he swiped a cheese puff off a silver tray when a waiter passed by, "the hors d'oeuvres are really rather tasteless to boot." He popped it in his mouth. "Lydia, I'm glad you came. It's so hard to meet new people when you do what I do for a living."

They talked and toured the exhibit, and Marek now and then would say something casually educational about a painting. Lydia liked him more and more. He seemed genuine. It helped that he was easy on the eyes, but he was smart, too, and smart was hard to find these days.

"My son told me a funny story," she said. "About the museum. About the guy who is showing his drawings in the men's rooms here. Actually, the boy—though, he's not a boy now, is he? The young man is someone my son grew up with: He lived with us during the summers, and then he disappeared. Why am I telling you all of this?" Lydia realized, of course, that she had embarked upon an anecdote that she shouldn't finish. Timothy might get in trouble.

"Back up. Someone is exhibiting artwork in a men's room? Here?"

Marek had been amusing her and she wanted to amuse him back with a story. He would hear the news sooner or later. "And selling it." She relayed what Eric had told her.

"Clever," Marek said, "very clever. Of course, if a fire marshal happened to make a surprise visit . . . And the security really shouldn't be in cahoots with anyone. Once or twice might be fun, but with all that's been going on lately—"

"I hope I'm not getting anyone in trouble."

"Not at all. In fact, you're telling the right man. You don't know what would happen if someone like our director heard about this first, or even some of my colleagues—they'd call in commandos. It sounds like this young man has a sense of humor. And no exhibit lasts forever, they all come down eventually."

"This painting"—Lydia stopped Marek in front of a stormy sea-scape—"is my favorite so far."

"Oh, well, that one leaves me speechless. The clouds, the depth, the arrogance and eloquence of this worldview . . ." Marek was smart, and he was charming. He removed the pencil from his pocket and used the eraser end as a pointer. He ran his fingers through his hair nervously like a schoolboy. But Lydia was wary of charm. Charm had gotten her into trouble before. Charm was a protean creature who had appeared in many previous forms, in the shape of a boring financier, a paranoid writer-philosopher, a deceptively con-servative and arrogant expert in international relations, and other nonmarital impersonations in between—a philandering restaurateur, a self-involved ex-astronaut, a self-important computer executive. But Lydia had conquered the beast. She could trust Marek, and she already detected a bond: Neither one of them truly belonged here. She had not been intimate with anyone for longer than she could recall, which was her fault. Even before Eric's return, she had dug a moat around herself. This had to change.

". . . By mapping a landscape, the painter could in effect take a journey . . ." Marek spoke softly and to Lydia only, but as the thinning crowd became quieter, she got the impression that other people were only pretending to participate in their separate conversations and were listening in on hers, first surreptitiously, then overtly gathering around like disciples.

Later, she left Marek so he could shake hands and talk art, and after having retrieved her coat, she waved good-bye. He abandoned two bony-backed women and rushed over to her. "The Thornton Institute gets a great deal of support from the Thornton Family Foundation, doesn't it?" he asked.

"Not a lot. Some."

"I've heard that the Foundation is about to expand into arts-giving. Maybe you could help me figure out how NYMA should go about applying for a grant. Perhaps over lunch sometime soon?"

Lydia hesitated for a beat too long.

"If you'd like to—"

"Call me at the Institute," she said.

The curator blinked and then spun around and returned to his conversation, walked past it, it seemed, and into a painting, into a landscape, so that he stood on a flat field, under dubious clouds, and then strode off toward a distant town of thatched roofs and windmills.

The building across from Eric's new home looked neither like a warehouse nor a onetime factory nor even a tenement walk-up like the other structures on Forelle Street. Its rising, Gothic windows gave it the institutional stature of a college dormitory or a rectory or maybe a nineteenth-century chemistry laboratory. And when Eric peered out at the floor directly across from him, he saw faces—faces belonging to little boys who gazed back at him. They were ghostlike, faded, almost photonegative impressions rather than real boys, maybe a dozen of them assembled at a time, and they were all wearing drab, formless uniforms. Eric had noticed them on day one. Whenever he stared too long, the images of the boys evaporated into a curious apartment cat stalking a pigeon on the fire escape or a woman in curlers scanning the street or even an idle spider plant hanging in a window, and he returned to painting his loft.

He had removed the portraits of the Hollywood stars and carefully packed them into boxes following the specific curatorial instructions left by the cinematographer. He had covered the furniture and floor with drop cloths, spackled putty into all chinks and cracks, and already painted the high tin ceiling. Gray on gray. Now he painted the walls. He painted, and he watched the news. In three days, he had not gone downstairs. He had not left the building. He had not returned the Cycladic statue to the museum or given it up to the police, and instead, it lay hidden in a box among vintage photographs.

Eric took the idol out at least once an hour. The object was as smooth as a well-caressed worry stone. Its features (except for the nose) were so shallow that it cast no shadows. What he saw in the stone was what was there, yet at the same time, there was an aura of ambiguity about the woman, in her alabaster glow, her stance, her blank face, a vague warmth emanating from the marble, as if it could breathe. The temperature of the figurine changed with subtle shifts. It became cool if he stood by the window or when he touched it to his cheek, but then warmer, gradually, as it measured his pulse.

Timothy stopped by each day and invited Eric down to the café, but Eric claimed he wasn't feeling well, which was not altogether untrue—he had run across Central Park in the middle of winter with his coat open. He did not, however, have laryngitis, which was how he avoided lengthy conversations with Timothy, how he won his sympathy and got him to purchase the necessary paint supplies and groceries, and how he got to spend time alone.

Eric had been all set to march up to the Sixth Precinct the day after he stole the idol, but he decided he should practice his heroic-bystander speech in front of a full-length mirror, and when he did, he was appalled by how unconvincing he looked. There was no way he had wrestled the statue from art thieves, no way. Lying had never been his forte, which was a problem if he didn't want to go to jail, so he dreamed up another story. He would say that he had simply found the idol lying in the snow in the park. Or on top of a garbage Dumpster outside a Sixth Avenue pizzeria. Even better: Someone had tried to sell it to him on Fourteenth Street. It was lying on a towel next to some gold watches and chains, so he scooped it up, recognizing it from its pictures in the papers, and ran straight to the police.

Whenever his mind raced with fantasy, Eric grasped the Cycladic woman tightly with both hands. "What if they give me a lie detector test?" By day two he had abandoned any notion of going to the police. He figured he could just leave the idol somewhere, in a basket, for example, by the main portals of the museum right before it opened, like a baby left on a stoop. But he worried that he might get caught when he tried to drop it off. He had to unload it in as obscure a place as possible, where no one would notice him, like at a corner table in a Chinatown dumpling shop. He could order dim sum, leave the idol with the tip, and disappear. A waiter would find it and ultimately turn it over to the authorities. Ah, but what if the waiter decided to keep it?

Eric himself wanted to keep the carved woman. So he painted his walls November Nimbus, he asked Timothy to bring him the papers, and he watched the TV news with fascination and astonishment. He was the one person who actually knew what the entire city wanted to know. As each day passed, he became more confident about his anonymity: As far as he could tell, the police had no leads, and no leads were developing. Of course, the F.B.I. had been brought in, and the investigators surely were not telling the media all they knew. Nevertheless, in a great game of hide-and-seek, he was the hider, and there was an unexpected thrill in it. He looked the idol in the eye (or nose). "You're safe with me," he said. He was nameless in the big city.

When Timothy came by on the third afternoon, he collapsed into an armchair that was covered with a drop cloth. "It smells like paint," he complained. He had brought two bottles of beer with him and opened both.

"That's a strange thing for a painter to say."

"My kind of paint smells like art. Do you feel better?"

"I feel pretty good."

"I don't." Timothy tipped his head back and stroked his throat.

"There's probably something going around."

"I got kicked out of the men's room today."

"Oh, no."

"Just when things were happening. I sold another drawing, and then a curator named Derek—no, Marek—barged in and said that I was violating countless fire laws and that I'd had my fun and that if he ever caught me dealing art in the john again, he'd have me arrested."

"You better move on to another museum."

"It's because of the theft, you know. The people at NYMA are worried about how they look, but what they don't realize is that I was roping in customers for them. It's not like everyone was paying admission to see Rembrandt and El Greco, you know. Some of those people were coming to see me. I was on my way, Eric. It was only a matter of time before a dealer saw the show, but now . . ."

Eric threw the full weight of his body against his paint roller and ran it up and down the wall in long passes. He set the roller in its pan and picked up his beer bottle. "Tim . . ." Timothy was reaching under the drop cloth, pulling out framed photographs from a box. Eric wanted to confide in him. They used to motor a boat into the bay and cut the engine and drift. For a while, they told each other everything. For a while, but eventually they started guarding their secrets. Eric traded his bottle for the roller again. "There are plenty of other museums in this town. They all have men's rooms."

"I was able to get away with it at NYMA because I knew people there. Hey, who is this?" Timothy held up a portrait. "Do you remember staying up and watching this movie where she played a woman whose husband went off to fight in the French Revolution, leaving her behind to fend off the barbarians alone? It was a silent movie, and I remember thinking that when she was crying or screaming, nothing was coming out, no one was hearing her. It was very distressing. I wanted to shout for her. She reminds me of your mother."

Eric knew the film. "That was *City of Lights, City of Darkness*. And it was her brother and his best friend, who was also her fiancé, who went off to fight the battle, which wasn't the French Revolution—it was World War One, although it was France, and the star was that Belgian actress—" He dropped the paint roller into its pan, except he missed the pan, and the roller skidded across the floor, streaking November Nimbus across the floorboards. "Don't touch that!" He leaped across the room and kicked over the beer bottle—malt ran into the gray paint, into a quicksilver puddle that began to spread. Eric grabbed the picture frame.

"Okay, okay," Timothy said. "I'm sorry, I'm sorry."

Eric sipped what was left from the bottle. Meanwhile, the scope of the paint-beer puddle widened. "I'm still not feeling well, I guess. I didn't mean to snap at you."

"No problem. I'm in a pissy mood, too. Let's clean that up."

"I'll deal with it." Eric pressed the photo of Lilliane Dutoit against his chest as he followed Timothy to the elevator and waited until it arrived.

"You should get outside, Eric. I think that the paint fumes might be going to your head. Try to come down to the café later."

As soon as the elevator closed, Eric checked the box of photographs that Timothy had been rummaging through. Fortunately, Timothy had not lifted aside enough of the frames to reveal the idol, which after all was wrapped in a flannel shirt. Timothy probably hadn't noticed anything unusual. Just the same, it had been a close call, and if Eric wanted to hold the idol hostage, he would have to be more cautious. "You almost gave me up," he said to her. He found a shoe box in a closet. Swaddled in the shirt, the idol fit snugly into the box, and he placed it on a top shelf above a stack of film reels.

At the end of the day, one wall glistened in semigloss. Over by a radiator, however, a viscous, sweet-scented glue oozed out of the wall, and even after Eric wiped it up with a rag, the splotch reappeared. He cranked open a lower window at the street end of the loft to let in some fresh air. Sniffing the vapors, he smelled neither the usual city ethers nor his newly painted walls—instead he was enveloped in the aroma of coffee, which must have been wafting up from the café, although the Mystery Roast's windows were probably shut in the dead of winter. Maybe it seeped through the floorboards, up six flights.

He liked living here so far, but it felt temporary: At any moment the police could appear with a warrant, or down on Forelle Street someone might read his mind and finger him. All of New York would celebrate his capture. Yet gradually over the past three days, he had started to accept his new role as an unknown urban outlaw, and now at dusk, he remembered for the first time in a long while how as a child he'd been a thief, too.

Late one night at the end of the summer when he was nine, his mother had pulled off the main country highway, the way they usually came home from the movies, and onto an unfamiliar dirt road that carved through Long Island farmland. Timothy was sitting in the backseat with Eric, and it had been a big day: They had constructed an entire city in wet sand, baked under a dry sun, feasted on barbecued chicken, and watched a double feature. They had won permission to stay up during the illicit, adult hours of the evening. And Eric had been baffled by his mother's detour. After a while, it did not appear to be a shortcut, and he was old enough then to know that his mother was not the sort of woman who tried out new roads for the first time in total darkness. He grew suspicious.

He was impressed by how easily his mother navigated a sequence of unmarked roads, each narrower, more jagged, each darker than the one that came before. She hummed a song he didn't know. She slowed down occasionally and stared out her open window, and then finally, she pulled over to the side of the road and hopped out, leaving the engine running, the headlights on. "C'mon, guys," she said. She opened the trunk and pulled out a stack of empty buckets.

They stood on the edge of a vast field. Eric's mother crouched down behind him, reaching her arm around his shoulder, pulling Timothy in, too. "See? The farmers came through with tractors and collected the crop, but they didn't get all of the potatoes up in one sweep, and tomorrow they'll be back for the rest. Let's see how many we can get in our buckets." As soon as Timothy heard the orders, he bolted into the field, but Eric hesitated. "Go ahead," his mother said. She skipped away and began filling a bucket, hopping like a kangaroo, stuffing her pouch.

Eric followed a shallow trench. He scooped his arm into the soil and twisted a potato free. It was hard and cold. He tossed it into the bucket at the same time that he leaped forward. He fit his hand around a stalk, picked away leaves, sifted dirt, and plucked the next potato. This was more fun than just staying up late. He reached for a potato, snapped it up, and stepped farther away from the road. That was part of the game, too, to see how far into the illegal darkness of the field he could go. His hands were black by the time he had filled one bucket. He sprinted back to the car and grabbed another. He made a second pass.

The field was lit only by an August constellation, a piece of the moon, and the two conical beams reaching out from the car. When Eric thought he heard the buzz of a motorcycle, he froze until it dimmed.

Sometimes a potato was too big for his hand. He dropped a few. He started to giggle, as did Timothy, and Lydia shushed them, although she, too, sounded breathless with glee. The only noise became the earnest thump of the potatoes being pitched into the buckets.

Later, Eric recalled, his mother claimed that it was her father who had first taken her on a poaching spree, but given the little that Eric knew of his grandfather the banker, a man who became very upset if you played with the paperweight collection on his desk, this seemed improbable. And then again, the nocturnal raid was unlike anything Eric had ever seen (or would see) his mother do. The next day, she would no doubt be back to her old self: Eric, help me weed the garden. Eric, we need to scrub the boat. He would spend hours dreaming up ways to get her to move as quickly as she did when she stole potatoes.

They remained quiet, even after they had returned to the steady pavement of the main road, until Eric finally asked, "Are we running out of money because Dad left?"

"Oh, no," his mother answered. "No, no," she assured him. "We like potatoes." She sped up a little. "So what should we do with them? We have six buckets."

"We always have potatoes and parsley with lobster," Eric said.

"Baked potatoes," Timothy suggested. "Mashed."

"French fries," Eric added. "And potato salad."

"How about those scalloped potatoes—you know, with the cheese?" Lydia said. "Mmm, and some vichyssoise. I could go for some vichyssoise."

Stealing potatoes became an annual ritual, a tradition when there weren't many others. Each year, they came home with more than they could possibly eat, and Eric used to love to watch his mother offer bags to the neighbors: not tomatoes from the garden, not the fresh mint that grew out of control, not the standard offering of zucchinis, but instead these inexplicable new potatoes, which of course were graciously accepted, although with a few raised eyebrows.

The tradition ended with the last summer that Eric and Timothy spent at the beach: They were sixteen. That year, Lydia's second divorce had become final, and she looked lonely to Eric when she sat on the porch and reread her nineteenth-century novels and sipped her sun-tea. She looked like she wanted company, but every time Eric joined her, they ended up arguing about one thing or another. Timothy became irritable, too, and about the pettiest issues, like keeping towels straight in the bathroom. He had become such a sore loser at penny-ante poker that Eric ended up playing solitaire. Before the end of that summer,

Timothy left one morning without writing a note to say thank you or good-bye. Eric fought with Lydia more and more, and the following year, he stayed in the city and let her go off to the country alone. Then he left home and went away to school, and the year after that his mother sold the house.

And now a decade later, as Eric summoned the freight elevator, climbed aboard, and descended to the street for the first time in three days, he tried to recall one final, furtive harvest when he and his mother and Timothy came together peacefully in crime. Shadows bending through a dark field. The smell of the earth turned inside out. The silent victory-ride home. Eric remembered how they raced through the night, all the car windows rolled down, the wind carrying them fast. In each hand he clutched a stolen potato, dirty and cold, cratered, like a small planet.

here in Paris there might be rows and rows of small tables, the afterthought of a Manhattan sidewalk afforded only enough space for a single picnic bench, which was chained to the wall of the building outside the Mystery Roast. The café was empty when Eric went inside. The walls of the restaurant were washed in a mossy green, wet and glistening, free of artwork and decoration. A tin ceiling and exposed ducts and pipes that snaked around two fans were all painted in a shiny dolphin gray. There was an intricate design of fleurs-de-lis pressed into the edge of the plafond, but the pattern in the rest of the ceiling formed a more elaborate quilt, an Arabic geometry. Five marble-topped tables were arranged closely together on one side of the room. Behind them, along the wall, was a stretch of four deep booths with black-vinyl–cushioned benches surrounding larger marble tables. A tall bar balanced the tables and booths on the other side of the café, a bar of dark wood, mahogany probably, with four stools, and behind the bar, a row of machines lined up on a counter against the wall. Both the bar and the rear counter were topped with the same marble as the tables: a green stone veined with lavish swirls of burgundy, taupe, and ocean blue, like an out-of-focus panoramic photograph shot from a high-flying plane.

"Hello?" Eric called out. No one answered. He thought that he heard a cat meow. "Is anyone home?" Again no answer, and this time no meow.

A massive chrome machine with a polished, cantilevered beehive sat on the back counter, an industrial espresso maker with gawky levers and black knobs, but sophisticated and sleek at the same time, capable of fine-tuning: the beehive tapered to a delicate spout. Beside trays of stacked cups and demitasses, white china with single red lines around the brims, stood an elegant gold samovar crowned with a small white teapot. There was a shelf over the counter, high up, packed with two fat, cylindrical glass infusers that seemed clumsy and crude next to a set of swank, urbane Neapolitan filter pots. A simple, antique copper pitcher with a skinny handle sat alongside a contraption that belonged in a chem lab: It consisted of two glass globes connected by a tube, the bottom bubble resting on a burner. And next to the vacuum pot, Eric saw a more familiar appliance, an everyday percolator with a stained plastic lid.

The café reminded Eric of nothing that he had ever seen in New York. This was a place for toothless European pensioners to pass the afternoon at the bar, poring over racing forms, with a pair of adulterous lovers hiding in a booth against the wall, sharing a postcoital slice of cake, while loquacious students pushed tables together to smoke hand-rolled cigarettes and chatter about heady philosophy or underground politics or fashionable architecture or the woman who sat all alone in the corner, wearing dark glasses, a scarf pulled over her head, sipping espresso (making one cup last for hours), waiting for someone: who? Eric was an expatriate at heart, lost in America, but after two minutes in the Mystery Roast, he was miraculously borne back to a world for which he had always nurtured a nostalgic longing even if he had never lived in such an age—a sensibility, a fondness for places where you hung out for hours in the middle of the afternoon and then after quitting for the day and again late at night.

Timothy emerged from the kitchen door at the rear of the café. "I didn't think you'd make it. Welcome." He balanced a demitasse on a petite saucer in the palm of his hand, sipped some coffee, and looked worldly. He pushed the kitchen door open a crack and yelled, "Believe it or not, you have a customer!" Pointing toward a bar stool, he said, "Have a seat, pardner."

Seconds later, a man emerged wearing a red apron over black jeans and a black shirt. Eric instantly recognized him as one of Timothy's portrait-sitters.

"This is Eric, our new neighbor," Timothy said. "Eric, meet Andre Orso, coffee maven and coffee shaman of the Mystery Roast," to which the man half-curtsied with his apron.

"Welcome to Forelle Street," Andre said. "How do you like it so far?" To Timothy, sotto voce: "I thought we were going to have to wait for him to let down his hair so we could climb up and rescue him."

Timothy's rendering was really not all that faithful: Clothed and in person, his model was taller, slimmer, his hair was curlier, flecked with gray, receding more. "I like it here a lot," Eric answered.

"So, you're Timothy's childhood friend," Andre said, nodding slowly. "I didn't know that he even had a childhood."

"Always so witty," Timothy muttered.

Andre ran a rag over the bar. "You look like you need some coffee."

"That would be great," Eric said. "It's quiet in here. Not much business today?" He heard his father in this question: Check into matters of finance before you even have a drink.

"I wish," Andre said and frowned. "I get a so-so lunch crowd, sporadic at best. But in the evening, it's dead. On weekends, mornings are great, and that's it. If I were on, say, West Fourth and Charles, I'd be fending them off with my broom. But enough about me. Espresso? Cappuccino? American?" He said *American* with measurable disdain. "Decaf? Tea? Actually, skip tea."

"That's a handsome samovar," Eric said.

"It's on the fritz."

"It always is," Timothy said between sips of his coffee.

"It was working fine for a while," Andre corrected him.

"The spigot has always been shot," Timothy told Eric. "It makes a mess."

"No one wants tea anyway," Andre said. "People don't come here for tea." Again, *tea* sounded like a dirty word. "Café au lait? Mocha? A little Irish whiskey?"

"Shut up and give him today's roast," Timothy said. "Two, another for me."

"Today's roast?" Eric asked.

"*Deux cafés!*" Andre shouted toward the kitchen, although no one appeared. He turned around and started fiddling with the espresso machine himself.

"Andre's had the Mystery Roast for almost ten years," Timothy said. "He was thirty when he started. This has been the worst winter yet."

"I wasn't a day over twenty-five, and the season is hardly over."

"You have a great collection of coffee machines," Eric said.

Andre glanced up over his head. "Coffee is a way of life," he stated. A small circle of foam decorated the edge of the muddy liquid in the cup he handed Eric. "I assume that any friend of Timothy's takes his coffee black."

Eric preferred milk but was too intimidated to say so. The coffee was thin and chocolaty with a first bitter, then sweet, orange aftertaste. "It's delicious."

Timothy drank his second cup in slow, cherishing sips. "The best coffee in town."

Andre bowed from the hip. "Hey, you haven't guessed yet."

Timothy jiggled his demitasse. He closed his eyes and passed the cup under his nose as if he were judging a wine's bouquet. He sipped. Another taste. "Okay," he said. "Mocha Java." He took a generous swig. "Some Kenyan Kirinyaga, and a bit of that Jamaican Blue Mountain."

Andre smiled. He had full-roasted coffee beans for eyes. "What do you think, Eric?"

"You mean is it Mocha Java and whatever? I couldn't even take a stab. I don't know coffee all that well."

"You will, if you're living here," Timothy said. "Andre, is that job still open? Eric is looking for work."

"I thought I told you," Andre said, "or maybe I didn't. I realized I couldn't afford to take anyone on. Although I really need another person. As it is," he explained to Eric, "I cook, I wait, I'm always here. I live up there"—he pointed behind him, and at first Eric thought Andre meant the shelf of coffee machines—"on the second floor, and so the place is my life. I never escape." He leaned against the kitchen door. "If I can't give you a job, can I give you something to eat?"

"Two of whatever," Timothy ordered again. "On me."

Andre smirked. "You got kicked out of the boys' room and you can afford to be a big spender?"

"Wait," Eric said. "I still don't know the answer."

"To what?" both Timothy and Andre asked.

"Is it Mocha Java with Kenyan and that Jamaican whatever?"

An asymmetric grin broke slowly over Andre's face. "A novice," he said. "Let me get you boys something to eat." He disappeared into the kitchen.

"This is the Mystery Roast," Timothy said.

"I know."

"And the roast is a mystery." Timothy raised an eyebrow as if this koan brimmed with impossible meaning.

"The coffee? You mean Andre never tells anyone what the blend is." Eric nodded and chuckled, as if now he knew everything there was to know.

"He can't because even he doesn't know what goes into the daily roast. Andre's a little weird."

Andre Orso, small-eared, a teddy bear of a man, had always been a caffeine fiend, Timothy said, a man without vice, save coffee. Before he owned a café, he would venture to the finest emporiums in Manhattan and buy beans, all sorts of fine and exotic varieties, and then he would go home and experiment with blends of such rich subtlety that only a connoisseur could taste the exquisite contrasts and textures. One day, Andre was coming home from a visit to the coffee shop where he had made a complex purchase of beans. When he approached his apartment, he noticed that he had left the door unlocked, and when he stepped inside, he realized that he hadn't left his door unlocked at all and instead was in the process of being robbed. The burglar yelped when he saw Andre and came at him in an attempt to shake him up, clearly not wanting to hurt him at all, probably just hoping to grab a TV and get out. The burglar grabbed the bags of groceries and produce and started flinging them wildly in all directions. Fruits and vegetables flew everywhere, and so did the coffee beans, which burst free from their separate bags. Andre shrieked, and this was when the burglar finally ran out of the apartment.

There were coffee beans everywhere, on the floor, in the couch, behind books. Andre spent hours, days, trying to sort them. Vanilla Swiss Almond was easy enough to dig out—the beans were lighter and smaller—and even Tanzanian Kilimanjaro and Viennese Roast looked different enough. But they were hard to separate from the Colombian Excelso and Brazilian Sul de Miñas, which were themselves indistinguishable. And how could anyone pick out Celebes Kalossi from Sumatra Mandheling? So for weeks following when Andre would grind his coffee, he had to select handfuls of beans which formed a hopelessly intricate blend. He knew what varieties might be in the coffee he was drinking, but he could never be sure which had been included. Each cup was a mystery. Andre learned to enjoy this aspect about his coffee, ultimately reveling in it. It became a challenge to sip the brew and pick out the various components, and it became less frustrating not to know the answer.

"When he finally realized his lifelong dream and opened the café," Timothy said, "he continued to make a mess of his coffee."

"But he must know which kinds he orders," Eric said.

"He gets so many types that he can't keep them straight. And as soon as he acquires a new sack, he shovels the raw beans into several different bins. He roasts the mixed beans in a special oven in the kitchen. And when it comes time to make the coffee, he has no idea what he'll turn up with."

Eric drank the last bit of his cup—of what? Mocha Java, Kenyan Kirinyaga, and Jamaican Blue Mountain, as Timothy had suggested?—and was about to ask for another one when Andre reemerged from the kitchen, balancing two plates on one arm and carrying a large shaker of grated Parmesan and a pepper mill with the other. Spinach pasta shells were covered with a pulpy tomato sauce and a limp sprig of basil. Andre deftly sprinkled the grated cheese and ground a feathery twist of pepper over the plates. *"Bon appetit, mes chers."*

The sauce was sweet—Eric tasted carrots—and the basil made the tomatoes jump with mintiness. "You also know pasta," he said. It was the best he had eaten since the last time Margot whipped up one of her late-night numbers—in fact, it was richer and zestier and laced with some secret spice Margot's tomato sauce never knew.

"I am sorry about the job," Andre apologized.

"Me, too," Eric lamented because this was exactly where he wanted to come and hang out day after day, in the warm and empty café.

While Eric and Timothy ate their pasta, Andre arranged some recently washed cups. Out of the blue, he dropped a demitasse. "Damn," he said, and Eric assumed that he was referring to the shattered china. Andre covered the left side of his face with his hand.

"Are you okay?" Eric asked.

"Fine, fine."

"It's that twitch again," Timothy said.

"I'm fine." Andre took his hand away from his jaw. "I have this twitch that's been bothering me," he said to Eric. "Every now and then, it flares up and makes my whole face quiver."

Timothy rolled his eyes. "When are you going to—"

"Soon," Andre snapped.

"It's been going on for a while." Timothy whispered, "I can't see it, but he says it feels like he's going to have a stroke or something."

"Why are you talking about me as if I'm not in the room? I made an appointment."

"We lost Carlos," Timothy said to Andre. "Richard ran away. You're the only one from the old crowd who's left. You can't have a stroke on me."

Eric knew that Richard was the cinematographer to whom he was paying an exorbitant rent, but he didn't know who Carlos was. Andre returned to his chores. Eric assumed that he was gay, although he was the first to admit that he had never been very good at picking up on orientations and predilections. Homosexuality was a foreign language to him, like the Spanish chatter he heard all around him in the city. Actually, he had known several gay men, friends in school, some colleagues, Margot's best friend at the station, and Timothy, of course. Timothy had never formally come out to him. After that horrible final summer, he drifted away, and by the end of August that year, Eric heard from someone that Timothy was seeing an older man a few towns away. When Eric ran into him one last time right before Labor Day, Timothy was hanging out with two other guys, and something about the picture seemed both fitting and upsetting. Eric was splashed in the face with cold ocean water: Here was someone he thought he knew so well but apparently didn't know at all. Truths had been withheld. In retrospect, it seemed so logical and so right that Eric didn't ask his questions, even if he didn't quite understand the steps and phases that Timothy had journeyed through to arrive where he had. Eric heard a faint meow again.

"Melior," Andre called out, "come say hi."

From underneath a booth bench, a short-legged, dark brown cat with a white belly and white spats stepped forward with trepidation.

"He's handsome," Eric said.

"She. Melior tends to hide now and then. Actually she gets lost." The cat trotted over to the bar, leaped up to a stool and then to the counter. She sniffed Eric's breath. She purred a trill of approval.

"She gets lost?"

"At night, I have to take her upstairs with me because even if I just left the back door open, she'd never find her way home. Her full name," Andre said, stroking the cat behind her ears, "is Melior Earhart."

Melior looked back at Andre. Green eyes blinked faithfully.

A man walked in the café and slipped into a corner booth. After Andre presented him with a menu, he said, "Just an espresso and a pain au chocolat, if it's fresh."

"It's fresh. I'm fresh . . ." Andre stepped behind the counter, fitted a filter into the espresso machine, flipped on a switch, and then continued into the kitchen. Meanwhile, Melior jumped off the bar and trotted over to the man's booth, where she happily lay down beside him on the black cushion. The man mumbled baby talk at her.

"That's what she does," Timothy said. "If someone comes in alone, she keeps him company."

The café started to hop. A woman walked in. She was taller than she appeared in pencil, but Timothy's drawings of her were more accurate than his portraits of Andre were. She approached the bar with all the ease and tease of a runway model. Eric almost fell off his stool as he swiveled his body to face her when she sat on the other side of Timothy. She was wearing a bulky black overcoat that opened up as she sat on the stool to reveal a black miniskirt from which long, black-stockinged legs emerged. She crossed them. She was wearing a black sleeveless turtle-neck, and when she exhaled, her chest withdrew from her blouse, leaving impressions where her nipples had been. Then she filled the shirt once again when she breathed in. Her complexion was snowy, her eyes a pale jade. She tucked a stray sandy bang behind her ear. She was perfectly fashionable, trendy, but there was something uncontemporary about her, as if she had just materialized from off the pages of *Life* circa 1959. Eric's head spun with opening lines to deploy. She had been carrying a leather portfolio case and a matching attaché, which she propped up against the bar. What did she do? Was she an artist, too? "Gimme a vhiskey," she said to Andre. A low, simmering voice. "And don't be stingy, baby." That was what Eric heard, although what the woman probably said was something more like, "Andre, I could use an espresso. Make it a double."

Timothy kissed her on the cheek, a friendly, sweet peck. "Inca Dutton," he said, "Eric Auden. Eric Auden, Inca Dutton. Eric's moved into Richard's place." To Eric: "Inca lives below you on five."

"Are you painting it gray?" Inca asked.

Eric nodded.

"All new arrivals have to paint it gray," she said. Against her neck, little earrings of bright color dangled from long silver stems. The earrings were Rubik's Cubes. The tiny puzzles had been solved, the miniature planes of color perfectly arranged.

"Do your earrings move?" Eric asked. "Can you slide around the pieces of the puzzles?"

"I wouldn't want to. It takes forever to get all of the squares back in place. Because they're so tiny, not because I don't know the solution."

Andre served Inca a demitasse, and she closed her eyes. After one sip, she sighed and gripped the back of her neck, relaxing as if a fix were making its way through her veins.

Eric searched for something intelligent to say, but all he could think of was what he ended up with when a lull dragged on too long and he became nervous: "So you pose for Timothy?"

"From time to time." Inca's fingers tapped the counter.

"She's my best sitter," Timothy said.

Andre brought the man his pain au chocolat and coffee, and when he returned to the bar, he stood across from Inca and waited.

She sipped the coffee again. "Definitely some Kirinyaga influence. It's got a nice twang. A little fruity."

It occurred to Eric that Andre might have known the answer to the riddle, that the blend was not random, and that he was just putting on a charade of naïveté. He also, suspiciously, never offered his own opinion. "You know what it is, don't you?"

Andre bent over the bar and stared Eric in the eye. "I swear to you, I don't. You have to take my word." And although Eric had known him for less than an hour, he believed him.

"Tastes like the same old Colombian to me," the man in the corner booth said.

"No way." Timothy shook his head. "There's some Mocha Java in there."

"Too bitter for Mocha Java," Inca insisted. "More like Hawaiian Kona."

"What about Jamaican Blue Mountain?" Eric asked, because although he could not discern Jamaican Blue Mountain if his life depended upon it, not yet anyway, he wanted to impress her.

"Perhaps." Inca finished the rest of her cup. Melior had wandered away from the man sitting in the corner and hopped up to the bar again, where she assumed a Sphinx-like pose in front of Inca. "You're my one true love, Melior," Inca said and enthusiastically petted the cat's haunches. Oh, to be a café cat now, Eric thought. "I heard some gossip about the stolen idol today."

"What?" Eric blurted.

"Well, this guy at my office—"

"Inca invents gadgets," Andre said. "You should see some of the things—"

"What about the idol?" Eric's shoulders tensed.

"I heard that it was stolen by drug dealers. Narcoterrorism. It's a trend."

Eric sat back on his stool, relieved.

"The notion is," Inca explained, "that it's a lot easier to move art from country to country than it is to launder cash the old-fashioned way."

"I don't think so." Eric did not mean to say anything, the words just spilled out.

"You don't think so? And why not?"

"Ah, well . . . you see . . ." Eric stuttered. Everyone looked at him: Andre, Timothy, Melior the cat, Inca with her Rubik's Cube earrings, and even the man in the corner, whose upper lip was mustached with confectioners' sugar from his pain au chocolat. "You could be right."

"Timothy," Inca said, "tell this boy not to challenge me."

The last thing Eric wanted this handsome woman to call him was a *boy*.

"Don't challenge Inca," Timothy said, "and whatever you do, don't question her opinion about the day's roast."

Inca leaned in toward Andre, who was tipping one near-empty ketchup bottle into another. "You know what I saw this morning when I looked out my window? A new bald man leaving the building."

"Do you think there's a corner," Andre asked, "where they all hang out and where she can stop by after work and pick one up?"

"A bald man?" Eric asked.

"If you're going to live here," Inca murmured to him, "you should start to watch for the bald men who come and go."

"The woman who lives on three, Bea Ballard," Timothy explained, "has a thing for bald men. By day, she's a corporate lawyer. By night, she dates bald men."

"We chart her progress," Andre said. "The shinier their heads are, the longer they last. Also, she has a pet octopus in her bedroom."

"Billy the Squid," Timothy said.

"Can you imagine those moon-head lovers of hers?" Inca started laughing. "I mean in the heat of whatever, there would be this thing—"

"Stuck to the walls of the aquarium tank." Andre giggled.

"Making slurping, gurgling noises." Timothy approximated the sound.

"You must think we're catty," Inca said. "Really, Bea is a quiet neighbor with a great Big Band record collection."

"I don't think you're being catty at all," Eric said. "She lives on three? Who lives on the fourth floor?"

"The Faxes," Timothy said.

"Née Brody," Andre said.

"We call them the Faxes," Inca explained, "because he merges and acquires and she junks bonds, and when personal fax machines first came out, they were the first to have one. They had a party to show it off. Ostensibly, it was a tasting party—they'd gone to Napa for a long weekend in search of the perfect dessert wine—but the fax was sitting on their coffee table next to the cheese and crackers."

"You'll never see them," Andre said. "They don't deign to come down here."

"They eat only grilled fish in TriBeCa," Inca reported.

"It's us," Timothy said, looking at Andre and Inca and the cat, "and them."

"Um?" The man in the corner raised his hand. "Check please?" Andre pulled a pad from his apron and totaled the man's bill.

Us and them, Eric thought. The Mystery Roast Café could become his warm hearth, the kitchen of a large manor, home to the Us-family.

Inca collected her portfolio and attaché. "Gotta go. Loads of work tonight."

"You design gadgets?" Eric asked, stalling her.

Inca blinked. "I'm sure I'll be seeing you around." She extended her hand and gripped Eric's firmly as she shook it.

Eric watched her leave and then turned toward Andre. He raised his demitasse. "Hit me again."

That night, Eric lay awake in bed, regretting that he had downed five cups of the day's roast. The furniture, pushed to the center of the loft, formed an island in a calm gray sea. In the past few days, he had escaped his old self in so many ways, yet he still felt alone in the world. In the darkness, he tweaked the nose of the idol. He wrapped his finger around her neck, her ankles. He ran his finger along the curve of her knees. She was so old, he thought, ancient. He tried to imagine the artisan who had carved the stone, the anonymous Naxos Master working in his atelier, chiseling marble late into the night. And then he drifted into a pleasant dream.

He pictured himself in a house on a deserted rocky coast somewhere far away, all the way north in Maine perhaps, where he lived with the one true love of his life. The house rested on stilts on a cascading cliff overlooking the blue Atlantic. Out on a deck, he envisioned two chaises: one for him and one for her. They would sunbathe nude. She—whoever she was—had her back to him, and he couldn't see her face. He watched her sleep, lulled by the warm sun. A house on the beach: He could see its weathered clapboard, its white rooms. The woman turned toward him, stretching, shifting slowly, a curtain of hair falling away from her face—

Eric awoke, anxious and sweating. The radiators clanked. He turned on a lamp and set the idol down on a pillow. He and Timothy used to sit on the shore and talk until they caught the first glimpse of the day arriving from France. They were nocturnal creatures back then. The idol appeared to be levitating off the pillow. Eric avoided looking at the clock by his bed and decided to wake up Timothy.

**B**ut Timothy was already awake. He had never gone to sleep. He preferred to work late at night—morning, really—when high up in his lofty loft, he felt as if he owned the city, at least for a few hours after the nightlife had subsided and before the day began for most New Yorkers. He never painted by natural light, though maybe a little sunshine was what his current portrait needed. He was trying to blend a streak of persimmon into Andre's complexion, but it only made him look like a drag diva.

Timothy's project for the last months had been a series of oil portraits based on dozens of drawings, a series depicting the family of men he had joined when he stopped by an obscure café for a cup of coffee more than six years ago. He had already started and abandoned a portrait of Richard the cinematographer, who had fled to England after Carlos died. Carlos was the man with AIDS whom Timothy had nursed until he died a year ago. The painting of him was also unfinished. Now the portrait of Andre had become a prime source of frustration. Timothy set down the cedar cigar-box top he used as a palette and paced in front of the easel. All of his friends—which was to say, Andre and Inca—enthusiastically encouraged his art. They patiently sat for him, and they promoted the gig in the men's room, but lately Timothy was finding it nearly impossible to finish a painting. Portraits didn't speak the words that he wanted them to speak—they remained mute—and there was something unsatisfying about the play of color, about the light, the forms, the mood. Each day he identified a different problem in style or theme, but the simple truth was that his painting was not getting him where he longed to be in the world. He wanted people to study his images and relish and remember them, to talk about them and gossip, to crave more. He grew increasingly impatient, and he was afraid that he would amount to nothing more than one of the countless failed artists he saw wandering the Village on any given day.

In the deep sink in the corner of his studio, he washed his brushes. His studio occupied the back half of his loft and faced south. A series of skylights enhanced the airy height. From floor to ceiling, the walls were covered with his drawings, sketched faces that monitored his every move. He retreated to the front part of his loft, where his bed, his television, and his exercise equipment were separated by a drywall partition that fell short of the ceiling. He sat on his rowing machine, clutched the oars, reached to his knees, and pulled his arms back into his gut, his whole body weighing against an imaginary current. The best cure for the artistic blues was exercise. Timothy rolled off the machine after a while, onto his stomach, and proceeded to raise and lower his body in push-ups, but sank before reaching his goal. He pulled off his T-shirt and sweatpants and stepped toward, then ran into his bathroom, to his shower. He liked to imagine the water in an upstate reservoir spilling into aqueducts and rushing through wide pipes down to the city, to Central Park, and from the park downtown to his street and into his building and then up, up to his shower: a long journey that made him drowsy to think about. He lay down on the floor of the tub while the shower blasted at full force. He found it soothing: This was his main indulgence, his cure-all. It was like lying down in the rain.

When he got out of the shower, it was going on five in the morning, and he didn't expect to find Eric lying on his bed, staring at the ceiling. A shoe box was balanced on his stomach. "You shouldn't leave your back door unlocked," he said.

"Apparently."

"I couldn't sleep."

"So I see."

Eric was wearing a button-down shirt and shorts. No shoes. He had pulled a blanket over his feet.

"What's in the box?" Timothy asked.

"Nothing."

"Nothing?"

"I was thinking about the time that you came into the city," Eric said, "and we had to wait for five hours to see a midnight showing of *Star Wars*. Do you remember? We ate a barrel of popcorn each and drank at least a vat of Coke. I was getting this flu—"

"You puked all over your doorman's shoes."

"I don't remember that part."

Timothy found a pair of paint-smeared jeans on the floor. Most of his clothes were decorated with smudges of the drab hues he favored.

"But I do remember," Eric said, "the time we ate bad hot dogs—"

"It was shrimp cocktail. We *both* got sick."

"We slept all day, and then at night, we stayed up with my mother and watched the Watergate hearings."

Timothy remembered how he had snuggled under an immense afghan with Eric and Lydia, watching television, his fever finally cooled. They ate pistachio ice cream.

"We used to be able to talk to each other," Eric said.

"I know. Yes. We did."

"You were very mean at the end of that last summer."

"I thought you were the one who was being mean."

"Me?"

"Well, you know, you were seeing Lisa What's-her-name, and I ran into you at Mae's, right? And . . ." Timothy stopped. He surprised himself by recalling details.

"I'm sorry if I snubbed you—"

"It wasn't your fault or my fault. We had, you know, different agendas." He was becoming uneasy, not so much because talking about any of this with Eric was embarrassing, it wasn't, but because being reminded of those uncertain days ten years ago only churned acid in his stomach.

Eric sat up. "Why didn't you ever tell me you were gay?"

"Why?" Timothy leaned against a wall and slumped down to the floor. He hugged his knees. "It's not like I knew myself back then. I mean I knew, but I didn't know. Do you know what I mean?"

"You told my mother."

True. Timothy might have moved in with the Audens during the summer months because he was best friends with Eric, but the truth was that he also wanted to share Lydia. She was the Queen Neat Mom of the Century, and Timothy was jealous of Eric, envious of how his mother treated him as an equal. Timothy had confided in Lydia first, and she wasn't surprised. She congratulated him as if he had won a scholarship. Telling her was a rite that he had passed through successfully. It meant he could move on, live the way he wanted to live; later he wanted to thank her for that shove from the nest, although he never did.

"Maybe I thought you'd think back to all the times we were sunbathing together," Timothy tried to explain, "and think that I was, um, hot for you or something." Which would not have been untrue: For many summers, Timothy did nurture a crush, although now Eric seemed as remote as a brother.

"That never really occurred to me. Well, maybe once or twice. It doesn't matter now. We shouldn't keep anything from each other."

"No secrets. Nothing up my sleeves."

"In the museum, you said you had been with someone for a while."

"Right."

"Who, if you don't mind my—"

"Andre," Timothy said. Pause. "Does that surprise you?"

"Should it?"

"No, no." The epic story of their romance was complex, and Timothy didn't want to chronicle it. He wasn't sure he could. "Like I said, I think it's over. Almost."

"You seemed to get along in the café."

"We keep up appearances for our public."

"When did—"

"It begin or end? I couldn't tell you. I started seeing him with a passion when a man I was taking care of died."

"I'm sorry. I didn't know . . ."

"Carlos wasn't someone I was involved with," Timothy said.

"You mentioned him before."

"We became good friends, close. This was his loft. He was rich, a bit of a dilettante, and he willed it to me. He wanted me to have a space to be an artist in. To become what he never became. We all were friends: Richard the cinematographer, Andre, Carlos, and I. I came to the party late. The others had been celebrating for a while."

"So how long were you and Andre—"

"Two years. Without any interruptions. Well, longer. Okay, five years, if you include all of the times when we broke up and the space in between when we were apart. We'd connect, disconnect, connect. . . . Everyone was stressed out when Carlos got really sick, and that was when Andre and I started, you know, needing someone to hold late at night. That was a while ago, and now I drink his coffee and he poses for me and I help him with the crossword puzzle, and maybe it's best this way, nothing more."

"You don't sound so sure."

Timothy didn't want to talk about it anymore. "I'm sure."

Neither of them said anything. Eric looked different than he did when they were younger—Timothy had noticed this in the museum. Oh, he always had that look of a scared and surprised cat, not sure whether to come when you called. He would half-turn and glance at you, wide-eyed, startled, not knowing whether he should smile or look serious. He always seemed to be on the verge of saying something important. That expression was the same, timid but wise. But now he seemed extra cautious, not just wary but uneasy.

"Your turn," Timothy said.

"My turn?"

"What's in the box, Eric?"

"The box? The box." He held it tightly. "There's something I have to tell you."

Oh, no, Timothy thought, Eric was going to come out to him. It had occurred to him more than once that people who resorted to stereotypes might assume Eric was gay. He had gentle features: hollow, high cheekbones, deep-set eyes, a sweep of wavy bangs. Okay, he looked a little winsome now and then and lacked swagger. But he had to be straight: Look at the way he behaved when Inca was in the room. He couldn't take his eyes off of her. He had to be straight.

Eric stood up, still holding the box. Maybe he had a new pair of shoes he wanted to model. "I have the idol," he said, his voice shaky.

"What idol?"

"How many are there?" Eric lifted off the shoe-box top and removed a wad of laundry. "The Cycladic idol from the New York Museum. The idol that greater Manhattan is looking for. The infamous Ausgraben Idol." Eric carefully unwrapped a flannel shirt and cradled an object that certainly resembled the stolen treasure.

"It isn't real." Timothy chuckled. "Is it?"

"Believe me, it's very real."

"Wait. How did you get it? Do you know who stole it?"

Eric grinned. "I'm afraid so." He placed the idol on a pillow.

"I don't believe you." Timothy touched the alleged artifact with his pinky. The stone looked fragile, as if he could crush it in his palm.

"I'm trusting you with my deepest, darkest secret. Promise me you won't tell a soul."

"Okay, I promise." When they were eight, he had shoplifted a Matchbox Lamborghini from a five-and-dime. Eric was appalled and made him bury it in the backyard. "I don't believe you."

"Listen . . ."

And Timothy listened to the details of Eric's escapade and at first, no, he still didn't believe him. But then again, Eric had always been rather inept at lying. When he did, his earlobes reddened and he smiled with too many teeth. Now his whole face was pale. "I can see why you didn't want to go to the police."

"Plus, I don't want to get rid of her. I like having her. You're going to think I've lost my mind, and maybe I have, but I've been painting the loft, see, and I'll take her out, and I'll just start talking to her, to the idol. And then—don't look at me that way—I begin to focus what it is that I want."

"What you want?"

"In life. It's hard to explain. I have dreams at night now, and I haven't dreamed in years. I feel less alone, can we leave it at that?"

It was late: Eric was punchy. Timothy was willing to accept the slim possibility that he had stolen the statue. "It's not that I'm an uptight person or anything, and I know that we've been away from each other for a while, but I just don't understand *why* you would steal something from a museum. Unless, of course, you've become a professional thief, which is fine, but—"

"No, no, no. I never once turned in a college paper late. I don't know why I did it, I'm still trying to figure that part out. I don't have an answer for you. I was simply . . . drawn to the idol. Seduced. I fell into a trance. It was like I was having some sort of revelation, a dream that I can't really remember now. Does that make sense? And like I said, I just scooped her up"—he grabbed a fistful of air—"and ran."

"What if the police find you?"

"That wouldn't be good."

"Aren't you scared?"

"Less and less each day."

Timothy studied the triangular face and narrow body again. With those folded arms, she looked less seductive than impatient. "Why did you show me this, if you don't want me to help you go to the police or something?"

"I wanted you to know. I just wanted us to be like we were. Is that hokey?"

"Not at all," Timothy said. Actually, he was flattered. Even if Eric was a bit crazy, he felt honored. "I'm glad you told me. But let's be practical. You can't hold on to something this hot." He was an amateur thief, bound to mess up. "You can't keep it. It's not safe."

"No one has found me so far," Eric said. "Although I'm afraid you're right. I figured you'd think of something. You led the way to the fish factory."

"*You* figured out how to get us out when we got lost inside." Timothy picked up the ancient idol. "We'll think of something together," he said. Now the head of the Cycladic woman tilted back in his palm. She smiled an invisible grin. No, she couldn't smile—but he winked back nevertheless. "Don't worry. We'll think of something."

henever the phone rang in the middle of the night, Lydia always knew that it was going to be either a wrong number or her first husband, between wives, drunk and lonely. Jack would pretend that he was calling with a stock tip when he only wanted to make sure that like him, Lydia was alone in the world. In recent years, he had stopped calling. Whenever the phone rang early in the morning, the news was grim. Lydia's father had died at 5:36 A.M., her mother at 6:10. The phone rang at a quarter past seven.

"Hello, Mother."

"What happened?"

"Nothing," Eric said, "no one died. I was up and assumed you would be, too." After he had moved out and gone to college, he only phoned Lydia once every few weeks, and sometimes they went for three to four months without seeing each other. One time, seven elapsed. "I thought I should give you my number."

"I was wondering. Shoot." She found a napkin lying next to the coffee maker in the kitchen. A pen was lying across yesterday's crossword, which she had completed on the phone with Marek, who she discovered knew the names of all South American rivers.

"Five, five, five . . . seven, six, two, oh."

"Excellent." Pause. "How are things down there?"

"Fine, fine."

Did she detect, perhaps, the tone of détente in his voice? She held the phone between her collarbone and chin while she made coffee.

"So what's up?" Eric asked.

"A satellite was launched at NASA yesterday. One we worked on. Actually, I met someone." Why, she wondered, was she telling him this? First of all, he probably didn't care, and secondly, whenever she confided in him, she was sure he was going to respond with an I-told-you-so, especially after their last encounter.

"Great," Eric said but added nothing else.

"I went to an opening at the museum. Everyone was hush-hush about the theft, of course. Have you been reading about it?"

"I've been really busy painting my loft . . ."

"It's a tragedy. Anyway, there was this opening of the Dutch landscapes show—"

"How did you end up at that?"

"Your mother gets invited to these things all the time. I usually don't go."

"Did you have a nice time?"

"I met a very nice person. A man, that is." It had been much easier to treat him like an adult before he became one.

"Great."

"He's smart. He caught me by surprise. It's difficult to be surprised by anyone new when you're my age."

"You're only fifty-four."

"This man is quite knowledgeable about art and the art world. His name is Marek Vanetti. He has blue eyes that are not found anywhere else on this planet. Very smart."

"The name sounds familiar."

"We're having lunch," Lydia said. "Hello?"

"I'm trying to remember where I've heard that name before."

"He's been quoted in articles about that dreadful burglary." And he always sounded articulate. "Marek also happens to know Jason, and he had bad news." Lydia sighed. "Apparently he's ill."

"That's awful." Eric sounded genuinely concerned. "I was thinking about him the other day."

"Don't bring up the facts-of-life talk," Lydia warned him.

Eric laughed. "Thank you, I had forgotten all about that."

Once, Jason (in Jack Auden's absence) explained to a seven-year-old Eric where babies came from. He drew diagrams and, for some reason Lydia did not fully grasp to this day, he felt the need to label the participants in his clinical tumble Pierre and Marie Curie. By the time Jason was done, Eric understood a little about radioactivity, but some of the crucial mechanics of baby-making remained abstruse. Weeks later, Lydia caught Eric covertly watching a late-night movie which, because of editing for television, contained some jump-cut love scenes that did not add up. Eric was brimming with questions the next day, and Lydia had to re-explain both birds and bees. She remembered asking Jason why he had insisted upon invoking the Nobel laureates in a way that denigrated their accomplishments. Jason later explained that he wanted to provide Eric with positive role models, to which Lydia responded, "What's wrong with Mommy and Daddy?"

"Will you visit him?" Eric asked.

"It hadn't occurred to me to try." A lie. But was he living in the same place? Would he see her? Calling ahead was out of the question. Jason probably didn't own a phone, and if he did, he probably never answered it.

"Marek," Eric said. "That's the name of the curator who shut down Timothy's exhibit."

"Oh"—Lydia tried to sound surprised—"Tim's not in the men's room anymore?"

"Some guy named Marek came in with the usual bureaucratic rant about how they had been generous up until now, but it was a—"

"Fire hazard."

"Yes, and—"

"Bad for security, especially in light of current events. Marek told me that he really was rather amused by the exhibit, but he didn't think it could last much longer."

"Timothy was under the impression," Eric said, "that the museum officials didn't know about his show. I guess they found out."

"Well . . ." Lydia hesitated. Go ahead, she told herself, Eric would understand. "I sort of mentioned Timothy to Marek. It slipped out, and I'm sorry I said anything. But I did say, didn't I, that Marek was quite *amused* by the exhibit? If he closed down the operation himself, you have to realize that he was saving Timothy from potential prosecution by another, less hip museum administrator. Maybe even from the police."

"Mother," Eric whispered, "if you hadn't told him—"

"Someone else would have taken Timothy away in handcuffs."

"Maybe that would have been a week later and in that one week Timothy might have caught the eye of a gallery owner or sold more drawings or—"

"He's lucky he ended up with Marek. Marek did Timothy a favor. I don't know why you're getting so mad." She hadn't caused Timothy's exhibit to close. It was doomed anyway.

"You shouldn't have told this man about Tim. It was a breach of confidence."

"You nonchalantly mentioned the whole business to me as if all the world knew."

"Mother, didn't it occur to you that you were getting Timothy in trouble?"

"I keep trying to tell you that had I said nothing, someone very well could have arrested Timothy. Marek is a good person," she insisted. "He's not your average art historian."

There was a long pause. "Mother, you always manage to hear what I say without knowing what I said."

That smarted. "Don't make a big deal—"

"You shouldn't have told your boyfriend about the men's room." And with this, Eric hung up.

He hung up. Well, Eric was Eric, she was not going to get angry. She gulped her coffee. She marched into her bathroom, straight into a hot shower. She concentrated on the lyrics of cabaret songs and sang an entire medley to avoid thinking about anything else.

Lydia had agreed to meet Marek outside the museum at one o'clock. Perfectly on time, he bounced down the steps. She expected him to be wearing a Chesterfield and underneath it a hand-cut, Italian, double-breasted suit, a silk tie, expensive loafers—that was her image of a museum administrator. But Marek wasn't wearing a suit, and he wasn't even wearing a coat. In a flannel shirt and heavy cardigan, in worn corduroys, he looked as though he had been chopping wood, not curating Mannerist masterpieces. His hair blew back in the wind: Lydia noticed a faint splash of gray by his temples.

Marek tried to hail a cab. "I enjoyed our chat," he said between unsuccessful bids.

"Me, too." Marek had called Lydia during the business day but she couldn't talk, so they arranged to speak at night. Like high-school chums, they had chatted for an hour, not about anything in particular, mostly about museum politics. "Aren't you afraid of catching a cold?" she asked.

"I never get sick." Marek nabbed a cab, and they headed down to Chelsea.

"You're on the front page again," Lydia said. Today a photo of the idol had reappeared. This time the headline read: MISSING, PRESUMED DEAD.

"Lydia, we must agree right now not to discuss the bloody Ausgraben Idol, or I will suffer grave, perhaps lethal indigestion."

Lydia herself was really rather tired of all the hoopla. It was, after all, just a theft. This city had a way of running away with stories.

"I only want to hear about you and your life." Marek patted her hand.

"Ooh, you are cold." She pressed his fingers between hers. Marek's skin was smooth like a young man's. He had to be at least forty-five.

The cab shot along a cross street that Lydia hadn't been on in years.

Some men wearing white aprons were shooting craps on a town-house stoop not too far from the shoveled basketball court where a squad of girls in parochial, plaid skirts kicked around a soccer ball. A group of dancers, skinny, in leg warmers and heavy parkas, was walking en masse, in step, to a rehearsal. And finally, farther west, the taxi arrived at Marek's favorite Caribbean hot spot, which he vowed was always deserted at lunchtime. The metal siding all around the onetime diner made it look like a lunch box, and a red neon sign read: TALLY ME BANANA. Inside, there were fake coconut trees everywhere, the trunks constructed out of coffee cans. A string quartet seemed out of place on the sound system, especially when it entered competition with the whir of a daiquiri blender. As promised, the place was empty. Marek asked to sit at a table tucked away in the corner, right beneath a wall display of shadow puppets.

After securing a bottle of Chardonnay and some fried plantains with lime chutney, Marek raised his glass. "Skoal."

"Skoal."

"You look a bit uneasy, Lydia."

"I have a vague feeling that I was here once with Jason. Did this place used to be a steakhouse? Maybe it was with Anders."

"There's a terrific Cuban kitchen around the corner if you don't want to eat here."

"No, let's stay."

"Were you with Anders Bruckner even when you were still at Matting? I'm sorry. I'm being nosy." Marek dunked a plantain in the chutney.

"You're not. That was the problem. Working with him after we split up."

The waiter hovered by their table. Marek selected the chicken-pineapple-mango-surprise and Lydia opted for the salad-special of Bahamian prawns with a side order of Cajun potatoes.

"This morning," Marek said, "I had to endure a difficult meeting and ended up with an assignment I don't relish."

"A show you don't want to do?"

"I would give anything to have been relegated to something like that 'Treasures of Bahia' fiasco from a few years back, but alas, this has to do with the stolen idol."

Lydia was about to remind him of their pact but let him talk on.

"I'm going to head up the task force which will coordinate the various investigations."

"There's more than one?"

"There are more than I can possibly count. There's the city police and the museum's own, of course. There's the F.B.I., the C.I.A., who thinks it's all going to be linked to narcoterrorism, the insurance companies, and there's more than one company, the guards' union who believe they've been unjustly blamed. . . ." Marek had been counting with his fingers, and with two left, he said, "The list goes on."

"And you're in charge."

"I'm in charge of making sure they all have access to whatever information they need while keeping them away from each other. In short, I have to solve the crime myself before I end up floating raftless in a sea of bureaucracy."

"I like that." Lydia sipped her wine. "I mean, the way you put it."

"Oh, I've just been choosing my words for you all morning," Marek said dryly.

"Why you? I thought you said you arranged a few shows—"

"And mostly oversee print acquisitions. It's complex. Internal affairs. Politics."

Lunch came. Lydia sampled a prawn, which came on a plate garnished with crayfish. "Oh, this is splendid," she said. The shrimp did not taste like shrimp at all, but rather like some crisp other seafood that had taken on the flavor of honey and apricot.

"Try this." Marek extended his fork toward Lydia. He had neatly skewered a morsel of chicken.

Lydia was going to take the fork from Marek, but he held on to it and gently inserted the bit of food into her mouth. The chicken morsel had a breaded outer coat that was dense with pineapple, and the inside was moist. "I'm afraid I like yours better than mine."

Marek switched the plates.

"Oh, no. I didn't mean—"

But before she could blink, Marek had taken a bite of a shrimp and swallowed and kissed his fingertips. "I want this," he said. "So we were saying . . ."

"I was saying that Eric is mad at me for telling you about his friend in the men's room."

"Is that what we were talking about?"

Lydia had become so relaxed that she had assumed she had been discussing what was on her mind. "Skip it."

"No, tell me about your son."

Lydia reenacted her phone conversation, and Marek immediately said, "I'm so sorry, Lydia, if I took measures that compromised—"

"Marek, please. Eric is hypersensitive. I'm not mad at you at all."

"You're sure?"

"This chicken is heavenly."

"You asked me to tell you if I heard anything more about Jason Maldemer's illness, and I have. It's secondhand news of course." Marek fingered his spoon, hesitating. "I heard that he has incurable prostate cancer."

Lydia gasped. Her whole body shivered.

"I shouldn't tell you these things."

"No," she said. "I was in love with him a while ago, but . . ." But she couldn't let him die without seeing him one more time.

"I'm sorry." Marek reached across the table and placed his hand over hers.

She suddenly wanted to trade every fact and worry from her life with him, from her fears about Jason to her concern about Eric's welfare, from her boring job to her lonely bed. But what did she know about him? All he had told her about was the museum or how he found cold weather invigorating, but for all she knew he was— "Wait."

"What?"

"You're not married, are you?" And then Lydia laughed at her own bluntness.

"No, no," Marek assured her. "Never have been."

"Really?"

"There was a woman I was with for a long time. Natasha."

"Sounds foreign."

"We've both lived in many places."

Maybe that explained why he had a peculiar way of speaking, a slight trace of an accent, a bit French, a bit Slavic, but without clear origins.

"Natasha and I split up about a year ago. No, more like two, come to think of it."

"Sorry." Lydia tried to check a smile.

"Natasha is history. I am alone right now, and I have been for a while. Even when I was with Natasha I was alone, if you know what I mean."

She did: a loneliness more desperate when sharing a bed than when sleeping alone. She pictured Anders's back, in pajamas, breathing slowly.

"When I broke up with her it was horrible," Marek said. "Like a dreadful play. What were your divorces like?"

"The first one was long and ugly. Jack fooled around, but he didn't want to give me a divorce. With Jason and Anders, really, there was no fanfare. Although, with Anders . . . I was participating in a symposium which we used to have at Matting from time to time—like the ones we have at Thornton, but it wasn't televised."

"Wasn't one on Channel Thirteen recently?"

"The one about freedom of the press during military actions. I slept through it. I haven't taken a seat at the round table in a while, but at Matting, I always did. And Anders and I were on opposite sides of this war game, an end-of-the-world hypothetical. Anders was a high-ranking official in Country X, while I was just a demi-assistant-under-secretary in Country Y. And I sat there, and I listened to Anders going through the cities in Country Y, my home, which would be taken out in retribution for an assault that Country Y had launched against X, and I realized something: Anders really isn't all that nice."

"It was a hypothetical, no?"

"I had to get out."

"I'm glad you did. And are you happier at Thornton?"

"To be perfectly honest: no."

"Have you thought about leaving?"

Lydia nodded. "But never too seriously. It's hard to think about picking something else up—"

"I know exactly what you mean. Then it's probably best to stay."

"Stay?" No one ever appreciated her point of view.

"Stay. Regimes change. The weather changes: You know, some summers it's hotter than others. It snows more some winters. I've learned at the museum to lie low and wait out the dull seasons. Tell me something, do you ever go to jazz clubs?"

"Not in about thirty years."

"If you don't want—"

"I'd love to," Lydia said. "It sounds so . . . old-fashioned."

"I hope things don't get too crazy with this idol hunt."

"Missing, presumed dead."

"My big fear is that it's been traded on the black market. It's the only explanation as to why something so minor was stolen. That's one theory. It would be easier to unload, less recognizable. If the Japanese get it, forget it. The statute of limitations on purchasing most stolen property in Japan is only two years. I must confess something, Lydia."

Her heart beat faster.

"I've told a bit of a fib. I was complaining about having been assigned to head the investigation task force, when in truth I volunteered."

"That's not such a big fib. Why did you volunteer?"

"I want to get the idol back. I really do." Marek slapped the table.

"I'm sure you will." Lydia's thoughts kept returning to her second husband. "I haven't seen Jason in so long. . . ."

"He would never agree to talk to me. I made him angry."

"How?"

"I was under the impression that all one had to do was utter his name at a party when he wasn't there to earn his disfavor."

"Jason was always a funny man," Lydia said.

"Yes."

"Insane."

"Quite."

"Paranoid."

Marek frowned.

"Sorry. Let's talk about something else."

"Lydia"—he held her hand—"talk about anything, I don't care."

He was a bit much, she thought, a little creamy with the charm, yet Marek seemed able to make fun of himself at the same time—he exaggerated to be playful. She had never maintained close friends. She kept up with a few college chums with whom she corresponded at Christmas and phoned on birthdays. Men friends were lovers. She amazed herself by how freely and frankly she spoke to Marek.

Lunch was over too soon and the cab that ushered them back to the museum sped far too rapidly. In the taxi, they ate the bananas that had been handed out in place of after-dinner mints.

"We never got around to discussing the Thornton Foundation," Marek said.

"We didn't."

"We'll have to plan another lunch."

The cab got stalled amid a demonstration in front of a furrier, but Lydia relished the few extra minutes she got to spend with Marek. Protestors brandished cans of red paint and someone had accidentally sprayed a passing cab. The driver started to fight with some of the activists, and it did not help that he himself was wearing a leather coat, which was duly splattered. Lydia's driver steered through the fray, but he laughed so hard at the scene that she was sure he was going to crash into the women fleeing with their shopping bags, holding their coats, fur or fake, tightly around their slim bodies. Lydia held Marek's hand.

"They go a little too far sometimes," he said. "Why are you smiling? Do you disagree?"

"No, no, I agree completely." Lydia tried to look a little more sober, but her face lapsed back into a curve of inexplicable glee.

fter confessing to Timothy, Eric resolved to get over his fear of being recognized as the museum thief, and went out to explore his new neighborhood. West of the fashionable brownstones, west of the gentrified tenements, there were still strongholds of light industry and cold storage, and although every block boasted a gourmet grocer now, or a graphic design agency or residential lofts, each building retained the raw, gloomy aura of a slaughterhouse. The streets of the meat-packing district looked like worn, patched jeans: Warped cobblestone had never been paved over, except where potholes had been repaired or gas lines mended, where the Department of Public Works had applied bandages of asphalt. Stray trees dotted the sidewalks, all of them as spindly and sporadic as weeds. The February winds swept off the river in brutal slaps, protecting a veneer of ice and bunkers of snow. And the stench of pig offal in unexpected gusts forced Eric to wear his scarf over his face as if he were strolling through a morgue. He watched the meat packers work: Under a tin awning, a truck backed up to a loading dock, and men in bloodied white jumpsuits and lopped toques wheeled dollies that were stacked with boxes labeled CHICKEN LEGS or GRADE-A LEAN GROUND SIRLOIN. A building marked NEPTUNE'S FISH AND SEAFOOD was boarded up like an abandoned arcade at a onetime fairground.

Mixed among the warehouses were shuttered bars and the occasional club, too, leather dens and Brazilian-beat discos, and seedy *boîtes* where at night limousines waited triple-parked, their engines running so chauffeurs could keep warm. Those buildings that were taller than their neighbors or next to vacant lots sported advertisements painted in once-cheery, now-faded colors. The ads ran across the bricks without stopping for windows so that a letter in a word might be missing. Maybe the signs were recent but their slogans belonged to a lost epoch, a boom time, an era of optimism. DON'T LEAVE YOUR FLAT WITHOUT YOUR NEWMAN FELT HAT. Down one street Eric spotted a deep green sign with magenta, cursive instructions: FIND

YOUR TRUE COLORS AT VAN GORDESMAN PAINTS. And: VISIT THE VISION PALACE AND SEE THE WORLD. Where paint had worn away, he saw scraps of the previous signs that had been covered, a harsh, impersonal realism that undercut the playfulness of the murals: Nothing, not even the promises of the signs, was permanent.

Eric could walk for blocks without seeing anyone, but when he least expected it, he would happen upon a breath of life: a shoe and hat repair shop with a display of boots and fedoras, a dry cleaner's where a woman sat in the window and hemmed a dress, a deli with a neon beer sign and a sidewalk rack of cellophane-wrapped carnations and daisies. He wandered beneath the deserted el. Snow trickled off rusty girders in a momentary flurry, clouding a parking lot that according to Andre used to be the site of a flower market. When Eric stared at the pavement, he saw petrified petals layered into the tar and gravel like remnant tiles from a lost mosaic: a flake of rose, the blue of iris, a flattened sprig of freesia. A perpetual haze disguised heaps of sleeping bodies and offered fair haven for prostitutes in neon skirts. He noticed deals going down in a far-off corner of the stretch, blocks away. People still bartered in the old market, except they traded new commodities now, drugs or sex or currency or who knew what. Maybe stolen art.

At one point, Eric heard a slow, measured clip-clop and the creak of turning wheels. It sounded like a horse and cart was coming down the street behind him. He smelled horse shit, too. He turned around and expected to find a mounted police officer or a wayward hansom—who else rode horses in the city?—but all he saw was a page of newspaper carried in the wind. And then when he looked back at the el, dormant for decades, a freight train soundlessly slid in from upstate, a train with links of cars as far as he could see, cars teeming with grain, cereal spilling off the rails in a fine mist. The train braked to a hissing halt. Amid a tide of steam, Eric blinked, and when he opened his eyes, the train and the steam and the grain were gone.

A prostitute, her halter and hot pants glowing like traffic lights, approached Eric, but when he looked away, she rebounded into the shadows. He stared again at the far end of the lot, toward firefly-like dots, the butts of cigarettes. And then, out of nowhere, a squad car—with no siren, just flashing lights—came rushing off the cross street onto the pavement under the el in a surprise attack. It skidded right up to the dealers. This time, Eric was certain that he wasn't imagining anything, and so he ducked behind a column. The fuzzy shapes in the distance held up their arms when the policemen leaped out of their cars. Another car appeared, and two more cops rushed out. They had rifles. The police cuffed the dealers. Eric realized that while he had been watching the arrests, the prostitutes behind him had silently scattered, leaving behind only a trace of perfume. He headed home.

Timothy sat at the bar of the Mystery Roast, Melior on the bar, and the only patrons were a man wearing raccoonish glasses far too large for his small face and a tall woman, her hair in a tidy bun, who was sitting with him. They shared a single piece of chocolate mousse pie. Andre automatically served Eric the day's roast.

"Mexican Pluma," Timothy said, sipping his own cup, "and Sumatra Boengie."

"Mexican?" the man in the corner asked. "I thought we ordered today's roast."

"And that's what you got," Andre said. "He's nervous," he whispered to Eric.

"See the video rental on the table?" Timothy asked.

"When I went over to bring them their coffee," Andre said, "I saw what it was: *The Fountainhead.*"

"It's his favorite film," Timothy said, "and horror of horrors, she's never seen it."

"And how do you know this?" Eric wondered.

"Eavesdropping," Andre said. "She just told him that she recently gave up on her lifelong dream of becoming a concert pianist. Now it's his turn."

Even Melior's radar-dish ears were focused on the couple in the corner.

"For a long time, I wanted to be an architect," they heard the man tell his date. "But then I discovered tax law, which affords equal opportunities for construction."

A boisterous group of four women, all with brush-cut, quasi-military, quasi-punk hairdos, burst into the café. Their conversation drowned out the Ayn Rand couple. And then, despite Andre's complaints about poor business, another couple, two men, slid into a booth. One of the men had brought along an atlas and a dictionary. The other opened a magazine to last Sunday's crossword, partly completed.

Melior arched her back, stretched, and lumbered as far as Eric's end of the bar before collapsing in front of him. "Hello," he said. She licked at the bit of coffee that had spilled onto his saucer.

"Two espressos and one éclair!" one of the men shouted to save Andre a trip over.

"Two forks," the other man ordered.

"Diets kill the economy," Andre mumbled under his breath.

"And Andre," the first man asked, "do you by any chance know a middle name in American architecture? Five letters."

"Lloyd," Andre said as if it were obvious.

The second man gently punched his companion's arm.

As Andre twisted filters into the espresso machine, he shouted, "*Deux cafés! Un éclair!*" and retreated into the kitchen. Eric pulled a menu out from under the dozing cat.

"Andre's a toad," Timothy said, "but his chicken salad is out there. Past Pluto."

"Have you guys been fighting?"

"He's a toad and a half."

Eric ordered a sandwich when Andre passed through the café again, prompting the chef to chant, "Kaiser roll, French bread, pumper-nickel, semolina, twelve-grain, rye, platter-special, oatmeal, toasted white . . ."

Eric couldn't decide. Melior meowed a yawn.

"Twelve-grain," Andre said as if the cat had voted.

The chicken salad was impossible to dissect. The meat was tender, sure, but what made the sandwich so delicious were the other ingredi-ents, the greenish mayonnaise, the carrots and bits of currants, if that's what they were. Andre wouldn't reveal the secret herbs that gave the mayo its verdant punch, and Eric had to speculate about dill or basil or parsley, maybe oregano, maybe tarragon.

Melior showed no interest in the chicken salad but was quite curious about the cappuccinos ordered by the table of women. Andre had set the cups down on the bar so he could shake cinnamon and chocolate flakes over the steamed milk. "Okay, okay," he said. He poured a small amount of coffee into a bowl, added some milk, and set it down in front of the cat, who hummed louder than Eric had ever heard a cat purr as she allowed the liquid to cool somewhat before lapping it up.

Inca showed up. Her hair was wet and combed back, her cheeks red with the cold. All café chatter subsided when she entered, a coincidence of lulls perhaps, but noticeable enough so that she asked the room, "Did I interrupt something?" She sat down between Timothy and Eric. Eric straightened his back. Andre presented her with a cup of coffee.

Timothy issued a warning: "Careful."

"Mexican influences?" Inca asked. She turned toward Eric.

"Sumatra something, too," he said like an old hand.

Andre faced Inca. "Listen, sweetheart, I won't be offended—"

"Now, now," she said, "you know I'd drink even your *robusta* beans."

"Puh-lease." Andre fanned himself with a menu. "Only the very best, washed, lightly roasted *arabica* in this classy joint."

Inca laughed hard, Timothy giggled, and so Eric smiled knowingly, too. If only he could speak the language of coffeephiles.

"Nobel winner in peace *and* chemistry?" the man with the crossword queried the Mystery Roast at large.

"Seven letters," his companion added.

"Pauling," Eric said.

"Pauling. Linus Pauling," Inca said a quarter-beat later and smiled at him. He thought he might melt. "By the way"—Inca turned back to Timothy—"it's Venezuelan Maracaibo. If it were Mexican, it would be Coatapec. Andre wouldn't get Pluma."

"That's cheating," Timothy said. "He doesn't tell us what he buys."

The leader of the table of women raised her hand. "Another round of coffees!"

"*Deux cafés, deux fois!*" Andre instructed himself.

"Eight-letter word, fourth letter Z," one of the puzzle-solvers said.

"A candy made from almond paste," the other said. "Marzipan, dodo," he answered himself.

"They used to make marzipan on my floor," Inca said to Eric.

"Sometimes"—Andre pointed to a blotch of wall behind the espresso machine—"you find sticky stuff oozing out of the walls."

"I have that problem," Eric said. "It's coming through my new paint job in one spot."

"It's molasses," Andre explained. "Sugar dust got into the walls, survived the fire, was heated up over time, and oozes through the cracks when you least expect it."

"It's like a phantom glue that lives in the walls," Timothy added.

"The spot will dry up," Inca said, "and then reappear a year later somewhere else."

"What fire?" Eric asked.

Andre winked at Timothy. "He doesn't know."

"Know what?" Eric asked.

"About the orphanage," Timothy answered. "Oh, great. Now he's off."

"The orphanage?" one of the four women asked. Conversation in the café subsided once again, and everyone looked at Andre.

"Once upon a time," he said, "long before the turn of the century—"

"Can't you just cut to the fire?" Timothy interrupted. Someone shushed him.

"—Forelle Street was the capital of abattoirs. Animals were brought in from farms all over, and the streets stank with slaughter. Here and there, however, there were blood-free havens where they made pianos or hoopskirts or beer or, in the case of this building, candy. Griffin's Candies was seven floors of magnificent sweetness, hard treats and taffy galore."

Melior licked her chops and yawned like a drowsy lioness.

"Another piece of mousse pie, please," the man in the corner ordered.

"Apparently, back then, you could smell the candy works all over the block. The clean, crisp fragrance of chocolate absorbed the meat smell."

"I'll take a piece of mousse pie, too," Eric said.

"And one over here," the men with the puzzle ordered together.

"A round of mousse pies," the table of women decided.

"Everything was sweet," Andre said, "until an orphanage went up across the street." His voice was low and languid, as if he were narrating a ghost story. He disappeared into the kitchen to get the dessert.

"I've seen them," Eric whispered to Timothy.

"Seen who?" he whispered back.

"The orphans."

"The building stopped being an orphanage around the turn of the century. You were probably just seeing the neighborhood kids."

"I saw them," Eric insisted.

Andre returned with a fresh pie and a cake server in one hand, a stack of small plates in the other. "The building across the street housed fifty fatherless, motherless boys who had been adopted by the state." He passed among his audience and laid down plates. "Their life was sober. A life without a great deal of amusement or play. And to make matters worse, day after day, the children had to sniff honey and caramel everywhere, in their clothes, on their pillowcases, but the candy was inaccessible." He served the pie. "Every Christmas, the factory donated a chunk of raw chocolate, but that was all the boys got."

Eric warmed his nose with the steam rising off a fresh demitasse of espresso. He cut a triangle of pie with the side of his fork. A rush of sugar made him light-headed.

Timothy tapped his fingers on the bar. "I think he makes up the next part."

"Quiet," Andre whispered. To the café: "One day the children were walking down the street, returning from school or daily chapel or from the factory where they sewed shirts all afternoon, walking home in a pack led by their headmasters, when a few broke rank. First a handful, then maybe ten, then all the boys, ran toward the candy factory. They caught the factory managers off guard and raided the stoves—the boys grabbed whatever candy they could and shoved it in their pockets and mouths. The police were called in, and it took an hour, but ultimately the orphans' riot was quelled. Little boys with chocolate smeared all over their faces were rounded up and led across the street sobbing."

"How awful," Eric said.

"It gets worse," Inca whispered.

"One night, an older boy skipped out of the orphanage. He had decided to run away. He couldn't stand the tease anymore, the smell of raspberries and cherries and lemons and chocolate in his hair, on his skin. Marzipan everywhere. But once on the street, he knew he had to do something for the comrades he was leaving behind. He set fire to the candy factory. The boy fled. The building burned. By morning, a shell of a factory remained, an edifice: It had been completely gutted."

"At least they didn't have to smell the taffy anymore," one of the men with the puzzle said.

"No, no," Andre said. "The fire turned the candy into a sugary vapor and the air was so sweet and thick that the boys were teased by the afterscent more than they were by the candy. For months and months."

"Sometimes he gets really maudlin," Timothy whispered to Eric, "and he says that the runaway was burned in the fire, too."

"The candy factory was not restored. A drape and curtain manufacturer took over the building."

"Here he goes," Timothy warned.

Andre tipped his head back slightly and spoke to the tin ceiling. "Even the hope of chocolate was destroyed." He swept offstage into the kitchen. The café applauded.

"Oh, please," Timothy groaned. "He made most of it up."

Eric was feeling queasy.

"Check," the man in the corner said when Andre returned. His date looked distressed. "The runaway boy did what he had to do," he tried to console her. "He couldn't let society trample his dreams."

"That story"—Inca rubbed her arms—"always makes me want a stiff drink."

"Are you okay?" Timothy asked Eric. "You look sick."

"You look pale," Inca concurred. "Although the walls in here do tend to make everyone look a little jaundiced."

"I'm feeling, I don't know, dizzy," Eric admitted.

"Here." Timothy grabbed hold of Eric's elbow. "Let's get some air. *I* need air."

Eric let Timothy lead him outside, and on the street, he did breathe easier.

"Stick to small doses of Andre's mousse pie." Timothy kicked a chunk of snow into the curb. "And small doses of his stories. He gets so carried away."

Eric sat on the bench. Inside, Andre was standing behind the bar, probably beginning another tale. He was on a Homeric streak tonight.

"We still haven't figured out what to do with the idol," Timothy said.

"I know."

"Each night, I expect to hear the sirens. I have visions of hiding you in the boiler room."

"Okay, okay. I'll deal." Having watched the police spontaneously generate under the old el, Eric, too, was feeling less confident today about his safety.

Up in his loft, he removed the idol from the shoe box. Lamplight from the street added a sodium tinge to the artifact's glow. He shut his eyes and touched the stone as if he were reading braille, following the slope of the woman's back, pinching her squared elbows, the divide of her legs, the suggestion of her breasts. "I feel like a duck in a pond," he told the idol, "just waiting to be blasted out of the water."

*There's nothing worse than a thief who whines. He always falls off his horse just when he's home free.*

"I want to keep you, but what happens if I get caught? It's only a matter of time."

*There are two kinds of heroes: the ones who are in the right place at the right time and do what any fool would do—rescue a child, save a damsel—and the ones who lead the charge, the ones who inspire everyone else to get on his horse and follow.*

"Then again, I keep telling myself that there are people who have stolen things and gotten away with it, right? They never caught the Brinks robbers, did they?"

*I like my heroes to take risks. I like them a little reckless, a little crazy.*

"Maybe they did. I wish I had time to figure you out. A few more days."

*No one gets anywhere without a risk or two now and then.*

"At least until I figure out what you're doing to me. What you want me to see."

The next day, Eric decided to research the Cycladic Age. He traveled farther from Forelle Street than he had since stealing the idol, all the way to the library in Midtown. A clerk brought him the books that he found in the card catalog, and Eric sat at a long table, switched on a banker's lamp, and paged through the musty texts. The closest he came to narrowing in on the Cyclades was to read brief paragraphs amid other chapters on early Greek culture. There was much better coverage of Minoan life a few notches down the time line, books and books about excavations at Knossos, about Linear B. Then there were volumes that came from the Fine Arts section of the stacks, Atlas-sized tomes about ancient art, which at least included pictures of Cycladic artifacts: bowls and dishes and idols. Most of the idols had more of an abstract, violin-shape than the one he had stolen. Most were stouter, none quite as elegant as his. One photograph was a good match, however, and when Eric read the caption, he realized that it was in fact the Ausgraben Idol. He rotated the book as if he were examining a centerfold. There was not much text about the figurine, just a paragraph explaining that the pictured carving was the best-preserved among the cache of idols unearthed by the German archaeologist Friedrich von Ausgraben, who was the most famous explorer of ancient cultures in the latter half of the nineteenth century. Eric, who once upon a time had considered becoming an archaeologist, had never heard of him.

He scanned the microfiche catalog. Nothing under *A* for Ausgraben or *V* for von. Under German archaeologists: volumes on Schliemann. With low expectations, he flipped through an older card catalog (consisting of actual index cards) which listed books accessioned before 1954. Bingo: He found two entries, two author cards for Friedrich von Ausgraben in the Rare Books Department. *Journal #9: Persia,* which probably wouldn't be too helpful, and *Journal #14: Greece.*

The clerk in the Rare Books Department was listening to a Walkman and didn't remove his earphones when Eric approached his desk. "Hi," Eric whispered.

"Hey!" the clerk shouted back. He bobbed his head to the music. "I'm looking for this."

"Why?" the man yelled. "Just kidding!" He plucked the request slip from Eric's fingers. He took ten minutes to return with a thin volume in a plastic bag. Both he and the book smelled like dope. Eric signed another slip and carried the thin volume to a nearby desk. He had to read *Journal #14: Greece* within sight of the clerk, this was the rule, although he probably could have scrawled all over the pages with a Magic Marker and the clerk, who was busy drumming his desk with broken antennae, would never have noticed.

The book was a translation from the German by a British historian. There was a brief introductory biography: Apparently Friedrich von Ausgraben undertook a well-publicized tour of the Cyclades one April and then disappeared and was never heard from again. Greek officials never found him, and it was assumed that he had either been murdered or met some nice woman and run off to Tahiti, as was the fashion. Then, a quarter-century later, another expedition, this time French, followed Ausgraben's steps on Naxos. They unearthed crypts, and in one, found a wonderful array of Cycladic artifacts, including what came to be known as the Ausgraben Idol. They also discovered human bones, which seemed fine at first since the crypt, after all, was a burial pit. Carbon dating would prove that the ulnae and femurs were ancient, but some of the bones were more recent. And then a few telltale clues, some mustache remnants, a mostly decayed journal, confirmed that the bones belonged to Friedrich von Ausgraben. No one ever knew whether the German had been trapped by an avalanche, punished for tampering with sacred ground, or had committed suicide.

*Journal #14: Greece,* it turned out, was a dry account of a trip to the Isles that Friedrich von Ausgraben made before his fateful trip, and scholars believed it explained why he journeyed back. Ausgraben concluded: "I have wandered the far reaches of the ancient landscape, but never before have I investigated a place that is so plentiful with profound and intoxicating mysteries. I must return to Naxos." Famous last words. Eric had found what he was looking for. He had found someone who would know what it was like to hold and appreciate and cherish the enigmatic beauty of a Cycladic idol. Well, Friedrich von Ausgraben was long dead, but Eric nevertheless felt connected to him, no longer isolated by his own peculiar daydreams.

He went straight home to Timothy, who was working out on his rowing machine, heaving with each turn of the metal oars. A V of sweat darkened his T-shirt. He spoke between strokes: "I went. To the. Museum. Today."

"You're kidding."

Timothy stopped rowing and caught his breath. "Is that so strange?"

"Only if you recently stole an ancient artifact."

"I talked to some of my guard friends. I thought I should get the scoop on what's happening behind the scenes."

"Do I want to know?" Eric wandered into the studio to look at the wall of drawings.

Timothy rolled off of the rowing machine onto the floor, onto his back. "I asked lots of questions. Like about how the statue is coded."

That had never occurred to Eric, but of course the idol had to have a catalog number. Maybe it had a homing device. What if it was sending out a faint signal from his closet?

"Lately," Timothy said, "NYMA's been using this glitzy, experimental way of coding its collection so that if something gets stolen—fancy that—it might be located, and if it's found, definitively identified. One method that's still being tested has proven quite effective in Europe. A harmless perfume—people can't detect it—is sprayed on the back of a painting so that dogs can sniff it out."

Eric tried to remember whether the Cycladic woman exuded a peculiar aroma, a taste of tea rose maybe.

"It turns out that only really major properties have been sprayed so far. The idol wasn't considered major."

"Maybe it's coded in some other way."

"One guard told me that the cops have gotten nowhere with their investigation."

"Good. I'm glad you found that out."

"So, it's not like they're going to take you away in handcuffs tomorrow." Timothy stepped into the bathroom. "But sooner or later—"

"I know, I know." Eric heard him turn on the shower. He shouted, "I went to the library!"

"Did you meet anyone?" Timothy yelled back.

"Like who?"

"I've always heard that the New York Public Library is a great pickup joint if you want to meet intelligent men."

Timothy took what seemed like an endless shower. He emerged wearing a bathrobe, his hair uncombed—or newly teased with gel, Eric wasn't sure which.

"I read a book that Ausgraben wrote. A travelogue," Eric said.

"Who?"

"The guy the idol is named after. He had a thing for Cycladic art."

"A kindred spirit."

"Ausgraben wrote that when he was in the presence of an idol—not mine, but another one—that he—"

"It's *yours* now?"

"That he started seeing things. Once he saw his sister standing next to him, her arm wrapped around his waist. He knew he was dreaming, but his sister looked so . . . real. Not only was she *not* in Greece with him at the time, but she had died years earlier when she was nineteen. Consumption. And then she started singing lieder."

"Whatever you say, old sport."

"I was afraid you wouldn't buy any of this."

"What else did this German dude write?"

"Never mind." Disappointed, Eric flicked on the television and sat on the edge of Timothy's bed.

"You're not mad at me, are you," Timothy asked, "for nagging you about returning the idol and all?"

"I'm not mad." Eric could have predicted that Margot would be on the news. She appeared every night now, tonight from St. Louis, where a popular Populist faced well-organized opposition for his House seat. The candidate had lined up his family for the standard photo-op.

Timothy pointed at the children. "You know that one is heavily into drugs. And I'll bet money that one's queer." When the report was over: "Is it hard to watch her?"

"I'm over her."

"It would bother me."

"Let's watch the news." Eric was curt. "Sorry," he apologized.

The final report of the broadcast was a fluff piece about a man in Queens who earned a living as a Caribbean-style santero. He had converted his house into a workshop where he whittled banana wood into bowling pin–shaped figures on which he painted likenesses of the saints. The santero's home was littered with wood shavings. One parlor room was devoted to the supplicant figures, shelves and shelves of them. The report went into some of the mythology involved and detailed statistics about the saint-worshiping demi-religions in Queens. Thousands of followers kept the centuries-old rituals alive, and the santero made a decent living. All the Santa Anas, San Miguels, and San Franciscos were eerie, their eyes abnormally large and bulging, white, at once naïve and all-knowing.

After the news, Eric and Timothy became zoo lions, caged and bothered, pacing, occasionally dropping into prolonged slumbers, Eric in an armchair, Timothy on a rug.

"We still haven't figured out what to do with the idol," Timothy said after a while.

"We don't have to do anything with it."

"C'mon, Eric."

"How about if I just keep it."

"Fine. See if I care. But you should at least go out for a nice dinner or something, because tomorrow you might be bunking up with murderers and arsonists on Riker's Island."

Outside, a rainstorm gained momentum. Timothy paced back and forth, and then out of the blue he bolted into his studio. Eric assumed that he had suddenly been inspired to paint, but Timothy returned to the front room carrying a stack of canvases, at least five. He balanced them on his knee while he opened his back door, and then he placed the stack on the landing. Without explanation, he hurried back to his studio. An unfinished portrait of Andre looked back at Eric from the stairwell. Timothy passed through the front room again. "Cleaning house," he explained as he dumped another collection of unfinished paintings on the landing.

"Why?" Eric thought he heard one painting cartwheel down the stairs.

"They're terrible. I'm never going to finish them."

"You never know."

"I know."

Eric opted for honesty. "Look, the work of yours that I've seen is good. Sure, it isn't as brilliant as Picasso yet, but—"

"You don't have to say anything." Timothy swept his studio with a broom. "My pictures aren't reaching anyone. They're holding me back, and if something is holding you back, you have to push it aside, move on. That's my rule. I want to do something visual, something people can see, but I don't know what it is." He stopped sweeping. "You said that the idol made you see what you wanted in life?"

"Sort of. Not the whole picture. Just a mood, an outlook."

"Maybe I should borrow it."

Eric joined Timothy at the rear windows of the loft and looked south. The city spread out before them was a blanket of scattered lights, lights forming petal patterns amid a quilt of dark rooftops, loose threads of smoke spiraling from chimneys.

"I read some chapters on Cycladic culture," Eric said. "You know, they didn't have just one idol in one museum. There were scads of them. Everyone owned them. Well, they weren't exactly household items, but they weren't rare either."

"Why are you telling me this?"

"I'm not sure." Eric stared at the World Trade Center's pillars of light. He breathed a heavy sigh, and then in one tower he thought that he saw—outlined for an instant in the pattern of lights turned on over the entire span of the skyscraper's century of floors—the shape, the head-to-toe silhouette, the definite angles and curves of the Cycladic woman. Then the other tower blinked the same image. "Tim, did you see that?"

"See what?"

"In the World Trade Center? Did you see the idol?"

"You always were obsessive."

"Forget it." But Eric's mind began to click. What was so extraordinary about talking to an idol? People talked to plants. People talked to trees. People would talk to idols. "Can you imagine," he said tentatively, "if there were other Cycladic idols around like mine? Lots of them, the way there were in Ancient Greece. Can you imagine if people kept them in their houses, in their apartments, if they weren't imprisoned in museums?"

"Your mind is shot."

Eric snapped his fingers. "What if anyone who wanted an idol could have one to talk to—you know, like people talk to plants—or just to hold and admire? She is intriguing to look at, isn't she? She does possess a certain aura and mystique, right?"

"She's neat. I'll grant you that."

"What if we could make them? Lots of them."

"That guy on the news, what was he called?"

"The santero?"

"He manufactured the—"

"Santos."

"Out of his house," Timothy said. "In Queens, nonetheless."

Eric spoke slowly: "There are too many loners in the world. And I'm thinking that other people who are alone to some degree—like you and me and the late, great Friedrich von Ausgraben, like half the people who come into the café, like most of the people you see on the street—could own idols. Maybe they would have bizarre daydreams or talk out what they want in life or simply feel a little less lonesome. Like me. Everyone would have his own personal goddess—"

"A goddess?" Timothy stroked his chin.

"A foot-tall, marble goddess who listens to you. A listening goddess."

"The Listening Goddess," Timothy said as if he saw a title illuminated on a marquee.

"Well, calling her a goddess might be heavy-handed."

"The Shrink Goddess."

"The Goddess of Heightened Perceptions," Eric suggested.

"The Goddess of Kvetching."

"The Goddess of . . . Hope."

"The Goddess of Desire."

"I like the Listening Goddess."

"The Goddess of Desire," Timothy said. "There's only one real one."

"But in ancient Naxos there were hundreds, thousands. That's what I'm trying to tell you. They were all imitations, one from the next. Who says it has to be ancient?"

"You're talking about making clones."

Eric's mind soared. "Think about it. The world can be such a cold, miserable—"

"Replicas of an idol, and not just any idol but the one that was stolen. Very trendy. We might make some money. I could definitely use some money. And you need to pay your rent."

The idol would be someone to chat with when you got home, a mysterious companion. Or at the very least, a novelty. The thought of other people owning an idol so that they could whisper their innermost secrets delighted Eric. Their innermost desires. Yes, the Goddess of Desire. Maybe she would whisper back.

"We could make them, set up a lemonade stand, and sell them. It's Pop Art. I've always wanted to try something Warholian." Timothy paced in short laps. "You know who loves stuff like this? Yuppies like the Faxes. They'll gobble it up."

"Do you think it's just a gimmick?"

"I think it will be an oddity," Timothy said. "Short-lived, fun while it lasts, and soon forgotten."

"The curio of the moment." Eric laughed. "Let's not get carried away."

"No."

"What we're talking about is making some replicas of the Cycladic idol so that anyone who wants one can have one and do with it whatever he or she wants." A democracy of magic: That was what he envisioned. "And what they do is their business."

"I'm with you."

"But you're not a sculptor."

"I have done some sculpting in my day. Not since art school, but I could get ahold of some equipment. I could get my hands on some marble."

They stared at the raining city. Eric rested his forehead on a cool pane of glass.

"We still have to get rid of the stolen one," Timothy said.

"That's my problem. Don't worry. And don't tell anyone, not even Andre or Inca, about how we came up with these idols. I mean, never say anything about the *real* idol. Don't get into it."

Timothy found a wrinkled tube of oil paint on a table covered with art supplies. He squeezed a gob onto his forefinger. He took Eric's hand and similarly pressed paint onto his first digit. "Our secret," he said.

Eric's finger met Timothy's in the air.

ebruary was Lydia's least favorite month, a month of unpredictable weather, a month of moodiness. She was lost in a trance of indecision when she wandered over to Central Park West. At dusk, she found herself standing in front of a familiar building, craning her neck. However, the setting sun was in her eyes, and the brown brick building with its small panes of leaded glass was too tall for her to see the upper windows from the street. She had come this far, she told herself, so she might as well try to visit him, although she was sure that the doorman would be instructed to throw her out.

"The only person Mr. Maldemer lets up is the grocery boy," the doorman warned as he dialed his phone. He looked her over a couple of times, perhaps to determine whether she was another journalist. Reporters probably showed up several times a year, each thinking he or she would be the one to break the philosopher's seclusion.

Lydia had not set eyes on her second husband in eight years. It had been over a decade since his last bestseller had appeared. Almost a quarter-century had passed since his outline for a utopia inspired a generation of agitated students.

The doorman shielded his eyes with the visor of his cap. He glanced up at Lydia and then whispered into the phone. "About five-seven, I'd say. No, it's graying, sir. Chiseled cheekbones? I'd say so. But not gaunt, no. Mmm . . . a strong chin. Dark complexion. I'm not sure, if I would go so far as to say Mediterranean. No, sir. Right." The doorman looked at Lydia's hands. "Excuse me? Could you please remove your gloves?"

"Maybe I should just be on my way."

The doorman spoke into the intercom. "Okay, yes, sir." He hung up. "You must be very, very important, that's all I can say."

The elevator clunked dubiously upward. In buildings this old, Lydia envisioned someone standing on the roof manipulating the ropes by hand. When the elevator gasped its last breath between the twentieth floor and the penthouse, she knew that there was no turning back.

She had met Jason that summer at the beach when she knew things were falling apart with Jack Auden. Jason, as a friend first, encouraged her to quit her job as the assistant fashion editor of *Snap* magazine, the now-defunct picture-weekly. He was of the opinion that she should go back to school and finish her doctorate in political science, if that was what she really wanted. He showed up at a lobster bake later that summer. Like goofy teenagers, they slipped off. Jason brought a telescope with him, and he set it up on the crest of a dune. They examined the constellations. They spent the night on the beach, wrapped in blankets, talking, holding each other. But that was then, this was now, and she did not want to have to update her life for Jason. No, bad idea. Dumb idea.

"Lydia, I'm rich, but I'm not a wealthy man," Jason Maldemer stated plainly when the elevator doors opened onto a familiar foyer. He stood in the bare room and seemed smaller, thinner, whiter than he had two decades ago when Lydia first met him. And where once he sported a shrub of curly hair, impossible to comb, famously messy, his hair was cropped close to his head and neck now and it resembled the fur of a winter rabbit. The only bit of red left was in flecks in his eyebrows. "What kind of trouble are you in?" Jason shook her hand with stiff formality.

"Why do you think I'm in trouble?"

"Okay, okay." He turned around and led the way to the living room. "Okay."

The marble floor in the foyer and the warped parquet beyond sent Lydia reeling back in time. She recognized the once-trendy Eames chair that Jason dropped into and the burgundy-striped Biedermeier couch she sat on the edge of. "You don't look so bad," Lydia said cheerfully. Actually he looked pale, a bit sickly. Ashen but fit. Maybe his cancer had gone into remission.

"I think this is when I'm supposed to offer you a drink." Jason had grown up in Virginia, and adulthood in the North had not altogether dissolved his patois.

Lydia noticed his accent now more than ever, maybe because she hadn't heard it in a while. "Don't worry about it."

"A whiskey sour, if I'm not mistaken." Jason had always possessed an infallible memory.

"Sure." She had long since given up that sweet drink for gin and tonics and then vodka on the rocks but didn't want to tell him.

"I have a craving for one myself." He paced over to his bar. "It's odd. I have all this alcohol, but I don't drink much. Not at all. I might get drunk very fast. This whiskey sour mix has been around awhile. Do you think it spoils?"

While Jason prepared the drinks, Lydia got up and poked around as much as she could without seeming nosy. The dining room table, chairs, and sideboard had been replaced with high-tech exercise machines, the kind advertised in the back of glossy magazines. A long black telescope sat on a tripod by the window. All the furniture from the patio had been removed. By the bank of broad windows, Lydia could survey the park below. The tops of the leafless trees formed a pattern which from this height looked like a worn hooked rug. Even when they were married, Jason had maintained a separate aerie on the opposite side of the park from her.

He handed her a drink. "The view's the same."

"Well"—Lydia raised her glass—"it certainly has been a long time." He was wearing the same old uniform of a blue oxford and chinos. Even though he was pale and lankier, he did seem as alert and active as ever. Yet he was older. And he was dying.

"I'm very happy you feel you can come to me," Jason said, "and I still get quite an income from those bloody books I wrote—" He interrupted himself: "You would not believe the number of calls and letters I get each week. People think I have all the answers. Anyway, although I am well-positioned, as my mother used to put it, that position does not enable me to—"

"Jason?"

"Lydia." Jason smiled. His teeth were always very even and very white. That was what Lydia recalled being attracted to first, his teeth.

"I've invested my money well. I'm quite secure."

"You don't want money?" Jason glanced nervously around the room.

"I came . . . because I heard about your illness. I'm concerned. How are you—honestly?"

"Honestly." Jason nodded. A knitted brow. He set his tumbler down with a clink on the glass-topped coffee table. "What illness?"

"I met up with someone named Marek Vanetti—"

"Ooh." Jason grabbed his chest. "That name does make me sick."

"He told me you were dying."

"All of us are dying." Jason looked toward the terrace.

"When were you diagnosed?"

"I haven't seen a doctor in, I don't know, twelve years."

Lydia sighed. How foolish she was. She ate up rumors just like everyone else.

"And you? You look swell, Lydia."

"Thanks. I'm sorry. I'm so relieved. Marek heard that you had cancer."

"Which should teach you never to listen to anything he says. Don't trust him for a second, don't blink, don't leave the room."

"I've grown fond of Marek."

Jason rattled the ice in his glass.

"How do you—did you know him?"

"I think he knew my editor. I think he knows everyone. He talks to everyone."

Time to change the subject. "And what do you do with yourself these days?"

With a completely blank face, staring out at the park again, Jason said, "I haven't left the house in over three years."

"Literally? You have your groceries delivered."

"In this city, you can get anything delivered."

"Why?"

"Why haven't I left my house in three years?" Jason ran his hand over the gray fuzz on the back of his neck. "Out there," the hip philosopher of the Sixties said, "there is nothing worth seeing, nothing worth participating in. I don't need to go out there, and they—whoever they are—don't need me."

There were days when Lydia pined for the solitary life herself, but Jason's approach was, as usual, extreme.

"Come with me." Jason walked down a hall toward the bedrooms. "I know what's going on anywhere in the world. I don't need to go outside."

His bedroom had been transformed into a mission-control center of the globe. A row of seven televisions had been built into one wall, all of them running with the volume turned down, each one tuned to a different channel. "Best thing that ever happened was cable news. News all the time. It's vital." On the opposite wall Jason had taped up broad maps of the continents. Each one was decorated with colored pins and felt arrows. "I like to chart regional conflicts and civil wars. You would be surprised how close they come to involving us."

Lydia looked at another set of maps, celestial maps mounted on cork board hung on the last wall free of windows. Jason adjusted some of the pins. The pins had tags, and Lydia realized that the labels referred to satellites.

"You have to know what's up there," he whispered. "There is so much going on in space. So much . . . debris." When Jason spoke softly, his drawl disappeared.

"I worked on Lonestar." Lydia pointed to one satellite's pin.

"Is that so?" Jason's eyebrow arched. He said nothing else.

To make a connection with his map at first made her feel legitimate, but then she wondered if she hadn't implicated herself in some master conspiracy Jason had construed. He often used to fall into eerie silences and swift mood swings. She had never known what he was thinking.

"Do you still—" he started to ask.

"Never." She did not even remember the last time she'd had a free moment to peer through a telescope and examine the stars. It made her sad to think about how long it had been.

"I see," Jason said with an unwelcome psychiatric overtone.

Lydia looked out the window and was dismayed to find a large dish for long-range reception planted on the patio and blocking this corner's view of the park. Then she noticed a pile of small dictionaries lying next to a leather swivel chair that dominated the room. Newspapers were strewn around the throne, dailies from all over the world. "You're reading Arabic now?" she asked.

"It's imperative these days. You know, I haven't seen you do a spot on the news in a while. Not in over a year. You were quoted when the Khmer forces moved beyond the Thai border."

"You have a good memory."

As Jason looked at his watch and then at a series of clocks above the continental maps, clocks keeping track of different time zones, Lydia remembered what it was like to read the paper with him in the morning. He would get up and drink a quart of grapefruit juice and he would "interpret" the news for her. Some of his cynical auguries, as insane as they sounded at the time, eventually proved true. He could smell a scandal long before it was cooked and served. But Jason, the once-optimistic futurist who had grown cynical, even pessimistic, during her time with him, had now blossomed into a full-fledged, bona fide paranoid holed up in a self-sufficient nest.

A computer sat on a small table pushed into the corner of the room, its logic board, power supply, and some of the other innards removed from the console. "Are you fixing your computer?" Lydia asked.

"There are a lot of viruses going around, and I wanted to make sure I hadn't caught anything. So how is Anders?"

"Anders Bruckner? We split several years ago. We just became officially divorced rather recently."

"You're alone now?"

Lydia hesitated. "Yes."

Jason shook his head. "Nobody should be alone."

This seemed most unusual coming from the king of the hermits.

"He's on television all the time, you know, Anders Bruckner, dishing out Neo-Con rhetoric about this or that. I imagine that he talks in nine-second sound bites even in bed."

"You know him without having met him."

"You left for the Thornton Institute. I'd see the name when you were identified on the news and I'd cringe. The place is immoral."

"Yes, well . . ."

"So what happened?"

"I don't know. Sometimes things change," Lydia said—this seemed to be what she needed to tell Jason today more than anything else—"and the evolution from what you knew and held dear into what is alien and cold is so gradual, you barely notice."

"So leave."

"The Institute?"

"You've shifted gears in life before."

"I'm at home there. People still call me for comments, you know."

"Don't stay there if you're unhappy." In this respect, Jason had not changed. He was always ready to dispense advice.

"I'm not unhappy. And you? You really don't see anyone?" Jason ran his palm over the top of his head now like a cat cleaning himself. "You invited *me* up."

"Curiosity," Jason said. "It's just about time for the evening news. . . ."

Under the pretense that she was using the bathroom, Lydia slipped into a bedroom across the hall. She wondered if Jason was truly too reclusive to allow someone else in his life. She didn't know what she expected to find on quick inspection—a bra or a pump casually forgotten. All she found was a broad, white bed and a series of precariously wobbling towers of books piled on Mexican rugs.

The stacks were alphabetically organized. Lydia found Jason's own books in the *M* pile. Some of the paperbacks looked as if they might disintegrate in her hands. Jason's books had become so popular in the Sixties and early Seventies because he prescribed communalism, world harmony, and environmental awareness at the same time that he asked each and every individual to realize his separate potential. The sum of individual achievements composes the sum achievement of society, he said somewhere. On the one hand, you were supposed to plough a field with your neighbor, but you were also supposed to cultivate your own plot of beans, and not just any beans, but your favorite beans. Life was a struggle between altruism and independence, and Jason's goal was to mediate between the two competing parties in the parliament of one's psyche. He had deposited many phrases, now used out of context, now trite: transcendence through conflict, creative ecstasy, the breakdown of inner communication, the progress of self-reliance. And now in every dictionary: re-evolution.

Lydia thumbed through *Esidarap Found*, Jason's one utopian novel, his most commercially and critically successful book, and recalled buying and reading it the day after first meeting him. This was the book that lasted, the one each generation discovered and claimed as its own, a book taught in colleges. Not too long ago, Lydia saw a television report about a group of Neo-Esidarapians who were still trying to live out an experiment on a commune in Guatemala. The adherents were particularly keen on a minor aspect of the book, Jason's notion of positive-reinforcement child-rearing, which Lydia always found so amusing since Jason had never raised a child himself, he just borrowed some time with Eric for a few years. Lydia wondered whether Jason had seen the report. He must have. And had he been flattered or did he think that his disciples were silly for having listened to him, for bothering to perpetuate principles he probably now considered useless?

Back in the master bedroom/media center, Jason was watching four of the seven televisions, adjusting the volumes with a remote when he wanted to focus in on one segment in particular. "Be careful with Marek Vanetti," he said to the sets.

"What's wrong with him?"

"We had a falling-out."

"So I gather. Over what?"

Jason looked away from the sets and up at Lydia. "Not over anything." He returned to his televisions, and when he looked back a moment later, he paused. During that moment before he spoke, Lydia expected him to explode with anger. He never used to become physically violent, but he would lash out in venomous, verbal assaults. Tonight he merely looked Lydia in the eye and said in a tired voice, "If you must know, I saw Marek for lunch one day many years ago, and I told him a story. It doesn't matter what it was about, that's not the point. A few weeks later, I was at a party. I brought a date. It doesn't matter who. Marek was chatting with us. I went off to use the bathroom, and when I returned, Marek was telling my date that same story I had told him as if he were the source and originator of the information. You can't trust him."

Over the years, other people had told Lydia similar tales of Jason. If he found out that he had as much as been discussed at a party, he would cut you loose faster than you could explain to him that you were actually complimenting him in some way.

"Just be careful," he said again.

She had not come to him for money as he had suspected, and maybe not because she worried that he was ill, but possibly, like the tireless faithful who constantly wrote him and asked him to lecture, either ignorant of his self-exile or hoping that he might emerge for an evening, like his abandoned disciples, she'd come for direction in a troubled time, for guidance in a cruel world. Guidance he would not, could not, offer, that was clear. Jason Maldemer was spent, withdrawn, retired from the world. Lydia kissed him on the top of his gray head as one might a child who was too old to be shown more overt affection, but a child still of an age to require food and shelter and attention and care. Here lay the paradox that had defeated their love long ago. Jason flashed a confused smile, eyes still on the news.

Nevertheless, as she descended in the elevator, Lydia remembered the way that her calves throbbed with a wave-like pulse the night after a long day at the beach with Jason. She pulled her scarf over her nose when she stepped outside. They would take endless walks and gather mussel shells, a saltwater spray washing her forearms. Back then, anything seemed possible.

Timothy knew about a warehouse in Brooklyn where sculptors could procure stone. Eric spent an afternoon with him picking through varieties of white marble and trying to choose the one that looked the most porous, chinked, and chalky, the one with the least luster, the least veining. They purchased a slab and cabbed it home. Next Eric spotted a listing in the classifieds: A retiring gravestone cutter in Westchester was selling off his equipment. When Eric and Timothy arrived, they found an old man in an empty barn, chiseling granite, incising his birthdate on his own tombstone.

It turned out that he had already disposed of most of his tools, but Eric and Timothy were able to acquire a powerfully sharp electric saw and the man's most prized mallet and chisel set. Back in the top-floor atelier of the Mystery Roast building, they cut their single slab of marble into smaller strips. Timothy positioned the real Cycladic idol in the green sailcloth armchair in the corner of his studio where all of his models sat, made some preliminary sketches, and then began to carve out a Goddess.

Which proved to be a difficult assignment. Timothy wasted several squares of marble before he started to get the hang of it. He had to pencil the figure roughly on the stone, cut it, mold it down, chisel it finely, buff it, incise the linear details, and leave the final replica rough and unpolished to approximate the ancient patina. And when Timothy worked, a thin white web of dust hung in his studio like a tropical mist. The first completely finished copy was, well, crude. Timothy hadn't quite captured the Ancient Cycladics' particular proportions for a long neck and square torso. He had to tilt the head back even further. He had to pare the woman's frame down to a Saint-Tropez slimness. "Sorry," he apologized. "My technique is rusty."

"You're getting better with each draft," Eric said, cheerleading.

Timothy's face and arms were smudged with white powder. He pulled a new slab from the pile and started from scratch.

"Maybe you should take a night off and begin again in the morning."

"I have to keep carving," Timothy said. "Actually, Eric, if you don't mind, I work best alone." So Eric went away, and from that point on, Timothy chiseled in isolation and secrecy.

Eric turned his attention toward Inca. She had been noticeably absent from the café klatch as February rolled along. Andre reported that she stopped by briefly once a day to assay the day's roast, but Eric kept missing her. Andre also reported that she was finishing up a "big project," which prompted Eric to ask for at least the fifth time, "What exactly does it mean that she designs gadgets?" Andre shrugged: No one knew exactly how Inca earned a living. Andre did testify, however, that she had the most discriminating taste buds of any coffeephile he had ever encountered, including the Seattle bean samplers he'd once met. Timothy had studied her nude body with an artist's eye, and he said that he loved to draw her because she could sit as calmly as a vase of baby roses among milk bottles, and of course, because she was beautiful, somewhere between glamorous and earthy.

For Eric, Inca became a rare book that he had spent years searching for in musty basement shops and dank garage sales. At night he pressed his ear to his floor hoping that he might pick up something telling, but all he heard was the occasional rattle of pipes. He imagined her in the shower, polishing her skin with a soap that gave her a mercurial sheen. Once he rode the elevator to her floor hoping that his key would work and he would be able to get off "accidentally," but his key naturally didn't fit. Once he knocked on her back door, and she didn't answer (although he was sure she was home). He wanted to get a glimpse inside her loft, that was mission number one. Maybe she kept a man in there no one else knew about. Impossible: Nothing escaped the tight patrol of the klatch.

He discovered that if he stood all the way to the left at his front windows looking out onto Forelle Street, he could peer eastward, up the entire length of the cobblestone stretch. From this vantage, he could watch children play army amid sooty snowbanks, meat packers drifting home at dusk, their aprons tied over their winter coats, pigeons pecking through ice at frozen candy wrappers, at scraps of bagels, and Inca when she came strolling down the street in her bulky overcoat carrying her attaché and portfolio. He had to ambush her: That was the only way he would get to talk to her, and so he committed himself to a tedious stakeout. Late one fine afternoon, the sun lingered in the sky just long enough for Eric to spot her. He didn't wait for the elevator; instead, he jumped half-flights down the back staircase.

"Hi," Inca said when she entered the lobby. She blew warm air on her fingers.

"Just going up." Eric, out of breath, held the elevator doors open. "That would be your best bet."

The elevator rose quickly like a hot-air balloon dumped of all its sandbags at once, up past Andre's second-floor loft. Eric became speechless, his throat dry. Why was he being so adolescent about this? Up to the third floor: crazy Bea Ballard's. Inca studied her snow-stained boots: The salt thrown on icy sidewalks had created a spat-like configuration over her narrow feet. Up to the fourth floor: the Faxes. One to go. Eric swallowed hard and pictured the broad brow and sharp proboscis of the Cycladic woman. The fifth floor: Inca turned her key in the lock by the panel of buttons.

"So, Inca . . ."

"So, Eric?" Inca held the door open.

It was too dark to see into her loft. "I've heard you invent gadgets." Oh, real smooth.

"It's a living." Inca removed her key but kept the door open with her foot.

"Do you ever accept ideas from other people? Because I have an idea. I don't want to talk about it here, but—"

"Come in."

He was the most nonimprovisational sort of person, and any jazz was inspired by his marble friend upstairs.

"Something to drink? I could use a beer. I just turned in a whole series of design modifications and pricings today. A big project." Inca led the way to the back of her loft and tapped on the pedal switches to two standing lamps that lit up a black leather couch and two black wood-and-leather armchairs that surrounded a steel coffee table with an acid-etched finish. Her loft, Eric realized, was going to be a theater set: Inca would stage her scenes carefully, spaces only gradually revealed. It was difficult even to see her directly across the room, behind the counter of a Dutch kitchen, opening bottles. She returned to an armchair.

"What were they for?"

"The designs?" Inca pulled off her boots to reveal socked feet (black socks, of course). She folded one long leg under her bottom, and the other foot extended to the floor, where it toyed with some magazines that had spilled off the coffee table. "It was a boring travel kit that I'd been developing for a while. My firm makes kits of gadgets and whatnot."

"I've missed you in the café." His eyes adjusted. Inca's loft occupied the same amount of space that his did—and Timothy's, too—yet it was a completely different world, a rambling cavern of shadows.

"I've been slaving away day and night."

"How long have you been designing things?"

Inca sipped her beer. "Fifteen years at least. I'm giving away my age."

Not really, Eric thought. How old was she, thirty-three, thirty-five?

"What's your idea?"

"My idea?" His idea was to undress her with great leisure and kiss her everywhere. "I have trouble articulating my ideas." Now he worried that he sounded moronic.

"Me, too." Inca pulled her free leg under her butt so that she sat in the lotus position in the steep armchair. She looked like a child whose feet couldn't reach the floor. "Basically, I'm visual. Words rarely work for me. So tell me, what were you doing before you painted Richard's apartment gray?"

Good, Eric thought, she didn't necessarily want to pursue his lie. "I lived in Washington. I worked in television. News research. I was married to the reporter Margot Brandon." Why was he telling her this?

"Past tense."

"Right."

"Too bad. I like her presence. She seems smart."

"Smart, yes. And you?"

"Am I smart?" Inca chuckled. "About some things, not about others."

Eric wasn't really sure what he meant to ask.

"How have you been supporting yourself? If I'm being nosy, you let me know."

Eric stared at her long face and long limbs, at her long neck emerging from a high buttoned collar, at her chestnut hair recently cut behind her ears, and he said, with all the modest sincerity balanced with self-deprecating sarcasm that he could affect, "Since we met, I've wanted you to be nosy about me."

"Well, okay," Inca said and grinned.

"I had this aunt who left me some money. It's almost all gone."

"An aunt?"

"Her name was Lucia Madsen. She—"

"You're kidding."

"No."

"You are definitely kidding."

"I'm definitely not."

"You're related to Lucia Madsen?" Inca set her bottle down on the table. "One of the greatest filmmakers of all time?"

"I've never actually seen one of her movies."

"See, that's a sin in my book. She's one of my heroes in my personal pantheon, her and Buck Fuller. I can't believe you haven't seen her films, especially if you've been living off of her legacy."

Scolded, Eric looked at the floor.

"You can redeem yourself. As it happens, there's a screening of some of her films at Revival East next month."

If Aunt Lucia was her hero, he reasoned, maybe Inca would go with him.

"How old are you anyway?" Inca undid a few buttons around her shirt collar.

"Twenty-seven," Eric said and then wished that he had lied and made himself at least thirty.

"Right. Timothy told me that."

Eric feared that he had failed a litmus test. He was an acid, she was a base.

"Back to your idea."

He took a long chug of his beer to avoid talking. He had been peeling off the bottle's label, and it came off in his hand. He didn't know where to put it, so he folded it and slipped it into his pocket. "I can't tell you."

"I won't steal—"

"It's not that. I don't want to sound more foolish than I already have, and actually, I have no idea . . . no idea what it is that you actually design, so . . ."

Inca got up and receded into the darkness at the street-side of her apartment, where she switched on a crane lamp, lighting a drafting board and desk. "C'mere."

Eric obeyed. When he leaned against the desk, he accidentally put his weight on the cross of the T-square that bisected the drafting board, and it flipped back at him, slapping him in the nose with a thwack. He tried to recover his fumble and nearly impaled himself. "I'm such a klutz."

Inca took the T-square from him. "You're cute."

Eric's heart thudded like a clock tower.

Inca pointed toward a table next to the desk and drafting board and angled her crane lamp to light it better. Eric's eyes drifted first to the litter of objects on the desk, stacks of drawings and tankards filled with pencils, a pile of compasses and proportional dividers, templates, and a bundle of triangular scales bunched like kindling. There were wide shelves filled with paper next to a filing cabinet, and two cabinets which provided support for the wooden table where he was supposed to be looking. Bits of black metal had been pushed to the perimeter of the table: electronic guts, robotic innards, veins of colored wire, transistors that looked like pottery shards, a set of tools, pliers and minuscule screwdrivers, and off to one side, what appeared to be a sci-fi ray gun and what was probably some kind of a soldering device. In the center of the table, Inca arranged a collection of objects that had all been cast in a black metal with a matte finish, a high-tech, industrial patina that resembled the skin of a radar-evading jet. It was hard to determine what these things were exactly just from looking at them. Inca pulled a small suitcase out from under the table.

"This is the travel kit," Eric guessed.

"The prototype before my most recent modifications. Look, I just want you to know this is not what I'm about."

"Okay."

"I designed a set of kitchen knives last year which is more interesting than this stuff as far as I'm concerned." Inca pointed at a squat canister. "It's a portable blender on one side, and over here"—she unscrewed one end—"there's room for tumblers and a jigger."

"This is a travel kit?"

"The *businessman's* travel kit." Inca placed the canister in the larger case, which contained several compartments of varying size. She handled a long box that looked like an answering machine. "An adaptable modem to hook your computer up in a phone booth." A slim rectangular bar: "It has a magnifying glass at one end—see? And nail clippers at the other, plus a compartment here for spare cuff links." Inca added these to the case, along with a lint brush/corkscrew, a dual cologne bottle and aspirin case, and a voice-activated tape recorder with a tie-clip microphone. The case had a long flat panel for ties and a spare shirt. "You put your pens, calculator, date book here, your newspapers and magazines in here, pads, file folders there. Oh"—she picked up a palm-sized walkie-talkie—"you can't go anywhere without your cellular phone." She flipped over the case and revealed an unexplored side. "Plus"—she opened a panel—"a portable fax. I haven't quite worked out where the fax paper goes."

"I'm impressed."

"The whole thing is a little *male* for my taste."

"And this is what your company makes?"

"High-priced things that the world would be better off without."

Around her desk, on walls painted a lighter, creamier gray than November Nimbus, more like September Smoke, Eric saw framed blueprints. "These are your designs?"

"I think that in the Eighties, I tricked myself into being proud of what I did. Over here"—Inca switched on another lamp—"are the plans for some toys I worked on. I had fun with that gig."

"They look like frogs." Eric tipped his head back to see all of the framed, broad pages of vellum which reached high up the wall.

"They are frogs. Wooden frogs in medieval armor. The Frogs of the Round Table. It bombed in a big way. I had the most success with the predecessor to the businessman's travel kit, the tourist's travel kit." Inca pointed out another framed design. "The wilderness survival kit. I don't buy into any of that sportsman crap, but a job is a job—is a job is a job."

Eric followed her along an L of other workbenches and tables, similarly strewn with electronic guts and hardware.

"An electric garlic press." Inca held up something that looked like an oversized nutcracker. From another table she grabbed a fairly standard-looking purse. When she opened it, it lit up like a refrigerator. "Kind of basic, don't you think?"

"What's this?" Eric fiddled with a camcorder that had no lens.

"An electronic restaurant map. You've seen those monitors people are putting in their cars? You know, you pop in a compact disc with a map of the state on it, and then you can tell where you are and how to get where you want to be. You have to connect up with a satellite of course. You've seen those, right? Well, this does the same thing, except the CDs hold restaurant information. You can walk around any city anywhere and find out where the nearest Thai place is. Or chi-chi French. Whatever turns you on. Plus you get ratings and updates on recommended dishes."

"Useful."

"Please."

Inca continued to steer him through the darkened loft, but in the center of the apartment, he passed and nearly tripped over a low and vast, black futon with Noguchi lamps all around it, which Inca switched on. Their destination was Inca's kitchen, where she opened two more beers.

"You're not happy with your work?" Eric asked. "But you're an inventor. You're the mother of invention."

"Shut up, Eric. The joke's been made."

Every kitchen counter was crammed with juicers and mini-choppers and bread machines and toasters, waffle irons and blenders and microwave ovens—and there was not just one model of each appliance, but several. Curiously, there were no coffee or espresso makers. "Freebies," Inca said. "Hey, are you hungry? Have a seat." She pointed to one of the two stools by the kitchen bar-counter. The counter was made of glass bricks. Eric noticed an ashtray, a square crystal one that Inca must have lifted from the Mystery Roast. In it were three lipstick-smeared butts of clove cigarettes, the lipstick smears in different colors, shades of coral and ruby, and lying next to the ashtray were her Rubik's Cube earrings.

Inca reached into the refrigerator and pulled out a large bowl covered in foil. She placed it in front of Eric and then dragged the second stool around to her side of the counter. He pulled his stool in closer and nearly crushed a shiny black ankle boot that was lying on the floor. Its sister shoe was standing up next to it, ready to walk away. "Sesame noodles," Inca announced and handed Eric a pair of lacquered chopsticks. "Dig in."

They dined on extraordinarily thin, cold noodles, which had been coated with some sort of marvelous paste. Now and then, Eric happened on a slice of carrot or a chunk of tender chicken or a crisp scallion. They plucked at the noodles and drank their beers, all without conversation.

Eric filled up quickly but kept eating because he didn't want the noodle orgy to end. He skimmed the spines of a shelf of books hanging over the sink. *Gnosticism Made Simple, All About Alchemy, The Ways of the Cabala, How to Conduct Your Own Seance.* "Inca, I hope you don't mind my asking you something."

"Depends."

"Why do you have books about magic and mysticism above your sink?"

"I had a free shelf there."

"Are you interested in that stuff?"

"It used to be a hobby of mine to try to find something to believe in. Have you ever read about the Cabala? I don't buy any of it. So don't look so worried."

"I didn't mean to imply—"

"But I love to think about it all. Or I used to. It would be nice, if some of that stuff were true, wouldn't it?"

"Sure," Eric agreed. He noticed a worn paperback copy of *Esidarap Found.* "You have my stepfather's book."

"Your stepfather is Jason Maldemer?"

"He was my mother's second husband. I haven't seen him in years."

"I'm not related to anyone famous. When I was in college, I was a bit of an Esidarapian. You know, you'd see people marching against the war, and they'd have that book hanging out of their back pockets. So what's he like, Jason Maldemer? I've heard he's insane."

"He was kind of strange. Neat, though. I miss him in a way."

When they had eaten all the noodles they possibly could and still had not reached the bottom of the bowl, Inca said, "You don't really have an idea for a gadget, do you?"

Eric rubbed his chopsticks together like mantis legs.

"You're cute."

He wanted to change the subject. "Thanks for dinner." What he wanted was maybe to go out on the town, dancing, or just to stay here in Inca Dutton's messy loft and chat all night.

To his dismay, Inca said, "I'm kind of tuckered out. It's been a long week—"

"Thanks for dinner," Eric said again, as if she didn't believe him the first time.

Inca showed him to the door (the elevator), and soon he was traveling one floor up to his place. He lingered for a long moment before getting off, and when he finally did, his voyage into the mysterious Inca Dutton's loft faded like a waking dream. But when he sniffed his hands, he could rest easy: Proof positive he'd been there, his fingertips smelled of peanuts.

hen he wasn't obsessively pondering Inca, and when he wasn't trying to see how Timothy's sculpture was progressing, Eric spent time with Andre in the café. Early one evening, only one couple occupied a corner booth. "They're sort of odd," Eric said. The man and the woman looked remarkably like each other, both with short dark hair all gelled and combed back, both wearing blousy, white cotton shirts buttoned to the collar.

"Could you keep your voice down, I have a headache." Andre stacked demitasses into a lopsided pyramid. "Those are your downstairs neighbors."

"The Faxes? I've never seen them."

The couple was supping on penne and Beaujolais, and while they ate, they neither talked nor looked at each other. Instead they flipped through Italian fashion magazines.

"I thought they never came down here," Eric whispered.

"Their pasta machine broke, and she told me that it was too cold to go to where they normally go." Outside, the wind howled on cue. "They're here by default."

"She knows just what to say. Isn't that Melior's second cup of coffee?" The cat merrily lapped up the contents of a wide-brimmed café au lait breakfast bowl.

"And that's no decaf either. Her meowing was splitting my head open. I gave in."

"Do you have a migraine or something?"

"It's worse than a migraine. I feel like I'm going to have a stroke." Andre reached below the counter and pulled out an aspirin bottle. He swallowed a handful of tablets without water. Then Mr. Fax mimed that he and his wife wanted coffee. Andre touched his hand to his temple. "Why did they have to come here? It's too cold. Everyone should just be in bed with someone, under blankets and quilts, if he's lucky enough to have a someone." He slumped on a stool and buried his forehead in his elbow. "You make their cappuccino. I'll teach you. I'll talk you through it from here."

Melior leaped off the counter and scurried across the room, then settled under a table.

"Thanks for the vote of confidence," Eric said to the cat. He stepped behind the bar for the first time, where a dozen brimming, small burlap sacks of coffee occupied most of a stretch of shelves. When Andre received a shipment of raw beans, say of Café Havana or Colombian Popayan or Timor Arabica, he haphazardly dispersed the new variety among a series of sacks in the kitchen. These mixtures were then roasted in the official Mystery Oven until they achieved the right pitch and hue, poured into fresh burlap sacks, and stored in the cool dry space under the bar. "How am I going to tell one coffee bean from the next if all I ever do is drink your blends?" Eric asked. "It's all a muddle."

"I'll reserve a sampling from each shipment for you to try. For now, take about a half-shovelful from one of those sacks—the one all the way on the left is the fullest roast, the best for dessert—and dump it into the grinder."

Eric dug a metal trowel into the trove and emptied the beans into the funnel of a vertical machine cleverly built into the end of the bar, hidden from the clientele. It was a simple enough grinder, and he was about to flick on the switch when Andre raised his hand: Stop.

"Whoa, boy. First you have to set the dial there for how fine you want to grind the beans. One is super fine, ten is super coarse. With espresso or cappuccino, you'd say you want the beans ground real fine, right? But set it on at least four, because otherwise the water will move through the filter too slowly and get backed up, and then the pressure will build up too much, and the whole machine will explode."

"Maybe you should—"

"Go ahead."

Eric set the dial on four and waited while the grinder issued a series of grunts and whines, alternately like a trash compactor and dentist's drill. He filled a thin foil filter with the ground coffee, and the filter fit into a cup with a handle, a cup with a small nipple-like spout through which the espresso would be forced at high temperatures. Eric inserted the filter apparatus into the machine and turned its handle to the right to secure it in place.

"More to the right to increase the pressure," Andre said. "If you don't turn it far enough, the coffee comes out too watered down and thin. Too far to the right, and the coffee becomes too bitter, acrid, not mellow enough, unless, of course, extreme bitterness is what you're after. And if you go too far, of course, the whole café will blow."

Andre maintained a reserve of spring water in a tank under the rear counter. "What good is coffee if the water is polluted?" he said. Eric poured the measured water into the top of the espresso maker and closed the canteen with a tight series of twists that firmly secured its gasket. "Tighter," Andre instructed. "You don't want the top to shoot off and break a window, now do you?" He had to whisper because his head ached, but the whispering made Eric feel as if he was being entrusted with a secret, an old family recipe. He poured milk into a carafe. He inserted one of the red-trimmed china cups under the filter spout. "Let 'er rip," Andre said, "but first shout, *'Trois cafés!'* for good measure."

"*Trois cafés!*" Eric yelled. The Faxes glanced up from their magazines.

The water gurgled and pressurized. It sounded like a faraway plane, an entire V-flying squadron, the planes drawing closer. Mud-colored liquid at first sputtered, then poured forth in a steady stream. Just as liquid started to enter the cup, Andre rifled out instructions. "Insert the carafe under the spout on the left and turn that knob to the left to release steam into the milk." Eric obeyed. "More." The steam rushing through the milk sounded like the aftermath of a bomb explosion. It began to froth. One cup was half-full of coffee when Andre ordered Eric to push it aside and dump a healthy serving of the steamed milk into the espresso to fold it into cappuccino and at the same time position the second cup under the filter spout. Then Eric had to steam some more milk and repeat the entire procedure again. The operation took only a few harried minutes, and he competently twisted on and off all of the knobs.

"*Trois,*" Andre said. "One more for you," so Eric went through the cycle of knob-turning and frothing and folding a third time.

"What about you?" he asked.

"None for me," Andre said wistfully. He popped more aspirin tablets.

Eric delivered the coffee to the Faxes, who didn't bother to look up from their respective fashion spreads to thank him, and then he returned to his first self-made cup. He sprinkled cinnamon over the cup and added a flick of shaved chocolate. He sipped the coffee. Heaven. Then he noticed that Andre was staring longingly at his drink. "Why are you abstaining?"

"I went to the doctor." Andre returned to his post behind the bar, where he emptied the filter into the garbage. "I've been diagnosed as a caffeine addict."

"That's terrible. I didn't know there were caffeine addicts."

"It's messing up my nervous system. It started with a tic in my eye and then it spread to my whole face. No one ever saw it, it was internal, but I thought I was going to have an aneurysm. The doctor said I had to go cold turkey, which is why I have this awful headache. Withdrawal."

"I'm so sorry," Eric whispered. He felt guilty about enjoying his cup, and then he touched the side of his own face.

"It's not contagious."

"What about decaf?"

Andre maintained a special series of burlap sacks devoted to Swiss water-decaffeinated beans, also randomly roasted. "It's not the same," he said. "I can't reach that coffee high that you get when you drown yourself in the stuff. Now I'm sleepy when I wake up in the morning, groggy until noon, tired at night. I'm doomed to live a life without real coffee, a semi-comatose existence."

"How can you stand to be around the stuff?"

Having found her way back, Melior hopped up on a stool next to Eric and issued a plaintive meow. He bowed his head, and the cat licked the corner of his mouth.

"I don't know," Andre said. "I'll learn. Right now, it's torture."

The Faxes finished up their coffee and left. When they opened the door, wind rushed into the café and rattled the stacks of china.

"I just realized," Eric said, "that I don't know anyone who is happily married."

Andre pointed to the table where his customers had stacked their dirty dishes and left a heap of crumpled bills. "The Faxes do just fine, I gather."

"What do they know that nobody else does?"

"They do everything together, it seems, but whenever I do see them, they look like those people in— Who's that painter who did the scene of the people walking down the hill holding hands?"

"Eakins?"

"They look like people in an Eakins painting: aloof, looking straight ahead, almost unaware of each other's presence."

"Timothy told me about him and you."

"You got the battle-by-battle of the Hundred Years' War?"

"He didn't give me the details. Only that Carlos died—"

"That was part of it," Andre said. "That was one excuse. Now, we've . . . Well, he's been really impossible lately. He's been holed up in his loft doing I don't know what. I hate it when he gets like this." He thought for a moment. "Why does the glue rot between any two people?"

Eric nodded, thinking the question was rhetorical.

"Because," Andre said, "one person learns too much about the other. You know, I was jealous when I first met you. I got over it. But you knew Timothy when he was a child. If you love someone, you can spend your whole life trying to figure out what his childhood was like, what that person's life was like before you met him, and the less you know, the longer you're likely to be in love. I thought that Timothy and I were kind of like a classic, simple dessert: chocolate ice cream with fresh raspberries, which is a great combo, if you haven't tried it. But now I don't know. I don't know. You have cinnamon on the tip of your nose."

Eric rubbed his nose and licked the sharp spice off his finger. The door opened and the café was splashed with another cold gust. Timothy walked in carrying a rolled-up towel, which he set down on the bar.

"Dr. Livingstone, I presume." Andre turned around to make Timothy some coffee. "We were just talking about you."

"What were you saying?" Timothy had circles under his eyes. To Eric: "I couldn't wait to show you."

"Nothing you don't already know," Andre said. "Thanks for coming by last night like you said you were going to."

"Sorry, I was working."

"The warranty ran out on that excuse," Andre said.

Eric watched Timothy gently unfurl the towel.

Andre looked over his shoulder. *"Qu'est-ce que c'est?"*

A cloud of dust floated into the air, the same powder that covered Timothy's clothes and smudged each cheek like war paint. When the dust settled, Eric saw a crudely chiseled but definitely recognizable replica of the Ausgraben Idol.

Andre's eyes widened. "Hey, is that . . . ?"

Timothy had matched the overall shape, though the neck was a little too thin, too long, and the demarcations of the legs and arms were too deeply cut. But he had copied the tilt of the head, the bend in the knees, the feet pressed together. And her face—her face was perfect. The marble seemed old and rough, but not ancient. Timothy's version was also much heavier and denser than the real one.

Andre looked toward the kitchen and then the street. "It's a different one, right?"

"You did it." Eric patted Timothy on the back.

"The neck still isn't quite right."

"It's very clever." Andre laughed. "For a minute I thought—but why?"

"We thought people might want their own personal copies of the stolen treasure," Timothy explained.

Andre massaged his chin. "Clever, très clever. So you made a mock-up from the pictures in the paper?"

"Right," Eric said.

"It is a rather mystifying object, isn't it?" Andre said. "I'd love one myself."

Proof, Eric thought, that the appeal was contagious. Timothy looked at him and when Eric nodded okay, Timothy said, "Take this one."

"Really? Thanks." Andre cradled the idol like a baby. Then he propped it up against the cash register. "I think you boys are on to something. Are you planning on making more?" He slid a demitasse across the bar to Timothy, who warmed his face in the espresso steam.

"That's the idea," Eric said.

It was Inca's turn to barrel into the café. She removed her gloves and touched her hands to her cheeks. "Look at that," she said right away.

"Timothy made it," Andre boasted like a proud parent at an arts and crafts fair.

"It looks real," Inca said.

Timothy bowed. "I'll take that as a compliment."

"And why, may I ask, did you do this?" she asked.

"They did it together," Andre said. "Now people can have their own personal copies of the stolen treasure."

Inca smiled at Eric. "This was your idea." To Timothy: "You're doing this together?"

"It really was Eric's brainchild," Timothy said, "and I'm sculpting them."

"I think it looks fabulous." Inca kissed Timothy on the cheek. She reached over to kiss Eric, too. Her lips were icy, but his body temperature rose. "And you're selling them?"

"We'll set up a lemonade stand on the street or something," Eric said. "Although it is February. . . ."

"Put them on display here," Andre suggested.

"The idol is something the whole city is looking for, and now anyone can have one for him- or herself," Inca said.

"Everyone can own a stolen idol," Andre added.

"A city of thieves," Inca said. "I'll buy the first one. How much are they?"

"This one's mine," Andre said. "A gift."

"I'll make you one," Timothy promised.

"No, I want to buy it," Inca said. "How much?"

Eric started to calculate costs. "The marble wasn't too expensive. But not cheap."

"Fifty even," Inca decided for him. "That's a fair price."

Andre handed Inca a cup of espresso. Eric couldn't help but stare at Timothy's sculpture. He imagined a whole row of idols, each an imitation, one copied from the next, but each unique, a chorus of carved women lined up on the bar.

"Dutch Chocolate Mint," Inca said.

"What?" Eric asked, concerned.

"The coffee, Eric." She set her cup down. "Just the coffee."

In four days, Timothy made three more idols, honing his forgery with each rendering. On the fifth day, two more were added to the collection. Inca bought hers, Andre had his, and four were on sale in the café. They were displayed prominently on the bar, propped up against the cash register. Andre placed one flat on a cake plate and capped it with a glass top as if it were a dessert special. The chalkboard outside the café stated simply: CYCLADIC IDOLS ON SALE HERE. And the name that Eric and Timothy had come up with stuck. The Goddess of Desire. There were a few curious inquiries, but no sales. Eric lowered the price to forty dollars. Days passed. Timothy continued to mint the replicas, and the last one he carved was so refined and convincing that even Eric was duped for a moment until Timothy held up the ancient and modern figurines side by side.

Finally, on a cold, cold day on the cusp between February and March, a man who had come to the café off and on for several years, a man whose face was hidden by a beard, thick glasses, and a tweed rain hat—a man whose intentions therefore were difficult to read—took a liking to the idol. Andre was the only one around when the sale was made, and Eric found out when he saw Melior napping in front of one less figurine on top of the bar. He ran upstairs to tell Timothy, who responded to the news with a moment of introspective silence and then a cheer. "It's showtime," he said.

Eric returned to the café, but before going in, sat on the bench outside. He stared at the sun and drifted into a summer afternoon long ago, an afternoon that had been punctuated by a total eclipse. All of the women and children at the beach were supposed to stay inside while the men followed the phenomenon through window screens to protect their retinas. Timothy took a screen from the Auden kitchen window, and Eric reluctantly followed him outside. For months following, he was positive that he was going blind, having stared ever so briefly at the simmering blackness, having been scolded by his mother when she discovered what he'd done. But time passed, and years later he could see just fine.

eanwhile, Lydia was meeting Marek for lunch on a regular basis. They never got around to discussing how the museum might win funding from the Thornton Foundation. One night they had dinner. And at four o'clock one afternoon, Lydia found herself yawning because the night before she had stayed up way past her bedtime talking to him on the phone. She had to close her office door and move the two leather wing chairs in front of her desk together so that she could stretch out for a ten-minute nap. Around five o'clock, Lydia thought that it was a colleague who knocked and opened the door, so she scrambled around her desk. She tried to comb her hair and slip her shoes on.

"Sorry to barge in." Marek hovered at the threshold. "You were asleep—"

"No," Lydia said and cleared her throat. "Hi."

"I didn't see your secretary—"

"Left early. Actually she quit today. Sit." She joined Marek at the armchairs, leaving them where they were, so that they sat close enough to play patty-cakes.

"She didn't like working at the world-renowned Thornton Institute?"

"She didn't like working for *me*," Lydia said. "I get these magazines"—she picked through a pile of *Cockpit Quarterly* and *Diplomacy Digest*—"and I don't have time to read them, so I make my secretaries skim the key articles, which are all so dull that they would sooner be unemployed than have to read more. To what do we owe this honor?"

"I wanted to see what you do for a living."

"I've told you all about it."

"Frankly it doesn't make a lot of sense to me."

"There isn't much sense to make."

"Well, give me a tour." He stepped over to the computer on Lydia's credenza and switched it off.

The Thornton Institute occupied a stately Jeffersonian mansion. Niels

Thornton had served as ambassador to a variety of powerful nations and in his will turned his family residence into the home of the present-day think tank. Lydia explained all of this as she and Marek wound down the four flights of bedrooms and parlors that had been converted into studies, offices, and conference rooms. On the first floor there was a grand ex-ballroom. Television cameras were pushed into the corners, and an Arthurian table dominated the center of the room. "There's going to be a televised discussion later about Antarctica."

"Where are your fighter pilots?"

"Follow me." She led the way downstairs to the basement, which looked nothing like the paneled upstairs and instead resembled a bureaucratic government office. The crowd down here was noticeably younger, less tweedy but obediently collegiate. Lydia steered through a corridor of cubicles. The back half of the basement was a computer center, a hive of glassed-in data banks, air conditioned and humming, and one room off to the side marked SIMULATION PROJECTS was locked.

Lydia dialed a number code. She flicked on a series of lights, which illuminated a rather large and blank laboratory filled with more terminals and a wall of blackboards on which stretches of programs had been scribbled. She approached a door to another room, but before unlocking it, paused. "Software. That's what my life is about."

"I thought you were an expert on Sino-Soviet affairs," Marek said.

"I am. Or I was."

"I thought you wrote your dissertation on the inevitable inability of historically dictatorial regimes to democratize according to Western models and the necessity for a better understanding of localized governmental traditions."

Lydia leaned against the door. "Somebody has to bring in the money to run the place. Watch your head now. The ceilings are low." The next room was a cramped space resembling the cockpit of a jet, complete with buttons and switches and throttles and steering wheels and a computer screen in the shape of a windshield. Marek sat in the copilot's seat, Lydia in the pilot's. She flicked off lights, pushed buttons, and in a matter of seconds, the windshield filled with a view of the ground as seen from the clouds. In the darkened room, she began to steer the jet through abstracted skies.

Marek peered over the nonexistent nose of the plane. Through stretches of wispy cirrostratus, they could see a make-believe continent. "You fly well."

"Right now we're in a Z-130 Night-Condor reconnaissance jet. No payload, so we can travel very fast."

"A spy plane."

"I told the guys upstairs one day that I was assigning the bombers to Dot and Winston, junior associates. I don't fly bombers. The whole business makes me ill."

"Lydia," Marek said shyly in his ambiguous accent—he said her name as if it only contained two syllables, Lid-ya—"I don't want you to be angry with me, but I must tell you something."

"What?" She pulled back on the steering wheel. The jet glided up to a higher altitude, and even though the journey was pure simulation, she and Marek both fell back in their seats, as if the nose of a real plane had been thrust upward.

"I don't think you should put yourself down as much as you do."

"Do I do that a lot?"

"You talk about the think tank as if you're embarrassed about what you do here. But you hold a position of authority and respect and, yes, power. You can fly spy planes. You should be proud of what you do. I'm in awe."

Lydia leveled off. "Someday I'll quit and do something else."

"Someday is someday. Now is now, and I'm very happy to be in the cockpit with you." Red lights from the dashboard dotted Marek's face.

Lydia steered the aircraft into a gentle descent, a carefree and casual drop. "I wish I knew more about what you did."

"I am mired in as much bureaucratic muck as you are. But would you like to do something before dinner? A little *divertissement*? I'll make a phone call."

Lydia had been staring at Marek, relishing the glint in his eye, and had neglected the plane. Suddenly the jet spun into a rapid and chaotic downturn. Lights flashed, and a warning alarm, a cloying buzzer, pulsed with ominous volume. Lydia tried to maneuver the plane back on course. "We're going to crash," she confessed in desperation.

Marek held on to his seat with both hands. "I hate flying."

The ground grew closer and closer, and just before a fateful collision, with a thousand feet to spare at most, Lydia hit an eject button. The screen went blank, and the blue sky was replaced by a green backdrop, sortie statistics rolling dreamily by like a credit crawl. For a while neither one of them said a word, and when they looked at each other with knowing sobriety, it was as if they had endured some near-death accident from which they both emerged unscathed, the tragedy which they survived bringing them closer.

Even as they entered an apartment house on the park, all Lydia knew was that they were visiting a Mrs. Stewart who lived on a top floor and who presumably was someone who had something to do with the art world. Before the elevator doors opened on to an elaborately gilded entrance hall, Marek whispered, "Polly is a major collector."

Polly Stewart was a thin, severely tanned woman with a lot of hair, overplucked eyebrows, and perhaps the largest apartment Lydia had ever seen, and she had seen quite a few in her day. Polly led Marek and Lydia through a series of vast rooms with vaulted ceilings to a smaller, rose-walled study with a select view of the museum a few blocks south. She picked up a pack of cigarettes from one table and a lighter from another. In a gravelly voice, her accent half High German, half antebellum Georgian, she asked, "Are you two on your way to the opera?"

"I'm afraid not," Marek said. "You're not, Lydia, are you?"

"No," she said, thinking, You know I'm not, you asked me out for dinner.

Naturally there were paintings everywhere, large and magnificent prints that looked like cousins of the museum examples studied in college. The huge canvases were surrounded by smaller portraits and drawings. Pictures climbed the walls from the wainscoting to the ceiling the way art did in old-fashioned museums.

"You don't have any news, I assume," Polly Stewart said, and then lit a cigarette, letting it burn awhile before puffing.

"I'm afraid not," Marek said. "But I'm sure this matter will be resolved soon."

"I hope so," Polly said. "I hope so."

"You're referring to the idol theft?" Lydia asked.

"Oh"—Polly clutched her gray flannel knee—"you mustn't bring it up."

"I thought we were talking—"

"We were," Marek whispered, "but apparently we're not anymore."

"So upsetting. So very, very upsetting," Polly murmured.

A maid stepped into the parlor and placed a silver tray on the coffee table.

"Thank you, Harriet," Polly said. "I can pour."

"Mr. Wilkins called back," Harriet said.

"And?" Polly raised what was left of her right eyebrow.

"He said that there will definitely be enough New Zealand lamb."

"Splendid, Harriet. That is splendid, no? I can manage," Polly said and began to pour coffee into the gold-edged china. Harriet left the room.

"You're planning one of your famous parties," Marek said.

"Aren't I always?" Polly smiled teeth which had been yellowed by decades of unfiltered cigarettes.

"Polly throws the best parties in town," Marek told Lydia.

"I've heard," she lied.

"Really, they're very simple to pull off," Polly said. "Although I'll tell you the key." She leaned forward to whisper her secret and made her guests endure an important pause to lend gravity to this bit of wisdom. "I don't wait for R.S.V.P.'s. I don't bother with reminder cards. I follow up on my invitations with personal phone calls, and that's the case whether it's a party of ten or a hundred. When my guests arrive, they all know that I want them there because I've called personally. Marek knows what I mean."

"Yes," he said.

"Talk of parties bores men," Polly said to Lydia. "What shall we talk about?"

Before Marek could bring up whatever had brought him here, Harriet returned to the parlor. "Mr. Stewart won't be able to go to the opera tonight."

"Splendid," Polly said. "Call Mrs. Givgrabb for me, will you, dear?" Harriet nodded and left. "I must tell you a story, Lydia. Lydia is such a pretty name."

"Thank you."

"Lydia, I was in a real pinch a few weeks ago. You were there, no?" Marek shook his head no. "I don't think—"

"We will have you over soon," Polly said. "It's been too long, Marek, sweetheart. I'm so glad you came by for tea." They were drinking coffee. "Well, I was in a pinch a few weeks ago. We were having endives, which Barclay, who is not my regular cook but the one I bring in for parties—and despite any rumors you might have heard, Lydia, I think Barclay is even better than Claude, my previous chef. . . . We were having endives, which Barclay steams in red wine and tops with a reduced cream sauce, and it turned out that someone, and I'm not pointing fingers, had not ordered enough endives from the market."

"Terrible." Lydia hoped that she sounded like she cared.

"I sent Harriet to a deli. They had endive, but—I love Harriet. She said that I would have had to return to Heidelberg, if I served that endive, they were so . . . ooh." Polly tried to wrinkle her facelifted forehead. "Harriet is brilliant, and she bought some of that Bibb lettuce. We threw out the endive we had already cooked, because Barclay wanted everyone to have the same thing of course, and he had the women with him fix up the lettuce in the same way. . . . I'm telling you"—Polly Stewart waved her palms in the air exuberantly as if she were singing in a gospel choir—"it was the hit of the party. The hit of the party. People are still talking."

"There's a lesson in that, I suppose," Marek said.

"Well, yes," Polly said. "There is, now, isn't there? Well, I imagine that you want to make sure I haven't given away your picture."

"I would love for Lydia to see it."

"It's a marvelous painting," Polly said to Lydia. "Larry Pearson can't believe I'm willing to part with it. And Richard Hawkes thinks I could get quite a bit for it. Which, by the way, is the opinion of Maxine Vogelberg, who has always loved the picture. But your man Marek here has something I want."

Everyone, Lydia thought, wanted what Marek had. Polly led them back through some of the rooms which they had passed through earlier, as well as through new ones, but they were stopped by Harriet before they reached their destination. Harriet announced that a Mr. Lazlo Cruthers was on the phone. Lydia hadn't heard it ring.

"Yes," Polly said to Lydia, "it's *the* Lazlo Cruthers. Forgive me if I take this call." Polly trotted across the room to a phone positioned under a portrait of a king.

Once Polly started talking loudly, Lydia turned to Marek. "The singer?"

"A pudgy tenor who escorts Polly Stewart around Europe. So this is what *I* do for a living."

"You pamper the Polly Stewarts of the universe."

"I have to spend all this time with this woman just to get one lousy painting for my museum. Although the picture you're about to see really is a gem. We're trying to bypass the auction houses, where we'd never afford it. That's a secret. Don't tell anyone."

"How will you manage that?"

"We're going to try to trade some things in our collection that Polly wants for hers, several smaller things that add up, more or less, to what her painting's worth."

"I see. I didn't know that was done."

"It's done very rarely." Marek beamed. "It screws the auctioneers, and they're very powerful, and they don't like it. That's why the deal is so secret: We can't let anyone catch on. When we do get the painting, it will be quite a feather in my cap, if you don't mind my bragging a little. NYMA will get a masterpiece. Right now, unfortunately, we're having trouble finalizing the trade, and Polly's getting impatient."

Polly returned. "Lazlo sends his love. You've heard Lazlo sing, Lydia?"

"Not in a long while, I'm afraid."

"Darling, we must correct this." Polly hooked Marek's arm. "He's the eighth wonder. We must correct this." She sang something which sounded like it was supposed to be a line from an aria.

The oil painting was an early-sixteenth-century Italian work titled *The Storm Nears*. The canvas was average-sized, maybe four feet long, three high. It was not an overwhelming work of art. In fact, its richness came from a rather inviting warmth, from hot, soothing colors and a kind of queer irony about the scene. In the foreground of the painting, on the left, a young man casually leaned against a tall wooden pole. He was wearing elegant, patterned pants and chartreuse leggings. His complexion was eggy. He wore a bright jacket, the only red in the painting. Across the stretch of grass, on a rock, closer to the dense forest off to the right, a woman wore only cloth, which was draped over her shoulder and which she also managed to sit on. She looked suspiciously at the viewer while she nursed a baby. The scene was idyllic. There was a Florentine stream in the background and a series of tall white houses receding with precise perspective into the distance. A white dome of a basilica could be seen far off. But the deep green foliage and the bright white houses were sharply articulated by a mysterious and daunting, aqua-colored fleet of rain clouds which lumbered slowly and portentously toward Lydia and Marek and Polly Stewart. A faint bolt of lightning tore through one cloud.

"It is a gem," Lydia said, and she meant it.

"It's been in the Ausgraben family for centuries, of course," Polly said. "And now it should be in a museum for others to see."

Marek offered his professional appraisal: "It's one of those paintings that really influenced other painters. Everyone wanted to copy it. Look at the—"

"Ausgraben?" Lydia asked.

"My father's family," Polly chimed. She patted her trouser pockets and frowned.

"Look at the way," Marek continued, "the impending storm has been used to illuminate the grass and the stucco. It's really a brilliant study in lighting."

"Quite," Polly chirped. "I think I need a cigarette. . . ." Which ended their all-too-brief viewing. "Well, I hope you'll be calling again soon," she said.

"Nice meeting you." Lydia shook her host's bony hand.

Polly's Chanel bracelet almost slipped over her hand when she waved good-bye. "Remember the lettuce," she said to the closing elevator doors.

As they descended, Marek yawned a sigh of relief. "Thank you for enduring that."

"It's a marvelous painting."

"Glad you think so."

"Ausgraben? As in the idol?"

Marek pushed the elevator's stop button and the carriage came to a jerking halt. "I'm going to entrust you with a secret."

"It's safe with me."

"One of the museum pieces Polly wants out of the trade for *The Storm Nears* is the Cycladic statue. The *Ausgraben* Idol, which she's had her eye on for years. She wants it back in the family now more than ever. She's a superstitious woman, and there are all sorts of stories about that idol. Don't ask me what. She wants it because she thinks it will reverse her bad fortune. You may have read about the SEC investigation into her husband's junk bonds. And the IRS probe that ruined her brother. Not to mention the family's little South African factory problem. Polly is convinced that if she gets the idol back, everything will be fine again."

"And it was stolen."

"And that's why, my dear, I'm so keen on finding it. That's why I had to get involved personally in the investigation, why it matters so much to me. So much is riding on that bloody idol. Now you can't tell anyone that I've told you this."

"I won't."

"If only I could find that cheap piece of primitive marble . . ."

"I wish I could help you," Lydia said. He looked so agitated, so anxious. Maybe if he gave her the clues, she could help him solve the puzzle. "What can you tell me?"

"It's top secret, dear."

"You've trusted me already."

Marek whispered even more softly: "We have a very weak eyewitness, a guard who thinks he saw a man in a tan overcoat walking away from him around the time of the theft, but it's nothing to go on. There were no fingerprints. The thief just came in and snatched the idol cleanly and quickly in a premeditated, surgical strike. All we have is the issue of motive." Marek released the elevator and allowed it to drop again. "It's all theory, but if the thief was after an obscure treasure, he could have chosen something equally unrecognizable on the black market yet something of greater value. Which is why we don't think it's being traded through regular illegal channels. Which is why we think the idol was taken for personal reasons."

"Like Polly's."

"Like Polly's, except without a planned, secret art trade. Some people actually think that Polly hired the thieves. Between you and me, I think that's a rather ridiculous lead. And that's all I can tell you. All I know myself."

Lydia wanted to help crack the case, and she would turn her analytical mind to the matter, but not tonight. "Now that we all know what everyone does for a living," she said, "can we go somewhere for dinner?"

Marek saluted the doorman. "You're not going to steam me up some lettuce?" The temperature had fallen so low that even Marek had to don a coat tonight, although he wore it unbuttoned. He flipped up his collar.

"Some other time." Lydia had left her gloves at the office, so she dug one hand into her own pocket and the other into the velvet depths of Marek's overcoat as they walked briskly down the wide sidewalk. The sidewalk—the city, it seemed—was all theirs.

fter the first idol was sold, Mystery Roast patrons continued to order Goddesses of Desire along with their pumpkin ravioli and their pear-hazelnut tortes. Sales increased on a steady and sure climb to the point that all idols were sold the day after Timothy made them. Eric accompanied him on another trip to the warehouse-quarry in Brooklyn, and then Timothy began to sculpt nonstop, most industriously after midnight. Whenever Eric stuck his head out into the back hallway, he heard the soft tapping of metal against stone. Timothy worked up to such a feverish speed—he could shape and refine seven or eight Cycladic women a day—that in two weeks, seventy-six idols were carved and sold. At the same time, the percentage of empty tables at the Mystery Roast dwindled. One morning a man came into the café not for the eggplant chili or the mushroom-pâté platter, not even for a cup of the day's roast, but only to purchase "that weird, weird, white thing I saw at my friend's party last night." Word traveled fast in the leonine wind of March.

Inca became inaccessible again while she completed preliminary designs for an apartment tool set, a kit of implements that doubled as smart *objets* to have casually lying around when photographers from interior design magazines stopped by. A screwdriver with its smartly grooved handle might look clever next to a vase of white tulips and a pile of art books. But they did have a date together marked on their calendars—well, Eric thought of it as a date. In the meantime, he continued to make coffee for Andre, who had become quite irritable. Withdrawal headaches made him snap at patrons who lingered too long over a single cup of coffee without ordering dinner or dessert (or an idol). It was safer for business if Andre stayed in the kitchen, and so he taught Eric some of his tricks, like the secret blend of chocolate and mystery roasted beans for his famous iced mochas, which were topped with a combo of crème fraîche and whipped cream and ordered all year round. Andre told Eric that cooking was all chemistry with a dash of melodrama. Unofficially, whenever he hung out in the café, Eric waited on tables, and then when traffic started to pick up, Andre was able to afford him a meager salary.

An eternity and a half passed, and finally Inca turned in her plans. Right before their date, Eric visited the stolen idol. Timothy was showering (he was always either sculpting or bathing), so Eric had her all to himself. "Wish me luck," he said. "It's been so long, I feel like I don't even know how to breathe when I'm with a woman."

*Explorers sailing for new worlds always get cold feet—they dawdle, they rechart the voyage a dozen times—but once they're out on the open sea, they race to the continent.*

"I feel like I'm about fifteen."

*The tide will be gentle and the water very blue. Blue enough for a swim.*

Inca was taciturn as they walked toward Washington Square. She picked up the pace, and Eric nearly knocked over a shoelace vendor who cursed him out. Across the street in the park, a man had stolen another man's beeper and knit hat to protest the poor quality of the weed he had just purchased, and nearby, high up on scaffolding and oblivious to the approaching sirens, restorers worked overtime, rubbing lotions all over the pockmarked statues of the founding father.

Something caught Eric's eye, a figment, a person. A woman was walking across the street on the parallel sidewalk, heading in the same direction. She wore a graduation gown and pressed a mortarboard and diploma against her chest. It was Inca. In the distance, Eric heard a cheer rise from a commencement. Inca in the here and now was taking long strides next to him, but there she was across the street, too, at the tender age of twenty-one, hurrying away from college and into the big bad world. She glanced over her shoulder every few paces, and when Eric looked back, too, he could see an elegantly dressed man and woman in pursuit. Why wasn't she waiting for them? Eric rubbed his eyes, and Inca in cap and gown vanished. A jogger wrapped in mittens, a ski mask, and neon sweats bounced by instead.

Even at the end of winter, the East Village was a summer carnival, a bazaar sprawled all over the sidewalk and spilling over the curb. People peddled muumuus and clock radios, two-for-five-dollar brassieres and pirated videos of current movies. Eric and Inca stepped over towels covered with jigsaw fragments and adult comic books, past stands of self-help paperbacks and plastic kachinas, past tables littered with tiny, illicit-looking vials of clove extract. Eric covered his nose with his scarf so that he didn't have to inhale the fumes of incense burning into the dusk, and he waved off a woman who was tailing Inca, the woman's arms draped in rayon scarves and leather disco bags. They had to wend their way through a pack of demonstrators who were marching up an avenue toward a hospital, and they had to bypass the congregation of Ukrainian women clustered around a stoop. The women clutched brooms: They had just chased off a fleet of motorcycles, a clan of loud, causeless Beatniks who were trying to find someone, anyone, to listen to their poetry.

A yard ahead of Eric was a woman his age—Inca again, Inca from the past. Her hair was long, pulled into a ponytail. She sashayed down the street with a tall man who hooked a proprietary arm around her. The man wore a suede jacket and chic baggy trousers and Italian loafers. He looked over his shoulder to smirk at Eric: I know her better than you do, and I mean I *know* her. With his free hand, the man carried a wicker end table shaped like an elephant.

"Eric?"

He had walked right past the cinema. "Sorry."

Revival East looked like a vineyard cottage, odd among the neighboring tenements, and there was a fermented smell in the air inside, too. The pile of the carpeting was flattened, sticky with soda. The hallway leading to the theater was decorated with dry-mounted photographs of Hollywood legends, all signed with Magic Marker, and all in what suspiciously seemed like the same handwriting. Inca liked to sit far back from the screen, which suited Eric. They watched fellow Lucia Madsen fans trickle in. Eric was hoping they would arrive with time to spare for conversation, but the lights dimmed quickly.

*Waterfronts* was just that and not much else. For eighty-six minutes, Aunt Lucia, looking young and Bohemian with a bob of inky hair, bracelets snaking up one arm, and wearing a gauzy half-slip qua toga—a part-Hellenic, part-flapper Lucia Madsen—danced free-form along an ocean shore. Then she danced around the perimeter of a Catskill lake. Finally, Lucia danced *in* a reflecting pool of what looked like a turned-off fountain outside an English country house. All action was silent, and the score was some sentimental Impressionistic piano concerto with plenty of virtuoso glissandos.

"Life can be rather monotonous," Inca explained over fudge brownies during the intermission. "And then something happens when you least expect it."

"Like when the fountain came on in the end."

"Precisely." Inca scanned the dingy lobby and sighed. "I used to come here all the time. My friends and I would get terrifically stoned and watch those Technicolor musicals they'd run from time to time. *Gigi* was surreal." Inca looked Eric up and down.

"What?"

"Your generation never really got into drugs the way mine did."

"My generation?" He wished he hadn't shaved that night. "How old are you, anyway?"

Inca grinned instead of answering.

"Is that funny? Did you do a lot of drugs?" Eric pinched himself.

"Not a lot. But you know, it was in the air back then."

"I smoked pot in high school and college. But I never liked what it did to my memory. That's why I don't do it now."

"Pot?" Inca asked as if Eric had said *ginger ale*. "Your generation understands computers. The graphics on the computer at my office are amazing, but it's just not natural to me. I didn't grow up with it."

"I'm not *that* young. I remember when hand-held calculators first appeared. I didn't have a computer until college."

"I remember when a calculator was a big room with vacuum tubes the size of Rhode Island."

"I remember . . ." Eric gave up. He couldn't out-reminisce her.

"Thirty-nine," Inca said and returned to the theater.

"Is that all?" What was twelve years, he thought, even if they were separated by the rise of microchips and the decline of psychedelic drugs?

The second film, *Piety,* was much livelier than the first. Instead of long takes of Lucia dancing, the film was one extended montage. Lucia, this time in a black Victorian frock, petticoats and all, appeared playing chess with a man with a goatee and monocle. Lucia held one hand over her midsection and with the other moved the white pieces. Then she was kneeling in the front pew of a church, looking penitent, praying. Then lying in a bed, clothed, daydreaming. A lacy curtain answered a breeze. Cut to a child running on a lawn. Then back to the chess game. The church. The child again, and so on. By the time it was over, Eric was dizzy and yawning. They walked home fast, the wind behind them, too fast for him.

"It was about motherhood," Inca said. "It was about the choices we make." Her gloved hands grabbed at the air.

"What was chosen?"

"Nothing. The choices were simply spelled out."

Eric groped for something profound to say because he knew that his late aunt was Inca's hero. All he said was, "It's too bad Aunt Lucia stopped making films." He expected that Inca would consider this to be one of the century's great misfortunes.

"Why? She made a major impact in the fashion world."

"I sort of thought that she sold out."

"From what I know about her, she tried to add spark and spirit to women's clothes, and at first she was considered a lunatic, a renegade, what with all of those long, beaded frocks and those low-cut halters. Not what the average matron was wearing in the Forties and Fifties. She didn't sell out. She *chose* to do something else with her life."

"I just remember her as this terribly old woman who did a striptease at dinner, which I don't think was a choice."

"Are you making fun of me?" Inca stopped.

"No, not at all."

"You're making fun of me."

"I'm not, I'm not."

"She was a woman who lived her life the way she wanted. Did she marry?"

"Never."

"Did she have kids?"

"No," Eric answered sheepishly.

"She was criticized for leading an unconventional life. She was a poet, first with a bold new medium, then with a more traditional one, but always revolutionary and daring. A feminist. I don't think you should grade your aunt according to some standard of what society expects of us, of women. She lived a unique life. Choices." Inca continued walking.

Eric went over everything he had said that led her to think of him as a narrow-minded person and possibly a chauvinist. Maybe she was trying to tell him something. Maybe she had made some choices. "Inca"—he caught up—"did you always want to be a gadget designer?"

"No, I was trained as an architect, but when I went to work for an architectural firm, I lost my mind. Quite literally. It was unbearably dull, and I was relegated to shit-work. I thought I would draw beach houses and museums and libraries. Boy, was I naïve. I had to work on apartment house renovations. I was assigned to figure out where the mirrors should go in lobbies. I'd go home and try to sketch out my own houses, but all I could think about was turning fireplaces into heating ducts. Then no houses came to mind at all."

"That must have been depressing."

"A blank page on a drafting board is very hollow."

"And do you ever want to design houses again?"

"Can we talk about something else?"

Now Eric couldn't contain his questions. "Where are you from originally? Did your parents name you Inca for any particular reason? How long have you lived here? Have you thought about living anywhere else?"

St. Louis. Her father was a Latin American historian who met her mother, an archaeologist, on a dig in Peru—thus her name. Since college. And no matter how hard it got sometimes to live alone in this city, she would never consider emigrating anywhere else, never consider it for a moment. New York spoiled you, prevented you from surviving elsewhere. Inca explained, "I have to live in a place where there's Indian food takeout and where there are skyscraper lobbies that you can constantly rediscover."

Turning onto Forelle Street, Eric was so engrossed in Inca's minor revelations that he tripped on the curb and fell on his knee. She extended a hand to lift him up, but he sat on the sidewalk for a moment. Odd: In the gutter, something silvery was flopping around, then flipping over like a fish yanked from a lake. It was a fish, in fact, struggling in the gutter.

"You okay?" Inca asked.

Then the fish became a single white glove being carried down the street by the wind. He could have sworn it was a fish. Eric held on to Inca's hand, and she tugged him into the air. She yawned. "Let's get some coffee. I haven't had today's roast."

Inside the Mystery Roast, even though a dusty Timothy and a harried Andre were chatting at the bar, Inca indicated that she wanted to sit in a booth. "But are you unhappy in your job now?" Eric asked, emboldened.

"It pays incredibly well, and this city ain't too cheap anymore, kiddo."

He dared to slip in a non sequitur. "Have you ever been in love?"

"Everyone has."

"Have you ever been married?"

"You would know that by now."

"Do you want to be in love?"

Inca looked Eric in the eye. "Love comes when love comes. Andre? A refill, babe."

At two in the morning, Andre yawned and winked at Eric. "Why don't you kids lock up," he suggested. He rescued Melior from under a table, retreated into the kitchen and up the stairs. Alone in the empty and darkened café—all the lights were off except for the dropped lamp over their booth—Inca began to testify without prompting: "By the time she was my age, my mother had given birth to all of her five daughters."

His mother had taught him never to ask a woman if she wanted children because you never knew if she was physically unable to give birth. But carefully, quietly, Eric asked, "Do you want kids?"

"I like children." One bang ot Inca's hair fell from behind her ear and covered half her face. She sat up straight, her face pale. "You're young."

"If you do the math—"

"It's an important twelve years. Not just any twelve years. You haven't had to revise yourself. Not yet. Sure, you were married and divorced, but you haven't had to revise yourself."

"I don't know what that means." Eric had a clue, but he was tired and this line bothered him as coy and slippery.

"I'm beat." She stretched her arms, climbed out of the booth, and shook her limbs like a swimmer loosening up before a Channel swim.

Eric was mad and tempted to express his frustration, but instead, he stood next to Inca in the elevator, conspicuously close so that he could feel her breath on his cheek, close even though there was enough room left for two baby grands. The elevator paused on the fifth floor. She inserted her key and waited for a split second, long enough for Eric to infer an ambiguous cue. He cocked his head so as not to bump noses and kissed her. She kissed back. That sealed a friendship. And then he kissed her again, and this time she wrapped her arm over his shoulder and hugged him. "I had a nice evening," she said as she pulled away and stepped into her apartment. " 'Night."

Eric entered his apartment and, in a daze, rewound the tape in his VCR. Just as he always did every night when he was out, he had recorded his favorite late news program. Margot appeared to report on a senatorial race in Indiana. Old money versus new money. Something like that. He wasn't sure because as he began to nod off, he saw Inca on the set instead of his ex-wife, Inca bathed in the pale light of the café booth. And then he fell sound asleep with the television on.

The next day, one quick month after the first idol replicas appeared, an article about them ran in a popular downtown magazine called *Tomorrow's Bread*. Eric heard about it from a woman wearing a leopard-spotted boa and lace gloves who had come to the café directly from the newsstand. She was so happy to meet Eric that she gave him her copy of the magazine. He dashed upstairs to show it to Timothy.

"We're credited as 'co-*artistes*,' " Eric said. "I've never thought of myself as an artist, let alone an *artiste*."

Timothy said something, although it was hard to tell what exactly because he had taken to wearing a surgical mask amidst the thick web of marble dust in his studio. He lowered the mask long enough to say, "This is happening, Eric, this is really happening. I never ever thought we'd make it into the *Bread*."

Eric skimmed the article. "I'm the 'conceptual force,' and you're the 'artistic force.' How does it feel to be a *force*?"

Timothy signaled Eric with a thumbs-up. Then he directed his up-turned thumb at the real idol and began chiseling again.

"Do you want to come downstairs and have a celebratory iced mocha?"

"Are you kidding? I can't stop now."

Eric had to wait until Inca came home from work to tell her. She stopped by the café and congratulated him with a handshake. She said, "Why don't you stop by my place later."

At eleven-thirty when the café traffic finally dropped off somewhat, he went upstairs. The Mystery Roast had been packed that night with a black-jean crowd that had flocked to the newly anointed place-to-be-seen, and he was tired. Inca answered the door wearing a silk kimono as shiny as opal. He followed her to her black leather couch and sat down next to her. "You'd be amazed at the business we did tonight," he said.

Inca shot up right away. "Beer?" She foraged in her kitchen and returned with two bottles and a bowl of fruit. This time, however, she sat in an armchair, not on the couch.

"I was serving a woman some carrot soup," Eric said, "and she kissed me. Her friends giggled. She said it was a dare."

"The Goddess you've created is going to surprise you."

"Oh, it has already."

"You don't know what you've got cooking in the oven. You're—" Inca cut herself off with a swig of beer. She gripped the back of her neck. "Look, we're both adults here," she said.

When Inca lifted her arm, her bell-shaped kimono sleeve slipped back to expose her bare shoulder. A small curve of flesh, the side of her breast, was revealed before she readjusted her sleeve.

"And I think we both know," Inca continued, "that there's kinetic potential."

"There's what?"

"I've given this a lot of thought, and I don't think we should get involved."

He held his breath.

"I know it sounds clichéd—this line has been thrown at me more times than I care to remember—but what I need at this point in my life is a friend. Not a lover."

"A friend."

"I know that you don't see it yet, but I may be a big help to you later on. As a friend." Inca stood up and tightened her kimono sash. She began to pace.

"I'm just wondering something. Is this what you usually wear to reject men, or am I special?"

"There's going to come a time, sooner than you think, when you're going to need someone with commercial savoir faire to whisper wise advice in your ear." The fingertips of her left hand were scratching a spot (where?) under the fold of her robe. "I'm sure you're very mad at me—"

"Mad? Me, mad? Do I look mad?" Eric wanted to stick his head out the window and scream and shriek until he woke the entire block.

"—but don't be." She extended her hand. Eric shook it as if he were sealing a reluctant deal, and she said, "Then we agree."

Later Eric couldn't sleep. He didn't check the clock when he wrapped himself in a blanket and knocked on Timothy's door. "Inca told me tonight that she just wants to be friends," he explained.

"Do straight people still say that?" Timothy was clutching a half-carved Cycladic woman. "Sounds like she switched the faucet handles on you. You turn on the hot water and you get cold instead. I hate that." Timothy stepped around the partition into his studio.

"I can't sleep." There was nowhere to sit, so Eric pulled his blanket tightly around his shoulders and slumped in a corner, then sank to the floor.

"There are other things happening in your life, my friend," Timothy said.

Eric stared at the ancient idol propped up in the green armchair and then at the pile of fresh Goddesses. When he squinted, the pile looked like bones. "This is true. A lot."

"Stealing that idol was the best thing you ever did. We're hot. Don't you feel it? Hotter by the minute. Soon we'll be so hot, no one will be able to touch us."

"Hot," Eric said. His eyelids became heavy.

"We're feeding the people, partner, and they want more."

Timothy chipped at the marble once again, and after a while, despite the light, despite the metered chiming of mallet and chisel, Eric managed to fall asleep.

**B**efore long, Lydia did not need to arrange when or where to meet Marek for lunch. He knew the owner of a serene trattoria halfway between the Institute and the museum who kept a table reserved until two. Their standing date had evolved into such a central and vital part of her daily routine that one afternoon when Marek had an auction to attend instead and phoned to cancel, she was overcome with melancholy. She roamed the aisles of a nearby deli where there was a lush salad bar, always plenty of marinated corn and three-bean salad and roasted sweet peppers—a virtual Everest of chick-peas each day—and went so far as to fill half of a plastic container with snow peas before she recognized that she had a craving that salad wouldn't satisfy. She was driven not toward something healthy but toward something greasy and cholesterol-rich. Definitely not souvlaki, and a hot dog wouldn't do at all, not even with an ample layering of sauerkraut. She made a beeline out the door and straight for a knish stand, but when she reached the cart, she realized that a knish would not suffice either. She found herself drifting west, and without thinking, she hopped on a crosstown bus.

When the elevator doors opened, Jason called to her from down the hall, from his media center. He was working at a map on the wall.

"I have a craving," Lydia said, "and I don't know what for."

"You used to get cravings all the time." Jason stuck a pushpin into the Levant. "I remember having to go out for sushi once in the middle of a snowstorm."

"Maybe that's what I want, sushi."

"I make my own now."

Of course he did. He was the most self-sufficient person on the planet.

"I'll make you some when I'm done. There's been some pointless diplomacy over here, but I'm moving the pins anyway, even if I'll have to move them back. That's why you came—for lunch?"

"No, just to see you again." Lydia had wanted to call him several times, but she knew from experience how difficult talking on the phone with Jason could be, especially when he took for granted that he was being bugged. "But I'll gladly accept your sushi."

"It's quite nutritious."

She inspected the room. The televisions were running, the volumes down low. A Congressional hearing, a women's basketball game, and several talk shows competed with soap operas. "Do you sleep any better than you used to?"

"Me? No. But I always thought that sleep was overrated. Plus, if you're out of the loop for too long, who knows what might happen?"

"Where?"

"Anywhere."

"Right." In one corner of the room, the last free bit of wall space had been covered since her last visit, papered with dozens of clippings, a map of the park outside, and a floor plan of the New York Museum of Art. The articles all focused on the stolen idol. Jason had apparently collected every story that had appeared about the theft in every paper in every language. His plan of the museum was covered with penciled arrows.

Jason joined her by the clippings. "Eric certainly is very clever."

"Why do you say that?"

"You haven't seen this?" He handed Lydia the latest issue of *Tomorrow's Bread*. "It's important to keep abreast of the downtown scene, Lydia, and your son is making his contribution to it. Along with that Rampling boy."

"What are you talking about?" Lydia started skimming the article. "Hey, how about that? The last time Eric got his name in the paper was when he won that He's-Got-the-Whole-World-in-His-Hands diorama contest at the U.N. when he was in the fourth grade. You helped him, didn't you? He won with a Norwegian scene, a fjord, I think."

"I recall the winning entry well. I glued cotton into an old shoe box of mine."

Lydia read more. "Co-*artiste,* not bad. Jason, it certainly is refreshing to see him doing *something.* I wonder what their reproductions are like. Maybe I should call him and get one. Marek would get a kick out of it."

"Out of a cheap imitation of a stolen museum treasure that your son is selling out of some Village hole-in-the-wall?"

"You have a point. I wonder if he's seen this yet. He hasn't mentioned it. He's been so busy lately coordinating the museum investigations—"

"Marek is? They'll never get the loot back now."

The map of Central Park was decorated with arrows and a series of dashed lines radiating from the site of the crime. "What's this?"

"The way the burglar escaped."

"How do you know that he ran across the park?"

"A hunch. Let's make sushi." Jason's refrigerator was crammed with identical plastic containers of food. He knew which ones to withdraw without checking their contents. "You've been seeing a lot of Marek, then?"

"We enjoy each other's company."

Jason pulled out a chopping block and then opened one container full of pressed seaweed. "Salmon-maki?"

"Mmm."

He placed a band of seaweed on a small mat of thin reeds. "My name come up at all? With Marek?"

"No, dear, I'm sorry." Lydia knew better. "It's so unlike Eric to do something vaguely fashionable. I can't get over it. I always hoped he'd do something creative, write a novel, pick up the piano again. This wasn't what I had in mind, but what the hell."

"I'm not surprised. He was a very spiritual boy. So earnest, so curious. We would walk on the beach at sunset. So many questions." Jason opened a plastic tub which contained cooked brown rice. "I make this"—he pinched a gob of the glutinous starch—"and mix in a little plum sauce in the process."

Lydia tasted a few sticky grains. "Delicious."

Jason packed a bed of rice on the seaweed. With his pinky, he spun in a thread of wasabi. Then he layered in strips of bright orange raw fish, scallions, and splinters of cucumber. He rolled the mat so that the seaweed wrapping became a rice-fish–stuffed tube, and then he placed the maki on a butcher's block. With a long knife, he sliced the black pipe into smaller cylinders. He made a second roll.

It was a cool, cloudless day, and the sun drenched the living room with almost too much light. The sushi was sweet. "I love the rice," Lydia purred. "The salmon, too."

Jason nodded thanks and scratched his gray scalp. "A guy down at the Seaport brings me fresh fillets when he makes deliveries to restaurants in the neighborhood. So tell me, what brings you up here today?"

"I told you. I enjoyed seeing you the last time. I wanted to come back."

"Last time you came at the end of the day. Today you're here in the middle of the day. You're getting unpredictable. So, really. Why are you here?"

Lydia swallowed a piece of Jason-maki and contemplated possible responses: Bellevue sent me over to ease you downstairs, where men in white suits are waiting with a straitjacket. Actually, I'm a spy for Interpol, and well, we've had you under surveillance since you were twelve. Jason, if you don't stop asking me why I come and visit you, then, fine, I'll stop coming. "I had a craving," she said. "Do you use your telescope?" She assumed the answer would be no.

"I depend on it. Otherwise, I might have to go downstairs."

"Remember how we used to—"

"I don't use it at night. I mean I do," Jason corrected himself, "but I don't look at the stars or anything. Here, come look." He opened the door onto the terrace, carefully folded the tripod legs, and then lifted the telescope like a small child. Out on the breezy deck, he set up the apparatus again and angled it toward the park. "I watch the people down there." He pressed his face against the binocular eyecups.

"You spy on people?"

"*Spy* is the wrong word. I find people. I follow them. I keep track of them. Somebody has to."

"That's very kind, given how busy you are monitoring the rest of the world," Lydia teased gently.

"Look."

She bent down to the telescope. As a child she used to venture to the observatory of her local community college when they held open house. She always had a crush on the nerdy graduate student with the slide rule in his pocket who helped visitors locate the planets. Somehow she never thought it would be possible to study the heavens professionally: She assumed she was not smart enough to do the math. When she looked into Jason's telescope, she saw that he had focused on the zoo all the way east in the park and downtown. She could actually see visitors—a woman, two children, and a baby carriage—by the corner of the zoo where the polar bears lived. It helped that the trees in the park were stripped of leaves. She watched the bears lumber about their cement terrain. Two ivory bergs of fur at play. The third one napped. "This is truly incredible," she said.

"*Ursus maritimus*. I love them. We share a fondness for fish. See the smallest bear of the three?"

"Is that the one that tried to escape?"

"She's lost weight. I think they might be drugging her. They have a veterinary shrink visiting her every day. No doubt full of useless ursine psychobabble."

"Where do you think she wanted to go?" The bear lay on her side, her flank rising and falling in slow sighs. Lydia could see the fog of her breath.

"Home. She was headed in the right direction. I feel for her, I really do. She's not doing well at all, but I think she'll pull through. Zoo bears are resilient. They're survivors."

Lydia continued to observe the woman and children. The children waved good-bye to the bears, and then the woman led them on to another part of the zoo but curiously left the carriage behind. "Wait. I don't believe it. Look."

Jason stared at the polar bear and then returned the telescope to Lydia. "Well, the other bears don't treat her well," he explained. "They're not as smart. They're willing to go along with the system, you know. They conspire against her and steal her striped-bass treats."

"No, I mean the carriage." It was still there when Lydia looked again. Was it possible that the baby wasn't in it? She couldn't tell. However, the woman didn't seem to be carrying an infant and the other children were old enough to walk. Lydia swiveled the telescope and located them again by the island of snow monkeys.

"Yes," Jason said, "there's a woman who comes and leaves her baby in front of the polar bears each day for about fifteen minutes to a half-hour. Longer in warmer weather."

Lydia panned back to the carriage and the bears. "Isn't she afraid of baby snatchers? Isn't she afraid the bear that tried to escape will come at the kid?"

"That bear's a pacifist, believe me, and drugged, like I said. See, my theory is that the mother or nanny doesn't wander too far away and keeps an eye on the carriage. She must want the kid to be raised by the bears."

"This happens every day?"

"Every weekday."

Lydia kept her eye on the carriage. Finally, a woman in a long down coat came into view and wheeled it away. "I hope she's the right person."

Jason checked. "That's her."

It dawned on Lydia that he knew everything about everyone in the park. This was his only contact with the outside world. This was why he did not have to go downstairs, as he said, because whenever he needed human contact, he simply took out his telescope and followed a jogger.

"Sometimes you see strange things in the park," Jason whispered.

Lydia had trouble hearing him over the din of cars and buses on the street below. She was starting to get cold and wanted to go back inside, but he seemed eager to tell her something here and now.

"I happened to be out here the day the idol was stolen from the museum." Now Jason gently swiveled the telescope to examine the back of NYMA.

"Did you see the burglar?"

"Not really. I can't quite see the museum on that side. There are too many trees in the way, even if they have no leaves at the moment. But I did see someone running across the park around the time of the crime. I didn't get a good look, but I did see that there was just one person. A man carrying a bag. I couldn't see his face. He seemed to be, oh, a little taller than you. Slender. Dark wavy hair. Dark skin. A long coat. For a while, he was running west toward me—he was running straight across the lawn. But it was so white that day. So much snow. It reflected the sun and made it hard to see much of anything with any clarity. Then I lost the guy in the foliage around the Free Shakespeare theater. I found him again when he emerged on the street—I think—although I'm not entirely sure, because there were other people out, too. It really was impossible to see his face. He ran into the subway, the downtown side, which I assume he rode somewhere."

"Marek will be interested in this."

"Lydia, no, no. You can't tell Marek." Jason became frantic. "No, you don't want to do that. Believe me, you do not want to do that. He'll try to call me. I have nothing to say to him." He stepped back from her.

"I don't know what I was saying. I would never tell anyone. I won't tell a soul."

"Besides, I didn't get that good a look."

Lydia shivered. She looked into the telescope one last time. She angled it herself and scanned East Side buildings. "I guess you can see into those apartments. During the day you can't see in, can you? At night I imagine you could."

"I keep track of people there, too. At night, yes."

"Hey," Lydia announced gleefully, "I found my building. You can see it really well from here." Her apartment house was a whole block in from the park, but because of the way the buildings were laid out, given the height of Lydia's, she could see a small square of her building rising above others. She counted down from the roof and found her floor. "You can see my place," she said. Then she became very quiet. Yes, she could see her apartment. She could make out the shape of the Swedish ivy hanging in her living room window. "Did you know you can see my place?" At night, with the lights on . . . She did not even want to consider this possibility.

Jason scratched his nose. "I had no idea. I tend to only study the buildings along the edge of the park." He peered into the telescope. "I see it now. Funny. All these years, and I didn't know." He folded up the tripod. "We don't live that far away, do we?"

"No, we don't." Lydia remained outside for a minute after Jason went in. From his nest you could see polar bears in the zoo and museum thieves on the lam, and you could see her apartment with a high-powered telescope. She did not believe for a second that Jason was spotting her building for the first time.

The ninety-third Goddess of Desire was purchased by someone famous, a rock star of recent acclaim, a woman called Sister Leigh who was known for her folk lyrics and tropical beat and who showed up at the Mystery Roast in a stretch limousine. She was about to hit the concert circuit but had been suffering from stressed vocal cords, and she claimed that the idol would protect her throat. Eric never knew how many people lived on his block until Sister Leigh appeared at three in the afternoon one Saturday wearing a bomber jacket over her signature pink silk pajamas, until fans came streaming out of onetime factories and erstwhile warehouses to press for an autograph or just to catch a glint of iris or pupil behind the rock star's dark glasses. Most of the other sales were more mundane. The one hundred and thirty-fifth idol, for example, went to a woman who pined for fame as a romance novelist, a woman whom Eric learned taught "business grammar" at an adult school in Gramercy. The one hundred and eighty-fourth Goddess was acquired by a paramedic, and the one hundred ninety-seventh by a Xerox repairman. The month of March became a parade of people who had never set foot in the Mystery Roast before, and the faster that Timothy sculpted the Cycladic women, the faster they were dispatched into the world. For the two hundredth sale, Inca gave Eric and Timothy a bottle of champagne, which they drank together late at night while Timothy shaped and buffed and gave a final antiquing—with a rubdown of his dusty palms—to the two hundred and first. The two hundred and fifty-third idol was sold to the first man who had bought one (his wife had swiped his original purchase when she left him the week before), and the two hundred and eighty-sixth idol was carted off by a neighborhood boy, no more than ten or eleven, who was so transfixed by his acquisition that he left behind the wad of takeout menus from a nearby Chinese restaurant that he was distributing door-to-door.

Eric had never expected to make any money dealing Goddesses, but with two hundred and eighty-six Cycladic idols sold, he and Timothy were well in the black, each having earned three thousand dollars and some change after expenses. As long as Timothy was willing and able to manufacture the idols, Eric did not really need to work in the café, where he spent most of his days and nights now, but he never considered quitting, not even when he burned his hand on a dish of chicken potpie, not when he had to cope with an entrée of salmon Provençal returned inexplicably to the kitchen, not even when Andre barked his cynicisms, which he was doing with greater frequency (his withdrawal headaches had abated, but he was perpetually grouchy). Before he arrived in the Mystery Roast, Eric had spent so much time doing nothing with his life that he truly feared even one idle afternoon because of the next that he was certain would inevitably follow. He had always wanted to swim in the current of the city, and now he had his chance, right here in the salon of salons all the way west. When Eric stopped to take a breather and have a cappuccino one day, he realized that for the most part he was happy, and he wondered if there wasn't something wrong with him.

But the month of March was a game of winds, too, with a climate that oscillated like the temper of a recovering caffeine addict. Closer to the equinox, the moods of wind gave way to moods of light. The planet was at a tilt that afforded angles of sharp sun and pools of deep shadow, and the streets toward the end of a weekday afternoon or early on Sunday morning, when Eric liked to break away from the café and wander, were deceptively long or wide, each turn revealing an unknown alley full of questionable shapes. For example, one day, out of the blue, an MG tore down a quiet side street. Eric hopped out of the way just in time. The car stopped at the end of the block, and Eric saw that it was his parents, Jack and Lydia, sitting in the front seat—except they looked as they did in thirty-year-old snapshots. His mother was wearing vivid red lipstick, a scarf wrapped around her head, and his father was chewing gum. They looked lost, and his mother unfolded a map while his father shouted, although Eric couldn't hear what he was saying. Then they zoomed away and were gone.

Another afternoon, Eric was looking out his window when he noticed a large assembly of suffragettes wearing long dresses and carrying picket signs march up Forelle to meet a militia of policemen with rifles. One cop fired a shot, and one woman fell: Blood seeped into the cobblestone. Fine. A bizarre and disturbing daydream all on its own, but then later, Andre happened to be talking to some women in the café and they were discussing just such a skirmish that had actually occurred in 1913. Andre told Eric that several centuries ago, a trout stream used to run where Forelle Street was today (the name of the street was a bastardized spelling of *forel,* Dutch for *trout*), and Eric remembered the fish that he had seen flip-flopping in the gutter. He saw a young woman leaving a party late one night a few blocks east, a fin de siècle debutante ball. She left the arm of her fatherly, top-hatted escort and stepped into the street, where she was promptly hit by an oncoming carriage, thrown, and killed instantly. It matched another story that Eric overheard two teenage boys discussing in the café, although the similar incident that they were gossiping about had just occurred in Scarsdale outside a junior prom. The visions, day-dreams, whatever they were, the history he was happening upon, both personal and unrelated to him, became increasingly gruesome. Finally, one Sunday morning, Eric was walking past a famous book bindery when he stopped to read a frieze of faded advertising—EACH BOOK A UNIVERSE OF FINE STITCHING—and saw flames shooting out of the top-story windows. The factory was burning, and firemen couldn't contain the blaze. Panicking employees, women in long dresses again, had begun to jump from the fatal heights of the upper floors. Eric closed his eyes in fear and horror—but then opened them to see that the windows were in fact bricked up. The building was owned by the city and, among other things in the here and now, used to store salt for melting ice on winter streets. By the following Sunday, Eric's daytime nightmares had ceased as inexplicably abruptly as they had begun. He assumed that this was either because the angles of light softened with April or because he had not visited the idol up in Timothy's studio in well over a week.

Sunday had become Eric's favorite day of café living. On Sundays people came to the Mystery Roast in the late morning and lingered for hours. Patrons arrived with newspapers, and over cups and cups of coffee, over onion bagels and Nova lox (the only day Andre made them available), they slowly peeled away the sections as they read them. Inca, too, read her *Times* while seated at the bar. She did the crossword with Eric and Andre. She read real-estate listings aloud. She oohed and aahed at the sketches of polka-dotted spring fashions, at the photos of Connecticut interiors. She had said she wanted to be friends, platonic and faithfully unphysical, and so Eric made his best effort to forget about his house on a deserted Maine coast—or at least he tried to envision someone other than Inca sunbathing nude with him on its cedar deck—but it was difficult. He threw himself into his work in the café. He asked Andre to teach him recipes and hoped that in the memorization of ingredients, he would get over her. With curried tuna salad, with split pea soup, with chicken cacciatore, he made slow progress toward that end.

Sunday morning inevitably gave way to Sunday afternoon, when Inca went upstairs to work on her designs and when the café was less crowded and visited by tourists who had heard as far north as Times Square that the Mystery Roast was a landmark in the making. Andre brought a small radio out from the kitchen and listened to opera, turning it up so loudly that conversation had to be shouted. Melior didn't seem to mind the noise, and she slept upside down on the bar, occasionally reaching a paw toward the ceiling when Tosca or Aïda groped for a high note. Learning the secret spices of Andre's tomato sauce (select fresh leaves of basil, a pinch of celery seed) had been easy and fun, but Eric was frankly intimidated by the more complex rite of baking the famous pains aux chocolats. Andre spread out the operation in the café, setting up baking trays on the bar. Eric cut out squares of flattened dough and brushed them with melted butter. And more butter. He bisected the square with a generous helping of Andre's chocolate mixture. He folded the pastry just so, but somehow his final assemblage looked like a poorly stitched baseball, nothing like his teacher's perfectly shaped hexagon. Andre rolled his eyes, sighed, and Eric was afraid he was going to be reprimanded for inept technique.

"This town is a swamp sometimes," Andre said. "Correction: It's a swamp all the time. It stinks, and before you know it, you're submerged in muck."

A group of six women approached the bar. One held a map. Eric turned the radio volume down a notch. The woman with the map handed Eric her table's check and said, "And could we have a half-dozen little women to go?"

Two hundred and ninety-two. Eric reached under the bar and pulled out the last of the Goddesses in stock. A gray-haired man sitting in the corner watched the sale. Eric whispered to Andre, "He's going to want one, too. We'll have to sell him the display idol." There was one last figurine in the glass cake dish. "You were saying—"

"I walk around"—Andre slapped pastry onto the baking tray—"and I see buildings where friends used to live, and I have to tell you, Eric, they're all tombstones."

"Andre . . ." It had to be a caffeine deficiency that depressed him.

"The whole fucking city is a cemetery. If people haven't died of AIDS, they've run away, or they're too shell-shocked to come out and play."

"Andre . . ." Eric didn't want to believe this.

"You don't get it." Andre's face reddened. "You didn't live through it. I promised myself I wouldn't run. But lately . . . I can't even drink real coffee. So you tell me, what's left?" He turned up the radio, louder than before.

"I'm sure it's changed," Eric shouted, "I'll take your word. But I like this neighborhood, I really do."

The man who had been watching from the corner all the while approached the bar. He wore a suit that was of the same hue as his silvery hair. Gray eyes, too. A red handkerchief in his breast pocket matched his tie.

"I know, I know, you want a Goddess," Andre snapped.

"Ignore him!" Eric yelled.

The man reached over to the radio and switched it off. "My assistant already brought me one." The man spoke with an accent, Italian, Eric guessed.

"I'm sorry," Andre apologized. "I didn't mean to bite."

"I had to come here myself and see the place where it came from," the man said. "I'm looking for either Mr. Timothy Rampling or Mr. Eric Auden."

Eric noticed that the man was holding a rolled-up copy of *Tomorrow's Bread*. "I'm Eric."

"Excellent. And I'm Eduardo Redelarte." The man's name rolled from his tongue like the name of a Renaissance painter.

"As in the Redelarte Gallery?" Andre asked.

"I have just learned that an artist of mine is going to have to pull out of my group show which opens in a few weeks. I'd like to talk to you and your co-conceptualist."

"Why?" Eric said, not because he didn't understand but because he couldn't believe what he was hearing.

"That's wonderful," Andre said. "That's extraordinary. You want to include the Goddess in your show?"

"Precisely."

"Timothy will flip," Andre said. "Oh, shit," he muttered. "Now, they'll be no talking to him. His ego will balloon."

"I'm . . . speechless." Suddenly, Eric felt a pressure to have artistic thoughts, which as far as he knew, he'd never had.

"You know," Eduardo Redelarte said, "I have a way of calling these things. And I think what you've done might just be of minor significance."

"You're very kind."

"The folding of history and current events into a bluntly nonsubjective format is altogether unusual and uncanny. It's new, yet old. Old, yet new. You've seen it before. You've never seen it. The possibilities are enervating."

"I'm getting bushed just thinking about it," Andre said.

"I'll be sending an assistant along shortly to make arrangements," Eduardo Redelarte said. "So you see, Mr. . . . ?"

"Orso," Andre answered.

"Mr. Orso, your friend here is right. The city is not dead. It wobbles, it gurgles its last breath, but it is full of comebacks and surprises."

After the art dealer left, Andre said, "You know who he is, right? This is what Timothy has always wanted. What he dreamed about when he was just a toddler hanging dirty drawings in the men's room."

"Eduardo Redelarte," Eric said. The name sunk in. The man had surfed the crest of every postwar wave. "He's in art history books."

"Look, I'm sorry if I—"

"No, I hear you," Eric said. "To quote Timothy: I came to the party late."

"The party may not be over yet, sweetheart, not for you."

"I'm going to go tell Timothy now." The news was still strange to him. Were copies of ancient art in themselves art? Eric skipped all the way up the back steps and was out of breath when he knocked on Timothy's door.

"Who is it?"

"Me." The door was open.

"Wait a minute!" Timothy called from his studio.

Eric stayed put in the front room. "You'll never guess who I just met and who wants to include the Goddess in a group show at his extremely famous gallery."

"Who?" Inca asked from behind the partition. Good, she was here, too.

Eric thought he heard Timothy whisper, "You don't mind? You're sure?" And then Timothy shouted, "You can come in!"

"Eduardo Redelarte," Eric said as he turned right, into the studio.

"You've got to be kidding. That's phenomenal," Inca cheered.

"Really?" Timothy asked. "Wow," he said softly. "Wow," as if he wasn't sure whether he was awake or dreaming. "He was in the café? You met him? What's he like?"

Timothy was naked, sitting on a stool, balancing his drawing pad on one knee. He was sketching frenetically and continued to draw even after Eric brought in the news. And then Eric saw the idol, the real one, sitting on the green armchair—or was it one of Timothy's copies?

*Long time, no see.*

And last—in the split second of recognitions—Eric noticed Inca. She was sitting on a chair positioned next to the armchair, her long legs crossed, her hands folded behind her chestnut head of hair, her elbows pointing downward. She wore not an article of black clothing. Her eyes were focused on Timothy; she looked at Eric briefly, then at Timothy again.

"Redelarte," Inca said. "That's quite a coup."

"I'm—I'm sorry—I—" Eric swallowed. If Timothy preferred men, then why was he naked, too? Eric was consumed with an intense desire both to study the unclothed Inca and to avoid looking. And why was the stolen idol out?

"It's okay." Inca must have read his radish-red face. "I'm just posing."

He glanced over at her folded elbows behind her head, her arms pulling apart her breasts. Perfect geometry: two perfect triangles in the air and two perfect spheres connecting them. And then he glanced back at Timothy, who continued to sketch. He'd propped up the drawing pad on his knee, and with his leg lifted onto a higher rung of the stool, his penis and balls were available for all the world to see. It was cold in the studio, and Timothy's nipples were hard, his left pectoral muscle quivering with the movement of his drawing hand.

"I should go," Eric said. "You're working." He could see that Timothy was concentrating on the idol more than on Inca. Both were in the portrait he was sketching.

"No, stay," Timothy said.

*Relax.*

"Stay." Inca smiled at Eric. "Pull up a chair."

"Um . . . Timothy," Eric started to say.

Timothy winked at him.

*Don't worry. She thinks I'm one of those ridiculous forgeries, can you believe that? I won't tell you what I think of her. And did I hear you say that some Roman art dealer wants to take advantage of me?*

"Timothy, that's an awfully good copy in the armchair," Eric said with cautious sarcasm.

"It's his latest and best, don't you think?" Inca asked.

*Let's not take leave of our senses, folks.*

Eric expected Inca to look over at the artifact, but she didn't.

"Pull up a chair," Timothy said.

*Either sit down or leave, but don't stand there looking like a confused puppy.*

Eric knew that he should leave. The scene disturbed him. Maybe Timothy was having an affair with Inca. Yes, perhaps they had been involved in a torrid exchange for years and years and Eric was the last to learn about it. He knew better than to stay, but he opened a folding chair because his heart was beating fast with envy and lust, and he was afraid that he would pass out if he didn't sit down. He sat quietly in the corner for about thirty seconds and watched Inca striking her pose, still and silent, seductively looking at Timothy, and Timothy, in turn, with knitted brows, drawing with muscular fervor.

Eric couldn't stand it. "Were you two . . . ?"

"What?" Timothy asked.

*Give me a break.*

"Nothing," Eric said, but a minute later blurted, "Tim, why are you undressed?"

*"Undressed"? Please. He's stark naked. You can say "naked," can't you?*

"He always is when he draws me," Inca said.

"Not always," Timothy said. "I've done you in clothes, and then I was dressed."

"True."

"Wait," Eric demanded.

"I always match whatever my models are or are not wearing to make them feel more comfortable," Timothy explained.

"It works," Inca said. "Plus, it gives you something to look at and think about. I'm sure I look more intriguing because, well, I'm intrigued."

"Anyone I sketch nude," Timothy said, "is looking back at nudity." His hand moved across the pad as if he were washing a window.

Eric became conspicuously aware that he was the only dressed person in the room. Even the idol was nude.

"Timothy said he had given up drawing completely," Inca said. "But I convinced him to take time out of his busy schedule to sketch me."

"No, I still like to draw."

"I was feeling tense"—Inca looked over at Eric again and then back at Timothy—"and a little lonely, and this always helps me focus and relax."

"Do you want to get in the picture?" Timothy asked Eric.

"What, me pose?"

*No, why don't you stand on your head and bark like a seal.*

"I'd love to draw you on one side, the Goddess in the middle there— and Inca, you would stay right where you are." Timothy set up the composition and then, balancing the pad in his legs, formed a square with his thumbs and forefingers to frame the shot.

"Join us," Inca said.

*Go for it.*

Now, why was Inca playing with his mind, inviting him closer? It was a cruel joke. He couldn't decide what to do. "Well, all right." Eric dragged his chair over to the left side of the armchair and sat down.

"Eduardo Redelarte," Inca said again, her eyes on the artist. "What a feat."

"It's incredibly amazing," Timothy said. "I don't believe it yet. This is it. Now I—now *we*—are reaching people." Timothy sketched now in even broader, more hurried strokes. "People will talk at parties. They'll talk at work. They'll talk in bed after sex at night. We're on a rocket, Eric."

"What?"

"A rocket that no one, nowhere, is going to stop. To Pluto, my man. Beyond."

Eric leaned back in his chair and discovered that he sort of enjoyed being drawn. Posing was in fact relaxing. It was as if Timothy were performing card tricks, and Eric's spine tingled the way it used to when he was a child and a birthday party magician drew bouquets of silk flowers and gauzy scarves from his sleeve.

"Eric?" Timothy asked. "Maybe you'd like to take off your sweater."

"It is kind of warm in here." Eric combed his hair with his fingers after pulling it over his head.

"And maybe your shirt," Timothy suggested a short while later.

Eric realized what was being requested. He stood up and stepped behind the chair, out of Inca's peripheral range. He kicked off his sneakers and tugged off his socks. His shirt. His jeans.

"Don't worry about taking everything off," Timothy said.

*What have you got to hide? Show her what you're made of.*

Off came his briefs. Eric returned to his chair and stared resolutely at the artist.

"I find sitting very soothing," Inca said.

"Soothing," Eric echoed. Out of the corner of his eye, he noticed her crossed leg. The plane from her kneecap to her buttocks reminded him of the flat part of an oar. Beyond the oar was a tuft of dark hair, mostly hidden.

"I feel sort of cleansed when it's all over," she said. She relaxed her arms, allowing them to fall, but quickly resumed her pose. Her hair had been slicked back with some kind of gel that roasted the chestnut color. In the soft light of the studio, part natural, part artificial, her skin glowed and blushed like a nectarine.

"Cleansed, right." Eric was close enough to hear her breathe. He wanted to stand behind her and kiss the back of her neck just once quickly. No, if he were granted just one kiss, he'd go for the stretch of flesh between her shoulder and breast. Then, if allowed to continue, he might nuzzle in the soft field of her stomach. Yes, and then he would hold her, and they would roll all the way down a grassy hill, cool and wet on a fall afternoon, and at the base of the hill . . . Eric felt a warm rush in his lower abdomen, then in his inner thighs.

Timothy said, "I knew this would happen, of course. I knew that it was only a matter of time before someone major took a hard look at what we've been doing, Eric. By the way, I love the line that your wrist and arm make."

Eric looked at his arm and then back at Timothy. "Thanks."

"Before you came in," Inca said, "we were talking about Andre."

*They were not. They were talking about you.*

"And?" Eric asked.

"I think Timothy should be nicer to him," Inca said.

*It started when she asked him what your ex-wife was like.*

"Andre is a snail on downers," Timothy complained. "We've been dance partners for a long time—too long."

"He's gone through sad-phases before," Inca said, "but never this dark."

*He told her that he'd never met your ex-wife, and then she asked him if he knew why you got divorced.*

"When Andre is sad," Inca said, "I think the whole building is sad. That's why I came up here. Timothy, you make me happy, but you should try—"

"I think it's about over, Inca," Timothy said. "It was over a while ago."

*He told her that as far as he knew, you and your ex-wife just grew apart, that you married too young.*

Eric sighed loudly.

"I'm sorry, I didn't mean to depress you, Eric," Inca said. "Hey, we should be celebrating." And Inca changed the subject and started reminiscing about some young artist who she once knew and who became famous after a Redelarte show.

Eric didn't listen. When he leaned back uncomfortably in his chair, his penis flopped back against his navel.

*Uh-oh.*

Timothy drew, and Inca maintained her stance and stare and went on about the artist—and the idol, Eric thought, began to release a sustained cackle, more of a muted scream than a laugh. He tried to conjure up awful images, orphans deprived of candy, but when he opened his eyes, he faced a handsome man and had a beautiful woman beside him: Nothing could dampen his hardening hard-on, not even a howling artifact. At the same time, he was angry with Inca—why was she toying with him?—and mad at Timothy, a practiced tease, who knew how he felt about her. Why had he goaded him into this orgy?

Eric stood up and took a clumsy step back, knocking his chair over. He picked up his clothes on the floor and said, "Excuse me," as he retreated into the next room and threw on his jeans and shirt. He shoved his underwear into his pocket. He returned briefly to the studio, and he would have said good-bye before running out, but he was speechless after looking at Timothy's drawing. There was Inca, arms folded behind her head, breasts swaying in charcoal uncertainty. There was the idol, sharp-angled, self-assured, arms also folded, presiding. And there was Eric, outlined, tentative, looking as if he were about to say something, and there he was, in full bloom, as Timothy had captured him for the history of art to embrace for now and forever. Eric was already descending in the elevator when he realized that he had forgotten his sneakers. Instead of going back for them, he got off at his floor and found a pair of loafers, then hurried downstairs.

Later that afternoon, Eric worked with Andre in the kitchen chopping zucchini and asparagus for pasta primavera, chopping cilantro and garlic, chopping anything in sight. When Eric stepped into the café at one point, he noticed that his sneakers had been left sitting on a bar stool. The sneakers were not exactly new, but they were not worn out either. When he returned to the kitchen, he tossed them in the trash.

e wasted a fine pair of sneakers, and for several days after running out of his first and what he hoped would be his last joint-portrait sitting, Eric successfully avoided both Timothy and Inca. If either of them stopped by the café, he hid in the kitchen. He didn't use the elevator. Finally one night, Timothy knocked on his back door. He held two identically cut, boxy, formless jackets on hangers. "I'm leaning toward the brown plaid as opposed to the green plaid," he said.

"I like the green."

"It's a better color for me, but I read somewhere that it's bad luck to wear green at an opening." Timothy stepped into Eric's loft and laid the jackets flat on the bed. He tried the green plaid jacket over his dusty T-shirt. He rolled back the cuffs to reveal the blue lining.

"You still have three weeks to decide."

Timothy slipped out of the green jacket and tried on the brown one. "There will be lots of photographers, which is why I'm opting for plaid: It reads well in the newspapers." The brown jacket had a pink lining. "What do you think?"

Eric sat on the edge of the bed.

"I didn't really come down here for a fashion consultation. You're mad at me, I know. I'm sorry about the other day. It was an accident. She showed up and I was so engrossed in my sculpting that I forgot that I had the stolen idol out. It won't happen again."

"That's not what I'm annoyed about, Tim, although that really was careless—what would we have told her if she figured it out? But that's not what I'm mad about."

"The other thing?"

"Yes, the other thing."

"I wouldn't worry. You know, you're really in fine shape and—"

"I'm embarrassed enough, thanks. I don't need your assessment."

"No, listen—I've seen some good-looking guys in my time, and you're definitely looking good these days."

"Let's talk about something else," Eric said.

"Don't be mad. I hate having people mad at me."

"We topped three hundred."

"I know. It's time to move our bishop."

"Who?"

"The next move, Eric. We have to plan the next move. Eduardo Redelarte's keen on us. And soon, he's going to want something brand-new."

"Why don't you show him those paintings you threw out on the back stairs?"

"Last year's colors."

"I'll leave matters of art up to you. I'll just deal with the idols in the café." Eric walked to the other end of the loft. An April drizzle had lifted. The cobblestones glistened. A woman kicked puddles as she shuffled along the gutter, aiming her splashes at a friend, a man whose gleeful yelps echoed up and down the street. Eric jumped when Timothy placed his hand on his shoulder and squeezed gently.

"You're really mad at me, aren't you?"

"No, I'm just sort of generally blue."

"If someone or something is making you sad . . ."

"You and your rules," Eric said as he punched Timothy lightly in the arm.

"I buy clothes when I'm down. You should see the wardrobe I've amassed thanks to Andre."

Eric thought for a moment. "I could bake something."

"You know," Timothy said and stepped away, "maybe plaid is the wrong statement. Now that I think about it, plaid is all wrong. It's so in, it's out."

"I've had a craving for brownies lately. I'm not sure why."

"Maybe I should buy a whole new outfit."

"I'll learn how to make brownies." Eric looked at Timothy and laughed.

"What?"

"Was my face incredibly red? I felt like I was on fire."

"Nobody was looking at your face, darling."

Early the next morning when Eric was still in bed, Lydia called. "I have two meetings downtown this afternoon with time to kill in between. Wanna get a corn muffin?" She sounded cheerful. That and the mention of corn muffins, which for Eric was beach food, triggered a nostalgic impulse, and he quickly agreed on a time and place.

Corn muffins, however, were not on the menu at the Flatiron-district bistro that Lydia had picked out, Café Demimonde, a commodious and loud restaurant with Deco sconces and pastel murals. Before Eric even sat down, Lydia was apologizing. "It was where I had my lunch meeting, so I kept the table. We can still escape to a diner."

Eric scanned the menu.

"I had the five-leaf salad, which I don't recommend."

"What were the five leaves?"

"Endive, arugula, radicchio—how many is that?"

"What are you having now?" Eric examined his mother's bowl. She was spooning something that resembled wet snow.

"Sassafras sorbet. Do you want my boysenberry garnish?"

A waiter in a long apron approached Eric. "*Pour le monsieur?*"

"Coffee," Eric said, "and the petits fours, thanks."

"Well, well, well," Lydia said.

"Well, well, what?"

"Congratulations."

"For?" Eric wondered why his mother was grinning so mischievously. It was the same knowing smirk that she used to put on after meeting his high-school girlfriends.

"I read *Tomorrow's Bread*."

"Oh, that," Eric said, trying to sound nonchalant.

"I think it's very clever."

"You do?" The last person Eric expected to be supportive of the Goddess was his mother. "I thought you'd think it was kitschy."

"Maybe, but I think it's clever. I had no idea that this was what you were up to."

"I was going to call and tell you all about it, but I got busy." And he was positive that she was going to disapprove.

"I meant to ask you to bring me one. Are they very different from the stolen one?"

"Um, not very." Eric's dessert arrived, a pueblo of square cakes laid out on a plain of mint leaves. He bit into one of the cakes: Its pink glaze was pure sugar, too sweet. The jam inside stuck to his teeth.

Lydia started to giggle, which caused Eric to chuckle in turn. He rubbed his teeth with his finger. He couldn't figure out what was so funny, what was making his mother so uncharacteristically giddy.

"You know I've been seeing a lot of this man, Marek—"

"The curator."

"Right. And as you might imagine, given where he's coming from, he's not very keen on the reproductions that you're peddling." Lydia cleared her throat. "That's putting it mildly. Anyway, I haven't told him that you're my son. I mean he knows you exist, but he doesn't know your last name, seeing that it's not my last name."

"You're embarrassed by me." Eric swallowed the next petit four whole.

"No, no, no. I'll tell him eventually. But I sort of enjoy the confusion. I can't explain it, but it's sort of like I have all the cards, and I can play them as I please."

"That sounds Machiavellian, Mother."

"I'm not explaining it well. See, it's fun not letting someone new know everything right away."

Wasn't this a rather important bit of information to withhold? "So I embarrass you."

"I'll tell him eventually," Lydia insisted.

"You've heard about the Redelarte Gallery?"

"No." She picked one of the glucose cubes off his plate while he updated her. "Eric," she said, "that's marv—"

"I know, you probably think the show is very slick and calculated."

"What I am thinking is that you stand to make a lot of money."

Eric sipped his coffee (quite inferior by his new standards). "The thought's crossed my mind."

"The people who Eduardo Redelarte shows always make it into interior design magazines—you know, they've got a villa somewhere where there's a lot of clay and views of the Adriatic."

"I have my own dream house in mind."

"This is really marvelous, Eric. Good news, and good to see you. Our last chat was rather unpleasant."

"Sorry."

"You don't know how lucky you are. If you make a pot of money while you're young doing something like this, then you can do anything you want later in life." Lydia picked a sprig of mint from Eric's plate, ripped off the stem, and started chewing a leaf.

As far as he was concerned, she was probably only championing his current project because she hoped that once he made some money, once he got these faddish pretensions out of his system, he might go on to make what she no doubt considered more significant contributions to humanity—he might find a cure, he might help correct a social wrong. He was sure that this was his mother's attitude, but she blushed with good humor, a mood he hadn't seen in a while, so he finished off his petits fours without comment.

"By the way, Jason is fine. He's not ill."

"Oh, that's great news," Eric said. He was truly relieved. "Great."

"He's just crazy. *L'addition, s'il vous plaît,*" she said to their waiter when he passed by.

"What?" the waiter asked.

Lydia scribbled in her hand. To Eric: "I've seen Jason a couple of times."

"You're kidding." Eric leaned in. "And?"

"He's still in the same place, that big, empty penthouse."

"Are any of the rumors true?"

Lydia looked into her coffee cup and grimaced as if she were noticing a new wrinkle in her dark reflection. "He is sort of paranoid, I suppose. And he hasn't left his apartment in over three years."

"What does he do all day?"

"You don't want to know."

"I was just thinking," Eric said, "about how he and I used to collect shells."

"Mussel shells."

"We would walk for hours at sunset, at low tide, and not talk, just collect shells. After we filled a bucket, we used to stand at the end of a jetty and dump them back into the ocean. What was Jason's line? We had to 'nurture nature.'" Neither Eric nor his mother said anything for a while. "Do you ever miss being with him?" he asked.

Lydia opened her mouth but said nothing. Eric was as surprised as she seemed to be that he asked the question, and he wasn't sure exactly what sort of an answer he expected or wanted while sitting here in Café Demimonde. "So tell me," she asked instead, "what do you do when you and Timothy aren't making these little statues?"

"I'm working in a really neat café called the Mystery Roast."

"That reminds me of this horrible pot roast from hell we used to have when I was in college: mystery meat."

"You should come by sometime. You'd like it."

"Your father and I once got very lost in the meat-packing district when we were trying to find a steakhouse." Lydia looked at her watch. "I'm sorry this has to be so brief. . . ."

Eric had been enjoying her company and was sorry, too. He watched his mother wade through traffic to a cab; sometimes he was amazed that she lived alone in this city, amazed that she survived. He felt as though he should be protecting her in some way as she grew older, but he didn't know how.

He didn't want to head home right away, so he drifted east and spent the next part of the afternoon browsing through Persian carpets in the rug district. He wandered in and out of showrooms where salesmen peeled back layer after layer of loomed mosaics, each pattern a medieval topography of a country with antiquated roads and unchartable rivers. He turned west after a while and sailed into another world: Instead of rugs, he entered a block-long kingdom of plants, a dense and wet jungle. It had been drizzling again, and after a sudden vault in temperature, the streets steamed. The stretch was lined with potted plants, vined and climbing, with rubber trees and ficus out on the sidewalk and, in among them, dress racks, each sagging with the weight of hanging ivies. Walking any distance in the city was inevitably disorienting: In a few miles, it was possible to pass through a half-dozen empires, each different and strange. Beyond rugs and plants, there were pockets of sewing factories, and then commercial printers and photographers—note the absence of suits on the street and the preponderance of safari vests, of men wearing huge key rings on their belts—and then a conglomeration of nursing suppliers with showrooms of septic fashion, and a stretch of discount electronics stores, and a bustling hospital a little farther south. Then west to a health-food grocery, outside of which three men in homespun caftans compared their bags of grain and loudly traded bran.

Even though the north-south street he walked down to get to Forelle was all torn up, Eric was relieved to reach his home terrain. A crew of city workers had carved out deep, almost lunar craters, shoveling piles of cobblestones into a dump truck. New pipes lay alongside the ditches, soon to be implanted into the street's neural infrastructure. And rising from two tall, orange-and-white-striped cylinders, excess steam washed the whole block in an eerie fog, so that when Eric stumbled upon Inca, her shape lost in a black raincoat, he was startled and forgot for a moment that he was supposed to be embarrassed to see her.

"I love this," she said. She was weaving her way around the various trenches and pits in the street, glancing into the depths of the gaping holes.

Eric walked with her. "You love what?"

"This. I love it when the city comes along and digs up a street."

"Why? Were you a sewer rat in another life?"

"I love looking inside. See?" She motioned toward a pit that had been temporarily abandoned while the repairmen lowered a pipe at the other end of the block. "Isn't that fabulous? Look at the strata." Eric followed her over to the hole. "Beneath the cobblestone is a layer of concrete," she said and pointed toward jagged stone, "and then you get the wires, electricity and phone and whatnot. Gas lines down there. Look down further, and you've got the water pipes, below them the steam. The sewer is another level down. Keep going and you'll hit the schist."

"The what?"

"The bedrock. Whenever the city is digging up a street, I'm there. I know it may be strange—"

"Not at all."

"—but you have to remember that my mother was an archaeologist. When she was home with me, we used to walk around St. Louis and crawl into construction sites when no one was looking. Someone once excavated a room somewhere around here or further downtown. It turned out to be a waiting area for the old pneumatic subway system. Its walls were frescoed, and there was a chandelier and a player piano."

The mist hanging in the air suddenly turned into a cold rain. Eric took a few steps toward Forelle Street. Inca didn't move. She squatted, and before Eric could say anything, she had climbed into the hole in the street. "Inca? Wait. Inca?"

"Come down."

Eric looked around to see if anyone was watching. He sat down on the wet pavement and pushed himself into the ditch. Inca caught his elbow. In the awkward space, she managed to crouch down as if she were searching for a lost contact lens. "What are you looking for?" he asked.

"I found a tin box once over on Greenwich Street. I used it for my stash back when I used to have a stash. I love the things you can find on the street, in flea markets. Basically, I love anything old that has a good design."

Eric wanted to help her mine, but there wasn't enough room. He tried to move out of her way and got wet while shielding her from the rain. He wondered if she was at all intrigued by him. *She's been keen on you for a while. Please—do you think she would be standing in a hole in the street in the rain with you, loverboy, if she didn't like you just a little bit?* But there was no way, Eric thought, that she could long for his company as much as he craved hers.

"Eric, look."

*Why are you so sure that you're the only person on the planet capable of feeling?*

"Look what I found," Inca said.

*She's falling in love with you on her terms. It's a game, her rules. Helen of Troy started a war, more or less. This woman may have some other scheme in mind.*

"Can you believe it?" Inca stood up to show him a necklace, a string of black plastic beads that she draped over her fingers like a strand of seaweed. She picked away some of the gunk and tried it on.

"It's you," Eric told her.

The crew of workers, now wearing Day-Glo slickers, was ready to cover the pit with a broad steel plate, so Eric climbed out of the hole and pulled up Inca. On the street, she straightened her coat. She played with the beads of her new necklace while they puddle-hopped home.

He started to see her every day. She came into the café for breakfast and then again as soon as she returned home from work. As the weeks passed, she lingered longer, all night at the bar, all day on weekends. Eric always offered her the first taste of whatever recipe he was perfecting, and she was always a blunt critic. In her opinion, he had mastered Andre's springy tomato sauce, but the bean soup was "too salty," tasting as if he had "already mixed in the cracker crumbs." His chicken salad needed work: "More of whatever those herbs are that Andre cuts the mayo with." It took him several tries to come up with a zucchini-almond bread that was nutty and soft. And the rice pudding was a deceptively complex challenge: If it wasn't lumpy, it was too sweet. But Eric attacked each dish with more discipline and endurance than he had ever brought to anything before, if for nothing else than to win Inca's applause. And then on his own one afternoon, without Andre looking over his shoulder, he baked a batch of decadently moist brownies, lush squares of chocolate that prompted Inca, after one bite, to give him a kiss. He tasted the cake on her lips.

One Saturday afternoon, Inca was sitting at the bar next to three men in bloodied butcher's aprons who were feasting on foot-long baguettes stuffed with chicken salad. One of the men said, loudly so the whole café had to hear him, and after only a few hasty sips of the mystery roast, "Antigua Blue Mountain."

Eric was not paying much attention. He was busy juggling cups of cappuccino in the far corner of the room, trying to avoid Melior, who was rubbing her jowls all over his legs.

"Wrong continent," Inca told the man.

Then another man who was sitting alone at a table and reading a thick science-fiction epic joined the fray. "It's Guatemalan Coban as I live and breathe."

"No, it's mostly Antiguan," the first man insisted.

"Guatemalan."

Inca spun around on her stool. "Excuse me, but you're both so wrong, I'm embarrassed for you. It's got all the bounciness of Tanzanian Peaberry."

"Are you out of your mind?" the first man asked, again very loudly.

"No, I'm not out of my mind," Inca said, matching his volume.

The whole café watched now. The man in the apron was elbowed and buoyed by his fellow diners. He stood up. "Honey, I've been drinking coffee for a long time—"

"My name is not *honey*."

Melior dove under a chair. Andre emerged from the kitchen.

Inca was firm: "If you sip it slowly, you'll see that it's a blend of primarily African—"

"You're full of shit, lady."

"Oh, I'm full of shit, mister? Who are you to tell me—"

"Guys?" Eric hopped across the room, raising his tray like a shield. "It is a *blend,* so maybe it has a little bit of this bean and a little bit of that one, right? Peace? Truce?"

The man sat down and joked with his friends, and Inca swiveled around on her stool, pouting. Eric knew better than to try to console her, so with calm restored, he joined Andre in the kitchen. "Amazing," Andre said. "I've never seen anyone do that to Inca."

"What, challenge her?"

"No, stand up for her. She hates chivalry of any kind, but she just let you rescue her from the butchers."

"I wouldn't say I rescued her exactly."

"It must be love."

Inca was full of surprises now. On the night of the gallery opening, Timothy had gone down to SoHo early, and Andre promised to come later, so Eric and Inca planned to walk downtown together and alone. When he knocked on her door, she pulled him into her loft by the elbow and twirled him around so that his back was facing her. Before he knew it, she was pulling off his blue blazer, which he had worn for almost every outing and special occasion for the last five years. She tossed it on a chair.

"Are you—" Eric was speechless.

Inca shushed him and turned him around to loosen his tie. "Take off your shirt."

This wasn't the sort of passionate, organic, mutual seduction that he'd had in mind.

"C'mon, we're already late." She presented him with two boxes.

"Oh." Eric caught on and unbuttoned enough of his shirt to pull it off with his tie still threaded through the collar. Inca had opened one of the boxes herself and was holding a white T-shirt with a mock turtleneck. He slipped it on, tucked it in, and when he looked up again, Inca had opened the second box. She handed him a gray linen jacket to put on. It had padded shoulders and a Nehru collar, a fine weave, and as it turned out, it made for a handsome complement to the tapered green trousers and black shoes that he was already wearing, which he assumed he was allowed to keep on since there were no more boxes.

"Inca, it's beautiful, thank you."

"You look very smart."

"So do you." She was wearing a collarless black jacket, an ankle-long black dress underneath it, and the beads she'd excavated from the street.

"I've done this before," she said when the elevator arrived.

"You've been to an exhibit opening?"

"I've been to a group show of new artists at the Redelarte Gallery."

"Oh, yeah? When was that? Was it interesting?"

"I was the date of a New Visions artist. His name was Jim. I almost married him."

On the street, Eric said, "You almost married a man named Jim?"

"A long time ago, Jim Stiles—and don't say you've heard of him, because I know you haven't—was an up-and-coming mobile-maker. We lived in Alphabet City. I was constantly running into Jim's solar systems. I got tired of ducking my head every time I crossed the room. It's a wonder I wasn't decapitated."

"So what happened?"

"We didn't get married."

"Right. But what happened?"

"I told you," Inca said—and it was clear that this was all that Eric was going to get out of her—"we didn't get married. We broke each other's hearts and that was that."

The Redelarte Gallery Downtown was the reigning establishment on West Broadway. It glowed with a green tinge at night, sharper than the hottest club. Eric's name came first and Timothy's was second from the bottom in the vertical listing of the artists that was stenciled in neat white italics on the window by the brushed metal entrance. That alone was all Eric needed to see, and he could go home thrilled. He was not so eager to go inside because the gallery was packed and brightly lit with no apparent corners or alcoves to hide in. The only bit of free floor space was in the center of the front, main room, where a narrow pedestal had been offered as a throne for the Goddess of Desire, where much of the track lighting was aimed, and where a large group of people were circling slowly with the awe and stunned zeal of Meccan pilgrims.

"They gave it the best spot," Inca said.

"Where's Timothy?" Eric wondered.

"Here somewhere, I'm sure. Let's check out the other New Visions."

They began to nudge their way through the gallery. Half the time, Eric had his eyes on the blond wood floor; he was trying hard not to step on anyone's foot, and hoping, too, to remain anonymous in the crunch of people. If it weren't for Inca, he never would have known when to look up to examine the work of his peers. He managed to grab a glass of champagne when a waiter passed, and then he nearly spilled it on a short man wearing suspenders and a floral-patterned tie, a man whom Inca later identified as the famous producer of that late-night comedy show that everybody but Eric watched. His date was a tall, vaguely familiar model who wore a canary yellow dress that looked like a slip and who Inca claimed had recently made a successful crossover into action-comedy movies. The producer and the model-actress stood right in front of a beige monochromatic field painting. Upon closer inspection Eric realized, however, that the work was not a painting at all but a collage composed of medical charts belonging to a patient in a mental hospital. Inca asked the producer to step to one side so she could read Eric the title: *Eve, Committed (Number Four)*.

"Do you think those are real medical charts?" Eric asked her, whispering. "They look real."

"If they are, they probably belong to the artist," she said. "This is *insanely* dull."

Eric agreed. They moved on to an installation titled *Lamps,* which was a grouping of ten or so standing and reading lamps all turned on and positioned closely together like a miniature forest. They passed some antidrug posters that had been hung in ornate, gilt frames. Then there was a series of photographs, all of the same woman. In each photo, the subject made a different face, a goofy grin or a horrific scream, and sometimes she wore a costume—a cheerleading outfit, a nurse's uniform, a Vegas lounge singer's gown. A woman dressed in an oversized double-breasted blazer and nothing else except boots stood next to one of these photographs, and given the anxious way she seemed to be measuring Eric's reaction, he assumed that she was the artist. "They're very provocative," he said politely.

"Eduardo's into schizophrenia, you know," she said. "It's a ticket in the door."

"No, I didn't know that."

"Because of his third wife and all."

"Oh, right," Eric said, "right."

"Hey," Inca said, "I found Timothy."

Timothy stood amid a group of women who either by accident or design all had dressed in white chemises, right in the archway between the two large rooms of the gallery, a prime position to monitor traffic. Inca tried to wave, but Timothy was busy grabbing hors d'oeuvres off the passing trays. So Eric and Inca cut straight through the crowd, skipping the trompe l'oeil paintings of Socialist newspaper pages, ignoring a sculpture of mannequin limbs, to reach him.

Timothy excused himself from the women in white. "They were telling me where to get the best tiramisu," he said, his words somewhat slurred. He sipped a glass of champagne.

"You look great," Eric told him.

Timothy had abandoned plaid in favor of a broad-shouldered purple suit, a crisp white shirt, and a simple blue silk tie. This play of color offered a nice backdrop for his hair, which he had just had cut so that it was short on the sides, spiked on top. "What a shindig," he said.

"Everyone seems big on the Goddess," Inca noted.

"Eduardo told me he's going to ask fifteen hundred for each one we do," Timothy said.

"Wow, that's a price hike," Eric said, awed. Suddenly he envisioned a park-side penthouse where he sat with Inca on a terrace miles above the city, eating a languorous breakfast. He gulped the rest of his champagne.

"Well, that's 'cause we're going to sign them along the statue's left thigh. And get this: Eduardo wants to sell a lot of Goddesses to spread them around town, maybe as many as seventy-five, and then—*then* is the operative word—then he says he wants to come back with something new in a much more limited way so that people will be falling over each other to get one. Supply and demand." Timothy replaced his champagne glass with a freshly filled one. "Hey, have you seen Andre?"

Inca stood on her toes and looked over heads. "I don't think he's here yet."

"I don't care if he comes. I was just wondering," Timothy said.

"Of course you care," she said.

"I really don't. Hey, champ, let's go talk to Eduardo."

Eric wanted to retreat to a corner with Inca, but Timothy had already linked arms and turned toward the center of the main room, where the art dealer was now holding court around the Goddess. They didn't make it too far before a man in tinted glasses and a pin-striped suit, the flag of some foreign nation pinned to his wide lapel, put one hand on Eric's shoulder, the other on Timothy's. "You're the boys of the hour." He squeezed their collarbones.

Eric nodded politely, and Timothy introduced himself by name.

"I've just reserved five of those splendid statues," the man said, "one for each of my homes and boats."

"Thank you," Eric said.

"Why not six?" Timothy asked.

The man coughed a laugh. "I should buy another boat?"

"Or house," Timothy suggested.

Along the way to Eduardo's inner circle, Eric lost hold of Inca, and she fell back into the crowd toward the buffet of cold lobster and runny cheese. His heart thudded with stage fright when Eduardo Redelarte reeled him and Timothy toward him, kissing each of them on both cheeks like old friends and longtime accomplices on the contemporary art frontier. "Allow me to introduce you to Dobbin Tremont," he said.

"The art critic," Timothy whispered in Eric's ear to identify the man dressed in professorial tweed, although Eric had not only heard of him but also sometimes read his column.

"I've been telling Eduardo," Dobbin Tremont said to Eric and Timothy and the other patrons who had stepped back to give him room to pontificate, "how much I admire your contribution." He formed a gun with his thumb and forefinger and aimed at the Goddess. "I'm going to write all about you," he said. He offered a faint smile at Eric, who got the impression that he was being hit on.

"I'm thrilled," Timothy said, "and honored."

There was a murmur of oohs and aahs as the entire gallery crowd focused on what happened ringside. Eric tried to find Inca, but the only person he could pick out was the woman in the double-breasted blazer, who was pouting, probably jealous of the attention that he and Timothy had won. Eric looked at the Goddess, at Timothy's sculptural rendering, and even amid the light washing the pedestal, there was something dull about her glow, some sort of false, inaccurate contour to her shape. But then he looked at Timothy in his purple suit—his friend was buoyed and high—and soon enough he, too, became infected by the spotlight. He finally located Inca, standing by the buffet, and she winked at him. She gave him a thumbs-up. He basked in the fame of the moment, and he felt handsome in his chic jacket, sexy and wanted. He could get used to this.

Responding to the critic's rave, Eduardo Redelarte clapped his big-boned, brown-spotted hands and indicated to a waiter that he should bring over a tray of drinks.

Dobbin Tremont turned toward Eduardo. "In the cab over, I didn't feel at all like inaugurating anything. Now, however . . ." The critic struck a thoughtful pose. He stared at the track lighting. "Artifactualism," he said. "That's what it is. The factual appropriation of history into the objective metaphor of artifacts. Artifactualism."

And so at 9:35 P.M. on the evening of April 27th toward the end of the century, a Movement was born. The tray of drinks arrived and Eduardo Redelarte handed out the champagne. He clinked his own glass with his ring finger. "Friends? Friends?" The gallery hushed. Everyone stared at the silver-haired impresario, who gave his glass to a nearby assistant and then raised both Eric's and Timothy's hands as if he were endorsing a winning Presidential ticket. The three men's arms formed an **M** in the air. Eric winked at Inca. Timothy looked like he might cry with glee. The art dealer held the silence and then said, "Friends, I give you Artifactualism." He retrieved his glass from his assistant and then tipped his head back for a noble swig.

The crowd applauded and clinked glasses and returned to the buzz-buzz of its conversations, which now no doubt focused on the newly baptized stars.

Eric looked around, and people looked back and knew who he was. He patted his trouser pockets and made sure his money clip was still there, which it was. So were his keys. He was still wearing his watch. He felt as though something had been taken away from him, although he couldn't put his finger on what it was. It didn't much matter, he was buzzed from the champagne.

"Congratulations." Timothy kissed him on the cheek.

"And to you," Eric said and kissed him back. "It's too bad Andre didn't make it. At least I don't think he's here."

"Fuck him."

"I'm going over there to Inca."

Timothy started to drift in the opposite direction, but he turned around quickly and pulled Eric toward him. "I mean I don't care—right?—but he should have been here. He said he was going to come."

"Sorry."

"Whatever." Timothy walked away.

Inca had taken off her jacket. She was cooling herself with a napkin she had pleated into a fan. "Let's get some air."

They made it to the sidewalk. Looking back inside, Eric could watch the steady stream of people still swirling around and paying homage to the Goddess.

"They're in love with her," Inca said.

"It continues to amaze me." Eric wobbled and leaned on her.

"I have to say something. I know that you think of yourself as an artist now—"

"Not really."

"—and art is a splendid thing, but so is commerce. I don't want you to think I'm crass—"

"Never."

"—but there's an egg that's been ready to hatch for weeks, if you'd just move your ass a little."

"You're referring to the Goddess?"

"In order to buy it, if you're not willing to pay for one of Eduardo's art editions, you have to go all the way to the Mystery Roast. Some people won't walk that far west. It's too scary for them, too industrial, too remote." She had been letting her hair grow long and she pulled it into a ponytail she held with her hand.

"So what are you getting at?" Someone with a camera popped in front of Eric. He smiled. Inca let her hair fall free. Flash, and Eric saw limes floating in the night.

"I have a twofold plan," Inca said once the photographer had flown away. "I want to hire some other people to make the idol. Just a couple of sculptors."

"Will Timothy go for that?"

"He'll be thrilled. He has his new project with Eduardo to worry about. I want to farm out the idol to increase production, and then— What are you smiling at?"

The magic of the ancient figure had inspired her, too, and he was thrilled. "Nothing," Eric said. "Go on."

"Then I want to distribute the idol to other places in Manhattan, other stores. I want to see how it sells elsewhere, what kind of a market there is. I told you a while ago: The Goddess has potential. Exposure in the art world will legitimize our enterprise in all sorts of markets that we might not normally reach. It's a gorgeous marketing spectrum. I'll say it once." Inca took a deep breath. She was dead serious, straight and sober. "You may have a *fad* here. In my line of work, that is what everyone hopes for and works toward and prays for and dreams of and dies never having attained. The idol is perfect. On the most basic level, it's completely useless."

"I wouldn't go that far."

"It has no apparent function. That's the fundamental requirement for a fad-object. With inutility comes infinite possibility. It's whatever you want it to be. You let the public shape the product, and then you follow their impulse and push the hell out of it. That's why I want to deploy it around town. Just you and me. We'll distribute it quietly. Measure the reaction. Then take it from there."

"Where?"

"This is just a first step, really. If this works, then . . . Well, one thing at a time."

Timothy wandered out of the gallery and stumbled over to Inca and Eric. "He's a bastard, you know. A real bastard."

"Andre?" Eric asked.

"He said he would come, he promised he would show up, but no. The shitter." Timothy started drifting down the sidewalk. He was headed south.

"Timothy?" Inca called.

Eric ran after him. "Are you okay? Do you want me to get you a cab?"

"I'm a little drunk," Timothy said, "but I'm fine. Just mad. I'm going to walk off this mood and come back. Really, I'm fine." And Timothy continued walking downtown.

"He's okay?" Inca asked.

"He's just angry. He's okay."

"So? Do you want to move some idols? Yes?"

The idea of Cycladic idols popping up all over the city was enticing, exhilarating, and frightening, too, disconcerting because in some vaguely self-destructive way, Eric felt as though something which had been his, only his, was gradually slipping from his selfish grasp—he was giving up a part of himself. He glanced back into the gallery once again, where men and women shuffled in orbit of the Goddess. Some people had noticed that he was standing outside, and so there was a line of bodies pressed against the storefront windows, everyone looking out at him, neither smiling nor trying to get his attention—complete strangers studying him, separated by a wall of glass but sharing his private moment with Inca just the same, taking something invisible and unnameable from him now, grabbing at the cloth of his new clothes.

"Eric?" Inca asked.

"Sure," he said. "Yes."

imothy was too mad to return to the gallery, and without really thinking about it, he had walked all the way south and west to a popular bar. The Toy Store was lit up all in blue— blue neon, blue strobes—which gave even the tannest of men an Alaskan pallor. This light made Timothy's new suit black, and he imagined that his scowl was enough to fend off anyone. But as he sat at the bar, which was decorated with a laminated mosaic of mirror shards, he had to answer quite a few queries, overt or implied, from men with nifty haircuts. Timothy was not rude, but he made it clear that he wanted to drink his gin alone to the beat of the mope rock.

How many hours did he stay there? He lost track of the time, and it was a miracle that someone didn't mug him or run him over as he zigzagged north on his way home. The Mystery Roast was still open. A handful of people were eating either very late dinners or very early breakfasts. Andre was behind the counter, but Timothy went in anyway.

"How did it go?" Andre asked.

"He wants to know how it went," Timothy said to a table of two men.

"I couldn't make it. I had a large crowd tonight. I couldn't break away." Melior finished up a bowl of coffee on the bar, and Andre lifted her on his shoulder, petting her as if he were burping an infant.

"A large crowd? Why do you think I care?" To the men again: "He thinks I care."

A woman in the corner raised her arm. "Could I have another plate of cold asparagus, please?"

Andre went into the kitchen. Timothy followed him. Once the door swung closed, Andre set Melior down on a counter and set to the task of arranging the green spears on a plate. "I don't know why you think I can just close the café whenever I please," he said.

"You own the place, you can do what you like. You said you would be there."

"You said you didn't care."

"That's not the point. The point is that you *promised*."

"Oh, that's the point. Well, I'm sorry, but I couldn't close the café."

"You're not sorry, so don't pretend that you are, because when you are really and truly sorry, you make me a cup of coffee and slice me a piece of your best cake and then you say, 'I have wronged you, can you ever forgive me?' "

Andre poured a stream of vinaigrette over the asparagus. "I never see you. You've either been holed up in your loft chiseling idols or . . . or shopping for that. Purple is not your color, by the way."

"Everyone thought I looked dashing."

A bit of vinaigrette spilled onto the counter. The cat sniffed it and licked her chops.

"You should have been there," Timothy said.

"You're so goddamned selfish, you know that? I told you. I couldn't close—"

"I wanted you to be there."

"You really expect me to turn away a huge crowd of people to—"

"I kept looking for you."

Andre stepped away, toward the café. "You know that this has nothing to do with whether or not I made an appearance at some opening."

"I hate it when you—"

"Excuse me." Andre left the room to deliver the asparagus.

Timothy waited. He stroked the cat. He waited longer. Andre was deliberately taking his time, joking with the clientele, deliberately making Timothy crazy. Well, he decided, he was not going to get mad. But while he waited, the alcohol in his body rushed from his stomach to his veins. He paced. He was hot, enraged, so that when Andre finally walked back into the kitchen, Timothy grabbed the first thing he saw—a sack of raw, recently delivered coffee beans—and threw it at him.

The beans spilled everywhere with a loud thunder, and at first the cat dove for cover. Once she reached the floor, she batted them with her paws, isolated one, and chased it the length of the kitchen.

Andre immediately fell to his knees and started to rake the beans with his hands. "Melior," he shouted, "stop that!"

Timothy breathed hard and fast. He would not cry.

"That's pure Yemen Mocha!" Andre yelled at him as he dumped a handful back into the sack. "Do you know how rare pure Yemen Mocha is? Melior!"

"It's all over." Timothy stepped past the cat toward the door to the back staircase.

"Understatement of the century."

"Good."

"We broke up a long time ago anyway," Andre said and continued raking beans.

"Fine," Timothy said. He tore up the stairs, up seven stories in a few breathless leaps, and once inside his loft, he slammed the door and peeled off his new suit and new tie and shed his underwear just as he stepped into the shower, where he turned on the faucets and shivered at first while the water warmed. He sat on the floor of the tub. The tropical rain washed away sweat and tears, if there were tears, and he calmed himself. He had a life now, the career he wanted. He was an artist who would be whispered about in the trendiest corridors of the city. He had fame. He would achieve an even bigger fame, and he did not need anyone. He stretched out in the tub and lay on his back. No one.

**A**nd whatever happened to Martin Fowler and Rita Schwartz?" Jason asked.

"Divorced," Lydia answered. "Ages ago."

"Herb Ridcoff and Cindy?"

"I saw Cindy about a month ago. She and Herb stopped selling antiques and are trying to produce a movie." Lydia checked her watch. She had just stopped by for a quick drink and a chat, but Jason was using her as a pipeline back to the real world.

"Gary and Eliza?" he asked.

"I'm not in touch with them."

"Astrid Margoles and Bertram?"

"Divorced."

"I saw Dale Simpson on the news. I see he's buying airlines."

"Wasn't he a Unitarian minister when we knew him?"

"Ah, the evil Eighties."

"Leona Simpson works for Rob Perez, I heard. She'd be a contender for cultural affairs commissioner."

"It will never happen," Jason said. "Perez is good, but he can't win. He'll lose everything when people get around to figuring out his finances."

"I'm having fun talking, but Marek is waiting for me."

"If you're having fun, stay awhile longer."

"I should head out."

"How's your little friend's investigation going?"

As everyone in the city was well aware, the investigation had led nowhere. "I think I left my coat in the other room."

"Your coat," Jason snapped, as if she had insulted him. And they had been having such a pleasant time. He disappeared down the hallway. Lydia waited by the windows. The street lamps and distant apartment windows and headlights outside vibrated like embers. She had a craving for a fire, although it wasn't really cold enough to warrant one.

She turned around when Jason came back in the room, and something caught her eye, a flash of white among the black and gray steel of the exercise equipment in the dining room: a stack of paper sitting on the seat of Jason's barbell bench.

"Here." He handed Lydia her raincoat.

"Oh—and my briefcase."

"Your briefcase," Jason said, and when he retreated down the hallway a second time, Lydia skipped over to the mini-gym.

Just as she had thought: It was a manuscript. The title page read, *Polar Bears Free,* a novel by Jason Maldemer. There seemed to be about a ream of paper, but Lydia didn't even have time for a cursory skim through the pages, not before Jason came back. She did not want him to feel like he was under surveillance. She made it back to the windows just as he returned.

"Are you sure you had a briefcase?"

"I guess I didn't."

"Well, you don't want to keep the brilliant and dashing Marek Vanetti waiting now, do you?"

"You certainly spend a great deal of energy putting him down, you know."

Jason pouted. "Don't get in too deep with him. He's slippery." Lydia knew that he was just baiting her into an argument and tried to ignore him. "You probably came by today just to make sure that I knew that you and he were cavorting all around town."

"*Cavorting?* Please." She poked the elevator button several times.

"You're full of secrets, Lydia. You think I don't know what goes on in the outside world, but I do."

"I'm full of secrets?" Fine. "You're the one who left the manuscript out for—"

"Ha!" Jason wagged his finger at her. "I knew it! I knew it!" he yelled. Whispering: "It took you long enough, but I knew it."

"You wrote a book and you're too much of a coward to admit that that's what you've been doing all this time."

"I didn't write a book. You just wait." Jason left and returned right away with the manuscript. "It's got a cover page, but flip through it. You shot at a clay duck, my dear."

To her chagrin, the pages were covered with equations and at a glance seemed to belong to a pop-physics tract.

"People still send me manuscripts for blurbs," Jason said. "And I saved one, and I added a title page to prove my point."

"Is the elevator working?"

"What do you want from me? Why do you really keep coming back here?"

Lydia was about to tell Jason to go to hell, but the question trapped her.

"You come back, and you snoop around, but what did you find? A decoy."

"You're a sad man."

"What do you want from me, what?"

"I heard you were sick. I missed you. I don't know why, Jason. I stopped asking myself difficult questions a long time ago." The elevator finally arrived. She stepped in and didn't turn around.

He kept talking, his voice quivering. "We're getting old, Liddy. We're running out of time."

Lydia let the elevator doors slide shut. On the street she found a pay phone and dialed Marek's office number. She clutched the phone between her cheek and collarbone and with one hand she covered a silver bracelet she was wearing on her other wrist. Tonight she felt vulnerable in the city where she had lived out her adult life, alone and helpless against crime.

Marek would buoy her. She felt safe in his company. For weeks now, he had been telling her that he had a "special evening" planned, and he would not reveal any details, although he had been querying her about her musical preferences. Lydia pushed Jason out of her thoughts. And when she met Marek on a nearby street corner minutes later, she was delighted by how handsome he looked, boyish in a turtleneck and an old camp sweater, its elbow patches coming unstitched. Handsome and charming and intelligent and reliable and very, very sane.

First they went to the sophisticated Apricot Room, a polished lounge atop a midtown hotel where Rose "Whippoorwill" Charone sang everything from scat to show tunes. After a set and a few drinks, Marek took Lydia by taxi to a downtown basement called The Hot Bed, where their knees were wedged together uncomfortably around a small table as a smoky haze filled the wine cellar–like room, blurring a T-bone master named Sloeberry Washington, who led his five-piece band through moody renditions of old standards.

"Buh, doo–doo and doo–ah . . ." Lydia sang outside the jazz club. The notes dissipated in the lilac May air. This evening reminded her of nights when she had first come to New York decades ago, when she and her friends would hop among jazz clubs, never really sure who was playing where—smoking too many unfiltered cigarettes, drinking martinis, and flirting with the trumpet players.

"I've never seen you so happy." Marek took her arm.

"Where now?"

"One more."

"It's a school night," Lydia reminded him.

"One more." Marek snapped his fingers and a cab appeared.

Resting her head on the backseat of the taxi, she watched the neon storefronts whiz by, the streaks of light making her feel as if she were on a carnival ride. "Buh, doo-doo and doo-ah . . . Buh, doo-doo . . ."

Outside the last stop on the tour, Marek paused. "Would you mind terribly if we skip Barry Tone and the Two Tones?"

"Not at all. Is something wrong?"

"No." Marek was staring at the curb.

"Something's wrong."

"Nothing's wrong at all. Is there anyplace you'd like to go instead?"

"I've been in the mood for a fire all evening. Isn't that crazy? It isn't cold enough for a fire."

"It's cold enough at my place. Follow me." He led her to a garage just blocks away and saluted a man in overalls. A few minutes later, a vintage green sports car with a raspy muffler and a convertible top that resembled a broken umbrella came racing down a ramp and screeched to a halt. "I don't have a fireplace here in the city," Marek said, "but I do have a rather grand one in the country. It's still chilly out there this time of year."

"Where in the country?"

"Hop in."

They had known each other for several months. She trusted him. Lydia pulled herself into the bucket seat and clutched the dashboard.

Marek pulled out onto the street in a smooth turn. "It's a good two to two and a half hours. Without traffic, I can probably do it in one forty-five, maybe one twenty."

Lydia decided that she would play hooky from work and make it a long weekend. She gave in to the tremors of the little car and neither of them said much during the first hour of the trip. They drove farther away from the city, past the slumbering Long Island communities with the multisyllabic names that used to make Eric laugh, and Lydia relaxed. "I can't tell you how happy I am to be getting out for a breather," she said at last.

"Me, too. Work has been tense lately. Open the glove compartment."

Resting among the maps was a Cycladic idol. Given that Marek would have probably told her the instant that the stolen idol was recovered, she assumed that it was one of Eric's copies. She pulled it out. It had heft: It might make a nice paperweight. She smiled at the object the way she might have grinned at one of Eric's teenage puns.

"They're apparently selling like hotcakes at that café," Marek said, "the Mystery Guest. I sent someone down there to fetch me one. The thing I can't get over is that Eddie Redelarte included one of these wretched rip-offs in his latest group show and called it art."

"Well . . ."

"I can't believe how Dob Tremont waxed about it. Artifactualism: What kind of flash-in-the-pan, bogus concept is that? I like Dob—he's always been very fair to me and my projects—but he's lost his mind. Now, according to my friend Martha Mazeborough in TriBeCa, every-body wants one."

"Marek, I have to tell you—"

"These creatures will kill me yet. Imagine having the whole city laughing at you. I don't want to sound paranoid, but you know what a small town it is. And that's what it's like for me, for us—the museum, that is—what with all of these forgeries out there, mocking us."

"Forget about it," Lydia said. "Leave it behind."

"Here, give it to me." He took the reproduction from her and at the same time rolled down his window. A gust of salty air blew into the car. They were traversing a causeway, the bay on either side choppy and black. With his eyes on the road, Marek flung the statue into the water as if he were chucking a stick for a fetching dog. He rolled up the window. "I feel much, much better."

"That's not exactly what I meant by leaving it behind," Lydia said. She hesitated. "I have to make a confession. I should have told you before." And she told him now.

Marek was quiet for a long stretch of road. "Lydia, I'm so embar-rassed."

"Oh, please, you shouldn't be. I understand where you're coming from."

"I hurled your son's creation into the causeway."

"Marek, it's okay. You didn't know. Really. It's my fault—I should have told you, and I didn't because . . ." The truth? "Maybe I thought you would be annoyed."

"At you? But it's your son who is minting the idols. He's not in your control. And really, I'm not all that mad at him. Not at all, now that I've thrown one of those bloody things out the window." Marek laughed.

How generous, Lydia thought, relieved. How understanding. "Well, you're sorry, and I'm sorry," she said.

"We're a sorry pair." He looked at her. "I could never be mad at you anyway. From now on, we must tell each other everything."

"Everything." She felt her shoulders release their tension. She watched Marek drive. He gripped the wheel with one hand, and his other rested loosely but confidently on the orb of the stick shift.

Lydia could see that his house was a naturally shingled Victorian with wraparound porches, towering over the dunes and the wide, bleached beach. As Marek had promised, it was at least twenty degrees colder out here. Just as they climbed out of the car, a curtain of rain drifted in from the sea.

"I haven't been here much lately." Marek unlocked the front door. He flicked a light switch and nothing came on. "Oh, no."

"No electricity?"

"A fuse must have blown." Marek tried a lamp in another room. "Wait." He scurried down a hallway and returned with two candles. "This way." He took Lydia's hand and led her into the icy living room. Her eyes adjusted and although it was dark, she could see that the room was white and full of windows. The blue tide beyond the beach moved in slow motion. There were two large couches positioned in front of the fireplace, where Marek quickly started to construct a pagoda of logs. Lydia rubbed her hands together and handed him kindling as he pulled matches from his pocket and ignited a blaze. The orange flames tented and ebbed, and the room, which she could see more clearly now, began to fill with the sweet scent of roasting sap.

"Wait," Marek said again and left the room. He returned with a quilt and spread it out in front of the hearth along with pillows and cushions from the couches. In the kitchen, he had found a bottle of Sauvignon.

Curiously, the wine was chilled. If the wine was cold (and they hadn't brought it), then the chances were good that the electricity had been working well enough to keep the refrigerator going. Maybe it had just gone out.

"Forgot glasses." Marek left the room again.

Lydia reached over to a standing lamp and switched it on. It worked just fine. She flicked it off before he returned. She was being set up for a romantic evening, and she asked herself if she cared. Not really.

Marek stretched out next to Lydia on the quilt. They sipped the cool wine and watched the ballet of the flames. Now and then, he prodded the logs with a poker. After tossing another log on, he lay on his stomach. He bellowed the collecting embers until they became bright and full, and then he returned to Lydia's side. She kissed him just as a knot of wood cracked loudly and shot a spark of maple onto the quilt.

Marek stomped out the ember with his foot, and in turning his body, he pulled Lydia on top of him. She began slowly to pull off his sweater, his turtleneck, a T-shirt stretched tightly over his firm stomach. She tugged the shirt free from his pants and slid her hands underneath the fabric.

The jazz that followed was pure improvisation, from the quick riff of snares to the sulky legato of a muted horn. Marek made her feel young. She was surprised to find herself moving with such agility. When she closed her eyes, the walls of the house disappeared, the rain ceased, and they were all alone on the beach, the warm sand shifting beneath them. The postplay was the best of all. Marek had curled them up in the loose ends of the quilt, but it was almost too hot, since the fire roared so furiously. He had deftly managed to keep tossing wood onto the andirons during their lovemaking. Now he let the quilt end roll away and, naked, he stood up. "Wait," he said.

Where did he think she was going to go? Right now, her only concern in the world was that the sun would rise.

Marek returned with a small, royal blue felt pouch, which looked as though it might contain a piece of family silver. He removed a large container of caviar.

"What, no toast points?"

"No toast points." Marek opened the shallow jar and scooped out a small amount of the black roe with his first two fingers. Then he spread it on the widest part of Lydia's forearm and proceeded to lick it off.

The coolness tickled, but Marek's lips warmed her. She ate caviar off his wrist, the salty eggs made saltier by the sweat from their fireside romp. Then it was Marek's turn, and Lydia's again, until they had spread the roe everywhere—and when they were done, the sun was beginning to reflect its first, exploratory rays off the ocean surface.

"You planned all of this, right?" Lydia asked. "The electricity is really working."

"Are you very mad at me?"

"I think it's funny. Funny and romantic." She nuzzled her nose against his neck, and they fell asleep.

Later that morning, Lydia woke up with a stiff back. Marek still slept on the quilt. He didn't stir. Slowly she got up and wandered. She walked onto an enclosed porch and saw a T-shirt lying on a chair, so she put it on. The night's storm had passed, and sunlight spilled everywhere. Marek's house had a splendid view. She knew that she was miles away from her own long-sold summer house, yet she got goose bumps when she imagined herself staring at the cove where she and Eric had spent so much time. Suddenly Marek's house became her old house, and the water rising with a morning tide became the bay that her place used to overlook. Then the water reminded her of something she hadn't thought about in so long that she wondered whether it had really happened or if it was something she had read about or possibly dreamed.

She was out on the water in the *Lydia* with Eric and Timothy one July afternoon. The last summer they were together at the beach, now that she thought about it. A lot of boats were out that day. The post-storm water was rough, the swells not for the weak-stomached. Where the cove opened into a larger bay, and then into the endless, choppy Atlantic, there was a tiny island of rocks supporting a small lighthouse, an automatic beacon really, that flashed day and night to warn of a sandbar and jetty and shallower waters moving inland from the high seas. Lydia skippered. A lot of boats were out: How many people saw the accident?

A speedboat, an aerodynamically clever cigarette, razored through the water at a speed that had apparently sent the harbormaster pursuing in his pathetic motorboat. The speedboat was piloted by a man and a woman, the man at the helm. They came into sight, whizzing by, the nose of the boat bouncing along the surface like a skimming stone. The woman pointed, not at the lighthouse, but toward the coast, and the man must have realized that he was steering the boat right toward the rocks and the beacon. He must have been ignoring the buoys. He was heading toward another boat, a sloop, and maybe he was trying to avert a collision and also trying to avoid having to slow down. He probably tried to turn the boat, but it was too late, and when the boat hit the rocks, it flipped, corkscrewed, flipped again, and tore apart as it flew over the outermost edge of the rock island. The accident was swift and, in its speed, perversely graceful.

Lydia ordered the boys to reef the sails. They motored away once it became clear that the speedboat had been destroyed and that there was no one floating in the water to rescue. A young couple died, newlyweds, the paper later said. She didn't remember much more about the accident because it had nothing at all to do with her family, with her and her son and her second, summertime son.

A pair of binoculars lay on Marek's windowsill. She scanned the bay—Marek's bay, not her old one—just to see if she couldn't find . . . what? Wreckage?

That day, they had motored back to the marina. Lydia could not then, or days later, bring herself to probe what she herself or what the boys felt about the accident. They had never discussed it. Yet she remembered it now vividly, and she recalled how she had felt like a failure. Somehow, she'd steered the boys toward ugliness and death.

She felt like a failure that day, but what was she supposed to do, protect her son from all inexplicable turns of fate? In retrospect, she wished that she could have comforted them, at the very least talked about what they had all seen. And now: She had just spent a sexy evening with a sexy man, so why, she wondered, did she feel so hollow and so sad?

A pair of dry lips kissed her on the back of her neck. "What are you looking for?" Marek wrapped his arms around her waist. "Sea monsters?"

Inca's company manufactured a five-by-nine-foot plastic map of Manhattan, which she taped to her floor. She stood on her couch so that she could survey the transparent island from above and then instructed Eric, in socks, to step across the grid of streets to position and reposition markers—his shoes, her shoes, magazines, an empty wine bottle, an ashtray—in key positions. "What we need," she said, "is another spot on the Upper West Side, one that pinpoints the intersection of old and new neighborhoods, the Yiddish and the Yuppies."

"I'll move your pump to Eighty-third and Broadway."

"That will do for now, but I'd still like to come up with a specific store." Inca shifted to the Battery-end of the couch. "Remember, we can't get trapped in—"

"Curiosity shops where the Goddesses will blend in with the usual ho-hum and bric-a-brac. We have to hit one-of-a-kind boutiques where clever people shop for offbeat objects." Eric stood on Central Park. "Key hubs where trendsetters hunt for new statements." He spun in a pirouette on the slippery surface and bowed.

"I have you well-trained."

"Ordinary venues where the unsuspecting can be ambushed."

"And what's the key play in our strategy?"

"To get store owners to go gaga over a product they wouldn't normally sell."

"Perfect score." She stretched her arms high. It was late. Planning sessions occupied the better part of Eric's free time. They had waited for the group of Jersey City sculptors whom they had enlisted to manufacture a suitable quantity of Goddesses, what Inca referred to as the *critical mass*. Thirty cartons were stored in Eric's loft. She plopped down on the couch. She scanned the map again, deliberated. "Okay. To the battlefield, soldier boy."

"Tomorrow?"

"Bright and early." Inca yawned like a cat, in a wide, quick snap. Eric kissed her good night and went upstairs. He punctuated his days by what time he would see her, when he would serve her coffee and lentil salad, when he would serve her coffee and a pain au chocolat, when he would plot their entrepreneurial gambit, when he would meet up with her the next day. They were not lovers, yet he lived his life as if they were: except when, inevitably, he made a solo retreat to his bed, to his tidy sheets and solitary blankets.

At around three, Eric was roused by a knock at the back door. Timothy wore a shiny silk shirt, buttoned to the collar, half untucked, and pleated linen trousers. He smelled of wine and nicotine. He was holding a tool box. "I've just had the most incredible dinner with Eduardo."

Eric crept back to bed and slipped under the covers. "Where'd he take you?"

"To La Vitesse. We sat at the first table. I had quail in lime sauce and grilled leeks, and Eduardo ordered a Bordeaux that wasn't even on the list. The sommelier cried when he uncorked it and—get this—Eduardo got up and sang a song after the first swig. Don't ask me, it was Italian."

"You and Eddie have become fast friends."

Timothy sat on the side of the bed as if he were going to tell Eric a fairy tale. "Yeah, well, I told him my mother was schizophrenic—"

"You're shameless."

"—so we've bonded, you know." Timothy set the tool box down on the blanket and pushed it toward Eric. "Say the magic words."

"Open sesame."

"Try the latch."

When Eric pulled the top back, a hinged tray rose toward him. The Ausgraben Idol lay on a bed of cloth, and beneath her knees was an official-looking slip of paper, a check. "Whoa." Forty-eight thousand seven hundred and fifty dollars. "From Eduardo? Is this for real? Wow, it's much more than I expected. Much, much more." On the one hand, he had harbored doubts about the simplest premise of Artifactualism, about the Goddess of Desire as an art commodity. But then again, unexpected profit definitely helped to soften his ambivalences. The bottom line was that more people, even if they had paid absurd prices, owned an idol, and now he could focus on his project with Inca, which would only widen the reach of the Cycladic woman even further. The Goddess of Desire was traveling to new places, and it mattered less and less to Eric how she got where she was going.

"I forgot to tell you, Eduardo sold another twenty-five at two thousand apiece."

*I only get better with age, but your friend here doesn't realize this. He's too busy deciding which new socks to wear with which new shoes.*

"And then he took his forty percent, of course," Timothy added. "They're all sold?"

*Which is why this gigolo thinks he doesn't need me anymore.*

"And how. So you can have her back. Eduardo and I are talking about the sequel to the Goddess. Look, I need to know if you want in."

Eric dug his arm under a pillow. "Inca and I are hitting the stores tomorrow."

"Fabulous. Soon there will be two idols in every pot—or on every mantel."

"You should go out on your own now, Tim. You're the artist."

"Thanks. I just had to ask for the keys to the car first."

*He thinks he can just dump me on you, but he isn't done with me. Nobody just kicks me out. Remember that. Nobody gets rid of me.*

"And you're sure you don't need her anymore?" Eric petted the idol's brow with his finger. He stroked her long neck with his thumb. He was glad to have her back.

"It's a good thing you're expanding, because Andre's turned against the Goddess. He doesn't want them in the café anymore."

"He told me that you are unwilling and unable to get on board for the long train ride of life, and that he's tired of waiting for you at the station."

"Well, he's a mule's mule, and I can't tell you how happy I am not to have him dragging me down all the time. Anyway, according to Eduardo, I've got to push ahead with the Artifactual agenda, so I looked in my old art history books and gave him an idea, but I'm not allowed to say what it is. I'll tell you, though."

*You won't turn me out in the cold, will you?*

"A bust of Nefertiti."

"Sounds neat."

"Eduardo says it's only a matter of time before I'm an *ArtNews* cover. Even I think that's pushing it."

*You'll show me a good time. You'll show me the town, won't you, loverboy?*

"Tomorrow," Eric said.

"Well, maybe not that quickly"—Timothy laughed—"but soon, Eric. Soon."

The next day, a Saturday, Eric and Inca rented a van. They spent the better part of the early morning loading cartons and getting sweaty since a humid fog had moved in overnight, rain clouds in tow. As Inca stacked the boxes, Eric balanced himself on the rear fender of the van and blew air onto her shoulders and neck to cool her down. She thanked him with a gentle and all too brief shoulder massage: She sat in the van while he stood on the street, and she worked her way from his blades up to his collarbone, twice slipping her hands over his shoulders to the top of his chest.

After breakfast they headed out into the city like a Fuller Brush sales force, full of faith in strangers. Inca drove. She raced through traffic at speeds Eric found both terrifying and thrilling, competing with each yellow sedan, drag-racing with them from stoplight to stoplight, darting across the lanes to jockey for a better position. Eric held his seat with his hands. She was wearing a sleeveless black turtleneck, and he could see her arm muscles and tendons at work as she maneuvered the steering wheel. Her whole body seemed to be one with the machinery of the van, and Eric, to his own modest embarrassment, got hard while watching her drive.

Their first goal was to find a new location in the Village. A woman in a Hudson Street storefront who painted portraits of people's dogs and cats knew all about the idols. One of her daughters had become a Mystery Roast habitué and had brought home the Goddess soon after the article appeared in *Tomorrow's Bread*. "They're kind of eerie," the pet painter said. "I'll line them up in my window." She took two cartons on consignment. Next, they dropped down to lower Greenwich Street, where they convinced a foreign-film video store owner that all of the TriBeCa movie stars who rented subtitled classics from him would gobble the idols up. The man agreed to take a carton and a half and decided to play Greek films on the store TVs as a promotional tie-in. He already had *Z* rolling when Eric and Inca left. They were two for two as they turned east to Mulberry Street. A woman with an arm of bangle bracelets and shoulder-length earrings, a customer in the Indonesian imports store, set down the cartoonish, banana-wood cat that she was about to purchase to check out a Goddess. "You know," she said, "I was going to buy one at the Redelarte Gallery, but it was so frigging expensive. This one is only fifty bucks?"

"It's unsigned," Eric said, thinking it was only fair to point this out.

"Signed, schmined," the woman said. "Who reads the fine print, anyway? I'll take two. No, three. Wrap two."

Farther down the Lower East Side, an old man in a blue pin-striped suit, his shoulders dusted with dandruff, tufts of wiry hair curling out of his ears, painstakingly examined every square inch of the idol. "No seams," he said. "It's very well made." But he waved his arms around at his store, at floor-to-ceiling shelves of down pillows, and said, "This is what we sell. For seventy years, just pillows. What do I do with a little woman like this?"

"You're in the sleep business, right?" Inca said. "So maybe your customers would put the Goddess on their night tables, next to their alarm clocks."

"Or *under* their pillows for good luck," Eric suggested.

Inca reached into a box on the floor to take out another idol. When her back was turned and she bent over, the old man winked at Eric and grabbed at the air with both hands as if he were squeezing invisible tennis balls. "Our discount is more than generous," she said, "and they don't take up a lot of display space." She placed a Goddess next to a pillow on a shelf marked FIRM. "See?"

The man chewed on a half-spent cigar. "Okay, sweetie, what the hell?"

Back in the van, Eric and Inca cheered in victory. "Under the pillow. Very clever," she said. "You know, a lot of very hip New Yorkers get their pillows there. That was a coup."

"You have a feather. . . ." Eric picked away a tiny plume of down from behind her ear. He pretended as if there were other feathers in her hair, three more, just to have an excuse to run his fingers through her ponytail.

The man in the store in the East Twenties known worldwide for his skill in stain removal and the narrowing of ties looked like he wanted to lop off the idol's head, but he accepted a box of Goddesses on one condition. "Let me press your shirt for you," he said to Eric, "free. It's a horror." Eric didn't think that his shirt was all that wrinkled. Nevertheless, he took it off and handed it across the counter for an ironing-quickie. Other men of all shapes and ages came into the store and stripped, too, so Eric did not feel so odd about waiting with his arms folded across his bare chest until he looked over at Inca, sitting on a bench and pretending to read a magazine, smirking, scoping men. Eric hurried to button his shirt, and while he got his bearings out on the street—feeling a bit dizzy in a steamed shirt on a warm day—he was startled by Inca's fingertips touching his chest as she fastened two buttons he had missed in haste.

The man who ran an out-of-town-newspaper stand in Grand Central thought Inca and Eric needed directions. The train information broadcast over loudspeakers reduced their pitch to mime, and when the man figured out what they were saying, he shook his head no thank-you, no thank-you. But he called after Inca and Eric when they were halfway across the station because he had found a practical use for the sample idol that they had left behind. The Goddess made for a handsome substitution for the metal bar that usually weighted down a stack of newspapers. The man took a carton, half to use, half to sell.

Some proprietors were amused, some skeptical about the enigmatic Goddess of Desire, but all of them were commercially optimistic and game to sell the new product. Eric and Inca engaged an East Sixties shop which otherwise only sold antique buttons and then a store where high-school girls spooned out pale flavors of gelatti. They were all set to do business with an exotic pet store further uptown, but the barking Lhasas and whining Manx gave Eric a headache, so he went across the street to a place that specialized in Neoclassical adornments, pyramid paperweights and marbleized picture frames. Now the Goddess watched over a shrouded woman who read palms and sold crystal balls in a cramped storefront on Upper Broadway. Now idols were interspersed among vintage blues records in a cellar store in the West Eighties. Now the idol was on sale at a Columbus Avenue bistro, an eatery where patrons were invited to doodle with crayons on paper tablecloths.

Eric rested a carton on a railing outside a designer sweatshirt and swimwear boutique housed in a Chelsea gym. He wondered today as he had before whether copies of an Ancient Greek idol could excite other people's imaginations the way the original artifact had fired his. Would the replicas he was scattering citywide work any magic at all? Would they speak sassy truths? Would they focus anyone's heart? He couldn't know for sure, but he was nevertheless confident that the Goddess would become a personal totem of some kind, whatever her keeper wanted her to be: a confidante, a confessor, an object of beauty and speculation, or a mere detail in an interior design. Each person would take from the idol what he or she needed—that was what Eric expected at the very least. And then, with admittedly manic optimism, he hoped and believed that others would be forced to respond to strange murmurings, that they would become engaged in a dialogue of desire.

Inside the gym shop, he watched Inca, who charmed a semicircle of muscled men, men oddly sweat-free after lifting weights. One man grabbed as many figurines out of a box as he could hold in each hand, four by their legs, and absentmindedly began touching his knuckles to his shoulders in repeated gestures. Right now, Eric didn't have time to worry about what the idol would mean to each worshiper, and if the truth be told, his foray today was less about the Goddess than it was about Inca, toward whom he was drawn with an ever greater gravity.

He could not stop studying her: the scrap of bang that came loose from her hairband, the shape of her knees in her stretch pants, the beat of her impatient boot.

When they left the gym, there was a single clap of thunder before an instant downpour began flooding the streets. They had to return the van to the car rental garage, but as the deluge thickened, traffic stalled. Eric's hand rested on the seat, and Inca started playing with his fingertips, plucking them and then letting them slap down against the vinyl upholstery. She hummed, horns honked. She gradually worked her way up from Eric's fingers to his knuckles, tapping them according to whatever song it was that she played in her head. Then she grabbed his arm. He had been pretending not to notice when she plucked his fingers, but now he looked at her. Inca fit her thumb and forefinger around as much of his left forearm as she could. "You have nice wrists."

His forearms were nothing special as far as he was concerned. The green lines of his veins thickened and warmed, and he could see them pulse faster.

"I have a thing about wrists. The first project I did for my company was a transparent watch. You could see all of the gears and cogs—we did really well with them. Anyway, I got to see a lot of models' wrists at print shoots. I dated a hand model for a while. He always wore white gloves. So I know all about wrists, about proportion and tone. Eric, you have handsome wrists."

He rotated his hands back and forth.

"Don't show off. Shit. This traffic is making me stir crazy." Now Inca honked the van horn, too. The windshield wipers were doing nothing to alleviate the cascade that made driving virtually impossible. "We have to get out of here."

Their van was trapped behind a cab and a bus in front of a Midtown hotel. Inca decided to cut between the two vehicles and skip into the slot in front of the taxi. It was a pointless maneuver, because they would only end up a few yards closer to their goal but still be caught in the web of cars. The cab inched forward to cut Inca off, leaving her on a diagonal. So Inca dug into reverse and swerved quickly to the left, but then the cab turned defensively back to its original position, and finally, the van ended up next to the curb before the glass-skyscraper hotel. A redcap opened Inca's door.

*Now or never, loverboy.* Now? *Now.* Eric leaned over her, his shoulder brushing against her chest, to speak to the attendant. "Can we park?" he asked.

"You're staying at the hotel?" the attendant asked back.

Eric nodded. He expected Inca to protest, but she played along. In fact, she was the one who told the clerk at the front desk that she wanted the biggest and brightest room on the highest floor. She didn't look at Eric after she was handed a key card, and she didn't look at him at the elevator. She didn't look at him until they had climbed up to the twenty-second floor. Inca pressed the emergency stop button. A deafening, sustained horn blared. "How many women were you with after you got divorced?" she yelled.

Zilch, Eric indicated with an O of fingers. It had been a long, long time.

"I've been tested."

Eric nodded, Good.

"Now is not the age to keep secrets of any kind!" Inca yelled.

Eric agreed, although there was one secret that he did hold on to concerning a certain notorious theft.

Inca released the button, the siren faded, and the elevator continued its ear-popping rise. They held each other in a tight hug, alarmingly platonic. Eric realized they were the exact same height.

Inside the Empire Suite, they kissed tentatively, as if asking a question. They answered each other in a second, frantic embrace. He peeled off her black sleeveless shirt and liberated her bare chest at the same time that she undid his belt, his fly. He unbuckled her boots, and she pulled off his recently ironed shirt and let it drop to the floor. They undressed each other in a hectic free-for-all, but when they were both naked, they each stepped back to look at the other with leisure. Eric had seen her body the day she modeled for Timothy, and he knew all too well that she had seen his. Now, however, he felt as if they had just met in the lobby. He pressed his hands against the side of her ribs, and she gripped his shoulders. They crept closer and slow-danced, waltzed and held each other tighter, then gradually regained their earlier frenetic spin.

They collapsed into a couch in the sitting room of the vast suite, but at some point, Inca slipped off of Eric and stood up. She steered him to the next room, to the bed, which she swiftly stripped of its hideous, chrome-fringed, crushed velvet spread. They plunged underwater, they scuba-dove; they kissed as if they were passing oxygen back and forth. Now and then, they surfaced only to plummet again farther into bluer, bluer, black depths. There was nothing around them for miles, just the sea and maybe in the distance a clipper driving closer, a rescue boat that Eric hoped would never quite arrive. They rocked and rolled with the waves, rising and falling, finally spinning out slowly, lazily in the Pacific breeze.

After making love, Eric always got his second wind. He watched Inca doze off. When she woke up, she asked, "What time is it?"

And he replied, "I thought, when she left me, that there would never be anyone again who would love me as completely as she did when we moved into our first apartment and started out. Back then I thought that I could not contain more love and lust for a single woman or I would burst." Then he started to cry.

Inca rolled over to face him. She stroked his chest until his crying subsided.

"I have to tell you something," he said a short while later. He lay on his back.

Inca's head rested on his stomach. She wrapped her body around his right leg. He didn't say anything else, so she squeezed his thigh.

"I stole the Ausgraben Idol from the New York Museum. I'm the one who did it."

Inca didn't move. "Is that supposed to be funny?"

"It's in a tool box at the top of my closet at home."

"I don't believe you."

"I'll show you later."

"You're serious?" She blinked. "I don't believe you."

"You will."

(The next night when she came downstairs dressed in her black kimono and opened the tool box and the idol popped out, Inca said nothing at first. Then: "Either this is a hoax, or I've fallen for a criminal."

"You've fallen for a—"

Inca punched Eric in the shoulder. "You idiot. You can't goof around. This isn't safe. They'll find you."

"So you believe me?" He stood behind her and undid the sash of her robe.

"I'm worried."

Eric cupped her breasts.

"Have you considered the consequences, if you're caught?"

He kissed the back of her neck, her spine.

"I'm flattered you let me in on the secret, but . . ."

He kissed her buttocks, the back of her thighs.

"I'm even sort of proud of you, although I don't know why."

Her calves, her ankles.

"And maybe a bit jealous. Isn't that weird?" She turned around and pulled Eric up. She closed her robe around him and tied the sash. "I never thought you were the sort of person who liked to live so dangerously."

"I'm not," Eric said. "Or I wasn't. Anyway, there's no danger whatsoever."

"Good. Because I want to borrow her. I want to sketch her, if it's okay with you. There are so many neat angles and lines. . . . What a design.")

Inca frowned as if she were missing the punch line to a very simple joke. She sat up. "I'm starving," she said.

Eric ordered Indian food. Without discussing it, they decided to stay in the Empire Suite all night (they were paying for it), and the rest of the evening was devoted to the game which Inca referred to as Sharks but which Eric in childhood had called Desert Island. You had to hop from one piece of furniture to the next without stepping on the floor. Inca broke the rules when she had to slip on Eric's shirt and answer the door for the delivery of their murgha tikka chicken and lamb shaag with a side order of raita and some poori.

The next morning when Eric awoke, Inca was gone. A note was taped to a mirror:

HAD TO RETURN THE VAN. GOING TO STOP BY MY OFFICE AND
CATCH UP ON SOME WORK. SORRY I COULDN'T WATCH THE SUN-
RISE WITH YOU. SEE YOU LATER. P.S.: I PAID THE BILL.

He wished that he had awakened first to see her lying next to him. Now he felt like a stranger. He could have been in any hotel anywhere. Had there even been a sunrise? The new day was as gray with rain as the previous one. *The sun always rises, silly man.* He knew that he was not alone anymore, yet he couldn't deny the fact that somewhere inside him was a hollow space, some truth echoing, fading, which he couldn't quite hear. No, no, no—it was nothing, he told himself, just hunger, and so he called downstairs and ordered a room-service breakfast, a prix fixe feast, the Pan Continental Deluxe. He dressed, and sat at the table by the wall of smoked-glass windows, a table that was soon covered with hot plates of eggs and bacon and pancakes and sausages and cinnamon rolls and toast. He left the metal domes on the platters and looked down at the busy street forty-six floors below him. Cars and taxis darted by like tiny fish pulsing against the current of a cold stream.

They made love all over Manhattan, on the plastic map taped to Inca's floor, although Eric kept having to peel Midtown off of his hip. The best or second best part of any romp came when he pulled the West Side over her body, and the two of them lay in the darkness and talked about their childhoods or politics or movies, or about Eric's attempts at Andre's Sacher torte and Inca's latest design for outdoor grill utensils.

Eric rolled Harlem into a pillow and tucked it under her head. She flipped onto her stomach, and he massaged her legs, gradually kneading his way uptown.

"I got a call," she said, "from the bookstore on Tenth. They had to sell the Goddess in their display case. Someone put a postage stamp of Gertrude Stein on the back of another one as a joke, and they had to sell that one, too, stamp and all."

"They've gone through three cartons since last weekend."

"Four. Have you thought about the plastic dinosaur shop on Amsterdam?"

"I think we should let them sell the idol, don't you?"

"But we did just start supplying the dried fruits emporium a block away."

"Let them both sell it."

After a first week of brilliant sales, they had restocked the stores and added promising new ones. Inca hired two more sculptors after the second weekend, and after the third week, she struck a short-term deal with a Hoboken collective to devote even more manpower to idol production. Almost as soon as she and Eric made their regular Saturday round of deliveries, the Goddesses vanished from the shelves. A gap in the flow of trade between Sunday and Friday only nurtured the swelling demand.

"Ooh," Inca said, "could you get that spot again? Over by the Lincoln Tunnel."

"So are you happy with the *New York* article?" Eric had been the subject of a short profile.

"And how. You looked cute, sounded clever. How are you keeping the idols in the air in the picture?"

He hopped over to the kitchen, where a box of idols sat on the counter. He withdrew two Goddesses and, with the same circus-dexterity that he had exhibited for the magazine photographer, managed to balance a Cycladic woman balletically *à point* in each palm. His hands wavered up and down like shifting scales. Then he let the idols fall, catching them by their ankles, and took a bow. "And for my next trick . . ." Eric skipped back toward Inca.

She pulled him down by his ankles and scrambled to pin his shoulders to the map. "Say uncle." She covered his ribs with wet, ticklish kisses. "Say uncle, if you want me to stop." She sat up.

"But I don't."

"The door," she said. She found her kimono on the bed and threw a sheet in Eric's direction, which he wound into a black toga.

Timothy was wearing a smart new double-breasted suit of the same broad cut as his purple one, this version done in raw linen. He carried a piece of heavy sculpture against his gut, something reddish, and he said, "Congratulate me," as he set the statue down on the coffee table. He pulled a cigarette out of his pocket, lit it, and released a puff. "Well?"

"Congratulations," Eric and Inca both said.

"Eduardo sold the last of the Nefertiti busts this morning to a very influential collector. An advertising mogul." At five thousand dollars for each Artifactual piece, Timothy could afford any new suit he wanted. "You know it's important *who* buys your work. Very key."

"And what's this?" Eric asked. The statue was a two-foot-tall man sitting in a chair, a book balanced in his lap, his hands clasped in prayer. Cuneiform was incised from the knees to the hem of the tunic he wore. His head was missing. The point of decapitation was rough, unlike the glossy, smooth surface of the rest of the crimson stone.

"It's this Babylonian dude named Gudea," Timothy said.

"You're moving back in time," Inca noted. "Where's his head?"

"I agree with Eduardo," Timothy declared, "that Artifactualism should embrace every ancient culture. So we're doing five Gudeas at seventy-five hundred each, and I'm shopping around in my art history books for something South American. I want something Pre-Columbian in the series."

Eric and Inca just looked at him. Eric ran his finger over the beheaded neck. "Couldn't you have put the poor guy's head back on?"

Timothy took an angry drag on his cigarette. "Don't make fun of me," he said.

"Nobody's making fun of you," Inca assured him. She pulled the lapel of her kimono tighter across her chest.

"Gudea's body is in the Louvre and his head is in the Boston MFA," Timothy explained. "An important part of Artifactualism is the measured effect of time. I have to take into account how the artifact is found."

"Of course," Eric said and tried to look convinced.

"Anyway, I just wanted you guys to see the first Gudea."

"You're all dressed up," Inca said.

Timothy exhaled a thin stream of smoke and handed Inca the cigarette to douse in an ashtray. "A bash for the ad mogul. His friends, Eduardo's friends. I'm late. Ciao."

"Is it my imagination," Inca said after he was gone, "or did somebody mug him and steal his sense of humor?"

"It's tough being an artist in demand," Eric said in his friend's defense. He shed his toga.

"It's tough being his friend." Inca let her robe fall off her shoulders. She slinked over to the map. "If I remember correctly, you were about to say uncle."

"I was going to say nothing of the kind." Soon the South Street Seaport became lost among their intertwined ankles.

May flew by quickly. Ginkgo trees flowered—this year even the nonflowering variety by some miracle of environmental warming appeared to foliate with petals. June arrived: Men and women began to sunbathe on their fire escapes, tourists overran the Village, and Eric's life overflowed as people queued up on the sidewalk as early as six in the morning to get a breakfast table, as late as 4 A.M. to claim the last iced mocha. Inca made it her mission to keep overhead low and profit high, and together she and Eric netted fifteen thousand dollars in one week alone. He was amassing an ample reserve of money that surpassed what he was used to or practiced at spending, so he stashed most of it in the bank. And still, he never considered quitting his job at the Mystery Roast, not even when Andre was at his most misanthropic, not even when Andre one day delivered an irrational fiat without explanation, no discussion: No more Goddesses were to be sold in the café. The Mystery Roast was vital to Eric in a way he couldn't quite explain to Inca, who in passing suggested he devote his full-time energies to the Goddess (although she was quick to say that she was not about to quit her own day job). No, the café was his keystone, his gravity-defying point of balance.

Nights were reserved for Inca. They spent much of the evening on her vast, black futon, which seemed to hold the rest of her loft, her drafting table and workbenches and kitchen full of appliances, in tenuous orbit. There was much to study in a new lover's home, which Eric did after she fell asleep. On the cube of lacquered wood that she used as a night table, he would find copper bracelets, a bottle of Liquid Paper, a black barrette, a half-eaten chocolate bar, a calculator, a bundle of incense, and one onyx tuxedo stud. Sometimes he wandered the dark apartment as if it were a city unto itself, journeying to the far neighborhood of her drafting board, for example, where he taped down a piece of graph paper and drew a doodle of circles with her finely calibrated compasses. He filled in the circles with her colored pencils and then left his collage for her to discover in the morning.

Finally, there were weekends. They distributed Goddesses each Saturday, sometimes Sunday, in a beat-up, white, rented van. Eric had already experienced fame to some degree—in the form of a gallery opening and a brief magazine bio, in the occasional salute from someone waiting to buy an idol. He enjoyed the glow. He knew that he was on the verge of a larger fame, true fame, the kind that defined you, the kind that you could never escape from, the kind there was no turning back on. He didn't know how or when it would come to pass, but he knew it would, partly because Inca told him it was imminent, partly because he was intrigued by the glory, desired it, and was eager to see how far he could ride it. For now, he had his work, his love.

On some evenings, Inca announced that she had work that she absolutely had to do, and so Eric had to leave her alone. "Can't I just read a magazine on the couch while you work?" he would plead.

"I need to be one hundred percent alone."

"You won't hear me turn the pages."

"Get lost."

Eric was allowed to return at an appointed hour—two, three in the morning—and he always asked Inca if she had accomplished all that she'd set out to. He guessed that she had, because no matter how late it was, no matter how deep the circles under her eyes ran, she would wrestle him to the bed and undress him, recklessly ripping buttons, and make love like a sailor at the end of shore leave.

On some weekend afternoons in June, after they had made their deliveries and returned the van, Inca took Eric to a parking lot which for the day was transformed into an immense bazaar, a dense flea market of tented booths and tables. Had Eric not been holding her hand, he would have gotten lost in the maze of attic antiques and basement collectibles.

One man dealt exclusively in incomplete sets of turn-of-the-century flatware, while a couple from Pennsylvania specialized in vintage military uniforms and bomb shelter memorabilia from the Fifties. A man hawked prewar toys: He lifted a pear-shaped rag doll in the air, its yarn-hair singed, and shouted, "Every treasure must go!"

Inca would pass a table covered with blue and orange glass bottles that had been dug out of an Albany backyard, bottles that once contained mouthwash or hair tonic or soda pop, and ignore all but one particular rat poison bottle, holding it up in the sunlight to examine the seam of the blue glass. It was marked seven dollars, and Inca bargained the seller down to five, only to then decline to buy it. When they had moved on to a collection of Mission rocking chairs, Eric asked her why she passed it up. "Oh, I never really wanted the piece," she said. She called everything a *piece*. The Tiffany lamp that she swooned over was a piece, and so was each of the hundred keys collected in a shoe box. They drifted among piles of Forties fashion magazines, books on manners and manuals on fishing, Depression glass wine goblets, cigar boxes full of buttons, a coat rack carved to look like a climbing grapevine, and a collection of panoramic photographs of Midwestern National Guards.

Whenever a dealer was selling arts-and-crafts pottery, Inca lingered. Eric finally started to figure out her pattern of taste: She wasn't interested in vases or planters with ornate decoration, pitchers with flowers molded into the ceramic. She avoided tea pots with glossy surfaces. But she did handle a spherical, matte-finished, lapis-colored bowl with a slightly chipped lip, and as she rubbed her palms all over the pottery, she purred. She told Eric about revolutionary technique, about the glazing process, about the simplicity of the line and curve in the design. It was only thirty dollars, a steal, she claimed, given current prices. Inca set the bowl down and walked away.

"My treat," Eric proposed.

"No thanks. As much as I love flea markets, I never buy anything."

"But you're always going on and on about how much you cherish antiques."

"I know, but there are collectors in the world, and there are pickers. I'm a picker."

Eric sneaked away from Inca at one point and doubled back to the pottery dealer, hoping to make a surprise purchase, but just as he arrived, two men were handing over the cash for the blue bowl. Nevertheless, Eric was determined to find something that Inca would appreciate, to bring some artifact from the current century into her loft. In the week following, he managed to get away from the café to wander the west West Village and walk as far down as TriBeCa. He became fascinated by the things that people threw away. Among some boxes of moldy Harvard Classics strangely left under the tin marquee of a one-time paint manufacturer, he discovered an antique radio microphone, a diamond-shaped pivoting instrument of mesh and metal with a lightning bolt etched into its casing. Inca loved it, so Eric was driven to forage further to see what else he might dig up. Outside a refrigeration company, he found a decanter, its plug missing, and five tin shot glasses, each engraved with U.S. Air Force insignia. Inca immediately found a use for them: She served sake in the little cups.

One day, when Eric was fishing through a pile of trash with all of the patience of an experienced archaeologist, he was startled by a woman wearing sequined hot pants and a generously filled halter. "Listen, pumpkin, I've already been through there."

Eric turned around and realized, looking at her Adam's apple, that she was a man in drag. "You never know," he said.

"What are you looking for? Cans, beer bottles? Ain't nothing here. So push on, pumpkin."

Eric assumed that he was intruding on a prostitute's turf. "I'm looking for something to give a friend."

"Mm-hmm. And she likes garbage? You ever try a bottle of perfume?"

"Look," Eric said. Patience had paid off, and from between two cardboard boxes he pulled out a long, brass object, a candlestick, a heavy pyramid cast in the shape of the Eiffel Tower.

"Ooh-la-la," the prostitute said. "Well, you got what you came for. Push on."

Inca, of course, adored the gift, but she said, "I love the things you bring me, Eric, but I always feel awful because I never have anything for you."

"I don't need anything." He didn't know how to explain that what he got in return was a rush that he had forgotten about: the urgency of being so enamored of someone that he had to do something to prove his love before the day was out. At least he did not have to explain how profoundly gratifying it was to watch her sleep. She was older, and he tried to find evidence of this as he followed the rise and fall of her rib cage. Maybe a roughness in the veins of her hand. No. Maybe by her eyes, the first clawing of crow's feet. No. Yet he knew she was older: She made a point of it in passing remarks. In my day. When I was your age. Not too long ago—but you would've still been a kid. Comments sprinkled here and there that Eric learned to ignore. One day he would bring up the age spread once and for all so that it could be shot down like skeet. That would be it, because he believed the decade that divided them was pure history, nothing more. So she had done a lot of drugs and been to war protests and spoke wistfully about screwing some boy while watching the first lunar landing, so what? History, nothing more, and she simply had more of it than he did.

Of course, as Eric traced the tautness of her thigh with his pinky—she didn't stir—he had to admit to himself that history was not only headlines. She might grow weary of sex before him. She might die before him. But did it matter? They had traveled an upward slope in their affair, a steady, fast rise, and he certainly did not want to reach the summit yet—or ever. *Show me a man who has skied down a mountain, and I'll show you a man who wishes he were back at the top.* At the same time, he worried that their separate desires for each other were not always equal. He was afraid that he would overwhelm her and smother her with too much passion. *There is no such thing as a ship, loverboy, that can slow down with its sails still up and the wind full and free behind it.*

At three one morning, he noticed a small box on one of Inca's work tables. In it he found at least a dozen hemispheric plastic rings mounted onto cheap metal bands: a stash of Mood Rings. Inca startled him by lighting the candle in the Eiffel Tower candlestick next to the bed. "What time is it?"

"Look what I found."

"Oh, gosh. You were probably just a kid when these hit, but for me, Mood Rings and moon shots just about define the Seventies."

Eric removed two of the rings from the box and gave one to Inca. Then he formed a gun with her hand. He slipped a Mood Ring over her forefinger. It was dark, but the single candle was bright enough to illuminate the change as the liquid-crystal gem shifted color to match Inca's rising internal temperature, from a cold black to a warmer green.

"Eric, I—"

"Don't say anything." He extended his finger.

"You move so fast, in such a hurry. I'm not going anywhere."

"I love you, Inca Dutton. More than you can know."

"No, I know." Inca fit the Mood Ring over Eric's finger in turn, and his gem shot from black to ruby in an instant. Both of their rings were bright red while they made love. Then they slept, their bodies cooled, and Eric woke to find their separate temperatures had turned their jewels blue or green or muddy brown.

Eric expected Inca to take the ring off before she went to work, but when she came home the next night, she was still wearing it. She had moved it from her first to fourth finger, and it was the only thing she had on while she and Eric lazed about the map of Manhattan. She stretched out over the central part of the island while Eric sat in the harbor so he could massage the balls of her feet.

Out of the blue, Inca said, "The time has come for us to take the next step."

He set her foot down.

"The Goddess is bigger than us, Eric. Bigger than this city." A deep breath. "We need to go mass-market." Inca stood up and began to pace. "It's always been my dream that we would arrive at this point. In fact, I planned it this way: First test the waters, then launch the armada. Still, I never thought we'd get here so quickly."

Eric was still wearing a pair of socks. He pulled them up his shins. "What do you mean exactly by mass-market?"

"I didn't tell you this before, because I didn't want you to worry, but now you have to know: We're vulnerable. If we don't seize the day, we'll lose everything. I mean the whole operation. I mean everything. We'll sink fast."

"Vulnerable?"

"To a company coming in and running away with our concept. A firm like the one I work for might come along at any minute and mass-produce the Goddess and mass-distribute it, all without our involvement. They'll make all the money and get all the press."

"But we—"

"Stealing an artifact doesn't give you a copyright on it."

"I see."

"But listen. *We* could hire a company—my firm, in fact—to manufacture the idol on a scale that you cannot even imagine."

Eric paced now, too, as if he and Inca shared a lane in a lap pool. Her enthusiasm excited him. "This would be incredible. And what you're saying is we have no choice. This is going to happen anyway, so we might as well—"

"I know just the person to bring in. His name is M. Scott Gold, and he's the Boy Wonder of fads. He was a major player during the Pet Rock craze. He made Dancing Flowers happen. He's taking his bows now for Snap Bracelets. Eric, we need to move fast. I can set up a meeting, but I don't want other people at the firm to know what's going on until we've got Scott on board."

"Bring him down to the Mystery Roast. It's so noisy, no one will hear us talking."

A few days later, Eric was serving lunch to two women who were negotiating a book contract in the overflowing café, and when a man who looked like he could have been Eric's younger brother, a man of similarly dark complexion and dark wavy hair, tapped him on the shoulder, Eric snapped, "Wait your turn."

The man skulked over to the bar and pulled a Goddess of Desire from his briefcase. He tossed the idol from hand to hand. Then Eric noticed that Inca was outside haggling with a cab driver.

"You must be M. Scott Gold," Eric said. "I'm sorry, I forgot we were—"

"It's heavy," M. Scott Gold said. He wore a paisley bow tie which matched the handkerchief in his breast pocket. "We've found that the consumer generally likes to buy things that are lighter. It could still be weighty enough to fulfill paperweight requirements yet also be feathery enough to carry in a briefcase. You've got to be able to buy it on the way home from work."

Inca stepped inside at the same time that Andre emerged from the kitchen carrying plates of chicken salad sandwiches.

"Eric," Inca said, "could you get Scott and me some iced coffee?"

"Andre, I have to take a break for my meeting," Eric said, clearing a table of quiche dishes.

"Now?" Andre swiped a pile of orders off the counter. He saw M. Scott Gold stroking the Goddess. "We have a rule about these here," he said. He grabbed the idol and returned to the kitchen before anyone could stop him.

Melior popped up from behind the bar. "Yipes, I'm allergic!" M. Scott Gold shrieked and pulled a napkin over his mouth.

Eric picked the cat up by her belly and set her down on the floor. She bolted off. He delivered the sandwiches to the book-contract women, and when he returned, the meeting was going on without him.

"Basically," Inca said, "Scott thinks the firm will go for the idea, if it can have full control over production and distribution and if we okay a modified design."

"The tabula-rasa thing is what does it for me," M. Scott Gold said. "You see whatever you want to see. Some people will see their lovers in the face of the idol. Or their exes, or their children, or their dead parents, or even their pets. That's the beauty. And it's already hot. It's already off and penetrating the consumer subconscious. Half our work has been done for us," he added and sounded ready to cry as if half of his fun had been taken away.

Eric pulled out two highballs from under the bar and a pitcher from the refrigerator. He poured the iced coffee.

Inca took a sip. "It's rich today. Resonant like Illy Café."

M. Scott Gold sipped the coffee and wrinkled his nose. He added four spoons of sugar. "Let's talk material."

"Wait," Eric said. "I have a question. I was wondering about the packaging."

"Right. Simple box, cellophane, nice rack-display." M. Scott Gold snapped his fingers. "Ooh, I have an idea. A brilliant idea."

"Run with it, Scott," Inca said and winked at Eric.

"I see a long, tall, white cardboard box," M. Scott Gold squealed slowly, painfully, "and it's fluted and cut on top to look like . . . a column. A Greek temple column. With a big flowery capital. And there's a window, and only the head of the idol can be seen. You have to buy the Goddess of Desire and rescue her from the temple column. People will be keeping the boxes, they'll look so sturdy and handsome."

"Cycladic culture wasn't building Classical Greek temples," Eric pointed out. "That would be anachronistic."

The fad-meister turned toward Inca: "Did I come up with the perfect package for the Crawling Spiders or what?"

"The octagonal web boxes," Inca said. "Eric, most people won't care if the column comes from one period and the idol from another. It's all Greek to them."

"Actually," Eric said, "I was thinking that maybe we could include a brief brochure about the idol. I've wanted to do this all along. We might include that Ausgraben legend I told you about. Maybe a little history—"

"Are you nuts?" M. Scott Gold stood up from his bar stool.

"Or maybe not," Eric said softly.

"People don't want to have to *read* anything." M. Scott Gold sat down again. "What's next on the agenda, Inca? Material?"

"In the cab over, Eric, we agreed that we have to replace the marble. It's too expensive, too heavy. I came up with hydrastone. It's a light substance, durable, and will look like it has an ancient patina. It's relatively cheap, so this could be a ten-dollar fad, like you said you wanted it to be, Scott. And I think we should add a discreet base, so the lady can stand on her own without having to be propped up."

Eric had no faith in M. Scott Gold to grasp the magic and mystique of the idol, but he did trust Inca. "I just don't want the Goddess to look too fake, too posed," he said.

"I'm with you," Inca answered.

"Next," M. Scott Gold said, "we need to talk about the other products out there. About the one you two have been selling all over town. It's got to stop."

That stung: No more weekends with Inca driving all over town in a rented van. Eric turned away to make a cappuccino for himself.

"We just can't have some artsy-fartsy version eating at the high end of the marketplace."

"He's right," Inca said to Eric. "As always."

M. Scott Gold fingered the loops of his bow tie. "How many should we start with in the initial run? A half-million?"

Five hundred thousand Cycladic idols at ten dollars a Goddess: Eric turned the frothing knob with no cup beneath it and splattered steamed milk all over his hand. "Ouch."

"Inca, Eric," M. Scott Gold declared, "I predict that we're going to make a really huge splash in an unsuspecting lake. But there's just one thing to make my wife lose sleep, because I'll be up all night eating popcorn and watching Westerns. There's a hitch. Something that would slow the momentum."

"What?" Inca asked.

"If the real treasure is ever found . . ."

Inca nodded. "I don't think it will be a problem." She winked again at Eric.

His Mood Ring turned beet-red.

"We want to take advantage of the theft," M. Scott Gold said while winding his watch (Betty Boop did a bump-and-grind on its face). "Let's not forget that. In fact, I'm going to get a friend at the *Times* to do a follow-up on the investigation. I'll leak the news about the mass-market Goddess. I'm going to have him interview you, Eric. Hype is vital. The coverage will spawn other coverage. Eventually, when the time is right, we can get you on a morning show." M. Scott Gold gave Eric a once-over. "Hmm. You're a fairly mediagenic kind of guy. Yes, we'll be able to use you well. Very well."

The first task was for Inca to redesign the Goddess. That night she removed the stolen idol from the tool box and studied her lines and shape with more scrutiny than before. She drew plans and projections and submitted them to the prototype department. A week later, Eric was fooled by the first model of the mass-market Cycladic woman, at least from afar. He saw it sitting on Inca's kitchen counter and didn't notice until he examined it up close that a cylindrical prop had been fitted and angled beneath the woman's heels. The prop was affixed to a counterbalancing square platform, very thin, and the whole Goddess—

body, prop, and base—was one piece, cast from a single mold. The hydrastone version turned out to be lighter than the real thing. And like the stolen artifact—more so than the first marble copies—the surface of the newest idol was porous and convincingly archaic.

The *Times* reporter followed him around for several days, and the article ran on the front page of the Metropolitan section along with a large photo. Eric was pictured in a booth at the Mystery Roast, surrounded by idols (samples of the new product), along with Melior, her ears peeking above the marble table. The article updated the museum investigation into the previous winter's theft, which both Eric and the *Times* agreed would go down as one of the great unsolved crimes of the year, but most of the feature consisted of an interview in which Eric explained how he had come up with the idea to replicate a stolen idol one evening by looking out at the World Trade Center and seeing the Cycladic shape in the pattern of lights. *The Wall Street Journal* was less interested in the creative process than in the financial prospects of a fad, which it described in monumental, reverential terms. The *Voice* wanted to know about Eric's politics: Was he making the statement that art should no longer be preserved by elitist, uptown institutions but instead be made available to the masses and to mass culture? ("Sure," he answered, "why not?") The *Observer* speculated about influences: Marshall McLuhan meets Brancusi, it decided. *MetHome* wanted to shoot his loft (which he explained he had not decorated, and so they photographed him in the café and published his recipe for brownies), while *Vanity Fair* wanted to know what book he was reading. *Tomorrow's Bread* did a follow-up on Eric and Timothy (who was wearing another new suit, a turquoise number, in an *ArtNews* feature that same week), and *Newsweek* devoted a paragraph to Eric in a survey titled "Fifty New Minds Alive in America." All of this publicity bubbled *before* the new idol had even appeared in stores. And meanwhile, no one could buy a Goddess of Desire anywhere. Every retailer had sold out his stock, and M. Scott Gold insisted that the town go dry to harvest even more demand.

Eric liked to linger under the covers in the morning and then use Inca's shower after she had already gone to work. He could have gone upstairs to his own loft, but if he cleaned his body with her lavender soap and washed his hair with her pineapple-scented shampoo, then he smelled like her for the rest of the day: He carried part of her with him. At eight-thirty one citrus morning in late June, Inca left, and at nine-fifteen, the phone rang. Eric couldn't find it. Inca's place was a mess. He extended his arm to feel around for the phone cord, and his hand touched something leather beneath the futon frame. When he looked, he saw a portfolio case which had been stowed underneath the bed. The phone was next to it.

"I tried your brownie recipe," his mother said. "When did you learn to bake?"

Eric didn't have a chance to answer.

"I've been trying to reach you."

"You should have left a message."

"You know me," Lydia said, "I hate answering machines." She worked on fighter jets, yet she deplored the mildest technology. "So what's this number?"

Eric had changed his message to indicate where he could be reached. "Inca's."

"What's that?"

"A person—a woman named Inca."

"Are you living in Machu Picchu now?"

Eric touched his Mood Ring with his thumb. "Possibly."

"Well, well, well," Lydia said. "You looked very debonair in the *Times*."

"Thanks."

"The *Times*! It's not every half-asleep mother who gets to open up the paper one morning to see her son looking so clever. It was a well-written story, too."

"Thanks," Eric said again.

Pause. "So I called to say hi and that I've been reading all of the stories."

"What's up? Have you seen any more of Jason?"

"Not lately. Listen, it's time you met Marek. He and I have grown quite close."

Eric probably hesitated too long before answering.

"After all, we all live in the same city—"

"I'd love to meet him."

"He's different, Eric. Very kind, very honest. What you see is what you get. We've been spending weekends out at his place on the Island. He grows his own parsley and chives, his own asparagus. He knows how to steam mussels. We had the most divine steamed mussels on the beach— I'm babbling. Why don't you come over one night for dinner? Just the three of us. Or, why don't you bring . . . Inca?"

"That's her name."

"How long—"

"A while."

"Good, Eric. I'm glad. You've really taken your Goddess enterprise far. I'm impressed. What are you doing with all of the money?"

"Putting it in the bank."

"Excellent. And what's next for you?"

Eric hesitated. "Why does anything have to be next?"

"You know what I mean. You're on a roll. I was just wondering what's next."

"When will I grow up and do something to change the world?"

"Is that what I asked?"

"Sorry."

"I know you don't believe me, but I *am* proud."

His mother did sound sincere. "Okay."

"I'm not so sure I should even say what I was going to say next."

"What were you going to say?"

"I am proud."

"I hear you. What were you going to say?"

"When you do come for dinner and you bring this Incan person, would you mind doing me a favor? As you know, Marek has been heading up the investigations into the museum theft—"

"He has?" Eric wasn't sure if he knew this. "Right."

"And it's gone nowhere, I'm sorry to say. They're just about to give up. So when you're here, remember the position he's in. This explosion of forgeries is embarrassing for him, that's all I'm trying to say: It drives home his failure to catch the thief. So we certainly can talk about your success—we should, I want to—but I just don't want Marek to feel too dismal. Okay?"

It wasn't asking too much. "Sure," Eric said.

"How's Saturday night?"

When he hung up, he reached under the futon and pulled out the portfolio. He didn't think twice about unzipping it to see what, if anything, was inside. He found blueprints. He found floor plans and projections for not one or two, but for dozens of houses. The drawings were dated, recently dated, and the one on top had been completed the previous day. Or evening. Last night, Inca had asked to be left alone in her loft, and now he knew why. She was not exactly designing high-concept can openers.

Flipping through the pages of houses, he found a design for a castle of vertical siding with an indoor-outdoor pool on a beach, the ocean beyond. A design for a white, square, luxuriously windowed palace in a flat meadow. A Spanish-style hacienda in the desert. A chalet for a glacier vista. A barn in the woods. Inca had imagined houses for every possible geography, and although they were different one from the next, there was a unifying motif in the projections. Wherever she could, she had incorporated pristine, classical elements: columns, domes, and referential follies of obelisks and archways. Her houses were geometric, plush with symmetry. But then Eric examined them more closely, and a darker theme became apparent, for there was something peculiar about these columns and domes: They were nearly all cracked or crumbling, rough and jagged, dilapidated with time. Bombed.

The sides of a manor to be built on a coastal bluff were uneven, measured out at shifting, irregular heights. She had drawn a large court-yard, but it wasn't a natural atrium. It was more like a deliberate gap, a lost segment in the floor plans. A flight of stairs broke off abruptly, leading nowhere. There was a turret with a missing roof. Missing walls. It looked as if someone had come along and constructed a new building amid ruins. Whether a house overlooked a beach or a ravine, a forest or field of reedy grass, this architect saw only a landscape of ruins: new ruins, ruins transformed, skeletons inhabited once again, but still skel-etal. A house and a destroyed ancient temple all in one.

She claimed that she no longer aspired to be an architect, yet that is exactly what she seemed to be doing when no one was looking. And what a mysterious and eerie architecture it was. Eric slipped the draw-ings back in the portfolio and pushed it back under the bed. He sighed. Inca had been keeping him out of her secret kingdom.

arek stood at Lydia's living room window and opened the curtains. "Darling, I don't understand why you always have these drawn. Does Eric like it dark?"

Lydia carried in a tray of Blue Saga, Eric's favorite, some Gorgonzola with walnuts, and a bowl of spiced pecans. "*I* do. Do you mind closing them?"

Marek pulled the curtains together. The intercom buzzed.

As Eric came in, he pecked Lydia on the cheek and said, his arm around a woman dressed in black, "Meet Inca."

"A Mood Ring," Lydia said. "I haven't seen one of those in a while."

"Neither had I," Inca said, "until Eric went rummaging through my desk."

"Marek, meet my son. Eric, Marek." She chuckled uneasily. "That rhymes." She watched the men grasp hands like diplomats.

"I've heard so much about you," Marek said.

"And I, you. Ooh, Blue Saga." Eric led Inca into the living room.

Lydia was expecting a woman her son's age, maybe younger. This woman was not quite young enough to be her daughter and not old enough to be her contemporary, which for some reason made her uncomfortable.

Marek spread cheese on crackers and handed them out. "Your mother tells me you're living downtown."

"We live in the same building," Eric said.

"All the way west," Inca added.

"It's the frontier."

"The frontier of what?" Lydia asked. "Drinks anyone?" She made a Scotch and soda for Marek, vodka on the rocks for herself, and opened beers for Eric and Inca, who were holding hands. Lydia noticed that he was wearing one of those hideous rings, too. Maybe they had eloped.

"Your mother was telling me," Marek said to Eric, "that on top of everything else you've been doing, you're running a café."

"Eric makes a mean iced mocha," Inca said.

"I think it's terrific when you're young and you can do all sorts of crazy things," Marek said.

"What do you do, Inca?" Lydia asked.

"I design gadgets."

"What kind of gadgets?"

"I just turned in plans for an automatic leveler—you know, to hang paintings. It also includes an electronic monitor to assess whether the painting's colors blend well with the existing colors in the room's decor."

"I suppose that color-blind astigmatics might find it useful," Marek said evenly, pleasantly. "And is that the sort of thing you usually make?"

"Unfortunately. I just got an assignment to put together my first trend box."

"People are always sending those to me at the Institute," Lydia said. "Does yours include the breakfast cereal of the moment?"

"That's requisite."

"And a swatch of the next decade's colors and fabrics?" Lydia tried to conceal her contempt for trend mongers.

"You bet. It always amazes me that people pay large sums of money for these packages," Inca said, "just so they can pretend to know for sure what hair color will be in or out. As far as I'm concerned, it's all a crapshoot. Research predicts ash blond, and watch, it'll be auburn."

A score for Inca, Lydia thought. She seemed to maintain a healthy perspective.

"Mother, did you see that Margot was in Nome?" Eric asked.

For months, Eric practically ran out of the room at the mere mention of Margot's name. "I did," Lydia said.

"It's a funny coincidence," Inca said, "that she's one of my favorite newspersons. I feel like I can trust her."

"Oh, Margot is very intelligent." Lydia felt strange discussing her.

"She certainly seems to have a firm grasp on Alaskan oil politics," Marek said, "which can be very slippery."

Crackers snapped. Ice rattled in glasses.

"Lydia," Inca said, "I'm not sure whether Eric told you—I'm a Lucia Madsen fan."

"Really? There aren't many people around who know much about my aunt Lucia."

"Inca's an expert," Eric said.

"I don't think your mother is aware of this," Marek said to Eric (why did he have to refer to her as "your mother"?), "but the head of NYMA's film department wrote his dissertation on Lucia Madsen. It was published in book form."

Inca clapped her hands in delight. "You know Yves Delfourt?"

"We started out at the museum together."

Lydia could count on Marek to know everyone.

"I've read all of his books," Inca said.

"Yves will be happy to hear that. He, Hugo Schell, and I used to share a summer place in Amagansett. This was years ago, though, when we were agile and cocky."

"Hugo Schell?" Eric perked up. "My favorite course in college was an archaeology class with Professor Schell. We dug up the Yard as an exercise and I helped unearth a seventeenth-century clock. I almost became an archaeologist because of Hugo Schell."

"I didn't know that," Inca said.

"And why didn't you?" Marek asked.

Eric shrugged. "I moved to Washington with Margot."

Lydia served a salad with a simple vinaigrette as a first course. Marek and Eric actually appeared to be getting along. Marek was telling war stories about his college days with Hugo Whoever and Yves Someone, and Eric was asking about Marek's past, which in a way Lydia herself hadn't. She got to learn new things.

"I thought I might go into the foreign service," Marek said, "so I majored in political science. A diplomat's life seemed romantic. But curators are diplomats of a sort, and you get to have your pick of pretty pictures for your office walls."

"Do you have a favorite painting? That's probably a dumb question."

"No, no. I do. It's called *The Storm Nears*. It's in a private collection. Lydia knows it."

Lydia cleared the plates; Inca helped. "Eric seems to be happier than he has been in a long time," Lydia said to her in the kitchen. "I worry about him. Of course, I'm his mother—"

"I worry, too. Right now he's flying," Inca said, "and he has to land sometime."

"I'm happy he's found you." Lydia always made a point of supporting Eric's choice in mates no matter what she thought of them. However, she intuitively liked Inca: She seemed very down-to-earth, open. "Designing gadgets sounds like an interesting career."

"I wanted to be an architect. I was schooled, certified. Left it all for the wonderful world of uselessness."

"That's too bad."

"I don't mean to sound depressing."

"Oh, be as depressing as you like. I hate plastic smiles."

"I was thinking today that I'm almost forty, and I'm not happy doing what I'm doing. If I'm not going to save the world, I should at least be satisfied in my work, maybe having fun."

"I know what you mean."

"Why am I dumping all of this on you? We've barely met. . . . I'm making a terrible first impression."

"No, no," Lydia said, but Inca had already begun to carry in the plates. She suddenly wished that the menfolk would skip the main course and retreat to their port and cigars so that she could talk to Inca alone.

"Lydia knows I love lamb," Marek said.

Thank God he was referring to her by name. She poured wine.

"The fennel sauce is delicious, Lydia," Inca said.

"My favorite potatoes." Eric popped some in his mouth. "Did you steal them?"

Inca and Marek both looked at him, lost, then at Lydia.

"Maybe." Lydia winked at Eric. The potatoes were nothing special—just brushed with a mustard-soy mixture and baked for an hour—but she had made them just for him.

After some discussion of local politics and the Yankees' recent comeback, Marek said, "Eric, about the Goddess of Desire . . ."

Lydia squinted a warning at Eric: Be considerate.

"I think it's brilliant," Marek said.

Lydia dropped her knife.

"Thank you," Eric said. "I owe a lot to Inca."

"We're having a lot of success," Inca said, "but it was all Eric's idea originally."

"It was a stroke of marketing genius," Marek said, raking string beans to one side of his plate, "which I myself wish that I had brought to pass."

Was the man seated to her left, Lydia wondered, the same man who once in the not too distant past had winged the Cycladic imitation into a dark body of water?

"Thank you," Eric said again.

"Of course, I have my reservations." Marek leaned back in his chair. "I hope that the mad rush of excitement surrounding the Ausgraben Idol doesn't cheapen our appreciation of its beauty and wonder and enigma. Or our concern for its well-being."

Why, Lydia wondered, wasn't he speaking his true mind? He'd admitted that the forgeries bothered him, and she had told him that she valued his honesty. In fact, the more frankly Marek expressed his disdain (which he claimed was growing proportionately to the rising popularity of the reproductions), the more Lydia appreciated him. The fact that they could live with this difference of opinion somehow strengthened their love.

"I don't think it will, Marek," Inca said. "If you look at the idol, I mean if you look at our Goddess version, there's a magnificence, a majesty. . . ."

"May I tell you a funny story?" Marek asked. "I've already told your mother," he said to Eric.

He was back to "your mother." Proof, as far as Lydia was concerned, that he was not entirely at ease with what he was saying.

"Through our insurers we've been able to post a reward for the stolen piece."

"You have?" Eric asked.

"I didn't know that," Inca said.

"We're offering a million dollars, no questions asked. We just announced it today, and it will be in tomorrow's papers. This all came about as a result of the new publicity. So in a way, I have you to thank for helping us revive our struggle. With the stolen statue in the press again, we can rally our forces in a battle that many assumed was already lost."

"I see," Eric said and saw his Mood Ring passing through the rainbow.

"The reward might bring forward some new information," Marek said. "That's what we're hoping. Well, word apparently got out right away at the Friends of NYMA meeting that this prize was being offered, and at the end of the day someone actually tried to return one of your witty imitations. Isn't that frightfully silly?"

"I suppose that's a compliment," Eric said.

"By all means." Marek waved his napkin and laughed from the gut.

"More lamb?" Lydia asked. "Beans? Eric, you must want some more potatoes."

"I've heard," Eric said, "that the investigation really has gone nowhere."

"I'll take some more lamb myself," Lydia said. "Inca, could you pass it down?"

"You might say that," Marek said.

"Well, given how much time has passed since the burglary," Eric continued, "given the fact that art thieves are rarely apprehended, given the fact that in all likelihood the idol has been smuggled to a country where the laws about buying stolen property are lax, Japan for example—"

"It's good to see you still read the papers," Lydia interrupted.

"Given all that, don't you think it's entirely likely that you will never find the idol, and that you should probably save your time and resources and stop looking for it?"

Inca was glaring at Eric as if to say, Cut it out. She obviously knew how Marek felt.

"Perhaps," Marek said. "But you see, thieves have a way of giving in. They prefer a ransom over having to find customers on the black market, thus risking exposure. We've in effect made an offer, and they no doubt think that they can negotiate. We've baited them. They'll slip up, go for the worm, and we'll reel them in."

"You have to admit: It is possible that you might never see the Ausgraben Idol alive."

"Dessert"—Lydia shot up from her chair—"is pear soufflé."

Eric helped her clear the table. "Really," she said in the kitchen, "you didn't have to make the stolen statue sound like the Lindbergh baby."

The phone rang. Eric answered it. "Hello? Well, hello. Wow. Yes, it's been a long time. It's good to hear your voice, too."

"Who is it?" Lydia asked. Was it Margot?

"Really? Yes, the *Times*. No, you're kidding. You get the newspapers from Singapore?"

Jason. How strange.

"So how *are* you?" Eric asked.

"Does he want to speak with me?"

"Right. Right. She's standing right here, do you—? Okay, I'll tell her." Eric paused and listened intently. "Well, it's great to hear from you, and maybe we can see each other sometime. . . . Me, too. Bye." He hung up. "Jason said, 'Tell Lydia I behaved like a child. Tell her I've been miserable since she left that night. Tell her I need to see her and that I have something to show her.' What is he talking about?"

"Who knows what Jason ever means?"

Eric leaned against the counter. "It just occurred to me that I always assumed that I'd never talk to him again."

"I know how you feel."

"He sounds okay, I guess. A bit anxious. What does he want to show you?"

"I have no idea," Lydia said. She didn't want to think about it.

Dessert. She had hoped to discuss the weather or recent obituaries, but Marek was game for idol-conversation.

"I often wonder," he said, "how you came up with the idea to replicate the idol, Eric. You told the *Times* that you were looking outside on a rainy night. . . ."

"It's hard to explain," Eric said.

"You know how it is," Inca added. "Ideas spontaneously generate in the shower."

"I wonder, though," Marek persisted, "what motivates you. *Why?* I often find myself trying to fathom, say, what sort of appeal light through a window has to Vermeer. Beyond the painterly questions. I mean, what is going on in his mind?"

Eric ate several spoonfuls of his soufflé before answering. "You get to hold works of art all day long. The rest of us aren't so lucky. Everyone wants to hold a piece of art. To touch it. To feel its age, its wisdom, its mystery, its—"

Inca cleared her throat. "This is a marvelous treat. How did you get the soufflé to be so airy?"

Seizing the moment, Lydia recounted at length the various steps of the recipe. At the other end of the table, however, Marek continued his spirited conversation with Eric.

After Eric and Inca were gone, Marek washed the dishes. It must have been Lydia's silence which prompted him to say, "You seem angry with me. Are you angry?"

"No. But I'm not really sure why you changed your tune on Eric's Goddess. You know where I stand: I think it's great that he's making all of this money. I think he's very smart, surprisingly savvy, but you . . . We've talked about your feelings on the matter."

"I want us to be one big happy family," Marek said. "Yes, those bloody rip-offs are the bane of my existence, but he is your son, and by extension my son now, and I want us all to get along fabulously. I think I can safely say that I won him over. Inca, too. Also, my dear, it was quite helpful talking to him about the Cycladic idol, quite helpful. I feel as though I have a whole new front to pursue. Nothing concrete, but if I can understand why people are drawn to that crude artifact, I might just plug into the motive of the thief. If I only knew *why* the thief stole the idol, I'd know his identity, I'm sure of it. I feel closer." Marek reached toward Lydia with a soapy sponge. "Closer."

The phone rang again. It was for Marek, who had given out Lydia's number in case of emergencies. "Something's come up at the museum. I've got to go."

"Can I tag along?"

The evening was balmy. On the way to the museum, Marek explained that after months of renovation, the wing of Greek Antiquities was nearly refashioned, and in order to get it ready for a gala reopening, the staff had been working day and night. And someone had just found something that might be important to the investigation.

Lydia followed Marek's example and signed her name in the ledger at the security post. Following Marek down a series of unfamiliar administrative corridors at night, she felt both criminal and privileged. She wondered if she was the first civilian to get a glimpse of the better lit, replastered, repainted, Ionically trimmed rooms of Ancient Greece. Once inside, her first impulse was to visit all of the old family favorites to make sure they were still in place. Coincidentally, Marek, too, headed right for the famed Brazewell Krater. "O'Brien, our chief of security, said he'd meet me here."

Dozens of museum workers, some dressed in overalls, some in jackets and ties, were painting trim while others stenciled dates on a map painted on a wall. Others positioned plaques. Marek frowned. "I was just thinking," he said, "that if our security system had been in place, this theft would never have occurred."

"I didn't know—"

"Well," he whispered, "the administration did not want this information getting out—we didn't need another scandal in the public domain. None of our security was in place when the theft occurred. Motion detectors, TV monitors, not to mention guards on the floor. Nothing. You see, the staff was in the process of removing the art for the renovation. The thief clearly knew something about our internal operations and seized this moment of vulnerability. That's the theory."

"So was the art actually out of its cases when the thief broke in here?" Lydia asked. "Was it sitting on the floor? I don't understand."

"Not exactly. The collection hadn't actually been removed, but some cases were open. Naturally, we dusted all the glass and encasements for fingerprints."

Lydia's mind clicked. "My son is right about people wanting to touch the stuff. It's forbidden, so people want to do it."

"Every time I walk through a gallery, I see a stray pinky reaching toward a painting."

Lydia examined the play of patterns and dancing figures on the Greek urn in front of her. "So the Brazewell Krater was exposed to the open air when the thief was here?"

"Right."

"And you dusted it? You dusted the art itself?"

"If the art wasn't stolen, then presumably it wasn't touched. Our assumption all along has been that the thief came in, made his strike with precision, speed, and predetermined specificity, and then retreated quickly."

"How do you know he didn't shop around?"

"We assume—"

"Wouldn't you shop around?" Lydia asked. "Wouldn't you want to inspect everything in the store?"

"Not if I were a professional burglar. For one thing, I'd have gloves on and I'd try to touch as little as possible."

"Why do you assume it was a professional burglar?"

"The theory is that . . . Screw the theory."

"I'd touch everything." Lydia leaned toward the glass case housing the Brazewell Krater. "I'd run my fingers all over that glorious urn."

Marek nodded. "I see what you're getting at. Marguerite Dantanzky, our chief curator in this department, is very sensitive about who handles what. Keep in mind, nothing else in the rooms was even moved around or displaced by the intruder." He paused for a moment. "I wouldn't be surprised if Marguerite prevented the police from applying any sort of fingerprint powder to pieces that were fragile. It might get in the cracks of the ceramic or eat at the glaze or react with the pigments or who knows what. They probably combed the art with magnifying glasses. Yes, I see what you're saying. But darling, if there were prints that we somehow missed, surely they would have been obliterated by now. Everything has been shuffled about lately."

"And everything has probably been cleaned recently," Lydia added.

"I would assume."

"Who knows how many people have touched the Krater alone in the last six months?"

"Exactly."

"It's highly unlikely, number one, that the thief wasn't wearing gloves. Or number two, that he picked anything else up other than what he came here for, and he probably knew what he wanted. Or number three, that prints would survive this long."

"Yes."

"Ignore me if you want," Lydia said. "But I bet you that the thief got his grubby paws all over these goodies and would have made off with other objects but may have run out of time. He could have put things back right where he found them, settling for just one little old Cycladic souvenir."

"First thing tomorrow," Marek resolved, "I'm going to have all of the art in here reexamined. Nothing will come of it, of course."

"No."

A man in a seersucker suit, a walkie-talkie clipped to his belt, approached Marek.

"O'Brien," Marek said across the room. O'Brien was carrying a small plastic bag. "I'll be right back."

Lydia pretended to examine the Brazewell Krater while she observed Marek's conversation over by the icing-white, Praxitelean discus thrower (sans discus), which was being repositioned on a new pedestal. She could not exactly hear what was being discussed or see what was in the plastic bag—O'Brien's back blocked her view—but she could tell that some sort of physical evidence had been uncovered, something small, which Marek examined with tweezers. After about five minutes of scrutiny, he returned.

He steered Lydia out of the room. He spoke softly, fast: "Something was found in the Brazewell Krater when it was moved to its new case this evening."

She looked back over her shoulder at the urn.

"It probably has nothing to do with the theft at all: Anyone could have dropped it at any point in the last months while the Krater was in storage. And then again, it might be something that the thief inadvertently dropped."

"Interesting," Lydia said. "It was *in* the urn?" They reached the hallway. There was a group of staff workers conferring under the new main portico of Greek Antiquities. "And what exactly is this *thing* that you found?"

Marek whispered in her ear: "A clip-on museum admission button. It's a green one, which was the color of the day when the Ausgraben Idol was stolen. That's not all. There are fibers stuck to the button. Some kind of red wool. Who knows where it will lead us? Although I am certain of one thing: You're very smart. Someone may have indeed been poking around the Brazewell Krater that morning. Maybe an amateur, yes, with lucky timing."

"I hope the new clue helps."

He kissed her. "We're back on track now. We're thinking like the crook."

I don't see why you had to discuss the you-know-what with that foolish man," Inca said in the cab home from the Upper East Side.

"He has no idea what's up and what's down," Eric said. "I can't believe my mother is in love with him."

"You made me nervous." She squeezed his hand. "You were definitely dancing a soft-shoe on a tightrope back there."

"He has no idea. I wouldn't worry." When they arrived home, Eric suggested that they walk around the block. "That dinner depressed me. I need the air."

"I'm afraid that I have to turn in designs for a desk set in the morning," Inca said.

"So I should go play by myself for a few hours?" She was going upstairs to draw some dream-château, and he knew it. "Look, Inca . . ."

A man carrying a glass of iced coffee and a piece of chocolate cake stepped out of the café and sat on the bench. Eric plopped down next to him. Melior, who was sitting on the windowsill behind him, poked her head through the open frame to sniff his hand, and he pulled her outside, then clutched her tightly in his lap.

"What, Eric?"

He looked at the man eating the cake, at the cat, and then back at Inca. "Why not just come out and say it? You have visions of an enormous log cabin on a lake, and you're going to go upstairs and map it out on your drafting board."

Melior wiggled from his hold and leaped back into the café. Inca stared at him, turned, and abruptly started jogging toward the river. Eric ran after her. She must have heard him, because she picked up the pace and dashed across the highway. He was trapped at a red light while she headed toward the embankment. He finally skipped across the lanes of traffic, narrowly escaping a honking station wagon, and hurried down to the floodlit pier, ready to apologize, but out of breath when he reached her. The sulfuric fumes of the Hudson made him gasp.

"You shouldn't have gone through my things." Inca looked straight ahead, at Jersey City, and sounded neither angry nor surprised, just cool.

"Your houses are magnificent."

"That's not the point."

"You're right, I shouldn't have looked under your bed."

"I'll suffocate if I can't keep a few things from you."

"Your houses are brilliant. Someone should build them." Cautiously, he put his arm around her shoulder. She didn't move away. "Unreal and cryptic. I loved your drawings. You shouldn't be embarrassed."

"Why do you think I'm embarrassed? I think they're brilliant, too."

Some sort of large vessel was ploughing its way downriver. In the night, it looked like a battleship, though it probably was only a garbage barge.

"Inca, I've told you everything. I have no secrets."

"What a person hides under her bed is her business."

"I would give anything to live in one of your houses."

She removed Eric's arm from her shoulder and took his hand. They followed the barge until it drifted out of sight, then walked home silently and crawled into bed without a word. They kept to their own established sides of the futon and watched a candle flame dance atop the miniature Eiffel Tower.

"I am sorry I snooped," Eric whispered, "but you don't need to explain why you keep your architecture secret."

"I wasn't planning to."

"Your houses look like ancient ruins. I don't know why, and I won't ask."

Inca crept close enough to fold her leg over his. She stroked his sternum, the line dividing his chest, the hair beneath his navel. "Ruins make a connection," she said, "with something we can never escape."

"The past?" Eric asked. She didn't answer.

The open windows allowed the cleansing aroma of coffee to wash the loft. When they made love, he wanted her to feel as though she were falling and he caught her. She reciprocated this strength when she rolled back to her side of the bed, pulling him with her. At first he was warmer, and then the temperature of her skin rose above his. Slowly they acclimated to each other, to one even, cool reading, a fragile balance that was lost when they fell away from each other, when they fell asleep, or in his case, into somnolent speculation about what might have motivated her architecture of ruins.

In the days and nights that followed, Inca allowed Eric to remain in her loft while she worked. She claimed that the house she was designing was coming along slowly, a more arduous labor than usual. She was uncertain about how the structure should lie along the bluff she imagined for it. And in a moment of utter panic and mental stagnation, she removed the Ausgraben Idol from the tool-box coffin. She held the woman's head in one hand, her feet in the other, pushed aside a stack of French curves, and set the artifact down. Eric pretended to read a magazine on the bed and watched Inca choose her weapons. She sharpened pencils. She held the blunt end of one against her lip like a cigarette. She pulled her T-square down her drafting board and drew a line, a single horizontal stroke. She positioned a 30-60-triangular template on the page and flew up its tall leg with another line and continued to measure out additional walls, but abruptly ripped the graph paper off her drafting board and crumpled it into a tight ball, which she chucked across the room. Then she drew exploratory lines on a new page, which she eventually discarded, too. And so on. Rather than use an eraser, Inca would move on to a virgin piece of paper when her design failed, although eventually she stopped crumpling the pages and instead let them fall off her desk.

After a while, she appeared to have hit upon a preliminary layout that she could work with. She started to draw wildly, all elbow and wrist. She slid the T-square up or down the drafting board and swept across the paper with graphite flourishes. She swung a compass into action. She plotted out a room with her triangular scale and then retraced the distance with her proportional dividers. The sharp, metal legs of the instrument, stepping point by point along the drafting board, looked like the legs of an infant learning to walk, awkward, falling forward. Two hours later, Inca showed Eric what she had drawn: a sprawling house nestled into the topography of a pretend cliff, a house that presided over the ocean at the same time that it blended in with the natural contour of the rocky scape.

The idol on the desk was lying on her back, staring at the ceiling.

"It's spectacular." Eric massaged Inca's shoulders. "I love the cupola. And I love the lotus-capped columns supporting the deck."

*In the winter people dream of summer, and in the summer people dream of winter—which is to say, the weather is never quite what anyone wants it to be.*

Inca stared at the drawing. "I don't know." She sighed. "It needs a lot of work."

*My business is always booming . . .*

"It's too cold, too forbidding."

*. . . because if I give them what they want, they come back asking for something else.*

"But I love the pergola," Eric said.

"The pergola is obvious. The whole layout is illogical."

"No," Eric protested. "I love the broken-roof skylight effect in the master bedroom. I love the bombed-out-turret eating-area off the kitchen."

"It's so unsubtle, so flamboyant."

"Inca, I'd live there in a minute. I've had dreams about a house on a cliff."

*The more they get, the more they want. I never get any sleep.*

"I loathe flamboyant houses." Inca ripped the drawing off the drafting board and let it slide down the slope of the table to fall on the floor.

Eric put it back on the desk, but she had already escaped to her bed, where she lay on her side and covered her head with pillows. "Inca? I think you should show this to an architectural firm or something, because to my untrained eye—"

"Well, that's just it, Eric. You've got an untrained eye. I need to be alone."

He tried to caress the dip in her pelvis.

She jerked away from him. "Please, Eric. I'll see you later."

The next day, they rented a car to drive to the factory in New Jersey where the new Goddesses were being manufactured and readied for shipping. Inca drove at her usual Grand Prix speed, and there was no conversation about the previous evening, no talk at all. Soon they arrived at the Evergreen Industrial Park, a meadow of factories and office complexes and lush sod. Outside, the hive-hum of the nearby highway was a constant drone, and inside the factory, there was a roar, the sound of cogs and gears turning, of heavy machinery pumping and gnashing and pounding. They walked past a glassed-in foreman's office where a woman at a switchboard waved hello to Inca. The woman pointed to her head, and Inca nodded back. From a pile of helmets, she pulled out two white hard hats, each equipped with goggles. And then they approached the source of the noise, an assembly line that stretched a half football field, maybe longer. The assembly line consisted of a series of large, anonymous metal boxes connected by a conveyor.

A group of men and women unloaded what looked like enormous blocks of soap from a forklift. There was something alienating about the factory employees, each hidden in white overalls, the white hard hat, goggles, and surgeon's mask. The goggles and masks made their faces impossible to read. The huge soap was actually the uncut hydrastone. Table-sized slabs passed along a conveyor belt into a gigantic cutter, where they were adjusted by a series of brushes that looked like the arms of a drive-in car wash, and then sent through other similar chopping machines until the blocks had been hewed into a series of idol-thin strips. The strips themselves were maybe ten to fifteen idols long, unbroken, and six or seven of these strips lay side by side as they moved along the conveyor into the next box of machines.

Eric peered through the Plexiglas windows that had been cut into the metal housing, and he could see that the strips were fed, bit by bit, into a series of clamps and metal hands that surrounded the hydrastone and compressed it into the rough shape of the Cycladic woman. The idols at this point were distinct within the longer strips, but barely defined, save a head, body, and what looked like the base. They slithered into the next set of machines, where the real molding took place. Doing away with the Naxos Master's expert chiseling (and, of course, dispensing with his alleged pigments), the machines pressed the curves of pseudo-marble into the blank face, crossed arms, and bent knees. The thin base and prop were connected to the idol, just as in Inca's model. A second pressing honed the replica, indenting the ancient sculptor's incisings into the figurine, and finally, a third pressing, which involved a thick steam, altered the patina of the object, transforming the soaplike hydrastone into five-thousand-year-old marble.

The idols emerged briefly and were shuffled into single file, headfirst, along the conveyor. Eric was about to pick one up when Inca grabbed his hand. She blew air over her fingers: hot. Next the idols were cooled by fans, and excess dust was vacuumed away. Quality controllers examined random examples from each batch. Then the product moved along to the boxer, the final organ on the alimentary journey. A crisp white box in the fluted and flower-capped shape of a Corinthian column was wrapped around the Goddess (surprise, surprise: M. Scott Gold had gotten his way). The head of the woman peeked through an oval, cellophane window. Boxed idols rolled off the conveyor and into cartons, dozens in each, which were sealed and carried away on golf carts, loaded into long white trucks, and sent off into the world. Any day now, to department stores.

Inca scooped up a box before it fell into a carton and directed Eric toward the employees' cafeteria, which had been soundproofed to some degree, although it was still noisy. Inca mixed Eric some powdery, presweetened iced tea. He examined the package and read the copy on the back of the column box:

DO YOU FIND YOURSELF WONDERING IF YOU CAN EVER BE HAPPY? PULL OUT THIS SLENDER AND SAVVY ANCIENT IDOL. TALK TO HER. TELL HER WHAT'S ON YOUR MIND. SHE'LL LISTEN. SHE'LL HOLD YOUR HAND. SHE'LL KEEP YOU COMPANY. SHE IS THE GODDESS OF DESIRE AND SHE'S WAITING TO ANSWER YOUR PRAYERS. TELL HER WHAT YOU WANT, AND YOUR WISH WILL COME TRUE. BASED ON AN ANCIENT GREEK STATUE KNOWN THROUGHOUT THE WORLD AND ACROSS THE CENTURIES FOR ITS MYSTICAL POWER, THIS IDOL IS MODELED AFTER A FAMOUS STOLEN TREASURE. AND WHO KNOWS? MAYBE YOU'RE HOLDING THE REAL THING. BRING THIS MAGIC WOMAN INTO YOUR HOME AND YOU WILL HAVE A LIFELONG FRIEND. AND SOON ALL OF YOUR WISHES WILL COME TRUE.

"Well?" Inca stirred her iced tea with her finger.

"It's okay, I guess."

"You guess? You look disappointed."

"I'm not sure the Cycladic woman should be portrayed as a genie in a bottle."

"That's what Marketing clearly thought people would relate to. They know what they're doing. It's not that big a deal, Eric, and it's too late to change."

"How much will it finally cost?"

"In New York? Eleven eighty-eight, with tax. Each one costs only one dollar and eighty-five cents to make. The retailer's discount is a little less than forty percent, so the profit margin is comfortable, even fatty, you might say. But what do you think?" Inca's Mood Ring had turned fire-engine red.

Eric wasn't sure why he was annoyed, and Inca seemed eager for his approval. "It's great," he said. He was such a lousy liar. "It's perfect," he said with more conviction. He hated himself when he lied.

One winter vacation during college, he was driving alone from Boston to New York to visit his mother. As always, he sped in the left lane. The highway near Providence was full of traffic. Suddenly—maybe he skidded over a patch of ice, maybe he was simply not paying attention—he lost control of the car. The power steering was too sensitive, and as he tried to decelerate, he veered the car to the right, almost into a truck. To recover, he swerved to the left, almost into the concrete divider. Luckily the divider ended abruptly, and there was a generous, steep valley of lawn between the northern and southern lanes of the highway. Eric's car dove down the slope of grass, and he pulled back on the wheel and turned right again. He kept turning right. The car spun around twice. If the concrete divider had not broken off, he would have either smashed into the truck or hopped over the low wall into oncoming traffic. It was the closest in his short life that he had come to death, and he knew it then, as cars continued to whiz by, which was why he didn't think about it—he would never have driven on. He steered the car back up to the road, waited for a break, and fell back into the traffic. He finished the trip.

As he sat in the factory cafeteria with Inca, he felt as if he was in that car now, the piece of machinery that contained him as it careened and swerved, at the instant before he plunged onto the grass. He was losing control now, that was the sensation, that he might crash.

He lived in a city of constant motion and constant change, a loose confederation of neighborhoods, each at one time or another inhabited by a flock of émigrés who eventually abandoned it and left behind a cuisine and a rhythm before a new colony moved in. In New York, buildings went up and buildings were torn down, allowing architects to pace through their redundant styles, their myriad revivals. And some buildings survived by reinvention: A candy factory became residential lofts, and near where Eric lived there was a onetime telephone company that now housed a theater for the deaf. For every condo conversion and tenement makeover, there was also a brownstone restoration, a resurrection in the name of history. A storefront might house leather goods and then a travel agency, a bakery and then a clock repair shop. Motion, change. Eric came from a republic of flux where anyone could journey through an odyssey of countless metamorphoses, larval to sublime, both cyclical and without pattern. Inside the city, he could transform himself, he was free to renovate and innovate, but outside its walls, he gave in to panic and sweat. He looked at Inca. "Can we go home?"

"I'm kind of tired," she said, "do you want to drive?"

"Not really."

Timothy sat in the middle of his studio surrounded by stacks of coffee-table books that documented the history of pre-Renaissance civilization in glorious four-color separation. Like a mail-order addict, he flipped through page after page of cave paintings and African masks and hieroglyphics and Carolingian coins. What next, what next? He had spent thousands of dollars on these books. He had thousands to spend. People knew who he was. The other day at a TriBeCa party, a man who someone later identified as the captain of the spaceship on a syndicated TV serial approached him and said, "I'm snapping you up now. I'll be able to retire on what you'll be worth. I'll only have to do the occasional reunion show."

It was three in the morning, the only time when Timothy had ever been able to think. He looked around at the drawings taped to his studio walls, hasty sketches of the Cycladic idol and the bust of the Egyptian queen and the headless Babylonian scribe and the Colombian votive figure, all belly and phallus, that Eduardo insisted be molded out of gold. "But I don't know much about working in metals," Timothy had confessed, and Eduardo told him that it didn't matter: "You can hire assistants to hack out the projects, and if you like what the workshop comes up with, you can sign the piece and just pay your assistants the minimum wage. It's the atelier system, and it's as old as Rembrandt." So Timothy didn't have to actually manufacture the art anymore, he just had to choose it, reclaim it from the past, and get Eduardo's approval. Five Eskimo-bone statues were in production. Twenty-five thousand a shaman. Then he'd do an installation, a Byzantine mosaic. And then . . . what? Timothy flipped past photos of Spanish shofars, Etruscan jugs. He tossed one book back in the pile, removed another. He must have bought a hundred tomes, museum catalogs and scholarly tracts alike. His eyes grew tired, so he headed for the shower.

He lay down and let the water hammer around his shoulders and neck, occasionally lifting his torso to let the puddles flood the tub and flow into the drain. He flexed his fingers. He had a hankering to use his hands. He never made anything anymore. The spaceship captain would buy the Eskimo mask, if he could claim one before the ad mogul, but the truth of the matter was that Timothy's only connection to the sculpture was his signature.

He washed his stomach. The shower massaged his lower abdomen. He began to arouse himself. He closed his eyes and this morning, as on other mornings, he heard a voice in his head: He heard Andre lecturing about an opera they were listening to in a darkened room, Andre complaining about the price of movies, Andre describing New York when he first arrived. Timothy could almost feel Andre lying on a bed next to him, reconfiguring the pillows around his body in such a way so as to hog three-quarters of the mattress and blankets. . . . But then Timothy opened his eyes.

He turned off the shower and dressed. He went downstairs and found Andre sitting in a booth with Melior, doing the crossword puzzle. Everyone had left, the door was locked.

"Oh, hi," Andre said, startled. "Long time, no see."

"Remember our trip to France? The one we took right after Carlos died?"

"Do I have to?"

Timothy slipped into the booth. "I thought it was incredibly decadent to have breakfast in bed, so you secretly ordered it the night before, and then this old woman knocked on the door at some ridiculously early hour and brought in these croissants and pots of jam and big bowls of coffee. We were in heaven."

"That was the trip when I got sick eating that rabbit stew."

"Andre—"

"No, it was that steak tartare." He looked down at his puzzle. "We're almost done," he said to the cat when she yawned.

Timothy walked across the room to the front door and picked up the Specials blackboard Andre had brought inside for the night. He carried it back to the bar, on the way grabbing a piece of chalk from the twenties slot of the cash register. He kicked off his shoes.

"What are you doing?"

Timothy pulled his shirt over his head.

"No. Don't do that. Nobody wants you to do that."

Timothy unzipped his jeans.

"This is how it starts each time. An innocent sketch."

Timothy stepped out of his pants. He sat on the stool, balanced the slate over his knee, and began sketching with the chalk.

"Then we go to an all-Mozart concert in the park. And we're sharing bottles of beer, spreading cheese on crackers for each other."

"Andre, let me draw you."

"Not this time, no. We can't do this again. We have to stop sometime. We have to move on."

Timothy refused to beg. He set the blackboard on the bar and pulled his pants on.

"I'm thinking of leaving the city," Andre said, looking back at his puzzle.

"A vacation?"

Andre shrugged.

"For good? You? Never." Timothy put his shirt back on. "You're serious? You can't."

Andre filled in a clue.

"You can't do that. You're joking, right?"

"I have to finish my puzzle. I have to get some sleep."

Timothy picked up his shoes and rushed back through the kitchen, up the back stairs, to the piles of art books. He flipped through the pages of a volume of ancient Kore figures, and then he stripped off his clothes yet again. The tub was still wet. He lay down in it without turning on the water. He knew that soon, in an hour, in a few minutes, over by the East River, the sun would begin to rise over the sleeping apartment towers. Not yet, he thought. He wasn't ready for it.

ydia did not visit Jason right away. Each day she thought about stopping by, but she procrastinated. She expected that when she finally arrived, she would find him poring over a map of Indochina or staring at his seven televisions. He would apologize in a roundabout way, and then they would pretend that they'd never tangled. But Jason greeted her in his foyer, his face obscured by a mammoth bouquet of gladioli. "I'm sorry I was such a cad." He handed her the flowers.

"They're gorgeous." She dipped her nose into the petals. "And fresh. How did you know I was coming today?" The only advance warning of her visit was Norton the doorman's call upstairs moments ago.

"I didn't. After I called, I had flowers delivered each day."

Lydia followed him into the living room, where a tall vase sat on the mantel, full of identical red flowers.

Jason tossed the day-old gladioli in the fireplace and put the new bouquet in the vase. "You can look at them while you read."

"While I read what?"

"A whiskey sour?" Jason hurried over to the bar.

"To be honest, I could really go for a vodka on the rocks with a twist of lime." The apartment was cold, the air conditioner on full blast.

"You're drinking vodka these days?" Jason mixed the drinks, sank into his Eames chair, and tried to wend his way through an explanation: "See, I planted that manuscript to see if you were genuinely interested . . . or if you were just trying to figure out what I'd been doing up here all these years. You know, spying for someone: a gossip columnist, a publisher, I don't know. I wanted to see if you'd notice, and then if you noticed, what you would say."

"I was genuinely interested."

"I realize that. And I'm sorry I set a trap. It was childish, I admit. You were the only person I ever trusted, Lydia, you must know that."

No, she did not. "The telescope," she said. "When did you get the telescope?" The black canister sat innocently on its tripod.

"When I got back to the city after that first weekend when I met you at the shore."

"You've been watching me all that time?"

"When we were together we kept the window open when we slept at night. Your third husband kept it closed. There were some others in between who kept it open wide, and some who cracked it just a bit. Marek apparently likes it closed completely. I would have thought that he was more the open-window type."

Lydia didn't know whether to be annoyed by his spying or flattered that he had cared for so long. "I don't know what to say."

"You don't have to say anything, I know I'm weird. Listen, I worry about you."

"I survive."

"Yes, but you know yourself, for example, that you've outgrown the Institute—"

"Don't start in on that."

"And with Marek—"

"Jason, you can't swoop into my life again and change everything."

"It's what I do. I may be rusty, but it's what I do."

"Well, my life is fine."

"Is it?"

Lydia decided not to argue. What had he seen through his telescope? Or maybe the question was, what hadn't he seen?

"What I want to do is . . . This is hard to say." Jason pinched the bridge of his nose.

Lydia sipped her vodka, waited.

"There is a manuscript. A real one."

"You really did write a new book? *Polar Bears Free*—is that the real title?"

Jason hesitated but then nodded. He looked as though he were co-operating with the police as part of a plea bargain, and even though a reduced sentence was on the horizon, he still had difficulty giving up information they wanted.

"I know it's a question you've never liked, but what's it about?"

"Hmm. What's it about? It's a utopian novel, a sort of answer to *Esidarap Found* for the Nineties. You know me, and you know that I'm arrogant, so I won't apologize when I say that I think the world needs to read it. And I'd like you to read it. If you want to, that is."

"I'm . . . I'm flattered and honored." Lydia didn't know Jason when he wrote his first book. He was already famous when she met him. And he had never shown her a manuscript before publication. "Of course I want to read it."

Jason ran his palm over his short-cropped hair. "In one sitting."

"If you like."

"And, of course, you can't take it out of my house."

"No? Of course not." She would have to camp out here.

"And I'd like you to read it now."

"Now? As in this particular Friday night?" Lydia had stopped by Jason's on her way to meet Marek. They were scheduled for a long weekend at his country house, complete with a picnic on the beach late tonight. Steamed mussels and cold asparagus. "I sort of had plans for the weekend."

"By the end of the weekend, I might destroy the manuscript. I can't believe I've waited this long for you. No, I'm not sure I will be willing to show it to you on Monday."

"Okay, okay. Don't be so histrionic." She looked at the telescope again: He was a man of extremes after all. "I'll read it in one sitting, here and now." Maybe she could simply join Marek out in the country later. "I just have to make a phone call."

"You won't mention the book to Marek."

"Of course not. I'll just be a minute." Lydia went into the bedroom and shut the door.

"I'll come fetch you with my car," Marek said.

She pressed the phone close to her ear as if this somehow brought her closer to him. "Marek, dear, I—"

"Guess what? We've got a new, crack forensics team on board. They've found a fiber of hair *in* the Brazewell Krater. They're going to run a DNA check on it and on the strands of wool that were attached to the button. It could be the thief's—or it could belong to someone on the staff. Of course, we can sample the DNA of the staff, and then determine if it belongs to an outsider. We can compare it to the codes of known criminals. If we do ever find the culprit, we'll be able to check his DNA against the DNA of—"

"Splendid news," Lydia said. "But Marek, I'm afraid I'm going to have to take the train out tomorrow or maybe even the next day and join you later on."

"What's wrong? You don't sound well."

"I don't? No, I'm not. Maybe I have that flu that's going around. I have a fever and chills and a headache. I'm going to take to my bed."

"I'll come take care of you."

"I need to be alone, dear."

"I'll call you every hour," Marek insisted.

"I'll be sleeping. I'll call you. Oh, listen, Marek . . ." She had been lying awake early this morning thinking about the museum burglar, and she forgot to tell him what she had been mulling over when he woke up. She had been trying to imagine what she would have done if *she* had stumbled into the museum and discovered all the art out and unattended. She would have tried on that gold Minoan necklace and matching headgear. She definitely would have looked inside the Brazewell Krater and appraised it with her finger. And what if, on a whim, she had grabbed the Ausgraben Idol. . . . Then what? She wouldn't try to sell it. She wouldn't know how. "You know how I've been trying to plug into the mindset of the thief, right? Well, if I had stolen a Cycladic idol, do you know what I would do?"

"You'd sell it on the black market, make a lot of money, and go live in Provence."

"I'd keep it for myself."

"Just keep it? And then what?"

This was where she was stuck. "I'm not sure. But I would definitely keep the idol and cherish and enjoy it and learn everything there was to know about the wondrous thing that I'd stolen."

"I see. Interesting."

"I'm sorry about the weekend."

"Feel better."

When Lydia hung up, she was dizzy with guilt. Jason had set out some wine and cheese back in the living room. The manuscript sat on the glass coffee table. He had gone so far as to remove her reading glasses from her purse and place them beside the stack of pages. When she got to know Jason, she was still married to Jack Auden, but they were more or less separated. Lydia had, however, been cheated on over the years by lovers and husbands, and now she felt as if she herself was committing adultery. Marek thought she was home in bed, but no, she sat on a couch high up in the penthouse of a reclusive man reading a book called *Polar Bears Free*.

It took all night and most of the next day. Her reading was punctuated by snacks and ample meals served by Jason, who cast an anxious eye at her and otherwise hid out in his media control center. The experience of reading was taxing, and at one point Lydia paused long enough to call Marek to tell him that she was not better and therefore not coming out to the country at all. He sounded dismayed, but she had to finish—she wanted to finish. She became engrossed. Reading Jason's prose again after so long was like wandering through a neighborhood from her youth: At first she couldn't locate any familiar buildings—houses and schools had been torn down, replaced. But slowly she found familiar landmarks, important to her for distant reasons, a drugstore, a train depot, a church, and she began to feel at ease, at home.

*Polar Bears Free* was about a band of urban loners who had quit their fancy professional jobs to follow around a sixtyish ex-Sixties guru named Dope Carson. There was more plot than Lydia expected from Jason: The group decided that in order to start saving the world, they needed to commit an act that everyone would take notice of, and so they schemed and schemed and finally one day figured out a way to free the polar bears from the zoo. Not just one, but all three. The three bears, however, were not caught on the other side of the park. Dope's gang helped the bears travel up through Westchester and New York State, overland all the way, up to Canada, and home at long last to the arctic hinterland. There were many trials and tribulations along the way, chase scenes and skirmishes with hunters, but ultimately the bears went free. Also along the way, Dope Carson assumed a camp-fire pulpit—this was a philosophical novel after all, a utopian allegory—where he delivered stirring sermons. Jason kept using one of his old words, a term Lydia had thought that he'd disavowed long ago: re-evolution. The only way to achieve any progress in a fast-spinning world of careless, greedy morals was to make a radical break from a past full of gluttonous gratifications and self-serving decadence, followed by a gradual branching and expansion into new frontiers of altruism, harmony, and concern for every living creature. You quit your job, that was the radical break; you saved some bears as a bold gesture; and then you followed an uncertain, winding path toward fulfilling renewal through constant, meaningful action. Not even Dope could tell his followers what came next, except that the world had to become a place where man respected fellow man because the alternative of self-destruction, of famines and deforestation and overpopulating annihilation, was too grim, too possible, and too close.

"So, what did you think?" Jason asked when Lydia announced that she was done. He stood before her like a small child waiting to be disciplined.

She honestly could say, "I loved it. It was moving in parts, heady in others. Dope's speeches went on a little long now and again, but I loved it."

Jason broke into a relieved grin that he immediately suppressed.

"Your opinion matters a great deal to me, Lydia. You're not just humoring me—"

"I'm not. No, no. In a way you're singing some of your old themes. I liked hearing them again."

"You think so?" Jason rubbed his hands anxiously. "I hope I don't sound like I'm just trying to make a buck on regurgitated dogma."

"No," Lydia insisted. "It's all very relevant. Really. I'm not just saying that."

"Yes, well, I suppose a man can only have one idea in his life and dress it up only so many ways."

"Why now? What made you finally write something again?" Lydia asked.

Jason spoke slowly: "I sit here and I watch the news and my instinct tells me that people don't read anymore, that people are complacent, flabby-brained, lobotomized, that you can't excite college students to do much more than recycle soda cans—and yet . . . And yet. I'm damned to be an idealist, try as hard as I may to the contrary, and I'm doomed to optimism. I guess that every thirty years or so, it seems necessary to say these things. And we—America, the world—have just survived an incredible war with our petty, selfish selves. We're on the brink again of healing. We're teetering, and we can fall either way at this point: back to our VCRs and home shopping networks or out into the streets again, to block parties and camping trips in the mountains. I won't lecture— you just read the book. Phew! I am so glad you liked it, so relieved and thrilled."

What Lydia did not tell him was that while she believed in what he had to say, she knew that polar bears were not the only animals rattling their bars. In his words, she heard a plea from another zoo creature, and it made her both happy that he cried for freedom and sad because she wasn't sure what to do, how she could help unlatch his cage.

Before she left, they hugged long and hard. Lydia had forgotten what it felt like to be in Jason's arms: It was no different really from being held by anyone else, except that his hands were warm with honesty when they swept across her spine and shoulder blades, passionately sincere. When the elevator arrived, she regretted pulling away.

T|he night before the Goddess of Desire went on sale again, Eric and Inca took a long walk to Herald Square. One Macy's window looked like a miniature stage for a Forties movie-musical. Tiers and staircases, all painted red, white, and blue, set against a backdrop of Old Glory, were now occupied by dozens and dozens of the Cycladic idols, a mammoth chorus of fake marble, each dancer in step. TELL ALL TO THE GODDESS, declared the slogan painted on the window. An Ancient Greek ritual figure had been transformed into an all-American icon, an immigrant star born from the melting pot. And the Goddess of Desire could only reign in America: Marching down the steps of a Macy's diorama, she represented promise, hope, invention, and mass production.

The scale of the phenomenon that followed could never have been predicted by M. Scott Gold or his ace market analysts. So far it had been a summer of movie sequels breaking box-office records, a summer of pitchers throwing no-hitters as often as they spat tobacco juice, yet nothing took off and soared as high as the Goddess of Desire. In the first three days in the metropolitan area alone, seventy thousand idols were purchased. Each subsequent day, sales continued to snowball—there was no drop-off, only more frantic demand—and even before a third of the idols manufactured had been sold off, M. Scott Gold had ordered a second large minting. Department and grocery and discount stores alike carried the idol. The fad became locomotive, it had a life of its own, spreading from New York to the entire Eastern seaboard, then the rest of the nation. Some of the previous generation of idols had already made it to Los Angeles, where the Cycladic woman's uncanny resemblance to the Oscar statuette made her all the more enticing. Next she would be bound for Europe, then Japan, then . . .

Eric began to breathe an alien and ineffable ether in the hot city air this summer. People wandered up and down Forelle Street for hours waiting for tables to free up at the Mystery Roast. And then, once seated, the average customer would order as many as five or six iced mochas (extra crème fraîche, please, more whipped cream). Andre's pains aux chocolats were more popular than ever. Perhaps the sultry, stagnant air made men and women susceptible to fantasy and infatuation, which could only be sated with chocolate. Even Melior, normally immune to moods in weather and people, seemed anxious. A local alley tom had taken to visiting at all hours. He sprayed the bench outside the café and made his intentions known by serenading like a Romeo at four in the morning. Melior, who in the warm months was usually allowed to step out on the sidewalk—Melior, who was spayed—was not allowed out for fear that she might elope. So she pawed at the door and bolted past the legs of entering or exiting café patrons whenever she could. She meowed plaintively when someone scooped her up halfway down the block and carried her home.

It seemed to Eric as if more New Yorkers were staying in the city on weekends, avoiding the beaches and even the cool cinemas, aimlessly drifting along the sidewalks instead, listless and thirsty. The light always lingered longer in July and August, but this summer, the sun set later and later: It was light out at ten at night. The heat was extraordinary, extreme and dry, so that park meadows browned into crisp deserts and air conditioners broke down—people would give up on the machines and defenestrate them into air shafts—and baseball players collapsed in their outfields. Eric read in the paper about a man who stabbed another man over a cab (and it wasn't even raining). Petty theft was on the rise; people were mugged for plastic jewelry. The stock market followed an erratic jag, peaking to new heights and dipping in steeper single-day plunges. Hysterical crows took over benches, and lost gulls wandered in from the shore; they began nesting in maples. More families than usual sat on their stoops, eating multi-coursed dinners on the steps, carrying out portable televisions, too. There was a run on ice cream and calamine lotion (mosquitoes went on a rampage). On one breezier afternoon, Eric saw a hopeful kite lofty in the hazy, blue (bluer) sky, a kite in the west West Village. Unleashed dogs strayed wildly, veering rebelliously away from their owners. More men than ever walked around shirtless, in tight, skimpy shorts; more women wore lipstick, sporting brighter, coral colors. At night, when the city lights finally, reluctantly dimmed, there was a sweat in the air current that wafted down the rivers, the sweat of bodies lying closer. A tide of Desire.

Eric drank a lot of iced coffee and walked around with most of his shirt unbuttoned and made love to Inca with a fervor that seemed to come from outside him. They left the lights off to keep the loft cool. They lit dozens of tea candles and aimed fans at themselves. Eric slept less, and at unsafe hours of the early morning, he pulled on a pair of tennis shorts, a tank top, and roamed the neighborhood. Sometimes when he wandered the meat-packing district he heard a faint echo, a sustained wail like beasts keening before the slaughter.

Timothy had more or less disappeared into his new world, Eric never saw him, and Andre had stopped talking to anyone altogether. Eric argued with Inca. Surely this was only the next phase in their rapport, getting angry over silly matters: Eric flicking TV channels around too quickly, Inca hogging sections of the Sunday paper. Yet differences ran deeper. Inca the gadget inventor oddly lost interest in the Goddess. The mass-marketing had been her initiative, yet she was more than happy to let Eric read over the sales reports, for Eric to answer the phone calls and do the interviews and even collect the checks. She seemed to be withdrawing from him, drifting. She continued to design houses while he was in the loft: houses for no one in particular, houses drawn the way a painter selects and records a landscape, houses strictly for her own pleasure. In fact, Inca took advantage of her accumulated vacation days in order to devote more time to her blueprints. Eric would ask her what she was working on, but she never answered. If he asked too many questions, she said that she felt watched and couldn't create. He had to back off, spend less time with her. She wore her Mood Ring on a chain around her neck: It was a cold, black pendant.

Inca sliced balsa and Styrofoam and constructed scale models of each mountain cabin or town house, planting them on boards of plywood to which she added contoured cardboard landscaping. The models were left white, never painted, as if they were made of meringue. Her loft became a virtual village of tiny homes, and Eric had to be careful where he stepped and sat down. At night, when the side of her right hand was covered in graphite and bits of Styrofoam were scattered through her hair, she was exhausted but high, elated in a way that seemed false and temporary, manic.

He wished that he could simply be content with the fame and fortune that he reaped (and it truly was a fortune at this point—in no time, he would be a millionaire), yet each day that the idol fad spread farther, he grew more moody. One night at four in the morning, Eric was sitting behind the counter of Inca's kitchen, insatiably spooning triple-chocolate, double-mint, fudge ice cream straight from the carton, when it occurred to him (not for the first time, but now with new meaning) that if he died tomorrow, his obituary would read: ERIC AUDEN, 27, PROMOTED IDOL FAD. He was not so sure that this was how he wanted to be remembered. He should have been quite happy this summer, right?

*Right*. But he wasn't. He wanted something else, something he couldn't grasp hold of or find at the bottom of an ice cream carton. *What do you want, big boy? Tell me.*

Inca woke up and saw him in the kitchen. She got out of bed, pulled on her robe, and crossed the loft to her drafting board. As she turned on a lamp, she said, more to herself than to Eric, "That last house looked okay, but it's not quite right. It's missing something. Maybe if I cantilevered all of the bedrooms . . ."

"Inca?"

She maneuvered her T-square. She measured a line with her scale.

"Look at all these models." He motioned toward the ant-sized urban sprawl.

"Give it a rest." They had wound through this conversation earlier that night, and Inca ended up in the tub, the bathroom door closed and locked.

"You're out of control," Eric told her now.

"I've never been happier, and you're condemning it?"

"I'm not condemning anything."

She made a break for the bathroom. Eric stuck his foot in the frame before she slammed the door. "You're the one who's out of control, mister," she said.

"You've become manic-depressive. The whole city has become manic-depressive."

"And you have become an arrogant, self-absorbed—"

"Do me a favor and try not to sound like my mother."

"Well, do me a favor and try not to act like my son. Her son." Pause. "I'm not exactly sure what I meant by that."

"Me neither."

"Why are we fighting?"

"We love each other."

They held each other in the dark loft and stared at the humid street.

"Artichokes," Eric said.

"Excuse me?"

He picked up the idol. "We're all artichokes, with layers of leaves, and she picks at us. Slowly and deliberately down to our hearts."

*You might say that the world is my artichoke.*

"Artichokes?" Inca whispered. "Listen, I think that I should take a bath, and maybe you should get some air." So she hopped into her cool tub, and Eric descended to the street, where he sat on the bench outside the café until dawn.

August lumbered along. The Goddess fad showed no intention of abating. Stand-up comics in comedy clubs used the idol to prop up one-liners during their routines. Newspapers appropriated the Goddess for editorial metaphors: Be it European neo-nationalism or South American rain forests or the federal deficit, the Cycladic woman was invoked. One editorial concluded: "Perhaps the best solution would be if each and every one of us had our own Goddess of Desire, if all of us tell her that we're tired of the drugs eating at the very infrastructure of our city. Then the violence might end." Advertising like that was a fad promoter's dream. What could be better than the Mayor appearing at a photo-op with his Goddess clenched like a Rotary award in his pudgy hands? The Mayor, who resembled an ostrich, pressed his beak of a nose to the blank face and kissed the statue. "I gave her my number," the candidate for reelection told the press.

One afternoon, Eric was working in the café when he noticed a man rapidly scrawling all over a legal pad. He filled several pages a minute and ordered extravagant amounts of coffee. Eric asked him what he was writing. "The Great American Novel," the man said, "in longhand." The man stroked a Goddess lying next to him on the booth cushion and then continued scribbling. In fact, there was a lot of writing going on. Eric picked out at least three other people absorbed in letters or stories or rambling poems. One woman asked Eric if she could buy his pencil from him because she had just gone through her third and last pen. An idol was stretched out across the Indian print fabric of her lap. Eric gave her his pencil and wandered out to the street.

Increasingly, he had been drifting away from the Mystery Roast during the day, without announcement, on pure caprice, leaving Andre stranded with a full café. Eric walked east. He saw the Goddess of Desire peeking over a sewing machine in the window of a tailor. He saw one in a plastic vase of water next to a tub of wilting daffodils on a sidewalk stand outside a deli. He saw an idol enjungled among potted plants in an apartment window, and several of them in place of impatiens in the window boxes outside an antiques dealer. A man in a park square had pulled a Goddess free from the mound of empty soda cans that he had piled into a grocery store shopping cart, and he was ranting incoherently at the hydrastone. A young, plump nanny sitting on a bench was doing the same. Her conversation, however, was intelligible and loud: "I know he's going to come back. She can't cook for shit, she doesn't know the Yankees from the Mets, so I know he's coming home." The girls in her charge, deep in a sandbox, were busy burying another idol up to its neck. And at the other end of the square, Eric watched one boy trade a model rocket for a Goddess. Farther east, on the bench outside a sushi bar, he saw three old women resting while their aging mutts panted. Each woman held her own brand-new Goddess (they were still in the boxes). The women, Eric observed, had lapsed into reminiscences about the screen idols of their youth.

On the subway, a man stretched out over a row of plastic seats was asleep, his grip loosening around the idol's legs. Peeking out of a woman's public-television-donor tote bag was the curved brow and bridge of a sloping nose. A young girl who rode the F train with her mother wore a T-shirt, the front of which was silk-screened with a golden rendition of the statue's shape. Under it: LET ME BE YOUR GODDESS. And then leaving the subway, Eric noticed a button worn by the woman selling tokens in the glass booth. In neon pink, her button read: DESIRE ME.

He wandered into an uptown department store. The packaged idols formed a ziggurat near a cash register. As soon as customers snatched the column boxes from the display, a clerk added more.

"Thanks," a rotund woman in a faded plaid raincoat said to the cashier.

Eric approached her as she zipped up her handbag. "Excuse me," he said politely.

The woman checked her watch. "Four twenty-five."

"Thanks, but I wanted to ask you a question, if you don't mind."

"Aren't you a college friend of my daughter's?"

"I'm afraid not. I was wondering what you were planning on doing with the Goddess when you got her home."

"Where I'm going to put it?"

"Not exactly. What do you expect from the idol? Do you expect anything at all?"

"Damn straight," the woman said. "I'm going to give it a piece of my mind about that jerk my daughter married. Of course, I'm going to pray that they work out their problems and save their marriage."

"I see. Thanks, I was just wondering."

"Buy one," the woman said. "You look like you need it."

Eric touched his eyes; his insomnia had made them puffy. A man was at the register now, counting out change. Eric stepped over to him and said, "Excuse me, sir. I was wondering what you were planning on doing with the idol."

"What's it to you?"

"I'm . . . conducting a survey."

The man hurried away from the counter. Eric followed. "All right," the man said, "for science. This little lady is going to help me find a job. I figure I put the babe on the want ads in the morning—you know, let her sit on the newspaper to warm them up—and something good will pop out at me."

Eric looked back at the line of customers creeping toward the register. A teenager with a shopping bag full of glittery halter tops used her mother's credit card. A man in a summer suit checked off items in his date book while he waited. One woman was negotiating a deal on her cellular phone. Another woman, once she had stepped a mere ten paces away from the sales counter, ripped open the package and set the idol on the ground. She dropped to her knees and began to meditate, right in the middle of Ladies' Handbags and Umbrellas. No one passing by seemed to notice her or care.

While Eric was watching her, another woman who had just purchased a Goddess tapped him on the shoulder. "Excuse me, but aren't you . . . ?"

He tried to sight the nearest exit.

"I saw your picture. . . ."

Other people started racing toward him. The woman pulled her idol out of the box. She found a felt-tip pen. Eric signed a hydrastone thigh. Then others closed in and demanded his autograph. Customers began to crowd around just to find out what was going on. He couldn't see beyond the circle of strangers thrusting idols at him. A swarm materialized out of nowhere. Nobody asked him questions or tried to engage in small talk: Everyone wanted his signature, nothing more, and he began to scrawl anywhere he could, on the idol's back, across the span of her crossed arms. He scribbled his name, then half his name, then illegible squiggles. His head spun. Shoes and sandals shuffled toward him. Strangers closed in.

"Excuse me," Eric said, "excuse me." He pushed through the wall of bodies and made his way to the perfume counters. The crowd trailed after him. He nearly knocked a man over as he tumbled through a revolving door. He dashed around the corner and crossed the street and wove his way back into the anonymous throng of people milling about Rockefeller Center.

There was a young woman selling food from a cart, and amid the steam and haze of hot-dog water and pretzel smoke, Eric recognized a pointy nose. There was no escape. *Face it, I'm irresistible.* This summer the ice-skating rink was being kept chilled at great expense, and skaters wearing shorts and T-shirts enacted a winter ritual with surreal nonchalance. Eric tried to lose himself in the motion of the skaters, he tried to forget everything on his mind, but when he looked more closely at the pack of skaters below him, he saw that they all were gliding along in a singular and peculiar path: not a circle, not a figure eight. No, all the skaters in the Rockefeller rink collectively traced a pattern of curves and swerves as if they were outlining one grand Cycladic idol in the ice. *Look what you've done, loverboy. I'm everywhere.*

Once in the not too distant past, Eric had moved about the city with the caution and paranoia of a felon who expected to be arrested. Now he traveled again in fear. His picture had appeared in newspapers and magazines, enough so that he could be identified by the man on the street. The American Dream was all about individuals who offered their ingenuity to the masses and who were rewarded with profit, so he had become a hero, but a hero, however, who knew it was only a matter of time before he was found out, before idol worshipers came after him, broken-hearted, disillusioned, tired of waiting for dreams to come true, tortured by unanswered prayers, wanting someone to blame for their despair.

M. Scott Gold, all the while, ruled over the fad like an arrogant regent running a nation on behalf of a boy-king. He more than monitored it—he nurtured it, played the game carefully, with strategy and cunning. He managed all publicity. He tightened his bow tie and released Eric to the public a little bit at a time, starving a growing cult of personality and then feeding it. He had been offered, for example, a coveted spot on a morning TV show early on, but he had held off on arranging the interview until August when the press had died down somewhat. This way he could set off a new wave of coverage.

M. Scott Gold was in the limousine that picked Eric up before dawn. He said that he wanted to coach him on the way to the network studio. "There's just one thing that troubles me when you do interviews," he whined.

"And what might that be, Scott?" Eric's tolerance for this man was thawing. "I'll say whatever you want me to say."

"When people ask you how you dreamed up the Goddess—"

"What's wrong with an idea hitting you in the shower, or in my case, while staring at the World Trade Center?"

"You sound a little simple. The public wants to see that a complex mind is at work."

"I can talk about Ancient Greece and the historical development of Cycladic—"

"Eric," M. Scott Gold said, annoyed, "cut with the Harvard crap and tell them who you sleep with. Why don't you make up a story?"

One studio beautician patted Eric's face with Pan-Cake makeup while another moussed his hair and blow-dried it to perfection. He was led to the set during the segment that preceded his. He stood on the edge of the sound stage, behind the cameras. He was alone with M. Scott Gold, who whispered, "So what will you say?"

"How did I come up with the idea for the fad?" Eric stared at the monogram on M. Scott Gold's shirt: MSG. "To tell you the truth, Scott, I stole the real one from the museum. And I stared at it for a while, and I came up with the idea of reproducing it."

M. Scott Gold gulped and chortled. "You should incorporate that sort of humor into your persona when you're on the air."

Eric refused to smile.

"You're joking, right?"

"Right now the idol is wrapped in cloth and sitting in a tool box under a drafting table in a former candy factory in the meat-packing district."

M. Scott Gold continued to chuckle but stopped abruptly.

Eric felt free.

"You're joking."

After all this time, the truth was amazingly easy to reveal. He felt as though he were breathing thin air at a higher altitude.

"Eric?" M. Scott Gold did not like to be teased. "C'mon . . ."

A woman wearing a headset approached them when a commercial interrupted the broadcast. The host of the morning show, Greg Dent, nodded hello as Eric was seated and fitted with a microphone tie clip. A makeup man washed Greg's face with a cloth and gave him a touch-up. The host, whom everyone agreed was evening-anchor stuff, dripped saline onto his contacts. "Relax," he said. "We're down in the ratings this week, so there aren't nearly as many viewers watching as you think."

Eric's heart pounded. His throat became dry.

"I'll introduce you and ask you a question or two. Like how you thought up this crazy thing."

Five, four, three, two . . . Greg Dent welcomed back the audience, commented on the spell of nationwide humidity, and reiterated headlines. Then he balanced the Goddess in his palm for Camera 2. He introduced Eric. He began asking him about his background, ascertaining that Eric had no previous experience in business or sculpture. "How then," Greg Dent asked, "did you ever conceive of this . . . crazy thing?"

Camera 2 focused on the idol again. The red light lit up on the camera aimed at Eric. He could count valuable, promotional seconds ticking away.

Ever accommodating, Greg Dent began to answer his own question. "I read somewhere that you were looking out at the World Trade Center one night . . ."

Eric glanced over at M. Scott Gold, who was wearing a grim face of concern and puzzlement.

". . . and if I remember your comments correctly, you saw a vision of the silhouette of the Cycladic idol, the one stolen from the New York Museum of Art last January. . . ."

Everyone was looking at Eric. Greg Dent, M. Scott Gold, technicians offstage, viewers at home. Eric blinked at Greg, glanced over at M. Scott, and then back at Greg. "I know it might sound strange to some people, but that's basically how it happened."

Later, M. Scott Gold bear-hugged Eric. "You really had me fooled, kiddo. For a minute there, I thought you were going to go psycho on national television. But I couldn't have asked for a better performance."

"Great," Eric said, moving swiftly toward an exit. For an instant, he had pondered a confession before an unseen audience, transmitted, on tape, irreversible. He would have been free, but the moment was lost.

At home, Inca was waiting for him by the elevator. Her eyes were red. "Great show, but I have bad news." Her hair, long now, was falling loose from a braid. She had been crying.

"That goddamned idol," Eric muttered. "She did this to you."

"The idol didn't *do* anything. But it's gone."

Eric hopped over scale models. The idol wasn't on her usual muse-throne on Inca's desk. The tool box was wide open, empty. "What do you mean *it's gone?*"

Despite this alarming revelation, Inca was eerily rational: "Someone or some people broke in here while I was watching the show with Andre downstairs, and they stole the idol. We've been burglarized, Eric. Yes, it's gone, I looked everywhere."

"Maybe the police came and—"

"What police? There weren't any police, Eric. Look, they took most of my freebie appliances, too." Most of the blenders and bread makers had been cleaned out. "They also took some of my more expensive architectural equipment, my silver fountain pen, some cash, and I'm sure they went into the tool box thinking that they'd find power tools or jewelry or something."

She had apparently had time to apply reason to the wound, but he panicked. "This is not good. This is definitely not good."

"We live in a city where a million people are burglarized every minute."

"Yes, but now I'm afraid that whoever stole the idol from us will try to sell it, and then the person who buys it will fuck up and be picked off by the F.B.I., and in a plea bargain, the black-market trader will point his finger at the burglar, who will point his finger at me, because I am, after all, the bigger fish."

"Will you calm down? Whoever stole the idol probably thought it was a Redelarte spin-off. A gallery version, if that. He's going to get five grand for it in some dark alley, but he's not going to know that it's the real thing. No way."

Eric acknowledged the irony with a nod.

"Look," Inca said, "I feel as horrible as you do about losing a museum treasure like that. It's terrible. But there's nothing we can do. Nothing. We can't exactly call the cops. We just have to live with this and move on. Just let the idol go, Eric. Let it go."

Let it go? On the one hand, he was relieved not to have to worry about ever being caught with the museum artifact in his possession, but he still felt vulnerable. Vulnerable and lost. He massaged his temples and happened to glance at the building across the street. Wait. On top of a loudly rattling air conditioner, he saw the idol. It made sense: Whoever lived across the street had spied on him and Inca as easily as he looked back now. An unknown neighbor had seen the real idol and come in for the kill when no one was home. No, no, no. He strained his eyes, and he could see that the figurine on the air conditioner across the street was standing erect by its own volition—well, with the aid of a manufactured base. It was factory-made, never touched by ancient hands.

He could not let go. He had to find the idol. But there were a million Cycladic figures out there, and he had no idea where to begin looking.

Later that same morning, Timothy knocked on Lydia's door. He didn't really expect her to be home on a weekday, but she greeted him in a bathrobe, and he thought that he saw another person, a man, pass by in the room beyond the foyer. "Hi," he said shyly.

"I thought the doorman was playing games with me," Lydia said and pulled him toward her in a hug. She looked older: thinner and grayer. "Come in."

Timothy didn't move. "I didn't think you'd be here."

"I've been taking Fridays off this summer and heading out to the country early." She tucked a loose lock of hair behind her ear. "We're running a little late today—"

"I just stopped by to say hi."

"Don't you want to come in? It's good to see you. It's been a while."

The man walked past the doorway again, in and out of view too quickly to get a good look. "I don't know if you remember," Timothy said, "but when I would, um, want to talk, you used to take me to Mae's Diner—"

"Just me and you. Sure, I remember." Lydia nodded. "There's a coffee shop around the corner. Let me put something on."

The coffee shop was designed to look like a country garden: One wall was decorated with a whitewashed wood lattice in which plastic vines and white Christmas lights were interwoven. Timothy's impulse was to order a milk shake while in Lydia's company, but he decided to be a bit more sophisticated and asked for some coffee. One balmy summer night she had taught him her trick for removing a lobster tail from its shell. He remembered now how she held his hands. She guided a knife steadily along the belly-side of the lobster. The white meat magically slipped out.

"I thought Eric looked smart this morning on 'Hello, World with Greg Dent,' " Lydia said. "Although he needs to pick up the pace with his answers. I should know, I used to do the occasional spot on the news. If you don't fold everything into neat, crisp sentences, they won't use your clips."

"Eric was on television?"

"He did look a little tired."

"I haven't see much of him lately," Timothy confessed. "Or anyone."

"Well, well, well. Congratulations."

"Thank you. For . . . ?"

"I've been following your rise. I always knew that you would do something with your art, Tim. I always knew that if you wanted to—"

"But Mrs. Maldemer—I mean . . ."

"Lydia."

"This is my problem: I'm not who everyone thinks I am, and I don't really like who I'm supposed to be." He described the past months, his success, his loneliness. He talked in honest terms that he never even allowed to surface when he was lying under his shower. "Let's face it, I'm a poseur."

"You're being very hard on yourself." Lydia sipped her coffee and winced. "You know what I really want? A malted. Waiter?"

Timothy pushed his coffee cup against the wall. "Make it a double order."

"I owe you an apology. You know your exhibit in the men's room at NYMA last winter? I'm afraid Eric told me about it, and I know a curator, and I spilled the beans to him—"

"Those were the days. But please, you don't need to apologize."

"You don't have to do everything Eduardo Redelarte and his minions tell you to do. You're the boss. You've made some money and established your name, so take some time off. Figure out where to go from here."

"You always make everything sound so easy."

"Sorry," Lydia said.

"I meant that as a compliment. I have another problem. There's a man named Andre. He owns the café—"

"Men. Say no more. I mean, say more if you want to."

"I remember that last summer we spent together, you, Eric, and me. Eric kept inviting Lisa Bloom to the house. She came out practically every weekend."

Lydia rolled her eyes. "That girl needed a good washing. And I desperately wanted to clip that hideous macramé bracelet off her ankle. It was so filthy."

"I used to clear out of Eric's room at night so Lisa could come in from the guest room to sleep with him. He thought you didn't know."

"I knew," Lydia said. The waiter placed a tall chocolate frappe in front of her.

Timothy slurped his shake slowly. "In the mornings, she used to take her shower, and Eric would walk in and out of the bathroom like they were married. It drove me nuts. He was way ahead of me in some unspoken competition because he wasn't a virgin anymore. I used to try to peek in when he opened the door, not because I wanted to see what Lisa looked like naked, but because I wanted to know what it was that Eric was attracted to. What he wanted, what I could never give him. That was when I knew what was what and who I was, which I didn't really want to believe. I came to you, and we went to Mae's. . . . You were amazing when I came out. I've always wanted to tell you that."

Lydia leaned back in the diner booth. "I did not think that I was amazing. There you were being honest and courageous, and all I thought at the time, I remember, was that you were making a wrong choice. It was as if you were choosing a college whose reputation I questioned."

"You didn't let on. You congratulated me."

"It took a while for your news to sink in. But I'm glad, if I helped," Lydia said. "I know it's a little early in the day for French fries, but . . . Waiter?"

"And some onion rings."

Soon Timothy and Lydia were dipping various deep-fried vegetables into puddles of ketchup and drawing in chocolate malted milk shakes through bent plastic straws. This was the sort of coffee shop that still gave you the extra frappe in its metal blender cup.

"So what about this Andre man?" Lydia asked. She reached across the table and placed her hand over Timothy's. "Did he break your heart?"

"It's been going on for years, Lydia, years." Timothy offered a terse outline of his romantic life. "I was relieved when we broke off once and for all, but now I want him in the worst way. He told me that he might be leaving the city, and I felt exactly the way I did when I realized why I was stealing peeks at Lisa Bloom's bony hips, and it wasn't for the reasons I tricked myself into believing it was. See, I always thought of Andre as temporary: We were traveling somewhere together, and then we'd say good-bye when we arrived at a grand, Victorian train station, where there'd be lots of smoke and ladies with small dogs. He'd hop aboard one train, I'd get on a different one. But now that he's announced that he wants to move away, I know that he's it for me, he's the one. We're supposed to be on the same train."

Lydia sat back in her chair, tears welling in her eyes. "You grew up."

"The thing is . . . I've said 'I love you' so many times, I don't think he believes me anymore."

Lydia wiped a gob of ketchup from the corner of her mouth. "I believe you."

Timothy almost said, That's because you're my mother. "I've cried wolf."

"Just take a deep breath"—Lydia inhaled, breathed out—"look the guy in the eye, and say—"

"Another shake?" the waiter asked.

Timothy nodded. "It's good to talk about it."

"Eric never came to me for advice," Lydia said. "He's like me. He has to fight the world alone. I envy you. You can send out for help. It's a talent, you know."

"All this time has passed, and I haven't even asked you what's going on in your life these days."

"Oh, you know. Work. I've been seeing that curator I mentioned."

"You don't sound happy about it?"

"I don't? Oh, no, no, I'm quite happy. Yes, he makes me feel young and—" She stopped as if to ask, Why am I telling you this? "Do you remember Jason Maldemer?"

"He once told Eric and me that he wanted to go fishing, so we got Eric's father's old fishing poles down from your attic, and the three of us got up really early the next morning. But it turned out that Jason's idea of fishing was to visit a hatchery and watch a fish lay eggs. Very strange. But we had a lot of fun anyway."

The waiter delivered two more chocolate milk shakes.

"I've been seeing a bit of him, too," Lydia said.

"You're kidding. I didn't know that Jason Maldemer was out and about. I heard somewhere that he had either founded or joined some cult in New Mexico."

"No, he didn't do that, but he's not exactly strolling the streets either."

"So you're seeing two men at the same time?"

"Yes," Lydia said. "I mean no. No, no. I'm *seeing* Marek the curator, and just *visiting* Jason."

"Jason had a way of making obsessive behavior seem perfectly normal."

"Right now I feel like I'm seventeen," Lydia said. "Eating French fries and gossiping about the boys." She sucked on her straw. "Look, about Andre: Sometimes the best people are the ones you go back to over and over. The people you fight with—the people you *can* fight with. The ones you . . ."

"The ones you what?" Timothy asked intently. He hung on her every word as though she were assigning him a mantra. "Lydia?"

"The point is, you just have to get back on the horse. Ride that wave all the way to the shore. Oh, no. I'm mixing my metaphors, I think."

Timothy decided to walk home. His T-shirt was soaked with sweat after only ten blocks, yet he felt energized, at least as powerful as the parching sun. At one point he passed a man standing on a relatively empty West Side corner, a man wearing just a raincoat, nothing else except sneakers, and Timothy was sure that he was going to be flashed. When he passed him, the man pulled a paper grocery bag out of his coat. "Camcorder," he said in a gravelly voice.

Timothy stopped and turned back toward the man. "For real?"

"Hundred bucks."

The bag looked like it was weighted with something. "Where'd you get it?"

"A truck."

"Not from someone's house?"

"What the fuck—who the—what do you think I am, buddy?" The man rubbed his unshaven face. He combed back greasy hair. "In all my . . . Never, never," he mumbled and walked away.

"Wait!" Timothy called after him. "Can I see it?"

"Potluck," the man said, dangling the bag.

Timothy took a step back to count his cash. "Forty-three, that's all I've got," he bargained.

The man handed him the bag at the same time that he took the cash, and then turned the corner and ran away fast, his coattails flying up behind him. Timothy was pleasantly surprised to find a video camcorder in the bag. In its box, too, brand new. He knew he was a fool to think that it was going to be functional, not for forty-three dollars. He walked into a hardware store and bought batteries and a blank cassette tape with cash from another pocket. He held the camera to his eye and pulled the trigger. The tape heads moved and the camera buzzed. The record light went on when he pointed it at a passing truck.

Timothy continued walking downtown and started filming snatches of whatever intrigued him, images that caught his eye: a woman screaming Bible passages at a line of people buying half-priced theater tickets, a girl showing off her gleaming new braces to a friend, a messenger in tight bike pants, cardboard tubes strapped to his back. He walked past a small park where some boys were playing with a golden retriever, tossing a Frisbee to the dog over and over. He got a good shot of the dog, faithful and tireless, waddling back to the boys with the saucer in his mouth. Then Timothy's tape ran out. He wandered around until he found another store that stocked blank cassettes, and he bought a dozen more.

ric knew that he was a thief, a grand larcenist at that, but he couldn't think like one. Somewhere in the big city, however, there was a black market in art. He didn't know where to begin looking for it, so he started a probe close to home amid the murky agora under the abandoned el. Some prostitutes told him to talk to a man sitting in the backseat of a long white sedan parked in the darkest corner of the stretch. When Eric rapped his knuckles on the tinted car window, the man opened the door and invited him in to his office. Eric left the door open and kept one foot planted on the pavement. The man wore a white baseball cap and white fur coat despite the temperature, sunglasses in the darkness, and he was in the process of trying out his newly repaired car fax, which he said was constantly breaking down from overuse. He had not heard about any stolen art floating around, no, but he could offer Eric some "grade-A flesh-squeeze." Eric declined, and the man told him where he could get some "super-classy smoke" over on West Fourteenth. Eric said no thank you. Finally, the man in the fur coat sold him an address for fifty dollars. The address was of a local used-typewriter repair shop, where a woman was surrounded by shelves of dinosaur-era office machines. She was hard to understand, what with a type bar hanging out of her mouth like a toothpick, with her head half-submerged under the hood of a vintage Selectric, but Eric ascertained (for another fifty dollars) that he should explore the world of pawn shops. One in particular. If Eric had nothing to sell, a pawn-shop dealer all the way east on the East Side told him, then he would have to put down a C-note for information. Eric learned about a place that unbeknownst to many was the true headquarters for the illegal bartering of highfalutin commodities. So next he waded through the dense human traffic of the diamond district, through the web of men in black frock coats, coats covered in dandruff, coats bulging with cash-filled manila envelopes. He ended up quizzing two elderly brothers whose beards looked like spun sugar and whose small store of glass counters and mirrored cabinets was so packed with their crystal wares, their raw gems, that Eric felt trapped inside a prism. He asked where he should go if he was interested in making certain acquisitions (he was as ambiguous as he could be), but the men were no help. They were only interested in selling him the largest emerald he had ever seen. It looked radioactive. Eric returned to the pawn-shop circuit, but after a week of random investigations and expensive tips that led nowhere, he was convinced that his search was futile. He gave up.

Inca showed no interest in helping him, which was in itself a source of frustration. In fact, she became angry with Eric for bothering to hunt at all. "I don't see why you can't just let it go," she said more than once. "It's gone forever. Frankly, Eric, I would have thought that you were the sort of person who by now would have accepted what's happened and moved on." At first when they lay in bed at night, they faced each other. Then Inca turned away, and Eric inched over so that he could kiss the back of her neck, her shoulders, so that he could reach his arm across her stomach, her thigh. But she wiggled out of his grasp. He pursued her to the edge of the bed. She shot up, and he called after her, pleading, but she said, "It's so hot in here," as she nevertheless donned her kimono and retreated to her drafting board, where she worked under a hot crane lamp. Eric ended up in his own loft, lying awake in the gray stillness, and then in his bathtub, where he pointed a fan at the water. Before long, he was sleeping alone twice a week, then every other day, and then every night. Inca didn't come into the café when he was there, and he made no effort to visit her loft. He felt like a satellite falling out of orbit, spinning slowly in a gradually narrower spiral, only vaguely aware of his descent, until with a single plunge, he would smash into the wall of the atmosphere.

Finally one night, Eric went down to Inca's. She was out, he didn't know where, and so he stripped and climbed under the single sheet on her bed. He fell asleep and was jolted awake at some late hour when she came home, presumably saw him in her bed, and turned on every lamp. Eric's eyes refused to adjust, and Inca started prattling about the movie she'd just seen or something Andre had said. After puttering for a good half-hour, she unstrapped her sandals and sat at the foot of the bed as if she were visiting a sick friend. Eric sat up and reached toward her. "I don't think so," she said.

He fell back against the pillows, became hot, sweaty under the sheet, and when he could no longer stand the silence, he cleared his throat and asked, "So is this it?" He was more shocked by how easily the words came to him than by the horror of what he suggested.

"We should never have let it get this far," Inca answered, even and aloof, staring at the floor. She stood up, retreated to her drafting board, and threw herself into the uncharacteristic tidying of her desk.

A thousand pointed rebuttals came to mind all at once, but Eric's throat went dry. He couldn't swallow. After so much intimacy, he was suddenly embarrassed by his nudity. He wrapped himself in Inca's sheet, quickly collected his clothes from the floor, and made his way to the elevator, still wrapped in the bedding.

He sank into a familiar jet lag, a specific numbness he had forgotten about, a loss of all appetites except for sleep and wandering. He was furious at himself for putting up no fight, for oiling the cogs of the breakup by asking if the end was truly the end, and depressed by the inevitable cycle of predictable turns in his life, by a clock he naïvely believed he had learned to read. Most of the immediate anger he felt came from the frustration of not remembering pain: It all seemed new when in fact it should have been a cliché for him. This was how it began, with the methodical dismantling of everything secure and dear. Soon he would nap away the day; soon he would slip into a constant funk, the feeling that he was perpetually traveling to a distant time zone.

He enjoyed working in the Mystery Roast less and less until it became a chore, until he could barely tolerate the customers, who had grown volatile and impatient during particularly feral dog days. The ceiling fans whirling at full speed did nothing to cool tempers. Eric passed among the tables to deliver cucumber soup and cucumber sandwiches and was assaulted by loud, confident pronouncements: "Costa Rican Tarrazu!" from a man dressed all in white, hat to shoes. "No, it's Indian Mysore!" from a woman with lavender-painted fingernails who fanned herself with her menu. "Brazilian Bourbon Santos!" from an old man who tapped out each syllable with his cane.

They wouldn't accept a compromise of uncertain blends, not in this heat, not this summer, and Eric felt inadequate at first when he failed to ease their anxieties, then just angry that all of these people were nagging him, expecting him to provide answers.

"What do you mean you don't know for sure?" The man dressed in white accidentally dripped espresso on his lap and ran out of the café without paying. "I know I'm right. I'm right, aren't I?" the woman asked, desperate. And the old man grunted: "I haven't got the time for games, young man. I never know when I'm drinking my last cup."

At six-thirty one evening, Eric broke away, despite the packed early-dinner crowd, and escaped to his loft to watch the top news stories. A familiar face appeared. He hadn't seen her in months. "And so today's revelations," Margot reported, "about the tax returns that Robinson Perez failed to file from 1983 through 1986 have forced the former Congressman and Borough President to end his campaign for Mayor." The candidate was at a press conference. "Perez aides say that his bid was cut short not by scandal, but by a lack of necessary funds in an age of rising advertising costs. We will see in the upcoming days whether the Justice Department decides to order an official investigation. Margot Brandon, New York."

New York? He picked up the phone. He would tell her that he was sorry that she was losing the cornerstone of her series. He called Information and got the number for the network, then dialed it but hung up before the receptionist connected him. He brushed his hair, put on a clean shirt, cologne, and went downstairs. In fifteen minutes, he had taxied his way to Midtown and was speaking face to face with the same receptionist whom he'd just hung up on. A security guard combed a wand that looked like an electric toothbrush over his limbs and torso. The receptionist told him to wait in the lobby, and before he had a chance to change his mind or figure out what had come over him, his ex-wife, untelevised, sensibly dressed in a skirt of the season's length, a collarless jacket, and a string of pearls, was striding toward him down a ramped hallway, her arms outstretched, a practiced smile greeting him. Her hair was pulled back into a tight, sprayed ponytail, her small ears exposed, her stage makeup caked on. Was she taller or was it her shoes that gave her an extra inch on him now?

"This is a surprise, Eric. It's really wonderful to see you."

They kissed each other on each cheek like European school chums. They hugged quickly. Her body felt bony, frail.

"What brings you—"

"I just saw your spot," Eric said. "I was sorry to hear the news."

Margot glanced at her watch. "Were you watching in a neighborhood bar?"

"I was home. I'm living downtown. I took a cab. Listen, do you want to get some coffee?"

"Well, actually . . . Okay, sure. But we're doing a seven o'clock feed—"

"I'll wait. You look great."

"Lots to talk about," Margot said and rushed back up the ramp into the studio.

Eric sat in the lobby and watched the news as it was aired again for other cities in the country. Margot reprised her performance and sounded less anguished about the candidate's withdrawal this time.

"I can't go far," she said when she returned. "I'm doing the late show and maybe a couple of segments for the affiliates." Her shoulders and torso were lost amid the padding of her jacket. "Is the commissary okay?" He tried to remember where the real frame of her body fell within her clothing.

It had been a long time since Eric had been in a network cafeteria. It had been a long time since he sat across a table from Margot. They batted tidbits of family news back and forth. Margot told Eric about some of the people they knew in college, about a favorite professor who was retiring, about her mother's successful battle against cancer.

"I'm glad to hear she's okay," Eric said. "It's too bad about Perez."

"I liked him as a person. But hey, I got an exclusive interview. It's the business I'm in: One man's defeat is my victory." She pulled a black velvet bow out of her hair and let it fall over her shoulders, only to pull it back again. She retied the ribbon. "Well, you've been busy, and I must say that I'm astonished. I caught you with Greg Dent. I said to Ben, 'I was married to that man.' "

"Ben?"

" 'Hello, World'—that was great. What I'd give for Greg Dent's job. So congratulations. I never thought you'd do anything like this. You must be very happy these days. I hope you are."

Eric didn't answer. Who was Ben?

"Do you like being famous?"

"In a way, I think I understand some of what you were going through . . . toward the end. But you're really famous, Margot. I'm just a little famous for the time being."

"Still, it can be annoying sometimes, can't it?"

"I keep thinking about the time when we were celebrating our third anniversary of being together, before we were married. We were all set to go out to celebrate just by ourselves, dinner somewhere with candles and wine in a bucket, when Barbara Flashman showed up at the door."

"You were mad that I told her it was our anniversary."

"She gave us a bowl. It was a very nice bowl, but I didn't want to share that moment in our lives with her. I wanted it to be our secret. That's the way it feels now. I don't mean to sound paranoid or ungrateful, but I feel like something's been taken away from me."

"Without having met you, people think they know what makes you laugh. They think they know what your favorite color is and how you take your coffee."

"Don't talk to me about coffee."

"A man today just handed me a mug with cream in it. Cream! And after I did that comparative study of incumbents' high cholesterol counts . . ."

Eric wasn't sure why he had come to see her. What did he want to tell her? "This has nothing to do with fame or public exposure, but I think I'm messing up again, Margot."

"Messing up? I'm not sure I follow." She stared at the linoleum table as if she damn well knew what he meant but didn't want to discuss anything too heavy.

"Like I did with you. I found someone, and I've lost her."

Margot nodded like a therapist. "You didn't *mess up* with me, Eric."

"No, I know now that I wasn't very—"

"You were you, and I was whoever I was. We were growing up."

"I know that," Eric said. He did.

"You were always too serious."

"You're telling *me* this? You were very serious, too, my dear." Through all of her makeup, she seemed to be blushing. "Remember our trip to Santa Fe? And when we tried to use the self-timer at Ghost Ranch?"

"That was a terrible fight." Who broke the camera was the issue, at least on the surface.

"We should have laughed at ourselves, but we didn't."

"I wish we had."

"I'd laugh now. What about you?"

"I'd laugh. At least I hope that I'd laugh."

"Good. I've learned not to take everything so seriously. I don't exclusively go to serious, tearjerker movies the way I used to." Margot pulled a small, palm-sized mirror from her pocket and checked the corners of her mouth for crumbs. "I can't, if I'm going to spend my whole day reporting hard news. I can only afford to read novels that make me giggle." She paused as if she expected Eric to respond.

"Great."

"I'm off to Alaska again tomorrow. It's very calm and serene there. Very raw. Far away, but I like it."

"Not too serious a place, I hope, for your sake."

"So if I'm back in the city . . . ?"

"You should call."

"Maybe we can grab a late-afternoon salad or something. I know a place that makes a phenomenal salad."

"I'd like that." Eric knew she wouldn't call: For one thing, she didn't have his number, and he wasn't listed. He wasn't certain he wanted her to call. He stepped into the night and was sad not because Margot seemed unchanged or because he couldn't remember why he had been so deeply in love with her once, but because seeing his ex-wife reminded him of innocence and lost youth and all those hackneyed, sentimental presents that people from the past brought with them. He was only twenty-seven, almost twenty-eight, and age was a phenomenon he had become aware of. He didn't feel old, but he had a chunk of time to account for. History, time lost. Perhaps he had expected to see Margot and lapse back to a less complicated state of mind, but all the encounter did was rekindle an urge once again in his life to get on a plane, any plane, and travel to a place where he didn't speak the language.

When he returned to the café, the place was stuffed beyond its full capacity, and Andre greeted him at the door. He was covered from head to toe with smudges of chocolate and flour and cucumber peels. There was a slice of turnip stuck to his elbow, a sliver of carrot over his eyebrow. He looked exhausted, and Eric's response, a nervous, unexpected chuckle, was probably unwelcome. "Look, smarty-pants, if you're going to go out wandering whenever you feel like it—"

"I told you to hire a prep-cook."

"I did. Tonight. I had to. But he dumped too many olives into my gazpacho, not to mention the fact that he burned my croutons to a crisp. I fired him. So look, if you're going to go wandering—"

"What exactly," a woman interrupted, "does a person have to do to get some service around here?" She was wearing a gray suit and a matching tweed hat with a feather, and she was banging a rolled-up *Playbill* on the edge of the bar.

"I just can't do this anymore." Andre disappeared into the kitchen.

"What can I get you?" Eric asked the woman.

"I understand there's a splendid chicken salad platter here. I'll have that and a cup of tea."

He patted the defunct samovar. "Unfortunately, no one can have tea at the Mystery Roast. The samovar doesn't work. It's just for show."

"Well, that's absurd. I've just walked out on the most dreadful piece of theater, full of nonsensical screaming and cross-dressing, and now you're telling me that your samovar doesn't work? What's there not to work about a samovar? It isn't a broken spigot, is it?"

"I think that might be the problem."

"I've seen this before. We—and when I say we, I'm referring to the distinguished ensemble with which I had an affiliation for many, many years—we used to do a great deal of Chekhov. The gizmo just needs jiggling."

"I don't think I should play with it. Maybe I can find some tea bags in the kitchen."

"Heavens. Just put the water in, and I'll come around and fiddle with it."

"I don't know," Eric said. He looked through the diamond-shaped window in the kitchen door and saw that Andre was pacing.

"Go on," the woman said impatiently.

Eric removed the teapot from the top of the samovar. He filled a pitcher with spring water so he could dump it in the urn. He lifted the lid off.

*I've been buried in a crypt for thousands of years. I've been smothered in parlors filled with cigar smoke. I've been packed in a crate and flown across dangerous oceans.*

"This production was horrible," the woman waiting for tea said. She shuddered. "If the Bard wanted to see Lear in drag driving around the stage in a souped-up golf cart, he would have written Lear in drag driving around in a golf cart."

Eric stood on his toes. He had almost drowned the Ausgraben Idol.

*I was misplaced for two days in museum storage, but I have never, ever, in all my centuries, been trapped in a samovar.*

"Who put you here?" Eric whispered.

"Excuse me?" the woman asked.

*Get me out of here before somebody caffeinates me.*

"Shush."

"I beg your pardon?"

"I'll just take this into the kitchen," Eric said and carefully lifted the heavy urn.

"Really, all you have to do is jiggle the—" The woman stood up and watched him swing through the kitchen doorway. She looked ready to follow, but through the window, Eric saw her sit back down.

Andre, however, was waiting for him, fuming, his brow wet with the green steam from the artichokes he was preparing. "I have to know whether you're in or out. What are you doing with that?"

Eric set the samovar down on a counter. "Fixing it."

"Do you care about the café or don't you? I have to tell you that I've been thinking about—"

"Andre?" Eric grabbed a cloth napkin off a counter. "Are you asking me to quit?"

"Not exactly . . ."

"Then I quit. Okay? Is that what you want?"

"Eric—"

"I quit."

"Fine. Fine with me." Andre wiped his forehead with a dishrag, slung it over his shoulder, and walked into the café.

Eric removed the idol from the samovar, wrapped it in the cloth napkin, and hurried up the back staircase. Andre didn't exactly flinch at the sight of the broken urn. Who hid her? Whatever the answer was, Eric knew that he had to stash the artifact somewhere safe, a place that only he knew about and not in the Mystery Roast building. In his loft, he put the idol, still cloaked in the napkin, in a canvas shoulder bag. He rode the elevator down to the lobby. When he passed the café, he saw the woman at the bar, exasperated, wagging her *Playbill* at Andre.

Eric ran fast and looked over his shoulder now and then, although he wasn't sure who he expected to see following him. Then he slowed down and merely walked at a clipped pace so that he wouldn't draw attention. He entered the subway and made his way toward the only safe house he could think of. Of course, there was risk involved, but he didn't have anywhere else to go.

Lydia, unfortunately, was home, lying stretched out on the long couch in her living room, reading Hardy and making her way through a deep bowl of red flame grapes.

"Hello, hello." She was wearing a bathrobe. "What's the occasion?"

"I was in the neighborhood." He kissed his mother on the cheek and tore off a sprig of fruit. "Is Marek around?"

"He'll be here soon. I'm supposed to be dressing. We're going to a party."

"I don't want to keep you." Eric put the bag down on a chair.

"You're not keeping me," Lydia said. "But what brings you by?"

"Really, I was just in the neighborhood."

"I wish you'd called first. I could have planned to spend some time with you. What's up?" She walked into the kitchen and Eric followed. "Want a beer?"

"No thanks. Nothing's up. Hey, these grapes are delicious." They were unseasonably sweet. He smelled basil in the air. "What were you cooking?"

"Pesto, with basil from Marek's garden. Do you want some cold pasta?"

"Not really."

Lydia removed a plastic container from the refrigerator and placed it on the counter. "Help yourself. So, really, how have you been?"

"Great. Nothing new to report. And you?"

"Me? Same as I ever was. Too bad about Rob Perez, isn't it?"

"I thought you'd be wearing a black arm band. I went to the studio and saw Margot, believe it or not, right after she broke the news."

"No kidding? And how is she?" Lydia cocked her head at him.

"Great. Well, actually, she's the same."

"What did you expect?"

"I'm not sure." Eric was torn: He wanted his mother to disappear so he could hide the idol and at the same time wanted her to linger in the kitchen.

Lydia reached into a drawer and pulled out a fork. "Eat."

He opened the container and leaned against the counter. He twisted his fork in the fettuccine and swallowed several mouthfuls of it, which tasted verdant and cheesy. "Mmm. Want some? I'm not really hungry." He continued eating.

"I have to get in the shower," his mother said but stayed put instead and watched him, smiling the way she did on the days when by some freak miracle, he had eaten breakfast (even if a milk shake constituted a meal). She was graying faster these days. He couldn't remember what she had looked like when her hair was dark like his. Her cheeks were rough and there were lines above her brow, by her eyes, beneath her nose. She had lived and endured a lot. She was a walking encyclopedia of lore, full of tidbits about nineteenth-century novels and the latest in jet propulsion, not to mention the history of warring nations. His mother knew about other things, too, about how to use only the best, shiny, heart-shaped basil leaves for pesto, about nocturnal raids on potato fields. She knew things: Why did he always forget this? He wanted to sit her down and ask her: What do you think I should do with this ancient idol? Because he had to get out of this mess he was in. He had to get out and then travel far away.

"Mom?"

"Eric?"

He sighed. She waited. She probably knew that he was on the brink of saying something significant, but she was the most patient person in the world, perhaps too patient. He didn't know where to start because he was inclined to begin before the theft at the museum, before his return to New York. "Do you use just Parmesan, or is there some Romano in this, too?"

"Romano is vital: a quarter-cup for each cup of Parmesan."

"Pine nuts or walnuts?"

"Walnuts are meatier, grainier, so I use them."

"It's delicious." Pause. "You don't want to hold Marek up. I'll probably be gone by the time you get out of the shower."

"Call the next time you decide to stop by." Lydia didn't move, however. She looked him up and down. He almost expected her to tell him that he had grown an inch. She kissed him on the forehead and finally left him alone.

Once he heard the shower running, Eric grabbed his bag and pulled out the wrapped idol. The kitchen cupboards were stuffed. He thought about stashing the artifact behind some baking ingredients in the pantry—his mother never baked these days. But what if Marek had a birthday coming up and she decided to make him a cake? In the living room, there wasn't enough room behind the records in a cabinet, and given his mother's propensity for rereading novels, he didn't dare hide the treasure behind books. The linen closet was packed. Every closet in his old bedroom was packed. His mother never threw away anything and never threatened to. She had a bad habit of only cleaning when she was breaking up with a man. He skipped into her bedroom and was stumped. Lydia was singing in the shower, a pretty melody Eric didn't know. And then the song stopped. His mother turned off the water.

He was out of time, trapped, with only the minutes left that it would take for his mother to dry her hair. He bolted into her walk-in closet, a double-racked room with a geologically dense crustation of never-worn clothes. Think, he told himself, think fast. There was one dress, he remembered, with deep pockets, where he used to stash dope when he was a teenager—right under his mother's nose, where she'd least expect to find it, and she never did. Plump dime bags fit nicely into those pockets. Not the best hiding place, but he had no choice, he had to get out of here.

Eric crawled over shoe boxes to the back of the closet, to a second bar of dresses. It was the ugliest and most out-of-date frock, a minidress with no sleeves and big black buttons, a light wool dress in an oversized black houndstooth pattern. Had his mother ever really worn clothes like this? He pulled back the cloth napkin. The idol crossed her arms in indignation.

*I can't stand a hero who fights a few battles and then quits the war.*

"You've caused a lot of sorrow."

*I like my heroes to run the full course of a myth. There's no glory in retreat.*

Eric wrapped her up again and stuffed her into the dress pocket. *You can hide me anywhere you like, but it's too late.* He straightened the dress. *It's too late, because I am already everywhere.* He straightened the other clothes. *Everywhere.*

"Fuck off," Eric said and left his mother's apartment.

hat?" Lydia called out as she emerged from her bathroom. She thought that she had heard something. "Eric? Marek?" She wrapped herself in towels, wandered into the kitchen, and put away the pasta. Minutes ago, she had looked her son up and down, her near–mirror image, looked at him as she had countless times. He was handsome and smart: This wasn't a revelation, but a reaffirmation. If they had difficulty staying friendly, it was because they were so similar. Did he know that?

Marek waltzed in a short while later. "You're not ready?" He looked atypically well-groomed. His blue blazer was not rumpled at the elbows, and he had white sail pants on, crisp, pressed, and glowing. He looked different, handsome as always, but costumed.

"Do we really have to go anywhere tonight?"

"Darling, I loathe these soirees just as much as you do. I would love nothing more than an evening home, you know that. Alas, this is an important party. I've got to keep tabs on my painting, and I fear that if I don't have you by my side, I will—"

"Okay, okay." Lydia retreated into her closet. She filed through her dresses. A hand from behind pulled off her towel. "Frisky," she said and turned around.

Marek tossed his jacket on a chair, his ironed trousers on the floor. She pulled him onto the bed. When she closed her eyes, she and Marek were punting along a little-known English tributary. The river was theirs.

Later, Marek climbed out from under Lydia's duvet. "Now we're more than fashionably late." He retrieved his boxer shorts from under the sheets.

"I have an idea. Let's take turns reading *Middlemarch* aloud."

Marek had pulled on his pants and drifted into the bathroom. "Now, now, I just gave you something that you wanted—"

"What I wanted?" she whispered. "What *I* wanted?"

"—so you can do this for me. I'll help you dress."

Before she could inform her lover that she had been dressing herself since she was five, Marek, buttoning his shirt, was standing in her closet. "Do you even wear half of these clothes?"

"I think I wear the same seven dresses. Hand me my Tuesday one, will you?"

Marek peeled back fabric from the front rack to see what was in the back. "Look at that lamé jumpsuit."

"I bought it to cheer myself up when the Senate went Republican in 'eighty. I've never worn it."

"This pink dress is nice," Marek said, pulling out a jumper.

"Too casual."

Marek reached even further back in time and grabbed hold of a black houndstooth, short dress with big black buttons that Lydia remembered fondly. He was about to lift it off the rack.

"If you think I'm going to wear that—"

"It's very contemporary-looking. The Sixties look is in now. *Très chic, cherie.*"

"—to a party at Polly Stewart's, you are so mistaken that I wonder if you know me at all." She did not know what made her so angry.

Marek let the dress fall back into line with the others. "I'm sorry that I'm dragging you out. . . ."

Lydia pulled a red number out without really bothering to examine it. "No, I'm sorry that I snapped."

Marek sat on the edge of the bed and tied his shoes. "Oh, say. We may have found another piece of the puzzle. A small piece, but the most complex puzzles are made up of the tiniest tiles."

"What did you find?"

"It seems as if some people—one person, actually—went to the public library around the time of the theft and looked at some books that contained pictures of the Ausgraben Idol. These are books, mind you, that no one had requested for years and years. It probably won't add up to anything in the end. But that NYMA button we found . . . it might factor in. We think we know what the red fibers came from. We've got one tentative lead, a fish looking at bait, but we need to gather more evidence before we can reel him in."

"Marek, that's wonderful."

"Lydia?"

"Yes?"

Marek put on his blazer and straightened his cuffs. "I feel a bit silly asking this." He scratched his jaw. "I was thinking that it might help our effort if you talked to Eric about the theft."

"Whatever for?"

"I can't help but think that just in the way you put yourself in the mindset of the thief, that Eric . . . might do the same."

"If he knew anything that would help you, he would have told you."

"Right. I just think you should talk to him about it," Marek said.

Was he implying . . . ? "You don't think Eric knows anything, do you?" Would Eric withhold information from a criminal investigation? She laughed.

Marek laughed, too. "Oh, I . . . No. I just—"

"Sure, I'll bring it up. He was just here, though, and I don't know when I'll talk to him next—Marek, are you feeling all right? You don't look well."

Both of them sat on the bed. Marek heaved a sigh.

"You look like there's something you want to tell me," Lydia said.

"Yes, I'm afraid there is. I don't know quite how to say this."

"Take your time."

"I must tell you that I have a deep, dark secret that I've never told you. It's been festering. Consuming me. I love you more than I have ever loved anyone." Marek dug his head into her lap and hugged her waist. "I can't tell you how much I adore being with you."

"That's your deep, dark secret?"

"I've not always been honest with people I've known. Some women have hated me for it. But because I've fallen so in love with you, I have to make this confession, and I want you to know that this is the only secret I've never told you. The stolen idol . . . the Ausgraben Idol . . ." Marek sat up.

"Yes?"

". . . is probably a fake."

"A forgery?"

"A very old forgery, in itself an antique, but not the Ausgraben Idol itself. Nobody knows about this, save a few of my closest colleagues. We've suspected it for some time. Forgeries of ancient art have been turning up in other collections. And, well . . . I was going to deal it away before anyone discovered that it was a fake because Polly Stewart wanted it so badly and because if we had *The Storm Nears,* we'd be number one in the world." Marek took a deep breath. "That's it."

"That's it?"

"That's it." But he added, "I was going to pursue a trade even though I knew full well that I might be defrauding the other party. Oh, the artifact hasn't been proven yet to be a fake, but . . . there's something else. I arranged to have the statue authenticated. I arranged for a phony bill of goods. I hired experts who certified that it was a healthy sculpture because I paid them handsomely to do so. It was all set. But then—poof! The statue disappeared. I'm so relieved I told you. I love you, and there's nothing now about me that you don't know. Nothing. You aren't terribly ashamed of me, are you?"

"Of course not," Lydia said. "I can't say I approve of the cover-up, but I'm glad you're being straight with me. I've always admired your candor. And if you recover the idol, I'm sure you wouldn't try to trade it away, right?"

"Right. Well . . . Lydia, sometimes we must do things that aren't entirely truthful. NYMA would get *The Storm Nears,* a painting widely regarded as the most important work in an American collection, public or private. It's a painting that influenced so many other paintings. It's a tradition unto itself. It's worth it. Do you understand? I need for you to tell me you don't despise me for this dishonesty."

Lydia understood. If Marek won Polly Stewart's painting and knowingly dumped on her a fake figurine, he would be a hero in the art world, and he fully intended to do this. Polly Stewart would probably never know the difference. Lettuce worked in place of endive. Marek would have clinched the deal of the century. When he made his confession, he was almost in tears because he trusted her and wanted to divulge everything. "Of course I don't *despise* you."

"I knew you'd understand. I love you."

The last thing Lydia wanted to do now was to see Polly Stewart. In the elevator rising toward the penthouse, Marek said, "This party is all a front, you know."

"To pretend like everything is peachy even though Polly's husband is going to jail."

"Exactly. Now she wants the Ausgraben Idol back more than ever. She thinks it will bring her luck, and she can still save him on appeal."

"Naughty you," Polly Stewart greeted Marek in her gilt foyer. "I was afraid you two lovebirds weren't going to show."

Lydia heard a string quartet in a distant room. She kissed her host's lifted, stretched, Pan-Caked cheek.

"I'm glad you two finally made it to one of our little jamborees." Polly was wearing a gold jacket that matched the leafing of the wainscoting in her living room. She hooked Lydia's arm. "Have you met my dear, dear friend, Signore Lazlo Cruthers?"

"I haven't had the honor." Lydia grasped the swollen fingers of a man with a trimmed beard and a laugh (or normal breathing pattern) that sounded like a bellows. "And do you," she said to the tenor, "know Marek—?" When Lydia turned around, her date was gone. She saw him maneuvering his way across the vast room toward a circle of ascots and faded gold pinky rings, where Polly's indicted husband was holding court.

A waiter passed by with a champagne tray. Another waiter approached Lydia and asked, with the clear diction of a well-trained Shakespearean, "Would you care to try a Nova Scotian salmon-soufflé puff?" Lazlo took three of the hors d'oeuvres off the tray and looked as though he might juggle them. Lydia popped one in her mouth. She felt like she was swallowing salty, pink air. Now Marek had disappeared completely.

"I'm so delighted you came," Polly said. "Marek is one of my favorite, favorite men."

"Mine, too," Lydia said.

"I must ask you a question. Are you superstitious?"

"I think we all are, even when we say we're not."

The tenor grabbed two miniature croissants from another passing tray.

"Precisely my point," Polly said. "So tell me what you make of this. Thinking it was wide open, a big, black crow flew at my bedroom window when I was getting dressed earlier, and its beak shattered on the glass, and it plummeted all the way to the sidewalk."

"*Cara.*" Lazlo Cruthers clasped his heart with sticky hands.

"I'm fine, I'm fine," Polly said. "I called the Animal Emergency Hot Line, of course. We've given them money in the past, but there was nothing they could do. What do you think it means?"

"I'm not sure," Lydia said. "Probably nothing."

"Feathers all over the canopy. Very messy. I was just telling this story to my dear friend Burton Baggley, who you must meet, and Burton said that something dark is heading my way."

A tray of hors d'oeuvres passed by Lazlo too quickly, so he chased after it.

"I wouldn't worry," Lydia said. "A bird flew at your window—I'm sure it happens all the time."

"Yes, of course, but my question is, why was the crow trying to fly into my bedroom in the first place?"

"Maybe it admired a painting," Lydia said.

"The Constable over my vanity probably." Polly was apparently still shaken. "Such a noise: whoosh, flump."

A tall woman in a beaded dress crossed the room. "Polly," she said, "terrific shindig."

"Babe Gregarian, meet my dear friend Lydia."

Babe Gregarian half-smiled. "Polly," she whispered, "Burton told me about the raven that smashed into your window."

"Horrifying," Lydia whispered.

"You must do something very charitable at once. Loan a painting somewhere," Babe Gregarian said before flying off, no doubt to gossip about Polly's dark omen.

"Yes," Polly said. "Most definitely." She looked at Lydia and shrugged. "What can you do?"

"What can you do," Lydia agreed.

Polly hooked her arm and surveyed the room. Her eyes drifted among her guests at about drink-level to make sure everyone was outfitted with Baccarat. "Isn't that nice? The Maltese ambassador is talking with Maxine Vogelberg."

"Oh, is he here?" Lydia asked for want of something to say.

"Do you know him? You don't? You must meet him." Polly looked frail and taut, as if she might snap in two. Lydia wanted to tell her: My lover is defrauding you, and he definitely should not rank among your favorite, favorite men. And feeling sort of sorry for her, she allowed herself to be escorted past tycoons and ladies-who-lunch and major collectors in order to greet a dignitary with a polished heraldic badge prominently pinned to his tuxedo, a man whom she could have happily died never having met. She floated across the room simply because poor Polly Stewart would probably get some small pleasure out of thinking that Lydia would be impressed by an ambassador, and it did not seem like too much to ask to pretend that she was.

On the way, Lydia spotted Marek standing amid a circle of women who were attentively listening to a story he was telling. She tried to get his attention, but the string quartet was riding a crescendo, and Marek apparently was wrapped up in his narrative. So Lydia watched him for a passing moment. There was something in his hand, she couldn't see what. He was holding it like a dart. It was a cigarette. She had never seen him smoke before, never. They always sat in the nonsmoking sections of restaurants. She knew that she was overreacting, yet she couldn't deny that seeing him across a crowded room dressed in clothes he didn't normally wear and chatting so breezily to society women, to see him smoking a cigarette, troubled her.

People were animals, she thought. What was she? A cat seemed like the obvious choice to her. Jason was a tortoise. And Marek . . . She was beginning to suspect that he might be a lizard who blended in with dirt or grass. She had fallen for a lizard, she decided, and this began to worry her. A lizard reported tonight that he had no more secrets. But that was while he slithered in the grass. Right now, he was in the dirt.

ric wandered the city. He wore dark glasses and a baseball cap, more to mask himself from anyone he might know than to elude strangers. Some days he left home long before dawn, only to return, if at all, when the sun was rising the next morning. He roamed as far as he could and still remain within city limits, and for a while—he wasn't sure why—he was drawn toward water. Somewhere in Brooklyn, he watched two dogs bathe in a foamy current gushing from a hydrant that neighborhood kids had abandoned without closing. He made his way uptown to the Cloisters, where he could survey the widening Hudson below and beyond. He walked the fenced perimeter of the Central Park reservoir, where the same joggers passed him over and over, and he went to Coney Island one day, to the aquarium, where whales floated in their tanks like ancient battle-wrecked ships, occasionally rising to the surface, only to sink again into dark, warped depths. He ended up at a public pool where he watched kids compete in sloppy dives, women in flowered caps bob up to their necks, then shake the green water from the cleavage of their swimsuits, and the smallest New Yorkers dressed up as turtles splash and dare each other to float face-down. All of this water made Eric eager to get wet himself, and so he went into an East Village bathhouse during off-peak hours. In the steam room, he convinced himself that he was evaporating, that he was melting into the sweaty air, into the conversations of bitter, old Russian men, but this fantasy dissolved abruptly under the reality of a cold shower.

He wandered city cemeteries, visiting both the small Portuguese plots tucked into misshapen corner lots and the hilly Victorian parks of the dead. In cemeteries, no one would ask him to autograph an idol. And then he found himself staring into the interiors of brownstones. At night, he could see the occasional Sargent rip-off hanging over a mantel, somebody's gowned, imperious great-grandmother watching future generations through a pince-nez. He could look into bookshelf-lined parlors, beyond a track-lit Cubist drawing or a potted tree to see people gathered around television sets. Through open windows, he heard arguments and laughter. One afternoon, a realtor mistook him for the man to whom she was scheduled to show a Greek Revival town house, and Eric pretended to be the prospective buyer simply because he wanted to check out the high-ceilinged interior with its egg-and-tongue molding and symmetrical rooms. The realtor purred about original floors, about the thriving rhododendron in the garden. The place was white, elegantly pristine, empty, and restored, and for a moment Eric considered making an offer. The city was large enough: He could escape here, not tell anyone, and no one would know. He would buy very little furniture, live ascetically, start life over from scratch. A new name, no past. But what if someone recognized him? It had happened the other day when he took off his dark glasses to count his change for the ferry, and then again that night in a deli when he was buying soda. Then he would only have to escape once again.

Enough, he decided one day, enough. He packed the essentials and withdrew a large sum of cash from his bank (he would get the rest later). At the airport, he opted for an international terminal and an airline he had never flown before. He approached the ticket counter and a woman in a beige uniform asked him his destination. "You tell me," he said. "What are my choices?" The woman straightened her scarf, looked at him suspiciously, and began to recite an alphabetical list of South American capitals, checking her console to read the times of the next departures. There was a wait of at least an hour, which wouldn't do at all, so he decided to try another airline. But he never made it to the next counter and instead—maybe because he was so practiced at drifting—he headed for the terminal gates, as far as he could go without a ticket. He could see the runways in the distance, the potbellied aircraft miraculously rising and disappearing in clouds of exhaust. He watched people greet one another and send each other off. And then he was truly knocked off course, not that he knew what his course was anymore, because he spotted a familiar face amid the flood of European passengers flowing through security.

He saw Timothy in the crowd. Eric hadn't talked to him in weeks, and as far as he could tell, Timothy didn't notice him in turn, which was the way Eric wanted to keep it because the last time he unexpectedly ran into his old friend, he ended up on a journey he did not care to repeat. Timothy held a camcorder up to his eye and filmed a group of small children, two boys and a girl who were apparently waiting for someone to appear. Did he know them? Was he waiting, too? It was unclear whether the children even knew that they were being taped because they were so absorbed in scanning the faces that passed them, none of which belonged to the one they wanted to see. At long last, a gnarled old woman was rolled off the jet in a wheelchair, and the children dove under stanchion ropes to engulf her in kisses and to present a bouquet of suburban violets. Timothy shot the reunion but then walked away, and so did Eric, in a different direction. When he got off a down escalator, he spotted a free cab coming up to the curb, so he bribed a traffic guard, hopped the queue, and rode off.

He waited a day and decided to try the airport again because he had to get out of the city while he had momentum. That was the plan. He had to stick to the plan. This time, he decided on a specific place. "Paris," he told the man behind the Air France counter. "One way." He paid for his fare in cash. He carried his one bag with him and passed through security with flying colors. He converted an ample number of dollars into francs at a *bureau de change* and then waited in the lounge, where he got drunk quickly on vodka, his mother's poison, never his. The circular terminal began to spin slowly, nauseatingly. He waited and waited. Finally, a flight attendant began welcoming passengers aboard, and when Eric's row was called, he stood up, wobbled, but managed to make it to the ticket-taker. He handed a woman his boarding pass. Then he froze. The line of passengers behind him grew longer. Through a window in the gateway he could see luggage being stowed on board the plane, fuel lines withdrawing. "*Pardon,*" he said. "I forgot *quelque chose.*"

"Sir, the plane will be leaving shortly!" the woman called after him as he retreated back into the terminal. "Sir? *Monsieur?*"

Almost. He had almost escaped the city. "I don't care," he told a taxi driver. "Just go anywhere. I have lots of francs. Just drive, please. Fast."

It was just Eric's luck to have wound up in a cab whose driver had fashioned a Cycladic head, decapitated from one of the mass-market versions, into an ornament for his rearview mirror. A red ribbon was tied around the woman's long neck, and her head dangled upside down. The driver combed a broad mustache with his forefinger and thumb. "You gotta pay me something now, mister."

After the driver rejected the rococo, crinkly foreign bills, Eric pulled a crisp hundred from his wallet and handed it over. And so he toured the city, following a jagged path toward its core of bridges and tunnels, feeling less inebriated and sorrier for himself, if that were possible, as he worked his way back to Manhattan.

"Where you coming in from?" the driver asked.

"I never got anywhere."

"So you're from here?"

"Why all the questions?"

"A city so great, they named it twice."

"I'm trapped," Eric confessed. "I can't get out."

"Who are you running from?"

"Why do you think I'm running from anyone?"

"You know, you're gonna do permanent damage to your eyes if you wear those shades all the time."

"Did you find the Goddess head like that?"

"My six-year-old dropped it. Wanna see her picture?" The driver pressed a plastic-coated photo against the Plexiglas barrier that separated him from Eric.

"She's lovely."

"She's a fucking terror."

After driving in circles for a few hours, Eric asked to be let out on a random corner, and it wasn't until the cab had sped off that, irony of ironies, he realized he had been ferried back to his own district. He didn't know what else to do, so he meandered toward Forelle Street, feeling foolish and defeated: He was no Odysseus. He wished that he'd had the nerve to vanish. He didn't know whether he was more disappointed in himself for not going through with his plan or for not knowing what he truly wanted.

Dusk: a time of self-reckoning, a threshold. From across the street, Eric stared at the Mystery Roast, at its green awning, and then counted each floor up until he reached the roof. He realized that he had never taken in the view from the full height of his building, so he rode the elevator up to his loft, stepped out onto the back staircase, and climbed up the final flights. He walked out onto the roof, propping the door open with a cinder block.

The vista was astonishing, vast and endless. He had not expected to be so overwhelmed, to feel so small. He could look at the flat, blacktop roofs of the buildings all around his neighborhood, and then beyond as far as he could see. Each roof was an island, and the city suddenly became a continent of islands with an unnavigable, fractal coastline. Roofs and roofs everywhere he looked, some with triangular staircases and sheds, some with elaborate decks. Roofs with small metal chimneys and air ducts, the air ducts crowned with spherical bulbs of rotating blades, globe-shaped windmills responding to shifts in the wind. Skylights on some brownstones looked like miniature greenhouses. The water tanks that were exposed resembled squat, antiquated rockets awaiting lift-off, but many were hidden by elaborate minarets, faux temples with tiled ornaments, tracery, and empty belfries. Eric spun in slow circles. He picked out a favorite roof, a green mansard that capped a building of elaborate stone embroidery and drooling gargoyles. He lingered over the buildings with oxidized cupolas and gabled steeples and flaking gold domes that once upon a time stood proudly as the tallest edifices, each an achievement in engineering, each surpassing a vertical challenge, all of them humbled in today's world: They were early chapters in an ongoing epic. Here and there, Eric saw a building going up, just the frame so far, girders and beams that didn't amount to more than a massive fish skeleton. Roofs and roofs stepped away from him, and the rolling canyons of smaller buildings were dwarfed, finally, by the true peaks, by the architectural contest among the steepest mounts, the world-famous skyscrapers that defined the city's arrogance, its failings and its promise. At dusk, nobody else was out on his roof or any other roof, so Eric imagined himself as a lone pioneer. He recorded the view knowing that soon, tomorrow, it would look different after the arrival of other settlers, after the invasions of greedy nations.

From his roof, Eric began to see the world plainly and lucidly. He had examined the city from varied angles, but never this one, and somehow the freshness of the vantage, of this point of view, cleared his mind. He was completely sober now, and to maintain his clarity, he decided to spend the night up here. He went downstairs for food and a blanket. There was a shopping bag full of idols in his loft, leftovers from one of the Goddess's several incarnations. He carried them upstairs, too, because finally he knew what to do with them. He knew what they would be good for.

On his way back out, Eric tripped over the cinder block. The door to the roof slammed shut. It wouldn't reopen, it was jammed. The neighboring buildings were shorter by two floors, so he couldn't jump down. He probably could have won someone's attention on the street or even leaped down to the fire escape in the rear of the building, but since he had decided to camp out, he didn't bother.

The sun melted into the silicon haze hanging over the flat ports of New Jersey, into the refineries across the river. Farther north, a final curve of sunlight empurpled the Palisades, the last preserve of bare cliffs, and the lights on the narrow arc of the bridge over the Hudson became low-hanging stars. Everywhere, there were frames of light from apartments, yellow squares, and of course the monumental spires of the city which remained illuminated until midnight. Eric watched the lights turn off a few at a time. Others came on. He napped and woke up cold, wrapped himself in the blanket and drifted off again, although never into a deep sleep. He awoke finally with the first quiet mention of morning, an orange fog that made East Side projects look like they were on fire. Pockets of mist lingered, then dissipated.

At dawn, the city smelled like bread. Eric's blanket was damp. He stretched. His shoulder and hip were sore. The street below was still and quiet. For breakfast, he had chicken salad (swiped one night from the café after Andre had gone to bed) and warm orange juice. A bag of stale blue corn chips, too. Then, inspired by the taxi driver's daughter, he dragged the shopping bag of idols over to the edge of the building and pulled one out. He removed it from its box. He pinched the Goddess by her thin brow and extended his arm straight out over the street. He let the idol drop. The stone woman fell gracelessly fast, seemingly torpedoing with greater speed as she plummeted, and shattered into uncountable white shards all over the street. He let another idol fall. From this height, it sounded like he was smashing milk bottles. He dropped another figurine over the edge, and another. He smashed the statues in quick succession.

Gravity was wonderful, he thought, both kinds: the physics that could break apart the stone that fell seven stories, and the sadness within him, which through an alchemy he was only beginning to understand was the source of both his wallowing despair as well as his creative desire, both a recurring angst as well as a capacity to reinvent and revise himself in a city that for better or for worse, for now, was home. He continued to drop idols and a strange relief swept over him, like a cool rain in the heat of summer.

Eric released two idols simultaneously. A woman across the street stuck her head out the window. She didn't see him because she looked at the pavement and then straight up, as if the traffic helicopter hovering over the river were responsible. People started to surface. Two men read sections of the newspaper while they walked their twin dachshunds. A bakery truck zoomed by. The sisters who worked at the laundry around the corner biked up Forelle. Eric waited for a gap in traffic before letting another idol crash. He held the figurine over the edge of the building, but just as he was going to let it fall, he saw a familiar shape walking down the street.

The man drew closer, and when he yelled, "Eric," Eric froze. "What are you doing up there?"

They would probably live out a lifelong friendship, he and Timothy, partly because they would inevitably keep surprising each other by turning up when least expected. "I'm trapped!" Eric shouted back.

"Don't move." Soon Timothy was pounding on the other side of the metal door to the roof.

"Keep at it," Eric cheered. He heard Timothy throw the full weight of his body against the door to no avail. "Don't hurt yourself."

Finally, Timothy forced open the door and fell onto the roof, onto his knees.

"Are you okay?" Eric helped him to his feet.

"I'm swell, but what the hell are you doing?"

"Dropping Goddesses off the roof."

"You were standing on the edge, and for a second, I thought . . ." Eric pulled Timothy into a long, quiet hug.

"You're all wet." Timothy pushed away.

"I spent the night up here."

"Couldn't you have called to someone down on the street to help you?"

"I didn't want to. And you, where are you coming from at this hour of the morning?"

"I've been working on a project," Timothy said.

"I saw you filming the children at the airport."

"What were you doing at the airport?"

"Escaping. You're making a video?"

"I like to think of it as a film. It's good to see you."

"I feel like I've been flying a plane through a storm all night and just now emerged from the fog."

"You do look like you could use some sleep," Timothy said.

"What is your film about?"

"You'll have to wait for the final edit."

"Hey, try smashing an idol." Eric stepped back over to the edge of the building. He handed a Goddess to Timothy. "Just let it drop." He checked the street. "All clear."

Timothy held the idol over the street.

"Let go."

Timothy looked like he was waiting for the wind to shift directions. He changed hands and closed his eyes. Was he making a wish?

"Let go," Eric said.

And Timothy obeyed, opening his eyes before the explosion. "Wicked. This beats breaking plates." He dropped a second statue.

"I don't suppose you were the one who hid the idol, the real one, in the samovar, were you?"

"Did I do what?"

"Never mind. Keep going. I'm determined to get through the whole bag."

"So is this going to be the new craze, idol smashing?"

"Don't even joke," Eric said.

They took turns. All of the Cycladic woman's high dives were exactly the same: Like a cat righting itself during a fall, the figure flipped over once and always ended up landing feet (base) first. The impact, viewed from above, looked like the dandelion-burst of a bright firecracker, and the white flakes of stone littered all over the street formed a monotone mosaic, the tiles rearranged by each additional bombardment: At first, the image was a seascape of gulls in flight, and then it became a magnolia tree in full bloom, besieged by an unseen wind that scattered its petals.

"Hey!" shouted the woman from across the street, finally locating the source of the noise. "Stop that, or I'll call the cops."

Eric and Timothy defiantly smashed one last idol each. They went downstairs. Inside, Timothy said, "I'm going off to finish a rough cut. Then . . . I have a plan."

"I'm going to take a nap. I'll be in the café later if you want to catch up." And so as New York began another day, Eric retreated to his loft and to his neglected bed, where he lapsed into a miraculous and sustained slumber.

He had planned on dozing for only an hour or two, but he ended up sleeping all day, and when he woke up, it was dark out. It was the middle of the night, Eric wasn't sure what time. In fact, the only reason he finally awoke when he did was because he heard his elevator doors open. *Aren't you forgetting something?* Someone was in Eric's apartment switching on lamps, and before Eric's eyes adjusted and before he could duck under his covers, two men were standing next to the bed. *Aren't you forgetting, loverboy, that you are a hardened criminal?* Other people, a dozen it seemed, all in uniforms, all wearing surgical gloves, began to comb his home like ants at a picnic. Eric was pulled out of bed by his elbows and pushed up against the wall. *Just when you thought that you were safe . . .* He was naked. He was told to get dressed by one man, but a second placed his hand on Eric's shoulder and told him to stay right where he was. . . . *you got nailed.* Eric could only look down at the shiny black shoes of the second officer, so he did not see the man's face when he said, "We'd like you to come with us so we can ask you a few questions."

Eric rested his cheek against the wall and closed his eyes. He tried to convince himself that he was having a bad dream. That was all. A nightmare.

"You have the right to remain silent. . . ."

His eyes opened wide with alarm. He could have screamed in protest—This is a terrible mistake, you've got the wrong man—but the fact of the matter was that he was guilty of committing an unsolved crime, and anything that he said could not change the truth. He was going to jail.

hen Timothy left Eric, he went directly in to his studio, which had been redefined once again: All of the sculptural equipment was gone, and the room was filled now with an assembly of television monitors and expensive editing machines. He noticed that the message light on his answering machine was blinking frantically, but he had no intention of returning Eduardo's calls—ever—so he unplugged both the machine and the phone. He switched on his various appliances and played back the latest raw footage. The studio hummed with electricity. Timothy was sure he would blow a fuse. Maybe this anxiety was what propelled him to work at an accelerated speed this afternoon, or maybe it was the idol demolition that got him moving. He tried out new video images in the master montage. He took out some pieces and transplanted others. The editing process was like making a collage. Connections occurred to him, juxtapositions. The shot of the girl with the turtle, the boy in the tree. His film was taking on a final shape—he would call it *A Life of Summers*—and he tested bits of music alongside the visual narrative. An alternately plaintive and playful cello score worked perfectly, music to go with children wandering a forest. Then there were the title cards, just a handful, since this was a silent picture of sorts. "Grandmother arrives." "Grandmother is sick." It took most of the day to finish, but when he was finally pleased with a draft, he made a copy of the master tape, ejected it from the machine, and, with a fair amount of trepidation, went downstairs.

Andre was in the café, and when he returned to the kitchen and saw Timothy rubbing Melior's ears, he said, "I remember you," surprisingly without bitterness and even with a detectable degree of delight.

"We could pretend that I'm coming into the café for the first time. I'll just sidle over to the bar and ask for a shot of espresso."

"You've seen too many movies." Andre looked at his pile of order slips. He ripped some lettuce and threw it into a broad wooden bowl. He sliced a red onion.

"Actually, I made a movie. A video-movie of sorts."

Andre chopped scallions, a cucumber.

"Can you close the café and come see it?"

Andre shot him a look: You're not serious, are you?

"Just for a half-hour." Actually, the movie ran eighty-five minutes, but he didn't want to push for too much. Timothy waved the video-cassette in the air. "We can watch it on your TV. Just a bit. How about fifteen minutes?"

"How can I . . . ?" Andre tossed spinach into the salad and added oval wedges of goat cheese and scraps of herbed croutons. Timothy noticed that Andre's hands were shaking slightly, nervously, that he was being uncharacteristically sloppy, spilling greens and chèvre on the floor. "I'd like to talk to you about something, Tim, but not now. I have to . . ." He sighed. "Fifteen minutes." He waited for the current café crowd to dwindle and leave, and then he locked the front door, writing on the board that he would be back soon and that anyone who returned would get an iced mocha on the house, with extra whipped cream. He left all of the lights on and collected Melior on the way upstairs.

Andre's loft was a maze of Persian rugs and bleached oak. His walls were lined with shelves of flawlessly alphabetized paperback novels in Romance languages. Timothy said nothing. He drew all of the Levolor blinds, turned on the television, inserted the tape into the VCR, and then sat at the opposite end of the loft while Andre and the cat watched the film. During the initial sequence, the scenes of the children playing with sailboats in the Central Park lagoon, Andre didn't seem to respond to the tape at all, and Timothy was sure that a cruel critique would follow. He sat at a rolltop desk and stacked account ledgers and made paper-clip snakes. Andre continued to watch (a half-hour passed, then an hour), and as the scenes progressed, from the mock tea-party to the kids waiting for their grandmother at the airport, Timothy began to hear laughs and meows at the other end of the loft. He stretched out on a quilt on Andre's bed. Then he thought he heard Andre quietly crying during the cemetery sequence. The burial of the grandmother, children in mourning. All of these scenes, including the finale of the children splashing around in a swimming pool, were shot in bright color under a bright sun, and the music that Timothy had used happened to be Andre's favorite Bach.

"Did they know you were filming them?" Andre asked when the film ended.

"I tried to stay hidden, which is why you get some branches in the way and all those shoulders in the airport sequence."

"How did you find them? There were different kids in each scene."

"I walked around until I happened upon them."

"And the story, about their grandmother dying and all of that? Were you eavesdropping?"

"I made that up. Actually that was a pet cemetery where a family dog was being interred, but I thought it would be more poignant if it was the grandmother who died."

"So you'll show it to Eduardo Redelarte now? Is that your goal? What's he going to do, a video installation or something?" Andre yawned. "Oh, shit. I lost track of the time. I have to get back downstairs. . . ."

"I'm not dealing with Eduardo anymore. I have another idea."

Andre sat down in a cane rocker by the bed. "You're on the inside looking out with a major, major gallery. Do you have a fever?"

"I'm going to make a few copies of the video. I'm going to use a pseudonym so I don't get arrested, and because that appeals to me anyway. Then I'm going to sneak the cassettes into video stores, and when no one is looking, I'll remove other movies from boxes and insert my film instead. I'll stuff the real videos in my coat or something and leave the store. Then unsuspecting renters will be surprised by my film when they pop the tape in the VCR." All the while, Timothy had been staring at the ceiling and when he sat up, he noticed that Andre was grinning. "What?"

"You have a name that people know—"

"I want to start over. I know you don't believe me, and you think I'm as fickle as a horny rabbit, but I think that I've finally found my voice. Don't laugh. This is what I really and truly want to do. I know what you're thinking—"

"No, you don't. I think this is the best thing you've done, the most sensitive and least self-indulgent—poignant, in fact—and I'm just trying to remember where I put my thermometer so I can see if you're running a temperature."

"People can change." Timothy found a legal pad and a pencil on Andre's desk.

"In most cases, no. Maybe there are exceptions."

Timothy kicked off his shoes.

"I don't think we should do this," Andre said. But he wiggled out of his boots.

Timothy unbuttoned his shirt and unzipped his chinos.

"Slow down. There's something I've got to tell you." Andre kept up the pace and pulled off his black T-shirt, his jeans, his underwear. He crossed his legs and rocked in the chair.

Timothy drew in broad, sweeping motions. Andre's chin cast a long shadow. His face was full of neat lines, like the one separating his cheeks from his mouth, or the one that delineated his jaw from his neck. Or his hairline, ebbing, yet still full and curly. Some thatching here and there could capture the contour of his crossed leg. And then his shoulders, tilted back, rocking, his arms . . . Not overly muscled arms, but arms that looked like mountain ranges seen from far away. Andre shifted in the chair, slumped, then pushed himself up and out of the rocker.

He chucked the drawing across the room—the cat bolted from her nap when she heard the pad flying through the air, which sounded like a bird flapping its wings—and he pulled Timothy's ankles out from under him until he was lying on his back. Timothy knew as if by instinct to kiss Andre along the side of his rib cage; in return he received a massage to the backs of his thighs and the utmost attention paid to his shoulder blades. For Timothy, there was sadness in the air as well as relief. They had wasted so much time.

Later, he slept with his head on Andre's chest. He didn't dare mention the disappointed patrons downstairs and their free iced mochas. He also didn't dare ask why exactly Andre was letting him back in his life, why now.

"I can't believe I didn't open the café," Andre said. "I've never done that before."

Timothy wrapped the loose end of the quilt over their calves. "So you liked my film?"

"Praise goes to your head faster than the cheapest champagne. Yes, yes. You should make more. Tell me: Why children?"

"It's supposed to be about summer. A child goes through so much in the summer that's completely different from the rest of the year. Do you remember? You live a whole lifetime in a summer. And then you grow up and summer's never the same."

"Timothy . . . I'm not pretending like I don't know what just happened here, and I'm happy, believe me, sincerely happy, so don't think that I'm trying to get out of—"

"Spit it out."

"I'm going to leave New York for a while. I have to get away."

Timothy didn't miss a beat. "I know. I've been expecting this. I'll come."

"No. Half my life has passed. I can't drink real coffee. My friends have died or moved away. You know Carlos hasn't been gone that long, has he? I feel like I'm supposed to go find him now and tell him about us and all. He'd be thrilled. He'd put on his best tutu and dance an arabesque. And then I feel like it's been ages and ages since he died. Like I've been in mourning forever, like that's all there ever was. I'd be lying to you if I said that all this death didn't affect my thinking. I need to move on to something else, and I need to figure out what that something else is going to be. By myself. Alone. I'm going to close down the café and sell the space, my loft, too, and I'm going to take the money and travel out West for a while. New Mexico, Arizona. I don't know when I'm coming back, except I will come back eventually, I think, but not before I figure out what I want to do next."

Timothy pulled the quilt higher up their legs. "I'll wait."

"It may be a while."

"Will you let me wait? Will you wait? I mean—"

"I know what you mean," Andre said. "Yeah, I'll let you wait."

"I have a lot of films to make."

"It will be a long time."

"I'll make a lot of films."

"What if I don't come back?"

"You will. You have to."

"What if you meet someone?"

"I'm going to try to wait," Timothy said. "Can't you have a little faith in me?"

"Oh, sugar, I have so much faith that I could serve it downstairs all night and still have plenty left over for breakfast. Which reminds me . . ."

Andre sat up and swung his legs over the edge of the bed, but Timothy pulled him back. He wrapped the quilt over them completely, over their heads, pitching the tent with his knees. Andre tried several times over the course of the next few hours to get up and go fix some food, but Timothy successfully pulled him back and made love or described the films he wanted to shoot or changed the opera on the stereo. They stayed in the dark room all night.

At one point, flashing lights blinked on Forelle Street, and Andre arose to look and see if there had been a car accident. Timothy tugged him back into bed once again. "Forget about the rest of the world," he said.

lso that evening, alone in her apartment, Lydia cleaned house. She was going through her home room by room and getting rid of all of the junk she had accumulated over the years. She did not fool herself about her motives. Ambivalences of any kind drove her toward organization and neatness. After a dispute at work, she might rearrange her office furniture. Confusion about men led directly to a sweep of the pantry. And so she could not deny that it was her slowly fading trust in Marek that was making her clean with abandon, a more thorough purge than usual that began with the oven and stove. She was still seeing him, but the faith and fun of her romance had been eclipsed by her doubts. Doubts about her lover's integrity, which she would have loved to have confided in someone— Jason for one, except she knew that he would only issue a smug I-told-you-so. She couldn't tell him, so she tossed out fondue equipment long out of vogue and medically incorrect. She emptied bottles of various liqueurs she had fancied at one point or another, arrack during one affair, ouzo during her Greek phase. She cleaned off a foyer bookshelf of out-of-date travel books, and with some reluctance dumped piles of old magazines in the building recycling bin. In one hall closet, she found manuscripts among frayed beach towels, early drafts belonging to Jason which she would return. And then finally, she faced the most daunting challenge.

She took a deep breath and entered her walk-in closet. Into a large cardboard box destined for the Salvation Army, she chucked sandals and stoles and shifts and culottes. Without taking the time to inspect or reminisce about the garments, she tossed them across the room. Out went the black suit she wore to funerals in the Seventies. So long to a pair of plaid bell-bottoms. Adieu to a rainbow-colored wool poncho. A beret. White boots. She would miss that suede vest. Good-bye to an ugly houndstooth, sleeveless minidress (circa 1965). It had a scoop back and big black buttons. She looked at its two large waist pockets. She remembered finding Eric's marijuana here once. She had left it there, liberated mom that she was. She also remembered that she used to look good in this dress. She folded it in half and aimed for the box.

Odd, she thought, and unfolded the dress. There was a wad of napkins in the pocket. One napkin actually. She unfurled it and gasped. She touched the blank stone face with her pinky. Was it real? No. It was a fake, a knockoff. It had to be. But then why was it in her closet?

What if it was the real thing after all? The real statue, which according to Marek might be a fake. The idol was holding her arms over her gut, and her knees were bent as if she were about to double over in pain. What was it doing in her dress? Maybe Marek put it there, and this was part of some elaborate scam. Sure. That made sense. No, it didn't. He'd told her everything. Or he said he did. Well, Mrs. Hamilton, the cleaning lady, certainly didn't stash it there. Face it, Lydia told herself, it was Eric. Just in the neighborhood indeed.

She had been wearing her cleaning clothes, which she shed. Without a moment's delay, she slipped on the houndstooth minidress and buttoned it up. It fit. If anything, the dress was too large around her collarbone and made her look a little like a diet-pill addict. She grabbed a handbag from the box destined for the Salvation Army, a rawhide sack trimmed with four inches of fringe. Lydia placed the idol, rewrapped in its napkin, in the purse. She had to chuckle while the doorman hailed a cab. What did she look like in her houndstooth minidress carrying a fringed purse? She was probably setting off a new look: Mix and match among the decades. She wished that she had a coat because her arms were cold.

When the elevator opened, Jason snickered. "We barely survived that period. Must we relive it?"

Lydia set her bag down and headed straight for the bar.

"I remember that dress."

"No you don't. It predates you."

"I definitely remember that purse. You were famous with that purse."

"Maybe you remember the purse." Lydia poured herself a drink. She sat down at the glass coffee table and opened the bag. Then, while Jason patiently watched, she removed the idol and unwrapped it from its napkin.

Jason knelt down next to the table and studied the surface of the stone. "Exquisite. It's just like the one that was stolen."

"I think it *is* the one that was stolen."

He smiled politely, as if he were realizing the lame punch line to an obtuse joke. "It's a very good copy, but the real one is much more delicate."

"Jason, you don't know everything. This is the real statue, the one that was stolen. It was stuffed into this dress in the back of my closet. Eric—"

"Stole the idol."

"You don't sound surprised."

"I didn't get a good look that morning. I convinced myself that I was wrong."

"Oh, don't start with a story. I've got far too much on my mind."

"The day when the idol was stolen and when I was looking at the park with my telescope . . ."

"You spotted the thief."

"I didn't know if he was in fact the burglar, but the person running across the lawn that morning, I thought, was . . . Eric. I didn't tell you, because I wasn't sure. And then I decided it was absurd."

Lydia was silent for a long while. "If it was Eric, for some reason, I feel sort of proud. Isn't that odd?"

"He certainly made a splash in the news."

"I should be very upset that I've raised a criminal, but I'm not at all."

"Does Marek know you're here? With the idol?"

"The bastard knew all along. . . ."

"Now, now," Jason said. "He was caught in the middle, wasn't he?"

"You're defending Marek?"

"I was just saying—"

"Don't defend him. I wonder at what point he knew." Lydia wandered over to the windows and stared out at the city. She sipped her drink.

"You have every reason to be proud."

"My son is a felon."

"It could be worse."

"What are we going to do?" When she said "we" she surprised herself, but "we" sounded right. The idol lay in state on the glass table. She knew that she should have been considering the mess at hand, but the scattered lights in the night outside distracted her. "Come on," she said to her second husband. She opened the door to the terrace and said, "Take the telescope."

Jason followed her orders, but his eyebrows were raised with skepticism.

It was windy. The evening smelled sweet, like ripe apples. "Let's see," Lydia said, "where should we set this up?"

"You want me to show you how I tracked him?" Jason nodded toward the park.

"It's about time you started aiming your telescope in the right direction—up."

"I've tried that. There's too much haze in this city to see any stars."

"Excuses, excuses," Lydia grumbled. "Let's go up there." She pointed to the top of the elevator shaft, which stood a story above the rest of Jason's penthouse terrace.

"Lydia, no. It's cold. . . . Wait, wait."

There were no stairs up to that highest point of the building, but there was a wrought-iron ladder bolted to the brick wall which Lydia, feeling agile in her youthful dress, scrambled up.

Jason handed her the telescope and climbed the ladder. "We won't see anything."

She ignored him and scanned the sky to figure out where she should aim the telescope. There were some stars out, not many, just a few celestial specks visible as a result of a cold front moving in. Not much to look at. "It's pleasant up here," she said. "You should plant some trees or something on your terrace."

"On the street, shrubs on penthouses always look like pubic hair. I've never been one for shrubbery on buildings."

"But you are never on the street to notice." Lydia guessed where there might be something to look at, though frankly her estimate was based only in rusty adolescent astronomy and certainly not rooted in empirical fact. It was a futile attempt, she was sure, they would see nothing. However, when she did stare into the telescope, the smog and pollution and the city lights faded away. The night became darker, bluer, and what was left was the bright tapestry of constellations that one usually could only see on the most deserted beach or remote country field or atop the tallest Pacific mountain. It was a miracle. "Look."

Jason pressed his eyes against the telescope. "I'll be damned. I never expected . . ." He squinted at Lydia. "Did you do something?"

"Like what?" Everywhere distant, cosmic sequins pulsated with luster and enigma. She was a schoolgirl once again, visiting the local community college, where an older boy, nervously clicking a ballpoint, showed her how to find Saturn. She was in love with him, in love with the night.

Lydia and Jason took turns studying the sky, aiming the telescope randomly. "You can see Capricornus, the sea-goat constellation," she told him. "It looks sort of like a wounded kite that's falling back to the ground."

"I see, yes."

"And I might be wrong, but do you see that stick figure . . . a man with a rhombus-shaped body. He's missing his head and his right leg."

"Where? Oh, yes."

"That's Perseus, the hero constellation."

"Don't worry about the stolen idol," Jason told her as he tuned the lens. "We'll figure out what to do."

Once long ago, she had felt that her life, the earth, the night, were all limitless in Jason's company. She'd experienced this freedom with nobody else, and she was feeling it again. She was cold but didn't want to go inside. They took turns looking through the telescope for as long as they could before their eyes grew tired, and when they could no longer probe the night, she reached for him. To an improvised, mellow riff that he hummed a cappella, they rocked in a slow, two-step, cheek-to-cheek dance.

"Did you really spy on me all those years?" she asked.

"Somebody had to."

Lydia told Jason to wake her up early, and she spent what was left of the predawn hours on his living room couch.

The phone woke her up at nine o'clock. "Jason, damn it!" she yelled. She had wanted to get up two hours earlier. The phone kept ringing. "Are you going to get that? Jason?" She shuffled into the kitchen.

"Lydia," a man said, "I'm sorry to disturb you."

"Michael?"

Michael Brickthrone had a precise way of speaking. "I am afraid Eric is in jail."

"Oh, shit."

"The Sixth Precinct."

Why, Lydia wondered, had Eric called her divorce lawyer?

Brickthrone must have read her mind. "Eric said that I was the only counsel he could think of."

"Jason!" she called out. "Jason?"

"A man named Timothy suggested I try you there," Brickthrone said. "I had to have a secretary dig through old files this morning to find the number. It seems as though your son has—I mean, allegedly has—"

"Yes, yes, I know all about it. I'll come right down."

"There's nothing you can do, Lydia. He won't be arraigned until three or four, it seems. Possibly not until tonight. Backlog."

"Arraigned?"

"I'll call when I know more. Don't worry." Michael Brickthrone hung up.

"It's too late." Lydia slammed the phone down. "He's sunk. Jason?" She knocked on his bedroom door. The bed was made, and he wasn't there. The televisions were on in his media control center, the volumes down, but he wasn't sitting in his chair monitoring world events. "Jason?" Nor was he in the bathroom. Or anywhere else, for that matter. But he never left . . . She ran out onto the terrace and back inside. "Oh, no." Lydia looked at the glass coffee table where they had left the idol. It, too, was missing along with her fringed purse. She searched the apartment again, indiscriminately filing through Jason's closets, which were mostly empty.

"Norton?" she asked when she called downstairs. "Did Mr.—"

"What a wonderful day," Norton the doorman said.

"Yes. Did—"

"It's so breezy, the first cool day after a very hot summer, and Mr. Maldemer finally came downstairs. I said, 'Are you all right, sir? Shall I call an ambulance?' And he said, 'No, Norton, I'm going out for a walk.' And then he did."

ric had expected that he would be locked up in some dank cell, but when he arrived at the police station, he was placed in what looked like a conference room with a long table surrounded by folding chairs. There was a coffee machine on a table in the corner along with a video camera on a tripod and a monitor, unplugged. A torn love seat was pushed against one wall. Above it was a chalkboard, wiped clean. He was left alone and unattended. The door was locked. There was no phone. After an hour and a half or so of this confinement (he had to guess how much time had passed, because they'd taken his watch), he reasoned that his isolation was intentional. They would drive him stir-crazy and force a confession. He filled a Styrofoam cup with some coffee but drank only one sip of the cruel and unusual brew. Finally, two plainclothesmen entered the room. One wore a blue suit, the other tan. They looked spiffy and clean, as if they had just arrived for work. Blue Suit plugged in a phone and told Eric to call a lawyer. Eric was annoyed that his mother wasn't home. Tan Suit said that yes, Eric was allowed to call Information, if he had to. Blue Suit offered Eric some more coffee, but Eric knew better.

Then the two detectives rifled through a series of questions. One of the policemen would tell him something about the rights of the accused, and then the second man would speak in blunt clichés about how Eric could make life easier for himself by cooperating. "Why don't you just tell us what you did with the statue?" Eric, of course, knew not to say anything before his attorney arrived. He was preoccupied with the way that gel was drying in one man's hair, making the back of his head look like wet duck feathers, and the patterns formed by pulled threads in the second detective's tie. Somehow these details seemed necessary to gather in order to understand what was happening to him.

Eric was told that *They* had a lot of evidence on him and that *They* had been following him for a while. "So Eric, why don't you just tell us what you did with the statue?" The men admitted that they were impressed by his master scheme to capture the imagination of a city with a theft and then capitalize on the crime. Very clever indeed, they said. "But why don't you just tell us what you did with the statue?"

Eric began to sift through the detectives' redundancy. He wondered why, if they had so much evidence, if they had been following him, they had waited this long to lasso him. And it occurred to him that in order to solve the crime once and for all, they needed his help. Only he could provide them with the missing evidence. "Make it easy for yourself. Tell us what you did with the statue." Eric could smell impatience on their breath like a tart liquor.

Michael Brickthrone finally arrived, dressed for the theater. First he talked baseball with the detectives. And then, once they were alone in the conference room, he said, "Now, Eric, what I like to do is negotiate. I've won some substantial settlements in my day."

Eric wished he'd opted for a public defender. "They don't have the idol," he tried to explain. "They've been trying to build a stronger case, and they got tired of waiting—but they don't have the idol."

If Brickthrone heard him, he didn't let on. "I think we might be able to hammer out an amicable agreement, a seemingly fair split that will in actuality leave you with the larger share."

Eric shook his head no. The detectives returned and informed him that he would be spending the night in the slammer if he wasn't going to cooperate, and before he had time to change his mind and tell them where the treasure was stashed, they were locking him in his cell. The everyday holding cages in the basement were full (some boys from Jersey had gotten into a brawl in a piano bar), and there was no space for Eric. He was moved from the conference room to an office that was in the process of being cleared out by one occupant and assumed by another. There was an empty desk and some metal chairs. The bleakness of the room with its waxed linoleum and empty file cabinets did not bother Eric so much, but he had been spooked during his short walk through the station house: Fluorescent corridors were filled with clusters of murmuring officers, in-out trays overflowed with triplicated, twice-faxed papers, phone lights blinked, although Eric never heard any rings. The place was hollow, and he was frightened, truly scared now, because it could be only a matter of time before he was sucked up into the criminal justice system and lost forever.

He was alone in a dark room, left to ponder his demise. He thought about what he would do if this office had a window (which it didn't, except for the frosted glass panel in the door), if he could climb out and escape. He would retrieve the idol from his mother's apartment.

He would return it to the museum as covertly as he had stolen it.

After a while, he put his head down on the desk. For some reason, as he drifted, he pictured flow charts like the ones he had to memorize for high-school biology classes, charts detailing the phases of intricate, time-honed processes. Then he was trapped in a maze of tall hedges, and he could hear his mother telling him in a calming, comforting voice that in life after high school, he probably would never be called upon to recite the phases of photosynthesis or the Krebs cycle. He could hear Lydia—it sounded as if she was just beyond the pruned, leafy wall—but he couldn't quite reach her.

Eric was ignored for most of the next morning. It must have been around ten or so (he guessed) when an officer unlocked the office door and let Inca join him. She was looking svelte in black jeans and an oversized, cable-knit, black turtleneck, carrying a black jacket. She'd had her hair cut short again, into a lopsided pageboy. She kissed him on the cheek after the officer locked the door.

"Your lawyer is downstairs trying to push up your arraignment," Inca said. "Don't worry. We'll find a way out of this."

"Don't worry? How can you tell me not to worry? You have to do something. You have to go to my mother's place—"

"Your mother isn't home. She was out all night. Timothy just surfaced, and he told this Brickthrone guy to try Jason Maldemer's. Look, the important thing is not to say anything—"

"I know, I know. I haven't."

Inca switched on the overhead light, but it was so bright that she flicked it off right away. "There's something that I have to tell you," she said, her voice soft and small.

Eric nodded. "I found it in the samovar."

Inca sank into a folding chair and sighed. "Phew. I was looking everywhere this morning—"

"But the police might go to my mother's and find where I hid it."

"Oh, shit. We have to find her."

"You faked the business about being robbed." Eric sat on the edge of the desk. "You removed the appliances to make it look real."

"I wanted the idol out of your life. I wanted you to believe that it had truly been stolen. I wanted to cut"—Inca mimed a knife—"the jugular of your obsession."

"That's the sweetest thing anyone has ever done for me." Eric held her hand. Her fingers were cold.

"It wasn't sweet at all. It was a completely selfish act. It was a ploy, Eric. Manipulative. All I did was make you even crazier. I could have found you and told you where the idol was once I realized that my move had backfired, but I didn't, did I? No."

"It's academic now."

A sudden tear rushed down Inca's cheek. "When you start to hide ancient idols in broken samovars, you know you're in trouble."

Eric squeezed her hand.

"I don't know, maybe I wanted to hurt you. Maybe I wanted you to stop breathing down my skyscrapers."

"Are you drawing skyscrapers now?"

"I thought I could live without you, but I can't. I want to take long walks through the Village with you. I want us to eat Indian food together. Go to obscure art films. Flea markets. I want," Inca said, "to drink cups and cups of coffee with you."

"I won't go to jail, if they don't have the idol."

Inca pounded the desk with her fist. "I actually thought that I would come in here this morning, see you one last time, and then be done with you."

Eric's heart thumped. All his legal woes seemed relatively unimportant.

"Isn't that awful? You'd be shipped upstate, and I'd be done with you. Oh, fuck."

"I love you."

Inca paced the short lengths of the office-cell. "I got used to the idea that there wasn't going to be anyone else in my life. I convinced myself that I could live all alone. I like being alone, and I need to be left alone more, if . . ."

"I want to live in your houses, Inca Dutton."

"You know what will happen, don't you? We'll get back together now only to break up again in a month or in a year or in two years. Then one freezing winter day, we'll reunite, and we'll get to talking, and we'll drink a bottle of wine, lie in front of a fire, and go gaga over each other all over again. We'll travel to Greece or Morocco, where we'll pledge our eternities to each other, and then we'll return home and set up a new life. We'll do new things, collect antiques or learn to play squash, we'll raise a kitten, maybe talk about children—egad! But eventually we will split up for the same reasons we did the first time. The breakups will get uglier with each go-round, but we won't escape from this pattern of coming together and drifting apart, together and apart until finally one sultry summer day years from now, we fight and become estranged overnight. Then we won't speak for a year, maybe longer, but ultimately we will send cards, chat on the phone, meet for dinner, then talk until morning. After that, we won't be lovers anymore, except for the occasional dalliance, yet we'll become the best of all possible friends. We'll find other mates in time, and they'll become insanely jealous of our incredible friendship, of how we confide in each other, not them. In fact, our past, our tight bond of trust and faith, a bond that ages like wine and violins, will scare off our lovers. We'll live both together and apart in a way, spiritually existing as one, but always feeling slightly alone. Some people are doomed for marriage, and some, you and I, are fated for a more complex romance. We're only just beginning."

Eric sighed. "It's your optimism that I adore," he murmured.

"I quit my job," Inca announced. "I've been talking with a couple of architectural firms, and once I get recertified, it looks like I might take a position at Hangmore Perry Hyde. They have great offices downtown. All glass brick."

"That's wonderful news."

"They're doing the new Asian art wing at NYMA and they really liked my idea to replicate the Beaux Arts facade from the front of the building in the back and then break it up for the bombed effect."

"Try to get them to beef up the security while you're at it."

Inca glanced around the stark office-cell. "What the hell are we babbling about? How can we talk about the future? There is no future unless we plan your defense. Who nailed you, that Marek creep? We have to plan your defense. Otherwise . . ."

Eric stepped closer, close enough so that she could punch him in the arm. "Ouch." And again, harder. "Stop."

"Why the fuck did you have to go and steal an idol?" she shouted.

Eric put his hand over her mouth. He pointed his nose toward the outside world. "What they don't know for sure won't hurt them. We just have to hope that my mother doesn't do or say anything crazy."

He stepped over to the locked door, carrying Inca's black jacket with him, and hooked the lapels over the hinge and frame, draping a curtain over the frosted window. Standing next to Inca again, he felt her breath on his face, then behind his ear. They didn't touch. Then his lips brushed her neck, her collarbone. He pulled off her sweater, and she unbuttoned his shirt. He knew in only hours, minutes, he would face a grave destiny, but when their bare chests met, he felt protected and possibly invincible.

C entral Park, Jason rediscovered, was as idyllic to be in as it was to watch from above. The air was surprisingly cool. The grass and trees were wet after a mid-morning drizzle. He followed the path slowly, each step a little less tentative. He walked around a pond, and at one point had to squat down and wait for a wave of queasy sea-sickness to pass. He breathed deeply, stood up carefully, readjusted the fringed purse slung over his shoulder, and continued along the path.

A woman wearing sweats and a headset jogged toward him. Jason froze. He looked for a tree to hide behind, but he had entered an open stretch of lawn, a hole in the forest. He braced as the woman passed, but she did not even meet his gaze.

A gaggle of teenage girls was next, chattering about some boy. Jason examined their rosy cheeks. They passed him, too, and didn't as much as look his way. If they were old enough to know who he was, he realized, they probably wouldn't much care.

He followed the contour of the hills and picked up his pace. The purse bounced off his shoulder, and he stopped again. He wasn't thinking. The leather bag—it would draw attention. An older man with a familiar face and gait sidled by: He was someone Jason followed with his tele-scope. No, no one appeared to care about him or his bag. A woman pushed a baby carriage past him. The baby grabbed at the fringe of the purse, halting Jason, and the woman apologized with a smile as she peeled the baby's fingers from the tassels.

Soon—distances were shorter than he remembered—the stately New York Museum of Art appeared beyond the trees. Jason climbed the steep sweep of steps up to the main entrance, having timed his journey to coincide with the museum's opening. Guards hovered by the doors. In this day and age of terrorism (and art theft), Jason expected that his bag would be checked. The first hurdle.

He had stuffed the purse with anything that he found lying around— memo pads and pencils, a couple of paperbacks. And, of course, a boxed manuscript. When he opened the pouch for the guard, he pulled it open wide, even pulled the box aside. The purse must have looked bottomless with harmless miscellany. He looked respectable. He didn't look like he was about to blow up the place or mar an Old Master with spray paint. The guard barely glanced in the bag.

But there were so many people already milling about the Great Hall, people buying tickets and checking coats and surrounding the information desk. Jason was not used to crowds, and he became dizzy. He held his hand over his stomach. He thought that he might collapse. Okay, okay. He steadied himself as he attached a NYMA pin to his shirt pocket. Now where? He thought about climbing the palace staircase that rose up to the rooms of paintings. One of those galleries undoubtedly would be free of patrons and guards. But a chair or bench wouldn't do. He had to be more discreet. He remained on the first floor and entered the hall of medieval art.

The gaunt eyes of crucified saints stared down at him. Not here. He moved toward a hall of armor, the walls covered with hatchets and spears and axes and daggers. No, thank you—besides, there were too many children in there oohing and aahing. He needed to find a place that was empty, and so he meandered toward the American art wing, where, bingo, he spotted the perfect hidden corner.

The period rooms were virtually unattended. It was too early in the morning for patrons to have trickled this far back into the corner of the museum. They were probably all working their way toward the new display of twentieth-century art way over on the other side of the vast building or maybe exploring the renovated rooms of Greek Antiquities that had just reopened. The period rooms were unwatched by guards—perfect—because each room had its own built-in security, waist-high glass barricades that kept viewers from getting too close to the furniture and priceless knickknacks that were all positioned with intentional nonchalance. A layer of plastic covered the rug where visitors stepped.

Jason entered a particularly airy dining room. The walls were frescoed with a garden scene and chairs were upholstered in a candy-striped, pink and ivory fabric. The sheen of the long, cherry table in the center of the room had a Mars-like glow. A tureen the size of a small boat was the table's centerpiece.

He removed the pair of rubber dishwashing gloves he'd brought from his kitchen. He climbed over the glass barricade as if he were stepping over a tennis net. He reached back for his bag and removed the idol, which was wrapped in a hand towel. The marble felt silky in his rubber hands.

He heard some voices, two women chatting. He froze. Through the doorway, he saw them studying a floor plan. They were trying to figure out how to get to the Egyptian wing. Fortunately they got their bearings, and he heard them wander away.

No time to dawdle. Trying to take soft steps across the rug, afraid he would set off a motion detector, he crossed the room. A clock presided over a sideboard, its face encased in a rising sun–shaped, silver frame. On either side of the cabinet there was an obelisk made of some kind of red marble, the veins of the stone like blood vessels. He removed one of the obelisks and set it down on a chair. In its place he propped up the Cycladic idol. It looked good there, but after a momentary review of the room, he opted for the tureen on the table. It offered better cover.

Jason positioned the idol in the silver craft and nodded good-bye to it. The woman possessed a certain nobility. The idol was white and pure, stark and pristine, an elegant classic, as at home in the eighteenth century as it had been in the twentieth. For a moment, he seriously considered putting it back in his bag and leaving the museum and keeping it.

But that wouldn't help matters. And the artifact belonged here in the museum where everyone could see it. At some point, a book no longer belonged to its author but instead to those who read it. Yes, he and the idol were both going public again. He crept back to the glass barricade and gracefully returned to the place where patrons were supposed to admire the ornate ceiling with its depiction of some Bible story the Enlightenment folk had found enlightening. He left the room and hurried from the American wing back toward the Great Hall. When he reached the denser crowd of museum-goers, he realized that he still was wearing the rubber gloves. He pulled off the fingers in short tugs and stuffed them in the bag next to his manuscript. Next stop: his publisher.

But one thing at a time, Jason reminded himself when he got outside. He located a pay phone. Right now he had to call the museum with an anonymous tip: The idol was in a tureen. It was home, the crime undone. But he decided to call his place first because Lydia would no doubt be worried.

Odd: No one answered his phone. Had she gone looking for him? He dialed the number of the lobby desk. "Hello, Norton?"

"Mr. Maldemer, hello. Is the outside world the way you remembered it?"

"Yes, thanks. Norton, did Lydia Carver—"

"She left a message for you, sir, on her way out. Shall I read it?"

"Thank you, Norton."

"Let's see, it says: 'Jason—whatever you've done, don't do anything else.' "

Jason looked back at the fountains in front of the museum, the timed geysers rising and falling to their own looped choreography. Something was wrong.

arek's office was territory unknown to Lydia. She'd never been to his apartment either, though she curiously assumed that she had. "Where were you?" He greeted her with a kiss, a quick peck. "I've been worried. I've been calling and calling. We need to talk." He shut the door.

She had expected that his office would be a messy den of overstuffed bookshelves, paneling, a fireplace maybe—kind of like the denim shirt he was wearing, wrinkled and slightly untucked. But sober, white stucco walls were adorned with three carefully chosen paintings: a Flemish port-scape, an Italianate madonna, and a large portrait of one of the Hapsburgs, complete with a feathery, combed Vandyke and an enormous chin. Marek sat down behind a broad, Shaker-simple desk covered with tidy piles of exhibition catalogs. A Spanish candelabra stood in the corner, a twisted tree of black iron. This was the office of someone for whom Lydia had felt great passion, but a man, she realized this morning, whom she hardly knew.

"Darling, I told you that you would look lovely in that dress, and you do. You know the Retro look really is—"

"Marek, please." Lydia sat down in the chair that faced his desk.

Marek sat, too. "Yes." A dramatic sigh. "I'll be honest with you, Lydia. I know that you must be upset, but I begged you to talk to Eric. I begged you."

She did not recall being *begged* exactly. She wanted to say, Marek, you shit, you knew that my son was a suspect and you didn't tell me. But calling him a shit was not going to win his support. She wished that she knew more about museum affairs. She needed his help. "What can we do?"

"Naturally, I've been thinking about it," Marek said. "I'd like to help, but I'm afraid it's out of my hands."

"Nothing is ever out of your hands."

"What can I do? The facts are the facts."

"What have you got on him? You can't have much."

"We have hair," Marek said, "fibers of hair in the Brazewell Krater. DNA fingerprints. Fibers from a wool scarf. We have the museum button from the day of the theft. We have library records. We have—"

"It's a slim case."

"We have motive. Look at the idol phenomenon all over the city. That was his doing. The theft made it all possible. Your son has profited handsomely."

"But you don't have the stolen idol itself," Lydia said. A bluff: She assumed that Jason hadn't given it up. She didn't really know what was going on and would have to wing it. Cautiously.

"No," Marek said. "No, we don't." He played with a rubber band, raised an eyebrow. "But you know, if Eric turned it over, they might go easy on him. He might be able to arrange a generous plea bargain. Look, darling, you're right. There isn't much of a case, and with Eric's cooperation, it might all go away. Maybe no one will even formally bring charges."

"Please don't *darling* me. You're saying that they might let him walk for now. Fine. But I don't really want to wait and see. And if they let him go this time, I don't want there to be any lingering doubt. I don't want the police to come back in two months with new evidence. Eric has to be cleared. I want the case to be closed, Marek. For good."

"Lydia," he said. "Lydia," he repeated her name softly. "What can I do? I have been scheming all morning—"

"I'm sure."

"No, I have. I have been trying to come up with some way to"—he looked down at his blotter—"clean up this affair. And the best thing I thought of was to say that Eric was only a pawn in a larger syndicate. He was a novice flunky with no record. He didn't know what he was getting into, and he is, of course, full of remorse."

"So we're saying that there are other people involved in the crime," Lydia said.

"I suppose we would have to figure out who they would be. Eric could furnish names that unbeknownst to him were actually aliases. Maybe he'd get off on probation—"

"Marek, you're missing the point. Eric is still a criminal in your scenario. He's still guilty. I want him to have had nothing to do with the theft."

"But he did, didn't he? If Eric didn't steal the idol, then who did?"

"We'll say it was somebody else," Lydia said with authority.

"Who? And how do I know?" Marek asked. "Do I know who these people are?"

"I guess if you did, you would've had to turn them in."

Marek wagged a finger at her. "Unless . . ."

"Unless what?"

"Unless I couldn't. What if I had cut a deal with these criminals for the sake of the art? What if I'd paid a ransom to kidnappers?"

"The true thieves who have nothing whatsoever to do with Eric," Lydia added.

Marek stroked his chin. "Yes, I could say that I paid a ransom to kidnappers at the last minute to save the idol from escaping into the black market."

Lydia relaxed in her chair. "That sounds almost heroic."

"Well, I'd need to have the idol back," Marek pointed out.

Right. And he needed the ancient artifact, she knew, to complete his deal with Polly Stewart. He was cooperating much more easily than Lydia had anticipated, but she could not afford to lose sight of his angle. After all, he had plenty to gain. She could only hope that Jason still had the idol or knew where to get it.

Marek frowned. "But my dear, it would never work."

"Why not?"

"Well, for one thing, where would I get the money to pay out a ransom?"

"You have acquisition funds, don't you? You must be able to spend up to a certain amount at your own discretion, no?"

"It is not as easy as you think to cut a check. And then, darling, to whom exactly would I make out this check?"

Lydia thought quickly. "Say you paid the ransom out of your own pocket. Then reimburse yourself."

"And do what with the money?"

"Please. That would be the least of your problems."

"If I lie," Marek said, "it would mean that I went behind the museum's back, behind the director's office, behind the trustees, behind the backs of the very investigators I was assigned to coordinate."

"But you'd get the art back, and isn't that a greater deed?"

Marek slumped in his chair, and Lydia sat up straight. "Someday the director is going to retire," he said. "This little episode will be remembered. It's bad enough that I've been involved with the thief's mother."

So he was a man with priorities. He had his agenda. His mind was a set of scales that weighed one motive against another. He had it in his power to make the mess go away, he had the authority to remove all doubt, but he didn't want to. And then she began to consider what would happen even if he did play along, even if Eric were absolved and the idol were returned. What would happen after Marek had secured *The Storm Nears*? Maybe he would turn on Eric again, provide new evidence. . . . She had absolutely no reason to trust him. She didn't think twice now about drawing her weapon.

"Better a tarnished reputation," Lydia said quietly, "than being exposed for fraud. Better to be unethical than criminal. Am I right?"

"Are you suggesting . . . ?" She noticed a shade of complexion she had never seen before in Marek's face, a streak of vermilion along his cheekbones. And then a tone of voice, hostile and snide, that she had not heard before either: "You can't blackmail me. Don't be ridiculous."

"I think I just did." Lydia looked beyond him at the Hapsburg portrait: The king was blushing, too. "I guess you shouldn't have told me about the bribery. I don't want to go to the press with the story. I really don't. But even if the idol turns out to be real and not a fake, Marek, it doesn't matter, because the truth is that you had already set the scam in motion. This can be investigated and proven."

"I only told you about that because I love you." Pause. "Don't think I haven't been very, very careful. I left no trail."

"What's it gonna be?"

"Lydia," Marek pleaded.

"How long did you know that Eric was involved?"

"I asked you to talk to him. Didn't I?"

"I love you, Marek. I think you're smart and witty and handsome. But I can't believe you didn't tell me what was going on."

"How could I? My position here . . . If anyone ever found out . . ."

"What's it gonna be?"

Marek sighed. It did not take him long, apparently, to sift out the lesser of two evils. "I need the idol back before I can do anything."

Everything turned on the recovery of one small, enigmatic ancient figure. "You'll get your idol." Everything depended on Jason now.

"Will I?"

Lydia got up to leave.

"Will you call me?"

"I'll let you know when I can bring it to you."

"I mean will you, you know, call me after that?"

"I just blackmailed you."

"I love you despite all of this."

Sadly, Lydia believed him. "Marek, I'm—"

"You're leaving me," he said. "You don't have to leave me. I'm doing what you're asking not because I want to save my reputation and career or because I even believe that you could prove that any bribes were made—don't think that I wasn't *extraordinarily* careful—but because I want to do what makes you happy. We can make this work, you know. We can get past this."

She did not want to injure him more than she already had, but what could she say short of the truth? She woke up today, and she didn't love him.

"We can make this work." Marek opened his office door for her but stood in front of it. Before she stepped around him, he pulled his wallet from his trousers. He opened it to a set of photographs. Behind cloudy plastic, there was a snapshot of a young woman too young to be his wife or lover but not too old to be his daughter. Her resemblance to him was uncanny: They had the same eyes.

Lydia did not want to know who it was. "Stop."

"Her name is—"

"I don't want to know. Whatever you're going to tell me you should have told me before."

"I'm telling you now. Lid-ya?" Marek called after her. "Lid-ya?"

She figured that by now Jason must have returned home. He had to be home. She hailed a taxi and told the driver to pass another cab on the transverse.

When the elevator opened on Jason's foyer, he was waiting. "I just got a call from Michael Brickthrone. Eric's being arraigned at five."

"What did you do with it?"

"It's in a tureen in the dining room in the American wing. I was going to—"

"Oh, you're incredible." Lydia nearly toppled Jason when she hugged him. "I love you. You actually went outside. I love you."

"You forget how many people there are in this city when you stay in your apartment for three years."

"I have to call Marek. He's got his idol back, right under his nose." She hopped into the kitchen, on the way outlining her plot.

"I hope this works," Jason muttered.

Lydia dialed the phone. But she paused a moment before pushing the seventh digit. She was suddenly astonished by how easy it had been for her to commit blackmail. Blackmail, after all, was a crime.

ric thought that when the policeman and the detective entered the office, they were going to escort him to either a grimmer holding cell or possibly a courtroom. He held his wrists behind his back and anticipated the pinch of the handcuffs. But instead he was led downstairs to the sergeant-of-the-watch, who handed him his personal belongings—his wallet, his watch, and his belt—as if they were presents. Even his lawyer, who shuffled false-arrest waivers to sign, did not seem to comprehend fully why exactly he was being set free. Apparently, instructions came from very high up in the offices of prosecution. One cop reported (without elaborating) that the stolen idol was back in the museum.

It was a strange afternoon. While Eric was away from the world for a day, summer had ended. Now clouds stampeded across the sky, colliding into one another, and the sort of wind that can rip leaves from trees, even green leaves not ready to fall, tunneled through the cross streets. Autumn had arrived in late September with an all-out assault of gray light that washed ordinary objects, lampposts and parking meters, traffic lights and mailboxes, with an eerie animation. Eric was underdressed and shivered when he walked toward the river. He hadn't shaven or showered, and he felt as though he were returning from a long trip, just getting off of a plane that had shot backward across a hemisphere.

The Mystery Roast was full to the brim, and in a corner booth, everyone who mattered to him had assembled. The time line of his life had folded in on itself like a collapsed accordion. His family clapped for him, as did the rest of the café, although people looked a little confused, unsure why they were applauding. Maybe a day of incarceration had left him more paranoid than usual or maybe it was because everyone stopped talking when he walked across the room, but he became wary of conspiracy. All he could do was hover by the booth and smile an idiot's grin, all words escaping him at first. He kissed his mother hello. "I don't know what you did, except that I know you did something."

"I know a few tricks," she said.

And then Jason, looking pale and faded, slid out of the booth and greeted Eric first with a congratulatory handshake and then a fatherly hug.

"You're outside," Eric said.

"So are you."

"It's wonderful to see you."

"I think this is when I'm supposed to say that you've grown," Jason said. He glanced around the café and sat down again.

"I don't understand," Eric whispered to his mother. "You found the idol? How did it get back to the museum?"

"Oh," his mother said loudly, "you have Jason to thank for that."

Eric looked at him, waiting for an explanation.

Jason shrugged. "It was nothing."

"Thank you," Eric said softly. "I think you saved my life."

"Really, it was nothing. I just put it back. More or less."

Melior yawned a wide meow. Using her sixth sense to detect true loners, she had taken to Jason and been cuddling next to him, but now she hopped to the floor so that she could smell the precinct house and the new season all over Eric's shoes. She rubbed her jowls against his calves.

Inca blew Eric a kiss, and he winked back.

Sitting across from Lydia, Timothy was grinning. "I guess this means that Andre doesn't have to bake a cake with a nail file in it."

Andre said, "Ooh, maybe I'll bake a cake anyway, something with a lot of chocolate," although this comment was not directed at Eric but rather at Timothy as if it were a private joke. Timothy dutifully giggled, and Eric noticed that Andre's hand was flat against the seat, under Timothy's thigh. Andre was going to relinquish his seat to Eric, but Eric pulled over a chair.

"Did they mistreat you in jail?" Jason asked.

"There was some pretty bad coffee," Eric said. "I was shivering, and I finally realized at some point that it wasn't the station house that was cold, it was me. I was in shock. I saw years of my life just falling away. . . . And I saw people—all of you, reporters, the lawyers, and judges—asking me, Why did you take what wasn't yours?" A deep breath. "I'm still not sure. But I can't say I regret doing it."

"No, no," Jason was quick to respond, "regretting is unhealthy. It's not a question of regret—"

"Just don't go ripping off any more major museums," Lydia interrupted. "Okay? I don't have that many cards to play out."

Inca tapped Jason's shoulder. "Don't think I'm done arguing, by the way. I don't see how," she said, her voice angry, somewhat hurt, "you can say what you have been."

Jason dug his hands into his pockets. "Look at the last two decades."

"But how can you say that my entire generation missed your point? We read passages from your books to each other over dinner and after making love. We quoted you at rallies to stop the bombing in Southeast Asia. Is that missing your point?" She pulled him back into the fray.

"It's a neat café," Lydia said to Eric. "Reminds me of when I was a student in Paris. We used to hang out for hours, smoking those hideous Gauloises, drinking wine from juice glasses, arguing. We would take sides: some of us for Simone de Beauvoir, some for Sartre—some for Delon, and some for Belmondo."

Jason turned away from Inca. "Paris is pleasant, but I'm really in the mood for Athens."

Timothy looked as if he was whispering something to Andre: Actually he was nibbling on his ear.

Inca pulled Jason back. "Don't change the subject. You wrote that radical breaks had to be made with the past—am I wrong?—but you never described where anyone had to go after those breaks were made, where the gradual reshaping had to—"

"Well, you can read all about it soon enough," Jason quipped, "in my next book."

Lydia clutched his forearm. "Then you will turn the manuscript in?"

"I already did. Don't look so surprised," he said. "My old editor treated me like a rogue husband. He said, 'I always knew you'd come back to me.' "

Inca's temper softened: "I can't wait to read it."

"It's got a good story," Lydia said. "Polar bears get top billing."

Eric scanned the various empty coffee cups and glasses on the table. He retreated to the bar and with assembly-line diligence proceeded to fill six highballs with foamy espresso and coffee ice cubes. He spooned in dark chocolate syrup along with dollops of crème fraîche and steamed milk and mixed it all up. He added generous send-offs of whipped cream.

"Sublime," Jason said, wiping away a mustache of froth.

Inca beamed.

"I've had so much real coffee today," Lydia said, wide-eyed, "who knows what secrets I'll divulge?" Everyone looked at her suspiciously.

Melior licked a spoon.

"We were guessing the coffee before," Lydia told Eric. "A man in the corner thought that it was Colombian Medellín, but Inca set him straight and said it was something or other from Zimbabwe with a twist of Viennese Roast."

"She practically murdered the guy," Timothy added.

"You exaggerate," Inca said.

"So Jason," Eric asked, "does New York seem very changed to you?"

"Don't let him fool you," Lydia answered. "All this time, he's been watching the city from on high and probably saw more of it than you did."

Jason's gaze drifted toward the ceiling, as if he were looking for hidden cameras amid the heating ducts. "I went out for all of a few hours and when I came back, my doorman was watching soap operas on my televisions, all of them simultaneously."

"I could do a film about doormen," Timothy said.

"But doesn't the city look incredibly different to you?" Andre asked. "I feel like it's changed so much in the last ten years alone, and not for the better."

"Yes, sometimes what happens to a city is painful to follow," Jason said. "We all feel powerless to keep it from aging. But it has to, I guess. And cities have a way of surprising you when you least expect it. They revive themselves. They breathe with youth again. They can, anyway."

Everyone drank their iced mochas at varying speeds, Lydia lingering, Andre in a few greedy slurps. Eric made a second round, a third, and conversation centered mostly on Jason's observations on his first day out. Andre slipped away to the kitchen to fill orders and bake a cake, and Timothy looked a little mischievous a short while later when he left, too, saying that he was going to go help him. Lydia winked at him.

"I get the distinct impression that there's something going on between those two," Jason said.

Lydia patted him on the arm. "Nothing escapes you."

"So what kind of architecture do you do?" Jason asked Inca.

"She constructs the most fabulous ruins," Eric answered for her.

"You know, that's interesting," Jason said. "I've been thinking a great deal about ruins lately. Greece, in particular. Can't get the place out of my mind."

"Got a hankering to wander the Acropolis?" Lydia joked.

"As a matter of fact . . ." Jason pulled an envelope from the lumpy inner pocket of his tweed jacket.

"Airplane tickets?" Inca asked.

"No, no," Jason said. "I'll stock up on Dramamine and Valium and travel by slow boat."

Lydia leaned back in her seat. "You leave your apartment for the first time in three years, and then you go to a travel agency?"

"I have to leave the country," Jason explained.

"Apparently."

"You used to have a line," Eric said. "What was it? 'Publish *and* perish.' "

"I can't very well stay here and have interviewers crawling all over me like picnic ants," Jason said, "my lobby full of insect photographers and the likes." He withdrew a second envelope from the depths of his jacket.

"What's that?" Lydia asked.

Jason kissed her on the cheek.

"Oh, that's so sweet," Inca said, reaching for Eric's hand. She became teary.

"When?" Lydia asked. She looked at the date on the ticket. "Jason, I just can't drop everything and leave like that—"

"Don't be a drag, Mom."

"I want to travel with you, Lydia. I'm going to be gone for several months, maybe longer, and I want you to come with me."

"I'll have to think about it," she said and sipped her coffee. Silence. "I have to think about it, okay?"

Andre delivered bowls of bean soup, in demand now that the season had abruptly changed, and on the way back to the kitchen, he sat down in the booth. "I have to tell you something," he said to Eric. "I've given this a lot of thought, and I know that it may come as a shock, and I don't want you to be angry with me because I should have discussed it with you before, not that I had to, but I would have liked to . . ."

Timothy leaned over Andre and massaged his shoulders. "What he's trying to tell us is that he's selling the Mystery Roast."

"You're what?" Eric's heart fluttered. "You can't. People depend on you. People depend on this place."

"I'm sorry," Andre said. The café-at-large must have heard his announcement, because a hush fell over the room. "I'm going West."

"Bravo." Jason raised his glass. "I love it when someone makes a real decision."

"And just when I was thinking that after all these years," Lydia said, "I had found a downtown hangout again. . . ." She ran her fingertip around the rim of her glass.

"Did you know about this?" Eric asked Inca.

"Just heard the bad news myself, kiddo."

Eric tried to imagine what would replace the café: All he could envision was an empty storefront, its windows dusty, a few stray, broken chairs left behind.

"I do have a proposal, though," Andre said.

"You've got tons of money," Timothy said to Eric.

"I think the time is right for this," Inca said.

Melior hopped up on the table to rub her forehead against Eric's chin, and Eric glanced at his mother, who nodded approvingly.

Andre made the terms clear: "I want you to buy the café. It would mean a lot to me. If you want, I can probably get a good price on your loft, too—Richard wrote me that he wants to unload everything. I want you to carry on here."

Eric looked back again at the tables of diners and coffee drinkers who were trying (and failing) to pretend that they were minding their own business. "I just got out of jail. I'm supposed to roam the country now. I'm supposed to drift aimlessly."

"Don't be a drag, Eric," his mother said.

Everyone waited for an answer. He was ready to shake on a deal, but at the same time, he panicked. It wasn't the prospect of failure and the loss of an investment that frightened him, although admittedly that was a factor somewhere in the back of his mind. More important, he needed to know that there would be a way out should he want to escape to the airport. He could not be weighted down by the burden of a café. He had to be able to wander. "I'll have to think about it," he apologized.

Jason winked sympathetically. "A man needs a good wash after getting out of jail. First things first. A good meal, a good sleep."

Before he could be pressed further by the others, Eric excused himself and hurried upstairs to his loft, where he drew a hot bath, sank into the tub, and held his breath as he plunged under the water.

Lydia, meanwhile, said good-bye to Jason, who after so much time in his self-sufficient cage wanted to do nothing more than walk around town. She climbed up the back staircase of the building and nearly tripped over a cracked aquarium on one floor, a canvas painting on another. It was an unfinished portrait (although it was too dark to see the face), and then she reached Eric's floor. She knocked—there was no answer—and used Inca's key. "Eric?" Her voice echoed. She saw a door at the other end of the loft swing closed. The place was large and empty. Too gray, too somber in her opinion. Some flowers might freshen up the place, some plants. "Eric?"

"I'm in the tub!" he called from behind the closed door. A few minutes later, he came out wearing a towel, his hair dripping wet, combed back. "You're here to tell me to spend hundreds of thousands of dollars on New York City real estate, admit it."

"This place needs something living in it, a cat or two."

"I like it empty. There's room to think. Although if Andre leaves Melior . . . No, no, no."

"Mothers are supposed to tell their sons that they envy them, it's a cliché. But I really do envy you."

"Go to Greece with Jason."

"You have a life down here. You should stick with it for a while. Not necessarily forever, just a while."

"When was the last time you took a boat around the Isles? With Dad, right? That couldn't have been very fun." Eric found some beer in his refrigerator. He handed a bottle to his mother. "It's not like he's asking you to marry him again."

"It would help your tax situation, I'm sure, if you invested in some property. I'll get my accountant Faith to give you a call."

"You should just quit your job and go."

Lydia thought of a dozen reasons to say no. First of all, there were some major contracts at the Institute that needed to be fulfilled. But beyond that, Jason was insane. She would only be able to stand so much of him. And no, he was not asking her to marry him exactly, but she was not going to deny the growing love she felt for him, the reborn passion. She knew herself well, she knew him, and she knew that it was only a matter of time before they became lovers of some sort. They had failed once, and she did not want to fail with him again. Or with anyone.

"Nothing's keeping you here, Mom. Why can't you be spontaneous?"

"Why can't you?" she asked. "At my age, spontaneity needs to be planned. You have no excuse."

Eric picked out some clothes and went back into the bathroom.

The truth was that she had just broken off with a man, and how could she convey to Eric, to someone still so young, that when you grow older, you have to learn to live alone, to be happy by yourself, to be a little lonely? She had to prove to herself that she could fly solo, that she didn't need a copilot, that she could even fly in loop-de-loops.

Eric emerged from the bathroom looking quite handsome, Lydia thought, in a burgundy turtleneck and jeans. Barefoot. His toes were shaped like her toes. He said, "I'll buy the Mystery Roast, if you go to Greece with Jason."

"I suppose that I could take a leave of absence."

"And I could always sell the place, right? I just have to leave enough money in the bank for a one-way plane fare and some spending money for when I arrive wherever I go."

"I feel like one of those characters in a novel of manners," Lydia said, "making a long tour through the land of classical myths and ancient history. Those characters always get into trouble, and when they eventually come home, life is never the same."

"You love Jason, even with all of his quirks and question marks."

"I always have," Lydia confessed. Eric stood by the windows, facing her, his back turned away from the city at dusk, lights coming on in the downtown skyscrapers, a harvest moon traveling in its luminous orbit. She shook her son's hand. She held on to it.

"I hope you get into lots of trouble," Eric said.

"I'll think of you whenever I see a demitasse," she told him.

Later that night, when Eric walked around the café, he looked at everything with a proprietary eye. As soon as he agreed to take over, he started to plan changes. He would build a window seat, mostly for Melior to nap on. Maybe he would get a kitten for her to take care of. And he might add some hanging plants and some magazines and newspapers. A pile of paperbacks, a stereo system. He might hang some moody black-and-white photographs on the booth side of the room. And he might play with the menu. He would add his ultra-chocolate brownies, and more fish, cold trout. Grilled chicken. He envisioned bowls of kiwis and apricots out on the bar. He had been dreaming about food lately, about a cream-of-red-pepper soup. He would improvise a recipe. In the kitchen, he opened a fresh sack of Yirgacheffe and distributed beans among the raw ones waiting to be roasted, and back in the café, he ground a new blend. A patron paid her check and asked Eric to sign a Cycladic thigh. He hesitated at first, but then nodded and scrawled his name across the hydrostone flank.

Inca sat at the bar and drank her coffee slowly. "Maybe we should take a trip somewhere," she said. "We could meet up with Jason and your mother in Greece."

"I have a café to run."

"I know, but you could get someone to take over for a little while."

Eric imagined Inca on a boat, wearing sunglasses, a scarf, her hair blowing with the sails. "Maybe in the spring, if we last that long."

"Oh, we might last. We might last, loverboy."

"Don't call me that."

Inca sipped the last of her coffee. "I've got some work to do. . . . I'll see you later?"

"Count on it."

Her empty cup sat on the bar after she'd gone upstairs, and Eric tipped it, hoping that he might be able to read the patterns of dregs and stains. But then he tossed it into the bin of dirty china: He didn't necessarily want to know what the future held. He could go on what Inca told him, that fads fade. The Goddess of Desire was riding a wave now, but ultimately she would drift from the urban scene, and people would recognize him for a while, and then sooner or later he would be famous for different reasons, maybe for being the man who ran the neat café all the way west, maybe for something else. Fads fade, and love evolves, she told him. He had to be willing to let their romance twist and turn according to its own mysterious helix. He knew there would be nights when, all zen aside, insomnia would drive him into the cold and dark, and he would become a nomad among deserted streets, worrying that he was on the brink of losing everything, that time was slippery and fast. But then sooner or later he would turn a corner and come upon the café and the rising edifice above it. He lived in a building on the edge of the city that was home to a family, complete with its own unique rites and everyday pageants that both isolated it from and linked it to all other families elsewhere in geography and time. Eventually, he would get some sleep, and he would wake up, roll out of bed, and hurry downstairs to his kitchen.

Around nine o'clock, a boisterous quartet of men and women burst into the café. They sounded like birds discovering an abandoned loaf of bread, chirping and squeaking, and as Eric approached them to take their orders, he noticed that all four of them held on to factory-made Goddesses.

"It's wild," one of the men said to Eric.

A women hoisted her idol in the air. "If you hurry, you can get one," she told him.

"It's a zoo," the man said.

"Where?" Eric asked.

"A few blocks that way—"

"There was a truck—"

Eric called to Andre in the kitchen to say he was going out for a few minutes, and then he jogged outside and ran east. He followed the backed-up traffic along a main street of the Village. Horns complained about an unseen snare. And then closer to the scene, he saw policemen in riot gear, all helmet and vest. Strobes of red lights flashed along the storefronts and a flood of water rushed through the gutter, spilling over onto the sidewalk. He saw people rushing away with the carelessness of petty thieves, knocking over garbage cans and bystanders, everyone clutching at least one idol by its legs or holding an unopened column box. He passed a man who was pretending that the Goddess was a ventriloquist's dummy: The idol was his prop to beg for spare change.

The crowd thickened, and Eric saw more police and more water pouring across the street. Then he was close enough to see what had happened. A small truck had apparently skidded into a fire hydrant, swerved in the flood of water, and tipped onto its side. Its back doors opened in the crash. Once the doors flew open, people poured out of all of the neighboring restaurants and bookstores and apartment buildings. *They will never get enough of me.* Looters tossed Goddess cartons back to the sidewalk (under the initial premise that they had to be saved from the flood), and then slit them open and pilfered the idols right in front of the helpless, bruised truck driver's eyes. *I was around for a long time, millennia, before you came along.* Most of the supply was carried off before the police arrived. The masses prevailed in a riot in the name of Desire. *And I will be around for millennia to come. This isn't the end: I have a way of getting where I want to go.*

Eric moved back to the fringe of the crowd as the cops closed in and people scattered. A man, addled and annoyed, was pinching a Goddess between her breasts, holding her like dead vermin. The man pushed his glasses up his nose. "Do you want it?" he asked Eric. "Somebody just threw it at me, and I have no idea what I'd do with a thing like this." Before Eric had a chance to respond, the stranger had handed him the idol and bolted away. *I have a way of getting where . . .*

Eric began to wade through the crowd, breaking free on a cross street. He wrapped his fingers around the waist of the Goddess. *I have a way . . .* He tossed her and caught her like a baton twirler. He stroked her smooth contours, her curved brow, her long nape, her bent knees. *I have . . .* He tweaked the arrow of her nose. The air was brisk, suddenly free of ancient murmurings, and he knew, with all the confidence of someone who has successfully guarded and might forever withhold a secret from millions and millions of people, that what he held in his hands was nothing more than synthetic stone, and that its power lasted no longer than anything else born from magma or soil, no longer than the leaves on a tree. He chucked the Goddess of Desire into a trash can.

And so one evening in late September, a Cycladic idol was at long last back in a museum, behind glass, well-guarded. (Soon it would be given a display case all its own, and soon museum-goers would be lining up for a look at the artifact. Soon, too, Marek would send a note to Lydia, which she would read several months later when she returned home from her trip abroad: "Case closed. And by the way, the idol turned out to be real after all, no fudging.") That night, the polar bears in the zoo stayed up late, as long as they could, to celebrate the lower temperatures before they collapsed into sleeping hills of white fur, their clumsy paws reaching northward while they dreamed. Not too far away, women wearing gowns and gloves trickled out of a ballet premiere. A man and a woman who, spurred by rattling windows and rustling leaves, had just made love for the first time now jogged together around the park reservoir, crazy and dangerous though it was. Elsewhere, a man was braving the wind to collect deposit bottles from Dumpsters, squirreling away what he could before a more severe wind moved in. And all around the city, people were pulling out quilts from trunks, from closets, drinking cocoa, chattering on the phone to friends and family and lovers and ex-lovers, gossiping, talking mostly about the weather and an apparent freedom tonight from what had been a very hot and very strange summer. Somewhere uptown, a mother helped her son with the math he had brought home from a new school: She tried her best to recall the mysteries of algebra. And across town, another mother was using a plate of chocolate chip cookies, warm from the oven, to woo her son off of the fire escape, to end a stalemate in the negotiations for a new bedtime.

That night, Lydia Carver sat in her living room window, balancing an old, old manual typewriter on her lap, one she had found at the back of her closet when she was cleaning. She was composing a letter to explain her reasons for taking a leave of absence from the Institute when she noticed, without the benefit of a telescope, some kind of signal coming from a building all the way across the park. It had to be Jason flashing the lights of his penthouse terrace, switching them off and on according to a Morse-like pulse: But what was he saying? Lydia typed out something quickly, off the top of her head, and then laughed: She had gone for more than a leave and tapped out a letter of resignation instead. Before she had time to reconsider, she left for Jason's. In the elevator downstairs, full of doubt, full of resolve, she imagined that she was walking to the edge of a cliff, she and Jason together strolling into the Aegean breeze. A temple once stood there, and now only some columns remained. Three or four fluted columns and a strip of fractured pediment. White stone against a blue sea. That was all, that was enough.

And on that first cold night of autumn, the crowd in the Mystery Roast was somewhat smaller than it had been recently and cozier. A woman wearing three sweaters instead of a coat sank into a corner booth. She ordered coffee and chicken salad and soup, with the fresh chocolate cake for dessert. Melior lapped up a tepid bowl of coffee and did her best to ignore a spaniel someone had brought in. A pair of men stopped by, each dressed in the same fake fur coat (one wore blue, the other green). They wanted pains aux chocolats and the day's roast right away.

Eric Auden deftly juggled the red-trimmed china. He pushed one cup under the espresso spout. Into another he delicately dumped frothed milk, and onto the white foam of a third, he sprinkled cinnamon.

"Ethiopian Harrar," a man in the corner looked up from a magazine to say. "With some El Salvadorean Arabica mixed in."

"We think it's mostly Peruvian Chanchamayo," one woman declared after concurring with a friend.

Another man angrily dissented. "You're all wrong. It's Copenhagen Choconut."

Eric delivered a cup of coffee to a woman who was holding a map. She was lost and had come inside to get directions and drink something warm. She tasted the coffee and looked up at Eric. "Which is it?" she asked.

He returned to the bar, where another cup awaited him. He sniffed its bouquet and sipped it. He had never been very good at deconstructing a blend. "I'm sorry," he apologized. "If I knew for sure, honestly, I'd tell you." Which was a lie, because even if Eric did know precisely which beans had been combined in the roast, he would never divulge the truth.

He dug his hand into a burlap sack, grasping a fistful of the cool beads, as many as he could hold. Then, slowly and evenly, he let the coffee beans pour through his fingers.

## About the Author

Peter Gadol is also
the author of the novel *Coyote*.
He lives in Los Angeles.